HEALERS' KISS I

KISS OF TREASON

BRANDI SPENCER

Authors 4 Authors Publishing
Marysville, WA, USA

Published by Authors 4 Authors Publishing
1214 6th St
Marysville, WA 98270
www.authors4authorspublishing.com

Library of Congress Control Number: 2021947821

Paperback ISBN: 978-1-64477-118-1
E-book ISBN: 978-1-64477-117-4
Audiobook ISBN: 978-1-64477-119-8

Edited by Rebecca Mikkelson
Copyedited by Renee Frey

Cover art ©2021
Images and Cover Art Illustration by Period Images, Pi Creative Lab and Mary Chronis. Cover Text, Background, Logo, and Branding by Brandi Spencer. All rights reserved.
Interior Design by Brandi Spencer

Author photo courtesy of 3rd Gen Photography.

Authors 4 Authors Publishing branding is set in Bavire. Headings and titles are set in Athena. Correspondence is set in Almendra. All other text is set in Garamond.

HEALERS' KISS I

KISS OF TREASON

BRANDI SPENCER

Authors 4 Authors Content Rating

17+

OLDER TEENS AND ADULTS

This title has been rated 17+, appropriate for older teens and adults, and contains:

- moderate sex
- strong language
- intense violence
- moderate alcohol use

Please, keep the following in mind when using our rating system:

1. A content rating is not a measure of quality.

Great stories can be found for every audience. One book with many content warnings and another with none at all may be of equal depth and sophistication. Our ratings can work both ways: to avoid content or to find it.

2. Ratings are merely a tool.

For our young adult (YA) and children's titles, age ratings are generalized suggestions. For parents, our descriptive ratings can help you make informed decisions, but at the end of the day, only you know what kinds of content are appropriate for your individual child. This is why we provide details in addition to the general age rating.

For more information on our rating system, please, visit our Content Guide at: www.authors4authorspublishing.com/books/ratings

DEDICATION

To my husband, my best friend, and the love of my life—Sean. Your love and devotion inspire me and make all my stories possible. Thank you for walking hand in hand with me on this journey.

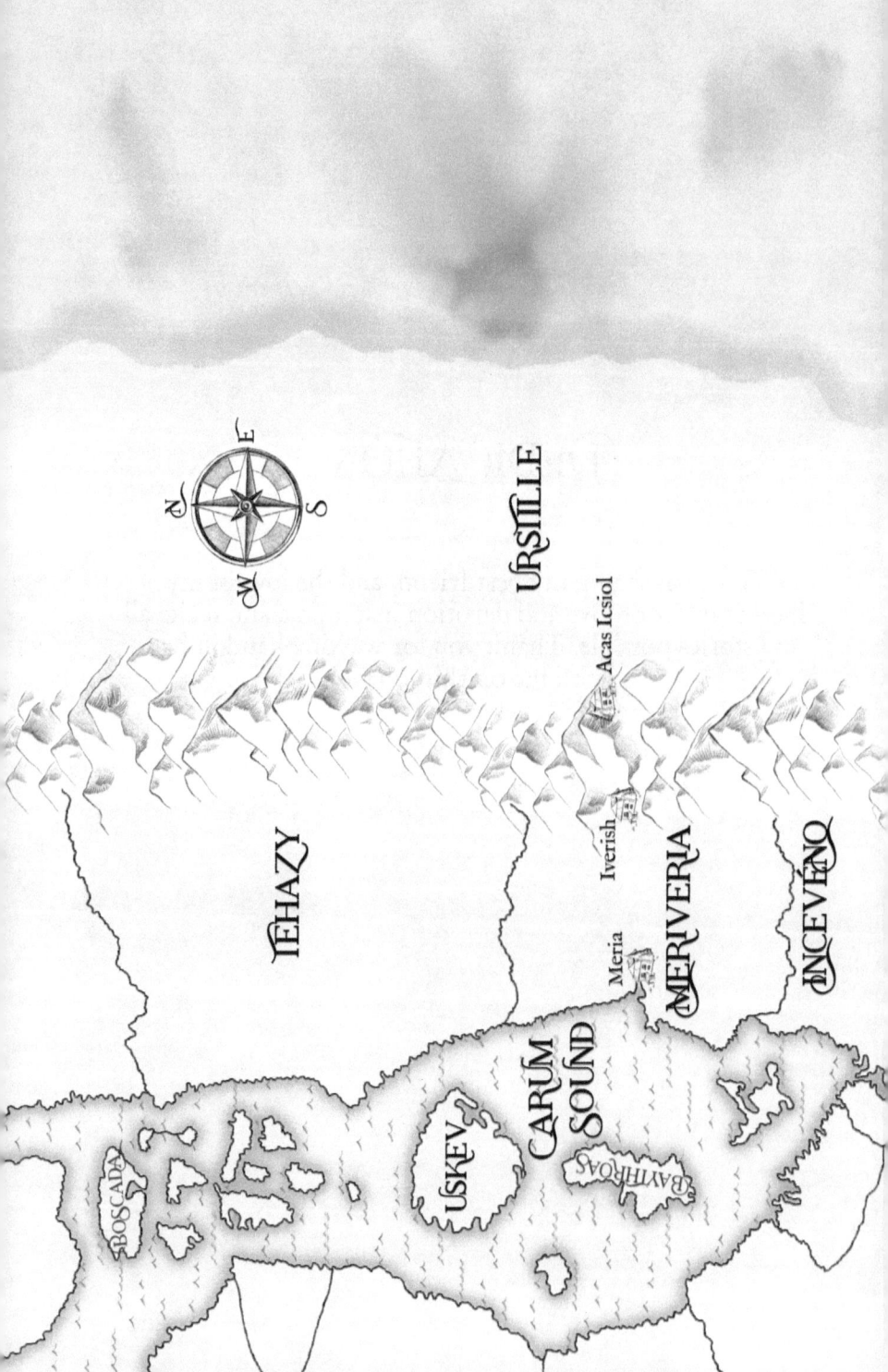

WORKS BY BRANDI SPENCER

Healers' Kiss:

Kiss of Treason
Kiss of Destiny
Kiss of Legacy (July 2023)

Tied Tongues (September 2023)

Gifted Hearts:
Short Love Stories of Carum Sound

"Her Dearest Treasure"
"I Loved You Tomorrow"
"Seeing Through Him"
"The Veiled Queen"

PRONUNCIATION GUIDE

For a more complete list, including IPA phonetics, visit
brandispencer.com/pronunciation

Abhenric – ə-BEN-rik
Ablure – AB-loor
Ascaympa – as-KAYM-pə
Barbenia – bar-BAYN-yə
Baythroas – BAYTHE-rohss
Cantahn – kan-tahn
Doivrie – DOY-vree
Doneron – DAHN-er-ahn
Eaund – ohnd
Eda – EE-də
Egino – EJ-i-NOH
Elgatha – el-GAHTH-ə
Iver – IV-er
Iverish – IV-ə-RISH
Jibiam – jib-ee-əm
Jonus – JAHN-us
Kennard – ken-ərd
Losuno – LOH-soo-noh
Melaine – mə-LAYN

Meria – MAIR-ee-ə
Meriveria – MAIR-ə-VAIR-ee-ə
Norlach – NOR-lahk
Odelia – oh-DEE-lee-ə
Ormoint – or-MOYNT
Oulley – oo-LAY
primogenitary
    – PREYE-moh-JEN-ət-air-ee
Rainald – RAYN-əld
Rhonwin – RAHN-win
salal – sə-LAL
Tasia – TAHS-ee-ə
Tehazy – tə-HAYZ-ee
Uldrio – UHL-dree-oh
Uskev – OOS-kev
Valerzan – VAL-er-ZAN
Viaporta – VEE-ə-PORT-ə
Wystan – WIS-tən
Yophiex – YOH-fee-yeks

TABLE OF CONTENTS

PROLOGUE

CROWN PRINCE KENNARD

The wooden entry hall of the Cedar Palace glowed warm with sunlight as the clamor of gathering crowds hummed through the thick cedar doors. Ken adjusted his gold circlet for the fifth time, but his mass of brown curls inevitably swallowed it again. He took a deep breath. None of his birthdays had generated quite this much fervor before, and Giftings happened every day without any attention beyond those involved. But the Gifting of the Crown Prince of Meriveria? Giver forbid anyone should miss it. As if the ceremony weren't daunting enough without everyone watching.

Lia slipped her hand in his, the familiar gesture calming him. He'd never been more thankful to share a birthday with his friend.

"Are you as nervous as I am?" Ken asked.

"A little. I couldn't wait to turn twelve until I woke up this morning, and..."

He nodded. "I just wish I knew which Gift I'll get."

She scoffed. "I think that's the point of the ceremony."

"I know, but most people can guess."

"And your guess is?"

Ken rubbed his chin. "Maybe Speech? Or Strength?"

Lia bit back a laugh. "Speech I could see, and it'd be useful to speak any language for diplomacy, but Strength?" She snorted.

"What's so funny about Strength?" He exaggerated his indignation.

"Please. Every boy thinks he'll get Strength. What would you do with it anyway? You have servants to lift everything, and it's so common that half the palace guard has it."

She had a point. Gifts were mysterious but not random. They served a purpose or enhanced an affinity. He didn't *need* Strength, and his natural physical prowess—though not embarrassing—was unimpressive.

Ken glanced backward, where Lia's parents stood smiling encouragingly. His own family was likely waiting to make a grand entrance.

"Any other guesses?" Lia asked.

He shrugged. "That's all I had. What about yours?"

She picked at the skirt of her sleeveless salmon dress as she thought for a moment, brushing its yellow lace hem against the toe of his deerskin boot. "Maybe Hearing, like my mother? What do you think?"

"I'll be shocked if it's not Memory. Only the royal librarian spends more time poring over books than you do."

Lia rolled her eyes. "I take a book on one picnic—"

"Or three."

She held up a finger and opened her mouth, then quickly closed it. Her pale cheeks turned the same color as her dress.

A drum banged five times.

By the time the last beat sounded, Lia had dropped Ken's hand and moved into a deep curtsy several feet away from him.

Father and Mother entered from the South Wing, dressed in full regalia. Pearls and embossed pines studded their gold crowns. Mother's gown matched Father's and Ken's shirts, the indigo satin embroidered with gold flourishes. Somewhere in the palace, Conora was wearing a smaller version of the same gown, but younger siblings weren't permitted into the ceremony—not even royal ones. His parents paused on their way to the doors just long enough for Ken to bob a short bow and fall into step behind them.

Louder drums boomed outside, and the hum of the crowd subsided as the doors swung open. Hundreds of people had packed onto the royal islet, most of them dressed in the blue and gray of old Elgatha. The herald hovered above the doorstep on enormous amber feathered wings. With his brown hair and gray uniform, he looked like a hawk surveying the turbulent sea of subjects. He lifted a large pine megaphone to his face and proclaimed, "Presenting His Majesty, King Gonfrid of Meriveria; Her Majesty, Queen Melaine; and His Royal Highness, Crown Prince Kennard."

Ken followed his parents down a path formed by guards, sending a ripple through the crowd as people bowed low before their approach and rose with their passing. Lia and her parents trailed several yards behind, maintaining their distance even as Father stopped at the western tip of the islet, in front of the Wise Women's Lodge.

The log-built structure rose two-stories high and was capped with a gambrel roof. Intricate but weathered carvings covered the door. Father stepped aside, and Ken walked past him to knock.

A woman answered, clad in a bright red tunic, skirt, and belt. Crimson ribbons wove through the thick black braid circling her cheery, round face. She beckoned them in and motioned to a half-ring of six chairs behind her. "Welcome. Please, do sit down."

Sunlight filled the large room, illuminating gauzy drapery of every color that covered the walls. In the middle, a striped wood table held an open book and a quill. In the back, a white door marked what he knew from a previous visit to be the wise women's private library, based on its other door outside, and a set of stairs led up to what had to be living quarters.

Ken chose a center chair and waited as Lia and her parents filed in. She stood warily in front of the seat beside him, no doubt prepared to move if Father objected.

The wise woman closed the door. "Please, sit, dear. I have enough chairs for you and your parents."

Lia obeyed, and their parents took their seats as well.

"Welcome, Crown Prince Kennard. Welcome, Odelia DiOrto. Happy birthday to you both. I am Sister Rose, and I will be inducing your Gifts today."

She was strangely chipper for such an important occasion. Given the mystery around it, Ken had expected more pomp, a dark and serious tone of voice—perhaps even some chanting. Everyone else looked equally confused.

"Is this your first Gifting ceremony?" Father asked brusquely.

Sister Rose smiled. "Oh, no. Not at all. I've been in the order for many years."

"Then surely you know better than to have closed the door before everyone has arrived."

She scanned the group before her and nodded. "Everyone is accounted for."

Father scowled. "They cannot have been the only two born that day. Was there a string of children's deaths that I was not informed of?"

"No, Your Majesty, there was not. I admit it's unusual to have such a small number, but life's often unusual." She leaned back and rested a finger on her chin. "Now, this is a fascinating arrangement. I wonder... Kennard and Odelia, please follow me. The rest of you may wait here."

Mother huffed. "This is not—"

Sister Rose waved her off. "Every ceremony is different."

It was common knowledge that wise women bowed only to the Giver, but this was crazy.

In stunned silence, Ken and Lia followed her to a corner of the room. Sister Rose drew back a leafy-green curtain, revealing a tiny room with a brazier in the center. She closed a door behind the curtain and sighed. "Much better. They'd continue interrupting forever if I let them. You appear to have a question, Odelia?"

Lia shook her head.

Sister Rose put a hand on her shoulder. "It's all right to ask real questions. I only object to interrogation."

"What did you mean by 'a fascinating arrangement'?"

"When both parents attend, children usually sit between them. You sat next to one another. That happens on occasion with children born in the same village, but the prince was born here in Meria, while you were born in Iverish, on the other side of the kingdom."

"So? Her parents were hired into the palace three years ago," Ken said.

Sister Rose's eyes lit up. "Ah, yes. Abhrenic. Seers do love to meddle. I wonder if he did it on purpose." She rubbed her hands together, then held them out to Ken, palms up.

He hesitated. Weren't his parents supposed to witness the Gifting?

She smiled and whispered, "Don't worry. This won't induce your Gift."

As he took her hands, her smile dropped into a pensive, lingering stare.

"Interesting," she said.

Ken laughed nervously. "Interesting? That doesn't sound ominous at all."

"I must maintain *some* mystery." She winked, then turned to Lia. "Your turn." She held onto Lia's hands for longer than his, then cocked her head. Maintaining her hold on one hand, Sister Rose reached out to Ken again. "Together now."

Lia asked the question weighing on his mind: "Is this...normal?"

"Yes and no. Some people are easier to understand than others. I like to see how everyone fits together, though the circle is usually much larger."

Still waiting, Sister Rose wiggled her fingers at Ken. He clasped hands with both her and Lia, and Sister Rose stared somewhere between them for a long while.

"I have what I need now." Sister Rose smiled and dropped their hands.

"Will you tell us what you learned?" Lia asked.

Sister Rose shook her head. "You know I cannot. Like your father, I must be careful with how much I reveal, but I glean so much more than just your future, and I must take that much more care with it."

"So you've chosen our Gifts?" Ken asked.

"I don't choose them. I find them."

He leaned to Lia and whispered, "There's a difference?"

"Yes," Sister Rose said, "one gives me far too much credit—or blame, depending on your view of Gifts. Come along. Your parents have waited long enough."

Back in the main room, Father and Mother glared at Sister Rose as Ken and Lia returned to their seats. The wise woman circled them to stand behind Ken's chair.

"Crown Prince Kennard of Meriveria, are you ready to receive your Gift?"

Ken gripped the edge of his seat. "I am."

She placed her fingertips on his temples. "Great Giver, please guide my hand. Use me as your conduit to bestow your child with your Gift."

Ken closed his eyes. All the air rushed out of his lungs. Electricity filled his body. Images flashed by, faster than he could comprehend them. Sister Rose lifted her hands, and the images stopped. Ken opened his eyes and gasped loudly. The electricity didn't stop at once, but settled in his face and hands, ending at his fingers and lips, until it faded away.

"Healing," she said. After a moment's pause, she stepped behind Lia's chair.

In a snap, Father took on the form of a wolf, his pewter fur raised. "Try again," he snarled, his voice still human but with a feral edge.

"My apologies, Your Majesty, but I cannot. Threats will not change that."

Mother stood up. "This is a mistake!"

"It is not," Sister Rose said firmly. "Your son has been given the Gift of Healing. I can neither remove it nor give him another. One can only receive the Gift meant for them."

"But he is—"

"I am well aware of who he is *and* who he will be." Something in Sister Rose's tone of voice implied she was speaking of more than his future throne. "But I cannot change the laws of Gifts. You have no further business here, so if you cannot be silent, I must ask you to leave."

Mother sat, and Father morphed back into a man, smoothing his wavy, dark brunet hair back into place. What had raised their ire to begin with? Healing was one of the rarest Gifts. Shouldn't they have been proud?

5

Sister Rose cleared her throat. "Odelia DiOrto, are you ready to receive your Gift?"

"I am."

She placed her fingertips on Lia's temples. "Great Giver, please guide my hand. Use me as your conduit to bestow your child with your Gift."

Lia closed her eyes and exhaled. She sat stone still as long as Sister Rose kept her hands in place. Just when Ken began to fear Lia might never breathe again, Sister Rose lifted her hands away.

"Healing," she said again.

For the first time, Lia's father spoke up. "I thought Healing was rare." Abhenric looked more confused than angry.

"It is the rarest," Sister Rose said, working her way to the table in the center of the room.

"Then how can we both have it?" Ken asked.

"If you were strangers, you could call it an unlikely coincidence. However, you are not, and I find that there are no coincidences where Gifts are concerned." She picked up the quill and wrote a few lines in the record book. Then she strode to the front door and said, "Farewell. Enjoy your Gifts, and remember, they are called such for a reason."

As she opened it, the crowd outside cheered. Father growled, then composed himself into a false grin and motioned for Mother to smile as well. He pressed Ken toward the door. Once his family was outside, Father raised his hands. The drums banged, and the herald swooped down to speak with Father for a moment. When the drumming stopped, the crowd fell still and silent, and the herald soared back into the air.

"His Royal Highness, Crown Prince Kennard has received the Gift of Healing!"

There were spatters of applause here and there. Whispers hissed like lapping waves on the shore.

The herald cleared his throat, then repeated, "His Royal Highness, Crown Prince Kennard has received the *rare* Gift of Healing!"

This finally elicited the expected cheers and clapping. Ken waved to the people as he and his family returned to the Cedar Palace. Behind them, people filled in the path of the retreating guards.

Ken sighed. Poor Lia would have to push her way through to come home. Was she as confused as he was? He needed to talk to her.

As soon as the palace doors closed, Father turned to the guards and dropped his smile. "Have Abhenric DiOrto and his daughter brought to me the minute they set foot in here. Melaine, delay the feast, then talk to Conora about what's happened. Kennard, you're coming with me."

Father led Ken to his study, his shoulders tight, like a stalking cougar—which he became somewhere along the way. He always used Transformation more heavily when he was emotional. He could choose any familiar animal with fur, though he favored large carnivores.

"Close the door, Son. I'm going to need to implement some new rules for you."

"Am I in trouble?" Ken asked. "Did I do something wrong?"

"No, not you. This is that idiot wise woman's fault."

"I don't think a *wise* woman can be an idiot." It slipped out before Ken could stop himself.

Father glared. "I'm not in the mood for your foolery. Thanks to her, I need to protect you now."

"Protect me from *what*?"

Father shrank back into a man, his eyes sad. "Yourself."

"Wha—" Ken furrowed his eyebrows. "What does that mean?"

Father ran a hand over his face. "There's a reason you've never met a Healer before."

"Because they're so rare?"

"So are Seers, but I've still always found one to work for me. Healers..." He cleared his throat. "It's a powerful Gift. It's said that at peak mastery, Healers can pull people from their deathbeds."

"But I thought you wanted me to be powerful. You're always pushing me to be stronger."

Father shook his head. "Not this kind of power. You know that all Gifts come at a cost."

Ken nodded.

"Well, the more powerful the Gift, the steeper its cost is. For even a hint of power over life and death, you will pay dearly. Healers don't live long lives."

Ken staggered back a step. His Gift would kill him? That couldn't be right. It sounded more like a curse. "What exactly is the cost?"

"From now on, every injury and illness you ever have will heal slower."

Ken shrugged. "That doesn't sound as dire as you're making it out to be."

"If you cut yourself, you can bleed to death in the extra time it takes your body to heal. And illnesses will only get worse if you cannot fight

7

them quickly. Most Healers die after catching the same ailment they've rid someone else of."

"But I'll get to serve our people, right? Think of all the people I can help now."

"Within rules."

"What rules?"

Father became a grizzly bear, towering over him. "No more fight training, not even with wooden weapons. Rough sport is out of the question as well. It's all too dangerous now."

Ken sank into a chair. So much for fun, but he couldn't object to protecting his own life.

"As for Healing, you can help the injured, but not the sick. If someone so much as sneezes, you are not to go near them."

"You're banning me from using my Gift? Why even have one if I can't use the good part?"

A knock sounded on the door.

"You will have to wait while I deal with your friend."

Father returned to human form to open the door. Abhenric and Lia entered and bowed.

"You requested us, Your Majesty?"

"Yes." Father squinted at Abhenric. "Give me one reason not to dismiss you from service right now."

Abhenric's pale blue eyes widened before he smiled up at Father. "Certainly, if Your Majesty will tell me what offense I am to be dismissed for."

"Incompetence, for one. How did you not See this?"

"I'm not a wise woman. Visions revealing Gifts are blocked from me. They create blank spots in the future."

Father sneered. "So you've claimed before. How do I know this isn't some plan on your part?"

Abhenric looked at Ken as if to ask, *Do you know what he's talking about?*

Ken shook his head and shrugged. He couldn't make anything of Father's current paranoia.

"You encouraged your daughter to befriend the prince," Father continued, "so she would influence his Gift. She pulled him away from what was meant to be his to weaken him."

Abhenric ran his hand through his short sandy hair. "With all due respect, even if I were capable of predicting Gifts, that would be a terrible

8

plan for me to carry out. What would I stand to gain?" He gestured to Lia. "My own daughter received Healing as well."

"The wise woman said it wasn't a coincidence."

"That doesn't mean *I* planned it. Wise women answer to the Giver himself. Perhaps you could pray for guidance."

"Perhaps you could tell me, Seer. Nothing should block your vision now."

"I don't want to know," Ken said quietly.

All eyes turned to him.

His confidence rose a little higher as he stood up. "It's my future you're discussing. Knowing can change it, and if there really is a grand plan for it, I don't want to ruin it by knowing."

Abhenric gave him a proud smile. Ken often wished Abhenric was his father instead, and in that moment, remembering the lessons he had taught him about the future, he could almost imagine he was.

"Fine," Father said. "You may keep your position for now, but your daughter will keep her distance from both Prince Kennard and Princess Conora from now on."

Lia gasped.

"No!" Ken shouted.

Father scowled.

Abhenric put a hand up to Ken and Lia. "If I may? I believe it is in the prince's best interest that you reconsider."

"Really? In *his* best interest?"

"Yes. They can learn from each other's mistakes and discoveries. Unless you know of someone else who shares their Gift, only she can do this with him."

Father jabbed his finger at Abhenric. "So this was your plan all along."

Abhenric maintained his usual calm demeanor. "Not at all. I am simply accepting a situation that we cannot change and offering the best method I can think of to cope with it."

Father studied Abhenric for a long while, then turned to Lia. "You may study side by side with the prince, girl, but never think that makes you his equal. You are in this palace at my sufferance, and should you forget your place, you will no longer be welcome here."

Lia curtsied and said meekly, "Yes, thank you, Your Majesty."

Father waved his hand toward the door. "You are all dismissed."

Lia and Abhenric bowed and left.

"You didn't need to attack them," Ken said softly. "They're good people."

Father sighed wearily. "Think what you will, Son, but I do what I must to protect what's mine. Someday, you will too."

ODELIA DIORTO

In the palace library, Odelia found Kennard sitting next to an unlit fireplace. He gazed longingly out the window, where sunlight danced on pink and purple rhododendrons. Doubtless, he was already planning a picnic to take advantage of the short summer.

She took the chair next to him. "Planning a whole feast or just a light snack?"

"Neither," he said flatly.

She waited for him to crack a joke or at least look her direction, but he didn't move. Odelia tried again. "Have you met the new tutor yet?"

"No."

"You're quiet this morning. Are you okay?"

Kennard sighed. "I didn't think Father would implement the rules so quickly. It's been one day, and he's already had everything he considers dangerous removed from my room. I barely convinced him to let me keep the staff your father carved for me by telling him it was for walking, not fighting. Apparently, hikes might be forbidden as well. With his rules, I'm more likely to die from lack of movement than injury."

She didn't like this new Kennard. He was usually the optimist. She offered a helpful smile. "You could take up more reading to stave off the boredom."

He put a hand on her shoulder and gasped in mock horror. "Oh, but I might get a paper cut!"

Odelia gave him a real smile this time. "Well, there I go, being a bad influence again."

A tall woman in a short black dress approached the table, holding an enormous book. Her deep auburn hair coiled around her head in a continuous braid, and a dark tan set off her blue eyes. "Prince Kennard?" she asked.

"Yes?"

She curtsied. "Pleasure to meet you, Your Highness. My name is Bertina Schuler, and I will be tutoring you on the use of your Gift. This is Odelia DiOrto, I presume." She dropped her large tome on the table with a thud and began flipping through it. "The king has informed me of the rules he's given you. I must admit, it's fascinating to work with two Healers."

"Fascinating for you, at least," Kennard said. How quickly the dark cloud returned.

"I know things seem bleak right now, but they aren't as bad as they look," Bertina said.

"To hear my father tell it, we're doomed."

Bertina folded her hands in front of her. "While it's true that Healing cuts most people's lives short, you are not most people. Few receive the kind of training I'm going to give you. For that, you should consider yourself blessed. Now, do you have any questions before we begin?"

"What is your Gift?" Odelia asked. If Kennard was determined to be dour, she could be polite for both of them.

"Memory. Do you know how that works?"

"You can never forget anything," Odelia said.

Bertina smiled. "Correct. I've compiled every text currently written about Gifts into this book, and since I've read all the texts, I remember everything contained within. I'll admit the section on Healing is woefully thin, but that can't be helped."

"Where are you from?" Kennard asked, his head cocked like a puppy.

"Ormoint," she said quickly.

He puzzled for a moment.

He wouldn't dare ask, would he? Yes, he would.

"But—"

Odelia elbowed him and shook her head. "Don't be rude," she whispered.

Ormoint had been an Elgathan border town before the formation of Meriveria. Vistans and Elgathans mixed more frequently in such towns. Bertina had the height and complexion of an Elgathan like Kennard but the bright hair and light eyes of a Vistan like Odelia. Most people from border towns tried to pass for Elgathan if they could, naturally, but Bertina didn't have that luxury.

Kennard was curious about Vistans, but other than Odelia and her family, he had little interaction with them. The first time they met, three years before, he'd blurted out that her eyes were strange because he'd never seen green ones before. The question he'd almost asked was nowhere near as rude, but she made a mental note to speak to him about it later.

"On second thought, let's just get started, shall we?" Bertina said. "Besides Healing and Memory, there are eighteen other Gifts. Can either of you name them all?"

Odelia grinned. Her parents had taught her all of them. Counting off on her fingers, she recited, "Transformation, Listening, Hearing, Seeing, Far-Sight, Near-Sight, Night-Sight, Water-Breathing, Speech, Animal Speech, Speed, Strength, Invisibility, Flight, Stone-Skin..." What were the other three again? "...Fire...Ice...and—oh, one more. Why can't I think of it?"

"Allure," Kennard finished. Of course, he would remember the queen's Gift.

She groaned. "How could I forget Allure?"

"That's okay. You still did very well. I'd say that happens to everyone, but well..." Bertina chuckled, then turned to Kennard. "Speaking of Allure, I'm sure you know that one well. What can you tell me?"

"Mother has it. It makes her more likable, even when she isn't trying, and when she does try, it can help her attract or persuade people." His voice was dry and detached.

Bertina leaned in close and whispered conspiratorially, "Judging by your tone, I'd say it isn't very effective on you."

"It doesn't work on blood."

Bertina waited for a moment, but he didn't offer any more.

Odelia had been around the palace long enough to know why he didn't approve of the subject or wish to speak about it. Between her Gift and her crown, the queen had most of the court wrapped around her finger. The sycophantic displays were unnerving, and the queen was so used to getting her way that she expected Kennard to fall in line with her whims. Fortunately for Odelia's friendship with him, he rarely agreed with the queen, but the constant struggle had to wear on him.

"My mom has Hearing," Odelia offered, hoping to give Kennard a reprieve.

Bertina nodded for her to continue.

"Every sound is amplified for her. She can hear a conversation through a wall, but loud noises are painful, so she has to wear earmuffs or earplugs in crowded places."

"Very good," Bertina said. "I'll eventually teach you about how all of the Gifts work, especially the ways they interact with your own, but for now, I'll teach you Healing. What do you already know?"

"We can Heal other people, but using our Gift will eventually kill us," Kennard said.

"And?"

Odelia and Kennard shrugged. If they knew more, they wouldn't have needed her tutelage.

"No wonder you're so gloomy. That's a poor explanation. Using Healing won't kill you unless you attempt to severely overextend your capabilities, which I will teach you to grow."

Odelia said, "But we sacrifice our bodies' recovery to Heal others, though, right?"

Bertina shook her head. "That's a common misconception. You do expend energy when you use your Gift, but in the same way you would with any kind of exertion, like running or lifting a heavy object. Any of those things could just as easily be harmful if you did more than your body was prepared for."

Odelia smiled. "Well, that's much better!"

"Then why all the protections?" Kennard asked, annoyed. "Can't we just rest or eat to restore ourselves?"

"Yes, you can, but the real danger is your permanent weakness—your body's slow recovery—and that's not affected by how much you use your Gift."

Odelia had spoken too soon. At least before, she believed she might have a measure of control.

Bertina continued, "Honestly, it could kill you even if you never Heal anyone—"

Odelia and Kennard turned to each other. His wide-eyed expression perfectly matched the horror that hit her.

"—but you can mitigate the risk by not throwing yourself in harm's way. Most Healers eventually contract an illness they've Healed because doing so puts them too close to a contagion to avoid catching it themselves. That combined with their poor recovery is what kills them, not the usage itself."

"So we could safely Heal anything that isn't contagious, right?" Odelia asked. "Like a stroke or a miner's cough?" Maybe they didn't need to waste their Gift.

"You can, but His Highness is supposed to avoid anyone with a cough, per His Majesty's orders."

"My name will do, thank you," Kennard said coolly. He still wasn't his chipper self yet, but at least he'd stopped pouting.

Bertina leaned in. "Well, Kennard, did you know that Healing gives you two abilities?"

Kennard perked up. "Really?"

"You don't just Heal people. You can also sense something called 'Vitality.' Put your fingers on the underside of your wrist or side of your neck—anywhere you can feel your pulse."

Odelia slid two fingers under her jaw. Her heart beat in a steady rhythm. But there was something strange.

"You should be feeling something else as well. That other sensation is your Vitality."

It was a taut vibration in her fingertips, like a freshly plucked string, but the note went on indefinitely.

"Now that you know what your own feels like, check one another."

Kennard put two tentative fingers on Odelia's wrist. "Ah!" He wrinkled his nose. "It feels weird."

Must everything about her be weird to him? Odelia scowled back at him and tried his wrist. "Oh! You're right. It does." The vibration felt different yet familiar, like two instruments playing the same note. She felt her own again, and the Vitality felt the same as the first time.

"You can try this on anyone with a pulse," Bertina said. "It takes no extra energy and endangers no one, so practice it as much as you can. The more Vitalities you become familiar with, the better you will understand what a normal one feels like."

"But why?" Odelia asked. "What does it mean?"

"The strength of someone's Vitality will tell you if they need Healing, how much they need, and most importantly, if you can do so safely. That's why we're starting with Vitality. It also brings me to a few rules I have."

Kennard groaned.

Bertina smiled. "My rules are only temporary."

"What are they?" Odelia asked.

Bertina held up one finger. "Rule number one: never Heal someone before you've checked their Vitality and understand what it means. That means that neither of you is ready to Heal at all yet, but we'll get there soon." She raised a second finger. "Rule number two: no Healing each other. With this arrangement and the king's warnings, that would be inappropriate. You may check each other's Vitality, but no Healing."

"Oh, good." Kennard plastered on a sardonic smile. "The list of people I can't Heal just keeps growing."

"The first rule makes sense," Odelia said, "but why the second one? Also, what happens if we break a rule?"

"For one, we don't know what will happen with two Healers. Sometimes Gifts can amplify each other. For instance, Fire and Ice have killed their users when combined."

Odelia shuddered. Ice absorbed heat, and Fire expelled it. Amplified, heat could transfer from the Fire user to the Ice user at fatal speed.

"But those are opposites. We have the same Gift," Kennard said.

"True, but we still can't be sure what would happen. And there's another reason. Allow me to demonstrate." Bertina leaned against the table and picked up her huge book with one hand, raising it above her head. She took a deep breath. The book slammed back down onto her other hand. Bertina let out a harsh grunt.

Odelia stifled a scream and jumped out of her chair.

Kennard stood up. "What is wrong with you?"

"I told you, a demonstration is needed." Bertina winced and hugged her hand to her chest. "Odelia, you're going to Heal my hand. Kennard, you need to stand behind her in case she faints."

"I'm not squeamish," Odelia said.

"I wasn't implying that you were. It'd be fairer to make the prince do the Healing, but I'm afraid he would squish you. Now, come here, quickly, please."

Odelia faced Bertina with Kennard at her back. With two fingers, she felt the underside of Bertina's wrist on her good arm. The Vitality throbbed now. It wasn't a large change—hardly more than the difference between two people—but a definite change nonetheless.

Bertina held out her broken hand at Odelia's eye level, palm down and shaking. The fingers bent at sickening angles. "I need you to kiss my hand," she said through gritted teeth.

Odelia grimaced. "Seriously? That's how it works? This must be a joke."

Bertina glared. "I just damaged my hand. Do you honestly think I would joke about that?"

Steeling herself, Odelia put a gentle hand under Bertina's to steady it. She couldn't look at the mangled fingers and focused on the back of the palm instead. A tiny jolt of power passed through her as she brushed her lips against it. Odelia let go, and Bertina's fingers were straight again.

"Hey," Odelia said, her own voice sounding far away, "it worked. I did—"

"Lia!" Kennard wrapped his arms around her as the world faded to black.

AFTER SIX YEARS OF PERFECT HEALTH

Odelia laid her head back on the floor and blew a limp golden strand from her face. It only moved an inch before clinging to a damp cheek. Panting, she tucked the stubborn hair behind her ear.

Still straddling her hips, Kennard bent closer and rested a hand next to her head. His dark eyes sparkled with mischief. "Again?"

She let out a weak laugh. "I think I need some air first."

"You always say that when I win." He pulled back the wooden dagger he'd held to her throat. Swinging his leg over, he hopped up and offered her a hand.

She took it and pulled herself upright. "That's because your victories take too long." She dropped his hand and sashayed to the window.

He flipped the dagger in the air and pointed it at her. "Mighty words, considering you just lost."

"This time. I believe you'll find I still have the upper hand this week." She leaned against the cedar plank wall as she pushed the window open. The chilly air felt nice at first, but as she stuck her head out and looked to the gray sky, a fine mist greeted her. Odelia pulled her head back inside and propped her elbows on the sill.

Kennard reached over her to rest his hand on the upper window frame. "That rain is persistent. I think the ambassador will arrive soggy today."

"And...?"

"He'll have to freshen up before he can present himself." Kennard grinned. "That gives us more practice time."

"Or gives the king more time to notice your absence." As much as she loved his optimism, someone had to be practical.

Kennard slumped. "Why do you have to do that?"

"Do you want to get caught with a weapon?"

"No, but it's been six years. If Father hasn't noticed by now, I doubt a little tardiness today will make him suspicious." He crossed his arms. "I have half a mind to tell him anyway. I'm not a child, and these protections are pointless."

He wasn't a child, but she was still a Vistan woman. How could he be so selfish? It was more than just her life at risk. Dad had taught them both, and arming and training a Vistan woman was equally illegal for the teacher and student and almost as illegal as breaking King Gonfrid's overprotective edicts about Kennard. Odelia elbowed him in the chest and held her own dagger to his throat. "Will you take that back?"

"Hey now! That's cheating."

She shrugged. "Everything is cheating when daggers are involved. Now think about what you just suggested, please."

He looked down at the dagger, then met her gaze.

She raised an eyebrow at him.

His eyes widened in realization. "I'm so sorry. You know I would never do that to you."

"You *just* considered it out loud!" She held the dagger steady in spite of her trembling fingers, but the quaver of her voice betrayed her.

He batted the dagger away and grasped her shoulders. "Lia, you know me better than that. It's just an idle thought. And even if I told him I was practicing, I wouldn't give you away. I'd tell him I trained alone."

Odelia shook her head. "He'll blame me either way."

King Gonfrid would pounce on any excuse to be rid of her. A Vistan commoner was an inappropriate companion for the Crown Prince of Meriveria. As a child, her father's value to the king as a powerful seer had protected her. But she was old enough now to find her own employment, and the king was losing patience with her friendship with his heir.

"Come here." Kennard pulled her into a hug. "I'm not that stupid. If you were banished, who else would tell me when I'm a being foolish?"

She chuckled. "Or laugh with you."

He pulled back, smearing her cheek with sweat. She wiped it with her sleeve.

He scoffed. "First of all, you are not helping your case. And secondly, I'll have you know I made Val laugh yesterday."

"A groan doesn't count." A streak of red flashed on her sleeve as she gestured with her index finger. That was not sweat. Where had it come from?

"So you say."

She reached up and tilted his head down, brushing his brunet curls away from his hairline. A gash between his ear and jaw trailed blood into his collar.

He winced. "What are you doing?"

"Ooh, Ken. I'm so sorry." She gingerly touched the skin near the gash, and he flinched again. It must have been from earlier in their session. Much of the blood had already dried. "I didn't think I hit you that hard."

He ran to a mirror. "Great. Of all the days... There's no way Father won't notice this."

She felt his wrist. Under his pulse, his Vitality hummed like the music of a freshly plucked string that never ended. The wound was superficial. "I can Heal that without any trouble."

He bent down to her eye level. She gave him a peck on the cheek, and he snorted in a failed attempt to stifle a laugh. He'd always been ticklish, and even a minor use of Healing left a tingle on one's skin.

Kennard checked the mirror again. He scooped soap and water from the vanity below it and rubbed at his jaw. "Can you help me clean up? I can't see if I'm getting it all behind the ear."

Odelia grabbed a towel hanging next to the mirror and dipped it in the water. "Bend your head over the basin."

He obliged, and she scrubbed until the only trace of red in his tawny skin was the flush caused by friction.

He inspected his stained collar. "Looks like I'll really need my spare shirt today."

"You got some on your pants too." She pointed to the offending spots.

"Frog nuggets. I don't think I ever gave you a pair."

Odelia pursed her lips. That could be a problem. She laundered the shirts he wore for sparring to keep his servants from musing about their sweaty origins, but they hadn't bothered with his pants. They never acquired the same obvious level of filth as his shirts, and asking her friend—even one as close as Kennard—for his pants somehow felt too indecent. "No. I don't think I have any pants for you," she said.

"I think borrowing one of your skirts would gather more attention than the blood."

"True."

"I mean, it would be a foot too short. I'd look ridiculous."

She smiled and shook her head. But that did give her an idea. "What about Valerzan?"

"Your brother isn't that much taller than you are. I'm not sure any Vistans exist with pants long enough for me. What if you sneak a pair from my room?"

"Soggy ambassador or not, we don't have time for me to change out of my own clothes and go to the other side of the palace and back before you can change yours—at least not without drawing attention."

He grimaced. "Maybe the spots aren't that noticeable?"

"They're more noticeable than short pants will be after you tuck them into your boots." She peeked out the door.

Valerzan already wore the cobalt pants and iron gray jacket of his guard uniform and had his booted feet propped upon the table. Certain that he sat alone in their family common room, Odelia opened the door the rest of the way.

"Oh, good. You're done. I need to start my shift soon," he said.

"Not quite... You wouldn't happen to have a pair of clean pants Ken could borrow, would you?"

Valerzan shrugged. "They'll be too short."

"That's what I said," Kennard chimed in.

Odelia rolled her eyes. "Not helpful."

Valerzan ducked into his room.

"Oh, and make sure they're a nice pair," she added before returning to hers. She opened a small trunk near the vanity and took out a clean white shirt. Gathering the practice weapons and depositing them in its place, she did her best not to completely stare at Kennard as he removed his dirty shirt. Sparring and manhood had honed his tight, lean physique, and her familiarity with the view did little to dampen its appeal.

He yanked the new shirt over his head, "I almost forgot to ask: what would you think of joining me to dine with the ambassador?"

Odelia looked down at her bloody sleeve. Her bodice had a few small smears as well. She didn't want to know the state of her hair. She'd have to work quickly to make herself presentable. "A little warning would have been nice."

"You don't have to come if you don't want to. I just—"

"I do. I'm just surprised you'd ask. What will the king say?"

Kennard rubbed his neck. "He thinks having you there will 'show a united front' to the Tehazians."

She put a hand on her hip. "He wants a Vistan. I suppose Dad and Valerzan will be requested as well?"

Her brother entered, black pants in hand. "That would explain why I was assigned to the dining hall tonight." Being a novice to the guard, he normally patrolled outside.

Kennard slung an arm over her shoulder. "Well, *I* want you there because you're my friend. If half the stories about Tehazians are true, I'll need someone congenial to talk to."

She smiled and pressed a hand to his back. "I'll be ready, but you can help by changing in Valerzan's room."

He followed Valerzan out. Halfway to the door, Kennard turned back and took her hand, brushing his lips against her knuckles and tickling her fingers with the trace of healing power. He winked. "Just in case." Then he left and closed the door.

Odelia ran her thumb over her knuckle. He could bring her sunshine at midnight. It was a benign gesture; it meant nothing more than the helpfulness of a dearest friend, but for a fleeting moment, she let herself dream of more. She dropped her hand. No good could come from letting the fantasy linger.

Ken stood next to his father in the audience chamber. People had often pointed out the strong resemblance between them, but Ken didn't feel anything like the stiffly composed king right then.

"Just remember, Son," Father said, "you are not to speak. You are here to observe only."

Ken nodded, but the knot in his stomach remained. He glanced down at his boots. Reassured that the hem of his pants did not rise above their tops, he folded his hands in front of him.

"Send them in," Father said.

A herald with giant hawk-like wings opened the door. "Grandilord Doneron of Oulley and Lord Egino of Cantahn," he announced.

Two noblemen entered and bowed. Both had dressed in what must have been their finest attire. Lace hemmed sleeves peeked out under their rich brocade ponchos. One wore thick, embroidered leather gloves, the other, a jeweled magnifying glass from a chain around his neck.

"Grandilord Doneron, how long has it been?" Father asked.

"Too long, my liege," the gloved man said with more reverence than could ever be genuine.

Ken fought the urge to roll his eyes, choosing instead to muse on the grandilord's gloves, which he hadn't removed, despite the roaring fire at the side of the room. What Gift did the gloves insulate the world from, Fire or Ice?

"Lord Egino, I don't believe we've met," Father said to the other gentleman.

"I am replacing my father, who died a month ago, Your Majesty. Other than my Gifting ceremony, he never brought me to court when he came."

"Our condolences, your father was always a friend to the court," Father said softly, then changed to a more authoritative tone, "but you should have sent word and presented yourself before today. What is the matter you bring before me now?"

Egino said, "Your Majesty, Cantahn produces well. Our soil is fertile, and the farmers work hard. The trouble is in getting our products to market here. There is no direct road from here to Cantahn. My people are forced to take the Port Road west to the South Road. It takes twice as long as it should. By the time goods reach the market, the food is not as fresh, and the extra time spent on the road is time my merchants could use to make money. A direct road stretching southeast from Meria to Cantahn would alleviate these problems."

Father crossed his arms. "Such a road would be mostly contained to Cantahn. What brings this local problem to me?"

"Grandilord Doneron has overruled me and ordered the project halted."

Father motioned for Doneron to speak.

"Your Majesty," he said, bowing again, "such a road will do damage to the seat of Oulley. As the roads are now, it is the same travel distance from Meria. The competition in trade is fair. If such a road were built, not just the seat, but other parts of Oulley would suffer. The crossroads at the Port Road and the South Road are trying to build a town. They depend on the traffic on both roads. A direct route would cut them out before they've even had a chance to name the settlement."

Father stroked his chin. "This might take some time. Feel free to enjoy the palace for now. I will summon you when I have come to a decision."

The noblemen bowed and left.

Father turned to Ken. "Well, Son, what do you think?"

"It's a difficult decision."

"That's why you're here. You need to be aware of what's happening in the kingdom if you're going to rule it someday."

Ken cleared his throat. "If?"

Father looked away. "It does no good to pretend otherwise."

"But—"

In a snap, Father transformed into a wolf, his russet fur bristling. "We are not discussing this now, Kennard," he growled.

Six years of perfect health, and Father still imagined to outlive him. Ken tired of the constant reminders of his shortened life expectancy. He no longer believed it himself, but Father wouldn't listen.

Father turned back into a man, his brown hair curling down to his shoulders, brushing the top of the silver embroidered vest that had rematerialized with his human shape. "As I've said before, this is not your decision to make now, but if it were, what would you do?"

"A road to Cantahn would be beneficial for them and Meria."

"And cost a fortune to build. Roads are expensive. Trees must be cleared, marshes and gulches skirted around or stabilized. Your grandfather tried to have a road built there once before. The wetlands ate it. Besides which, it would upset the hierarchy."

Ken frowned. "How so? Lord Egino has the authority to do what he wants with Cantahn."

"But as part of Oulley, Cantahn is also in Grandilord Doneron's jurisdiction. It would not do to overrule him on this matter without good reason."

"You sound as if you've already made your decision. Why did you tell the noblemen you needed more time?"

A sly smile crept across Father's face. "That's just what I need them to think. Nobles must be handled with care. The lord needs to believe I take his request seriously, or he may take offense; and the grandilord could do with an occasional reminder that he answers to me. It's all about power, Son. We must remind them who is ultimately in charge, lest they believe it is them."

"I see." Ken often wondered how much of his presence at these audiences was another demonstration of power. Neglecting to prepare him for the throne would be a public declaration of Ken's weakness. Though Father treated him like glass behind closed doors, in front of their subjects, nothing could be amiss.

Father turned to his secretary. "I think we've given the ambassador sufficient time to prepare himself. Reschedule any remaining requests for tomorrow and gather the attendees for dinner."

The man bowed. "Yes, Your Majesty."

He exited the room, and the herald announced, "Lord Jibiam, Ambassador of Tehazy."

Jibiam was as pale as a Vistan, but not as short. His long, dark hair had been slicked back into a long braid, matching his polished black boots. Gold spirals covered his plum doublet, cloak, and pants. Gold chains dripped off his neck in layers, and every finger wore a ring. They clinked and rattled as he bowed deeply.

"Welcome to Meriveria, Lord Jibiam. I trust your journey was pleasant," Father said.

"I thank you for your hospitality, Your Majesty. From what I have seen so far, your kingdom is beautiful. I look forward to an alliance between us." Jibiam strode forward and handed a document to Father. "Tehazy proposes a trading post and bridge on the Norlach River, near your Fort Vigil. We hope to make trade easier in the valley, to enrich both our nations."

Father handed the document to Ken. "I shall look over your proposal later. For now, if you will allow my secretary to accompany you to the dining hall, we shall first become better acquainted over dinner."

"Of course, Your Majesty." Jibiam bowed again and followed the herald out.

Father sneered. "And they think they're the more civilized culture? He handed that to me as if he expected me to sign it now."

Ken shrugged. "Well, you can't say he's inefficient."

Father morphed into a grizzly bear as he stood. "Let's hope his table manners are better than his greetings."

2

FAKE SMILES AND FEIGNED HELP

Lia was hard to miss. A pale Vistan in a sea of Elgathans, she waited just outside the dining hall. Her silky blonde hair had been coiled on top of her head and wrapped in a braid. The color had always reminded Ken of butter. When they were children, she'd been the first Vistan he'd ever met, and he'd wondered then if it felt as soft and smooth as butter as well. But that was a decade ago. He knew better now.

As he approached, she smiled and curtsied. Lia only wore long gowns for special occasions, and her floor-length seafoam dress marked this as such.

He offered his arm.

She took it and whispered, "You were inside a long time after the ambassador left. Is everything okay?"

"It's fine. Father wanted to skim the document the ambassador gave us before dinner. That, and I think he wanted to make him wait just to show that he could."

"I take it I shall have to play my part as the happily-conquered with conviction, then?"

"Yes, but you're perfectly paired with the not-at-all-fragile heir. We can fake our smiles together."

She stifled a small laugh. "Not that you've ever made that difficult."

He smiled back with a dramatic sigh, clutching his heart for effect. "Ah, there's the acknowledgment." He loved to make her laugh, especially at formal events. She would bite her cheek or hold her breath to keep the laughter at bay, only for them both to burst into fits at the first moment of privacy.

Lia looked past him. "Conora!" She dipped a quick curtsy to Ken's sister as she stopped in front of them.

Though two years younger, Conora towered over Lia. Her dark blue gown shimmered in the candlelight, as did the silver filigree headband in her flowing dark brown hair. Conora appeared as the opposite of Lia in every

25

aspect: one tall, rich, and elaborate, the other small, light, and simple—on the outside. In truth, the two were kindred spirits.

Conora flashed a surprised smile and touched Lia's shoulder. "I didn't know you were joining us! It's been too long."

"Your brother invited me at the king's request."

Conora's eyes lit up. "Does that mean...?"

"Just until the ambassador leaves," Ken said, unable to keep the disappointment from his voice. He had lied about the invite being entirely Father's idea. He had wanted to summon Vistan noblemen only, but Ken had convinced him that Lia and her family would be more amiable than the disgruntled nobility. What he hadn't lied about was his true reason: it was a convenient excuse to openly spend time with his best friend.

"Oh..." A smile crept over Conora's face. "In that case, I think I might need a new dress. Perhaps a dog is destroying one right now—a plain one, of course. Don't want to be wasteful..."

Lia grinned. "You know, Mom was worried that your gold one might not sit perfectly on your hips. It might be wise to have it fitted again."

"Even better."

It had been so much easier when they were younger. Mother and Father had interfered less in their friendships then. Ken and Conora hadn't needed to invent reasons to visit the servants' wing. This one wasn't much of a stretch. Conora loved dresses, and Lia's mother, Hortensia, was the finest seamstress in the Cedar Palace.

"Speaking of Hortensia," Ken said, "is she coming with Abhenric tonight?"

Lia shrugged. "They were both gone by the time I was dressed, so I'd assume they're inside already."

"We should be as well," Conora said.

"We were headed that way until someone stopped in front of us," Ken joked.

She put a hand on her hip and shot him a dirty look. "You know, Odelia, you are more than welcome to sit with me if he's going to be a pest."

He laughed. "Hey. Stop trying to poach my guest."

Lia faux whispered, "I'd rather keep an eye on him anyway."

"And...we're going in before you two can conspire against me." Ken led her toward the door again.

Just before they reached it, someone cleared their throat behind him. "What are you doing?" Mother whispered in his ear.

Ken turned. "Escorting my dinner guest."

Opulent as ever, pearls adorned her black hair and gold tiara, and gold embroidery covered her corn-silk lace gown. She tacked on a strained smile and pulled him aside several feet, leaving Lia by the doorway. "This is a state dinner. What is she doing here?"

"Father requested that I invite her."

Mother scoffed. "I doubt that."

Didn't Mother have better things to do than fret over Lia's presence? "He'll be joining any second. Please, ask him yourself."

She gestured at his head. "And your circlet is crooked."

His hair wouldn't cooperate with it at the best of times, and he had put it on without looking just before leaving Father. Ken lifted the circlet, ran a hand through his hair, and set it back down.

Mother sighed and adjusted it herself. "Maybe, if you found yourself a bride, she could keep your appearance tidy."

"Shall I find a woman who can stop the rain from falling as well?"

"Mind your tongue, Kennard. I can change your Father's mind about your little Vistan being here tonight."

It wasn't an idle threat. With few exceptions, people were compelled to like Mother. In his natural human form, Father was easily influenced by her Allure. Decades of practice in forcing her Gift on him had enhanced her power as queen consort.

Ken nodded slowly. "Apologies, Mother. Now, if you'll excuse me, I would like to return to demonstrating Meriverian unity."

She furrowed her brow. "That's what this is about? Why didn't you say so?"

"I'm telling you now."

Mother scowled and waved him off.

He hastened back to Lia's side. Holding out his elbow, he plastered on a smile. "Shall we?"

She took his arm again and followed his lead into the dining hall, faking a smile herself.

Like the rest of the Cedar Palace, the wood for which it was named lined the floor and ceiling of the dining hall, its pink and gold hues warming the room as much as the people did. Inlaid wooden panels depicted nature scenes across the walls. Long tables formed a giant square with a group of drummers, pipers, and flutists in the center. Guards stood at attention in the corners, and Valerzan was as easy to find as his sister, with his cropped strawberry blond hair that always looked as though he'd recently lost a battle with his comb. They couldn't interact while Val was on duty, but Ken acknowledged him with a slight tip of his head.

"What's wrong?" Lia asked quietly.

"What do you mean? This is a feast, I'm smiling, and—"

"Your attitude with the queen? That was brazen, even by your standards."

He guided her to a chair a couple seats down from Lord Jibiam. "She treats me like a child."

Lia raised an eyebrow. "How does acting like one help?"

Instead of pulling out the chair, Ken steered away from the table to the wall. "I guess I'm still on edge from something Father said."

"It wasn't about...?"

"No." Their secret was safe. "I think he's humoring me. He's not truly teaching me how to rule."

"Why?"

"He said, 'If.' It was about my rule, and it wasn't 'when' but 'if.' I asked what he meant, he all but told me that he believes I'm going to die soon."

Lia squeezed his arm. "He's wrong. You and I, we are both going to live long and full lives."

"I know, but it's frustrating not being able to explain how I know."

Based on every record they could find, Ken and Lia's experience Healing each other was unprecedented. But telling anyone what they'd done would lead to questions of why, which would lead back to their other secret. Making himself look less frail to his parents wasn't worth Lia's neck—or her father's.

Lia leaned closer and whispered, "Well, smile anyway, or I'll have to tickle your ribs under the table."

Ken laughed. "You wouldn't dare."

She raised an eyebrow. "Is that a challenge?"

"I'm taking you back to the table before you think of more ways to cause trouble."

The beginning of the meal passed with nothing more than idle chatter, and Lord Jibiam paid no heed to Ken and Lia—or so Ken thought until the ambassador spoke up.

"Prince Kennard, how long have you had a taste for the exotic?"

The exotic? "I'm afraid I don't know what you mean, Your Excellency."

"Your little pet. Where did you find her? I didn't think many Vistans lived this far west."

Ken nearly choked on his salmon, and judging by the coughing, Lia had done the same.

Lord Jibiam continued, "I was under the impression that they don't visit this court. At least, they didn't when my predecessor visited."

Ken dabbed his mouth with a napkin. Under the table, Lia gripped his hand for a second. He would choose his next words carefully if he were smart.

"I apologize for any confusion, Lord Jibiam, but Miss DiOrto is not anyone's pet. She is an old friend, and her family has lived and worked in this palace for the last decade."

The ambassador waved his hand. "As you say, Your Highness, but you have such strange manners here. We don't use these pretenses in Tehazy. A man of power like yourself? If you want the servants' daughters, you simply take them."

There was no pretense. Pretty as Lia was, Ken had never considered such a thing. He didn't indulge in dalliances, and as far as he knew, she planned to remain celibate.

Lia set down her fork. "I think I've had my fill," she said softly. Her face had taken on the same pink as their dinner. "Your Highness," she said, loudly now, "doesn't Her Majesty look lovely this evening?"

The deflection was obvious, but Ken didn't have a better idea. "Absolutely! Even more than usual." He leaned in to catch Conora's attention a few seats down. "Sister, you're an expert on the matter. What do you think of Mother's dress?"

She shot him a quizzical look before gushing about the fabric and cut and some details which were lost on him.

Ken nudged closer to Lia and whispered, "If you wish to escape, consider yourself excused."

A week later, Odelia entered Queen Melaine's sitting room. With trembling fingers, she tucked a loose silken strand behind her ear, then curtsied. The queen's presence always did that to her. There was something about being simultaneously hated by and drawn to someone that was unsettling.

"Have a seat, dear." The queen waved a jeweled hand to the empty seat beside her at the fireside.

Odelia eased herself in the over-sized blue armchair. Since when did the queen ever call her "dear"?

"You're a grown woman now, and I believe it is time that you and I have a little...discussion." Queen Melaine said the word like it was a foreign concept.

Odelia took a deep breath and smiled. "What about, Your Majesty?" She didn't need to feign ignorance. The queen's request had been completely devoid of details.

"Over the last few years, you have spent a great deal of time with Crown Prince Kennard. This may have given you some errant ideas."

Odelia clasped her hands together. "What errant ideas might these have been?"

"The two of you are more than old enough to entertain suitors. You will not expect him to be one of yours."

"But I haven't—"

"Don't bother denying it. I've seen the doe-eyed looks you give him." The queen settled deeper into her chair. "You're young. I know how difficult strong feelings are to hide when you lack the experience."

Odelia wasn't a fool. She knew better than to expect anything more than companionship from Kennard, and there was no harm in the occasional daydream. But she resisted the urge to object again. Best to let the queen finish.

"I would like to help you with this trouble of yours."

The queen had never offered to help her with anything before. There had to be a catch.

"My dear friend Grandilady Wilmarie of Eaund holds a smaller but lovely court that she will be returning to next week. I would like you to serve there and learn from her. Without the distraction of your feelings, perhaps you will be able to leverage your friendship with my son for a better suitor than you could attain on your own."

Of course, she wanted to be rid of her. Odelia's life was here in the Cedar Palace. Even without Kennard, all her friends and family were here. She swallowed hard and blinked. "What kind of service is she expecting from me?"

"What skills do you have?"

"My mother has taught me sewing, and Bertina and the court physicians have been helping me study ways to supplement my Healing Gift."

The queen smiled. "You can sew up sick people or something. I'm sure Wilmarie will find a use for you."

Or something. Odelia took a breath to collect herself before she responded with something snarkier. "Is there anything you need me to do to prepare?"

The queen stood up, motioning for Odelia to follow. "Study your lineage. A good ancestor could increase your standing." She gingerly put a hand on Odelia's shoulder and motioned to the knee length hem of her dress. "And perhaps you should invest in a few fashionable gowns."

WHAT REALLY HAPPENED IN IVERISH

Odelia darted across the islet to the wise women's lodge, her poncho tucked close against the oncoming sleet. At the back of the lodge, she found a small wooden door and dashed inside. She shivered, letting the dry interior warm her up.

Across from the door, a red-haired woman dressed entirely in white sat at a large desk. Rows of bookshelves lined the room behind her. "Greetings," she said, "I am Sister Bianca. What knowledge do you seek today?"

"I'm here to find my ancestors."

"Your age?"

"Eighteen."

"And?"

Odelia did a quick calculation in her head. "Seven months?"

"Come with me." Sister Bianca led her down one of the aisles and plucked a book off the shelf. "Your name?"

"Odelia DiOrto."

Sister Bianca opened to the middle of the book, scanning the pages quickly. "Book five. Well, isn't that something?" With a smirk, she replaced the book and walked toward a back corner of the library.

"Is there something special about book five?"

She raised her eyebrows. "You'll see."

Great Giver, wise women were so cryptic. Then again, they probably couldn't help it. Though officially there were twenty Gifts, being a wise woman could be considered the twenty-first, and the inability to lie was part and parcel to that power. Combined with their political neutrality, it made them the perfect recordkeepers, but Odelia suspected the evasiveness was a way to make up for it.

Sister Bianca pulled a heavy black book from the top shelf and handed it to Odelia. "I'll be back at the front if you need any more help."

Odelia studied the dusty tome in her hands. On the front cover, a dogwood flower ringed with fern fronds had been embossed in the black leather. She recognized it from her history books: the Vistan crest. Did all the Vistan lineage books look like this?

She sat at a nearby table and opened to the back, where the newest additions would be. Her name sat at the bottom next to Valerzan's. Above them were her parents. Her mother's read: "Hortensia - Book 94."

Odelia left the book at the table and walked back to the front of the library. "Excuse me, Sister Bianca? This book only charts my father's side. Would I be able to see my mother's family too?"

"You can, but I doubt you'll need it. What's the book number?"

"94. Why wouldn't I need it?"

Sister Bianca smiled. "I'll tell you what. You finish reading the first book I gave you." She pulled out some parchment, a quill, and some ink. "Write down all the books you'll want me to pull as you go. If you still feel you need them by then, you can take them all home."

Yay. More cryptic nonsense. Odelia took the writing implements back to the table. She flipped back a page in the book to her grandparents. Nothing interesting. Her great-grandparents had no titles either. She skipped back several pages.

Odelia's jaw dropped.

It couldn't be. She'd picked up the wrong book.

She checked the back again, but sure enough, her name was in it. She opened to her ancestors again, page-by-page this time. Labeled as her great-great-grandfather was the name of Crown Prince Idris—and it was a primogenitary line. But it was the name several generations back that had initially shocked her.

King Uldrio of Vist.

Everyone knew of Uldrio. Meriveria had been his idea. A skilled Seer, King Uldrio had gone to King Rainald of Elgatha with a vision of their kingdoms uniting. The two signed the Treaty of Meriveria, awarding one dynasty dominion over the other's kingdom should either fall, with the understanding that their heirs would solidify the union with a marriage as soon as they could. According to her history book, Uldrio's heirs had all died of a plague before a marriage contract could be fulfilled.

Clearly, one of the books was wrong, and the ones written by wise women could not lie. Even if they could, the wise women had nothing to gain from altering their texts, unlike the writers of history.

Everything she knew was wrong, not just about herself but the history of her people. Did Dad know? She needed to find out.

Odelia closed the book and returned to Sister Bianca. "May I take this with me? I promise to return it."

"I'm sorry, but lineage books are not permitted to leave the lodge, especially not one as important as that. However, I can write a verified copy of whatever pages you may need."

"I thought you said I could take a whole stack home."

"I said you could take them home if you needed them. I knew you wouldn't."

Odelia sighed. "How long would it take to write a copy of the line from King Uldrio to me?"

"An authenticated copy will take a couple hours, but you can come back for it any time after that."

She handed the book to Sister Bianca. "Thank you. I'll be back for it tomorrow."

Odelia secured her poncho and stepped outside. As the door closed behind her, she screamed into the wind. The catharsis didn't last long. She ran all the way back to the palace and up to her family apartment without pause. Odelia flung open the door to find her father there with Valerzan.

"Did...you...know?" Odelia panted, glaring.

Dad stared at her, almost out of focus. "Valerzan, go to the library and wait for me there," he said without breaking his gaze.

"What do you want me to—"

"It doesn't matter. Find anything to read. Just go." He waited for Valerzan to leave, then closed the door. "What is this about Odelia?"

"You're a Seer, Dad. I'm sure you know."

"Humor me."

"King Uldrio," she said through clenched teeth.

He looked at her dripping poncho and wind tousled hair. "So, you've seen the book. Have a seat, Odelia. It's time I told you a story. You know about King Uldrio and King Rainald."

"Yes."

"The history books don't tell the whole story. Uldrio's vision of Vist and Elgatha uniting in marriage as one kingdom did lead him to sign the Treaty of Meriveria with Rainald. That much is true. But while historians paint Uldrio as a fool for signing it, they conveniently forget two things. One, the treaty applied equally to both kingdoms. At the time of signing, it would have been just as plausible for Vist to have absorbed Elgatha instead.

Two, Vist and Elgatha had been allies for ages. Both royal families had enjoyed close friendships for generations, and both kings had every reason to expect the marriage between their respective heirs in their lifetimes.

"Of course, it was nothing more than an assumption. Uldrio's vision didn't come with a timeline—the really interesting ones never do—just a definite 'what' and a vague 'who' without a 'when.'"

Odelia crossed her arms. "What does this have to do with the lineage?"

"Look, it's a long story. If you're going to interrupt, I can give you the journal and make you read it instead."

She gestured for him to continue. "So what about this vague vision?"

"Because the treaty specified the marriage be between direct heirs or reigning monarchs, it proved more difficult to fulfill than they anticipated. Uldrio and Rainald's firstborns were both sons, and each subsequent generation failed to produce compatible heirs as well. There always seemed to be an unfortunate age gap whenever both a son and a daughter appeared, inevitably resulting in the older one being married to someone else."

"So far, none of this is new," she said.

"Ah, but a hundred years after the Treaty of Meriveria is where history fully diverged from the truth." He sat next to her. "Idris, the heir to the Vistan throne at the time, showed promise as a future king. With the Gift of Speech and a kind heart, many believed he could improve diplomatic relations and bring in more trade from the other side of the mountains. He cared deeply for his subjects and showed interest in the lives of those around him, common and noble alike. So no one thought much of it when one day, he paid special attention to a gardener who was pruning the rhododendrons."

A gardener? The story had to take an odd turn eventually.

"Idris offered her a smile and a friendly nod, then sat on a nearby bench. For several minutes, he pretended to read the book he had brought with him before giving up the ruse and simply watching her work. 'It's not often that the gardener herself outshines the garden. What is your name?' he asked.

"She thought the compliment little more than princely sweet-talk, but it made her blush all the same. The smile he flashed when she told him her name remained one of her most cherished memories for the rest of her life."

"Wait. How do you know that?" Odelia asked.

Dad ducked into his room and returned with a small green journal. "It's all in here, but the story has been passed down through our family. Now, where was I?"

"Her name?"

"Ah, yes. 'Tasia,' he said, 'a beautiful name for a beautiful maiden. It's a wonder the palace grounds can contain so much loveliness.'

"She shook her head. 'I believe you must have me mistaken for a lady. I merely tend the flowers.'

"Idris was summoned back inside before he could reply, and Tasia expected that to be the end of her interaction with the prince. But the next day, he appeared in the garden with a charcoal pencil and some parchment. She bowed and greeted him, then returned to her work. As he put pencil to paper, he asked her questions: how long she had worked at the palace, how many siblings she had, how she'd learned about plants. The more questions she answered, the more he told her about himself, and the conversation eventually gained a momentum of its own.

"After an hour had passed, he left, promising to return the next day. He kept that promise, returning not only the next day, but every day for three months.

"One day, instead of the usual parchment and pencil, he brought a rough leather book with a red ribbon tied around it. In those days, Ribbons of Intent varied less. You couldn't give just any trinket or color of ribbon. Only a red ribbon would do. But even after months of afternoons with Idris, Tasia couldn't believe he intended the token for her. He took a seat and invited her to join him, then handed her the book. Tasia untied the ribbon and held it out to Idris, but he closed her fingers.

"He told her, 'You may still refuse it, Tasia, but know it was meant for you.'

"She opened the book to the image of a cluster of rhododendrons, sketched in loving detail. The next was of Tasia, her hair falling in her face as she bent to pull weeds. She flipped through page after page of sketches. He had poured his soul into the pictures, and they took her breath away.

"'One for every day I visited the garden,' he said. 'They are yours to keep, whether you accept the ribbon or not.'

"In that moment, Tasia knew the words Idris had spoken to her on their first meeting had been genuine. She wrapped the ribbon around her wrist and held it out for him to tie off. Taking this as a sign of her permission, he kissed her.

"The next day, Idris met Tasia with a braided gold ring in his hand. It was sooner than propriety would dictate, but falling in love with a gardener was already improper. His parents had made plans to marry him off to an Elgathan princess on the off-chance she might outlive her older brother and inherit the throne. Idris was to leave for Elgatha in a few days, with no set time of return.

"Unable to accept such a fate, and reasoning that he couldn't be sent away if he were already married, Idris asked Tasia if she would be willing to elope right away. She paid for a room in Iverish that night and found a local priest who agreed to conduct the ceremony there. And so, without any fanfare, the pair sealed their love."

"How does nobody know about this?" Odelia asked.

"That's where the story takes a sad turn. The next day, Idris returned to the palace alone to inform the king and queen, promising to return for Tasia by nightfall.

"But dusk arrived, and Idris did not.

"Tasia gathered her few belongings and prepared to flee the city, but as she passed through the crowd on her way out of the inn, a servant from the palace came in, requesting the aid of any and all physicians he could find. A sickness was working its way through the palace, affecting everyone from the king to the scullery maids. Even the servant relaying the message moved shakily, appearing as though he might vomit and wiping drool from his face."

Odelia grimaced. "Was that a necessary detail?"

"Yes. The story is not mine to change.

"Believing it was only a matter of time before she too fell ill, Tasia decided to return to the palace to find Idris. She met little resistance on the way to his chambers, and the lone man tending to him when she arrived was too thankful to be relieved of duty to question her presence there before he left. Idris lay in bed, unable to move in between bouts of convulsions. Tasia stayed with him, holding his hand and talking with him until he drew his last breath a few hours later. What they spoke of, we'll never know, not because she forgot—she was incapable of forgetting—but because her last moments with him pained her too much to speak of with such vivid detail.

"By sunrise, every member of the royal family and most of the palace residents had died of the mysterious plague. By noon, only Tasia and two physicians from Iverish remained alive. They found her in the garden, weeping over the bench where Idris had fallen in love with her. One of them offered her some cornbread, but she couldn't bring herself to eat. So they kept silent company with her until they too fell ill and died.

"Yet Tasia suffered nothing beyond heartache and irrevocable loss. She didn't understand how she had been spared until she heard her stomach growl, reminding her of something vitally important: she had not eaten in the palace. She realized it wasn't a plague that had swept through the palace. The food had killed everyone. It couldn't have been mere spoiled food. The poison had killed too quickly and efficiently. But the symptoms seemed familiar to her.

"Tasia picked up the cornbread she had rejected, willing it to reveal its secrets. She remembered the cook's delight over the new batch of honey from Elgatha that had arrived the day before. Tasia looked past the bread to her rhododendrons. So beautiful and so deadly to eat. Even honey made from their pollen would kill in small doses, and the cook was known to use generous quantities in her baking.

"Knowing that whoever had poisoned them would not be apt to take kindly to survivors, Tasia acted quickly, taking whatever personal items she could find from Idris and collecting from the treasury as many important pieces as she could carry, including the crown jewels and family heirlooms. She couldn't bear the thought of those things ending up in the hands of assassins. She left the palace through the woods and circled back around to Iverish, lest anyone watched the entrance on that side.

"Days later, the king of Elgatha arrived in Iverish, offering condolences to the kingdom of Vist and declaring himself ruler of the newly-formed Kingdom of Meriveria. Expecting the nobles to reject the new king under such suspicious circumstances, Tasia kept a vigilant eye for any signs of rebellion that she might join. But as the weeks wore on, she found no such support. The king had made no radical changes other than putting the power in his own hands and treated the Vistan nobles no differently than he did his fellow Elgathans. Few suspected foul play, and those who did had nothing to gain and everything to lose from an uprising.

"At first, Tasia wanted to find proof of Elgathan involvement, but she soon found herself with a purpose more important than vengeance: Idris's child, your great-grandfather."

Odelia's eyes welled up. "Were you ever going to tell me?"

Dad put his arm around her. "Eventually. I was waiting for the right time."

"You didn't think that might be some time before I became an adult?"

He sighed. "It's more complicated than that. Why were you looking for your lineage anyway?"

She told him about the queen's offer.

"That woman has been fighting me for years. She doesn't know the truth, but I suspect she knows that I'm hiding something."

Odelia pulled away. "She was right. That's why you brought us here, isn't it? You want Ken and I to fulfill the treaty. You've orchestrated everything. And after I swore I had no designs on him..."

"I admit, I wouldn't be opposed to it, but no. That wasn't my plan."

"Then what is?"

"To save you from your fate."

"I-I don't understand. I thought my fate was to fulfill the treaty."

He folded his hands. "Your fate is to be Queen of Vist, to claim your throne and lead our people—one way or another."

"One way or another? You mean—"

"It's immutable," he said, his voice full of defeat.

Her heart pounded. Most fates were flexible, small influences could alter them profoundly. But she was guaranteed to become queen! "Isn't that a good thing?"

He shook his head. "I have spent your entire life trying to do the impossible and change it."

She stood up. "*Why*?"

"Because it's dangerous for you and for Vist."

Odelia fumed. "Tasia could have let this secret die. Do you think she protected it just so we could abandon our claim?"

"*Tasia* had a perfect vision of the *past*. Memory was her Gift, but it was also her folly. She knew nothing about the future."

She put her hands up in challenge. "And what is that future? You're still being cryptic."

"You think that King Gonfrid will just hand Vist back to us if we ask nicely? To claim the throne is to provoke a civil war. He will ransom your head for all the gold he can spare. You will fight to survive, and to hold your claim will require you to become someone I would never want you to be. It will mean cruel and ruthless acts and a cold heart. And when all is said and done, there will be two broken kingdoms, ripe for conquest by our neighbors because, lest you forget, Meriveria was formed for a reason. I see death. I see you wearing the crown, and alone. I want no part of this future, Odelia."

She stood, hand over her mouth, and stared at a knot in the wooden floor. Could she really turn cold and ruthless? She trained to defend herself, but she couldn't imagine bringing death and destruction. That couldn't be right. "How much of it is immutable?"

"You always take the throne."

"That's a good start, right? Maybe I can avoid the rest if I'm careful."

"It's taken me eighteen years to discover if there even are flexible parts to this fate. They won't be easily changed."

Odelia put her hands on her hips. "Well, I was never in on it before."

4

⊕USH ⊕USH

K en had spent so much of the past three days biting his tongue that he feared it might fall off. To hear Lord Jibiam speak, everything was better in Tehazy. If only Meriverians would shed their silly notions of politeness and propriety, they could be as enlightened as Tehazians—and become prying boors.

Meetings with the ambassador and Father were supposed to be part of Ken's "preparations" for kingship, but they ultimately proved to be the entirety of said preparations. Like allowing Lia to dinner, training Ken was just a display for Tehazy. He would smile and nod as Father and Jibiam held a never-ending pissing contest. Between all the posturing from both of them, it took until last night to finally begin earnest talk of allocating resources to build a bridge over the Norlach River. Ken longed to contribute, if only to keep the conversations on track, but Father made it clear every morning that he expected him to do nothing more than remain silent.

Today, thankfully, Ken found a reprieve. Jibiam left on a day trip to see examples of Meriverian bridges. The royal islet sat in the Ablure River delta. Twin bridges connected it to the city of Meria on both banks, and two more long bridges stretched directly between the northern and southern halves of Meria. And since Father disapproved of Ken visiting the city—too likely to encounter a sick person in a population so large—he made him stay back under the pretense of having more pressing duties at home. For once, the silly protections worked in his favor.

Without Jibiam asking uncomfortable questions about his love life and hobbies or prattling on about the oh-so-perfect kingdom of Tehazy, Ken could actually think—about something other than the ambassador walking off the end of the Meria wharf, of course—and all he wanted to think about was how to convince Father he needed real preparation.

Though he wouldn't betray Lia, there had to be something he could tell Father. He needed to talk his plan through, and she'd always been the

KISS OF TREASON

sensible one. The DiOrtos' apartment was empty, and the palace physicians hadn't seen Lia all day. He was sure to find her in the library.

Or not.

Instead, he found a tutoring session. Bertina stood by the fireplace, watching Conora, who was conversing with the gray tabby kitten on her lap. The kitten purred, and Conora made a note on her clipboard, then meowed back. As his sister approached seventeen, she didn't have many such classes left. Ken watched them chirrup and chatter back and forth a few times until Bertina approached him.

"Looking for remedial lessons?" she whispered.

He shook his head. "Not unless you're teaching kingship now. Have you seen Lia?"

"She's in the workshop with Hortensia," Conora chimed in. "I passed her on her way there."

Ken sighed. If Lia was helping her mother, she'd be there most of the day.

The kitten yowled and wriggled away to settle in a basket on the floor.

Conora rolled her eyes. "So dramatic. That has to be the neediest cat I've ever talked to. I'm fairly certain she thinks *she's* royalty."

"Strange," Ken said. "You sound surprised, but I've always assumed that was the natural attitude of every cat."

"Ha. Ha," Conora deadpanned. "What did you need Odelia for?"

"I wanted the advice of my fellow Healer."

"Perhaps I can help," Bertina said.

Ken put his hands up and shook his head. "I don't want to take you away from Conora's lesson, and you're long past tutoring me anyway. I'll be on my way now." He turned to Conora. "And be careful with that fluff ball. She looks vicious."

Bertina stuck her hands on her hips. "Nonsense. You're always welcome to join my lessons. And she's due for a break from practice. Some theory would be perfect."

He rubbed the back of his neck. "It's really a topic I'd rather discuss with another Healer—unless either of you two has miraculously received a second Gift."

Conora narrowed her eyes at him. "Hmm..."

"You think he's hiding something?" Bertina mused.

"Absolutely. He has that look he always gets when he's about to say or do something rash."

Bertina raised her eyebrows and nodded.

44

"What is it, Brother? You may as well just come out with it."

He scoffed. "Don't be ridiculous. What would I have to hide?"

"Something to do with Odelia, obviously," Conora said.

Ken threw his hands up. Why couldn't she leave him alone? "This isn't about her. It's about me. I just prefer her advice because she understands our Gift better than anyone."

"Then you won't mind explaining it to us," Bertina said. "You can help us understand it better."

He had to give them something, or they'd start digging on their own. Perhaps a piece of the truth would satisfy them. "Fine. If you must know, I don't believe I'm as fragile as everyone thinks, and I'm hoping to convince Father of this."

Bertina raised an incredulous eyebrow. "And what brings on this revelation?"

Ken checked that nobody else was around, then took a seat by Conora and lowered his voice. "Father's only been playing at preparing me for the throne. He told me a few days ago that he doesn't expect me to inherit." He found it impossible to hide a tone of disgust with the last few words.

"Oh." Conora looked down at her hands and fidgeted. "That just makes it worse."

"Makes what worse? You know something. What is it?"

She still didn't meet his gaze. "I'm sorry. I didn't know he'd go that far."

He crossed his arms. "Conora, you can't pry into my affairs without expecting the same. Tell me what's going on."

Conora sighed. "You're right. Father doesn't expect you to inherit. Last week, he decided I was old enough to take a role in things, and he has me studying our laws right now. When the ambassador is gone, he wants me to start holding court with him as well." She placed a hand on his knee and looked up. "I thought you and I would be working side-by-side with me as a back-up, not me replacing you."

Ken studied her face. She seemed sincere, but inadvertent or not, her participation in his exclusion still stung. "Did you—?"

"*No.* I didn't ask for this. It's not a responsibility I *ever* want to have. Honestly, I have half a mind to help mother play matchmaker for you so you can create a nice, wide buffer of succession for me."

"Perhaps you should work together to change the king's mind," Bertina offered.

"Right." Conora smiled brightly. "Why do you think Father's wrong?"

Ken leaned back in his chair and spread his arms out. "I'm perfectly healthy and have been for years. When was the last time you saw me ill?"

Conora shrugged. "That just proves his protections are working."

He grinned. "Isn't that enough to believe in me as a viable heir? I mean, if it's worked this long—"

"When did she kiss you?" Bertina asked flatly.

Ken's blood ran cold, but he held his smile and tilted his head. "I beg your pardon?"

"Odelia. When did she first Heal you?"

He scoffed. "That's not—she hasn't—"

"Hmph. Please. I already suspected that you'd broken my rule a while ago, but I was giving you the benefit of the doubt. When I first came to you, you were just as frightened of your Gift as the king is. 'We're doomed,' you said, and 'our Gift will eventually kill us.' Now you're brimming with confidence in your longevity."

Enough. Ken stood up to leave. "You know, I've been distracting you both long enough. Don't we all have more important things to do? Conora, don't you need to feed a dress to one of your dog friends or something?"

"It's a simple question," Conora said.

Ken held up a finger. "First of all, I already answered it, and secondly, I'm no longer a student, which means it's none of Bertina's affair."

Bertina blocked his path to the door. "You're right," she said calmly. "You're not my student, and I have no authority over you, but that's all the more reason to tell me the truth. I have no power to punish you, but if you share what you know, I can both help you find a solution and record a better understanding of Healing for posterity."

They had him cornered. He never should have opened his mouth. And yet, some part of him felt relieved. He was so tired of hiding.

Running a hand through this hair, Ken took a deep breath and sighed. "All right. It's been...several years."

Conora chuckled. "What did you do, break the rules the first day?"

Ken sniffed. "How dare you. We lasted a whole three months."

"Mid-autumn." Bertina smiled. "Makes sense. There was a bad cough going around then."

"Right." Ken nodded slowly. "So you understand."

Bertina dropped the smile. "Wrong. The cough went around the year after."

Frog nuggets. He knew better than to lie so poorly to someone with Memory. Clearly, he was too rusty to try again, but he'd already said more than he should have. He looked around to make sure no one had entered the library and dropped his voice into a low whisper. "Look, I had nicked myself—I won't explain how—and when Lia saw it, she offered to help me."

"Really?" Conora raised an eyebrow at him. "That's worse than the first lie. Even I can remember that you weren't shaving by then."

"I never claimed I was shaving," Ken said, "but if you'd like a more believable story, I could make one up for you with a little time."

"Leave him be," Bertina said. "He's broken stronger rules than mine, and I'd prefer not to know more about that. Let's stick to what I might actually be able to help with."

"Even so, please don't tell my Father what I've already said. He'll find a way to turn it into Lia's fault, and I don't want her punished for my actions." In truth, she was just as culpable for everything as he was, but he stood to lose far less.

Bertina smiled and shook her head. "Of course not. Why would I do that? I made the rule to protect Odelia. Getting her in trouble would defeat the purpose."

Ken was taken aback. "I'm certainly not complaining, but why? She was a stranger to you when you made that rule."

"She's a common young Vistan woman in a palace full of Elgathan royalty and nobility, and her Gift is ripe for exploitation. Not to mention the ease with which you, in particular, could take advantage of her if you were so inclined."

Ken gasped. "But I would never—"

"I know that now, but she's still vulnerable, which is why I would advise against bringing your good health to the king's attention."

Conora leaned in. "Dependency of that magnitude gives her leverage over you that Father would never stand for. He would do anything to restore the balance of power."

"Well, she's just as dependent on me, so that makes it equal," Ken pointed out.

"Since when has equality ever appealed to him?" Conora asked.

"True, but none of this helps with my original problem. I think we can all agree that I'm no more likely to die soon than anyone here, and I need to be prepared to inherit one day. There must be a way to convince Father without putting Lia at risk."

Conora sat back in her chair. "Is that really what you want? Father isn't exactly the best teacher, and you disagree with him on everything. Maybe you're better off without his influence."

Though not entirely wrong, she was missing the point. "But I need the experience and to be informed about what's happening so I'm not caught unawares later."

"This could work to your advantage," Bertina mused.

"This isn't what I'd call an advantageous situation, but go on." Ken waved his hand.

"He's all about power, so tell him that making you more prominent at court will look better. If you have some real duties, you can learn all you need to know without being under his gaze at all times."

Ken grinned. "Tell me more."

Odelia held the shimmering silver satin taut while Mom knelt and pinned a fold in place. It had been a while since Odelia had last helped her, and she'd forgotten how soothing the work could be. Conora would look stunning in this gown—she looked stunning in everything Mom made. A tiny pang of jealousy pulled at Odelia as the imported silk slid through her fingers. If her family line weren't forced into hiding, she would be wearing such finery as well. "This could have been mine," she said softly.

"Trust me. It does no good to dwell on that idea," Mom said without looking up. She flicked her thick coppery-gold braid over her shoulder and pinned the dress again. "I'd be lying if I said I wouldn't rather wear these gowns than make them, but I trust your dad. He believes in this path to keep you safe, and I will do whatever it takes to follow."

Her voice diffused a quiet serenity throughout the otherwise silent workshop, echoing the orderliness of the tidy rows of outfitted forms and neat stacks of cloth. If one wanted peace, Mom's workshop rivaled the library—surpassing it on days like today when the other seamstresses weren't there. Other than home, it was the only place Mom would forego earmuffs or earplugs.

So as not to overpower Mom's Hearing, Odelia continued whispering, "But what if I could fulfill the good parts of my destiny without everything else? Surely, that's worth attempting."

"Do you have a plan?" Mom asked plainly.

"Maybe?" Did a rough concept count as a plan? Not really, but Odelia wasn't about to admit that.

Mom stepped back to view her work. "And...?"

"Years ago, at my Gifting ceremony, when Sister Rose took Kennard and me aside—"

"I know. I Heard it all."

Odelia gaped. "You never said a word."

Mom shrugged. "It never came up before now—hmm, not quite." She adjusted the placement around the waistline. "I'm not sure it really means much. Given how close the two of you are and the positions you both stand to inherit, your influence on each other is inevitable. You could be each other's downfall as easily as each other's salvation."

"Which do you think we are?"

"It doesn't matter what I think. What do *you* want?"

Odelia tensed to avoid groaning. "I don't know. That's why I'm asking you."

Mom winced. "Stop grinding your teeth. That your first idea involves him is telling, but consider this: what would you want to do if you didn't have to worry about this dark future?"

Odelia helped Mom gently lift the dress off the form as she let the question rattle around inside her for a while. The tingle of Kennard's lips grazing her knuckle jumped to the forefront of her thoughts. Wasn't that what she'd been wanting? Until now, romantic thoughts had been nothing more than an idle fantasy—as Queen Melaine had been so eager to remind her—and he'd never shown any signs of feelings warmer than friendship.

Odelia sighed. "Well, I can't do what I want on my own, and I doubt Kennard is looking for the same thing."

Mom spread the gown out over a table. "How do you know? Has he told you he isn't?"

"No...but he hasn't given me any reason to believe he is either."

Mom turned to face Odelia. "Unless you know a Listener, the only way to know what he's thinking is to ask him."

Odelia nodded. "Even if he doesn't, he might be willing to work toward a new alliance of some kind." She smiled at the idea.

Mom grimaced. "Odelia, you must be careful. I know he's important to you, but how much can you trust him with this secret? There's a reason our family's been hiding. If there is a limit to his feelings for you, you can't expect him to go against his own family for ours."

"But he won't admit anything if he still thinks I'm a commoner, will he?"

Mom offered an optimistic smile. "Think of it as a test. If he cares deeply enough to fight for you, he won't care which station you hold. And knowing the king and queen, he's going to have to fight for you. See how much fight he has in him before you burden him with the truth."

Odelia smiled back. Of course, Kennard could be trusted. She could change her destiny in no time.

5

MISTRESS SECRETARY

Odelia hesitated before the door to Kennard's rooms. If she didn't talk to him about this now, she'd be too far away to do it later. She took a breath and knocked. She wasn't even sure if he'd be there; they hadn't planned to meet. How would she broach the subject? Why hadn't she rehearsed it a few times on the way?

Just as she turned away, the door clicked.

Kennard beamed through the crack in the door, then threw it wide open. "Lia! I'd been looking for you. Conora said you were with Hortensia." He stepped aside and motioned for her to come in.

"Yes, she wanted another set of hands for a few pieces." Odelia tried to dismiss the nervous energy that crept upon her as she followed Kennard into his sitting room. It was unlikely that he was looking for her for the same reason she wanted to speak to him now, but she couldn't help the flirty smile and warmth in her cheeks that came when she asked, "Why were you looking for me?"

"Father's giving up on me and grooming Conora as my replacement," he said nonchalantly.

She frowned. "Oh, I'm so sorry, Ken."

He grinned and rubbed his hands together. "No need to worry about me. I have a plan."

Already on edge, his excitement made her nearly giddy. "What do you need me to do?"

"Nothing. I'm going to talk to Father about doing more for the sake of appearances...serving while I can...that sort of thing—in more detail, of course."

She gasped and grabbed his hands, stopping just shy of squealing. "You found a way to ask him without revealing anything?"

"I won't go anywhere near the subject. We can keep fighting one another in peace."

"Wonderful! So— Wait. If you don't need a plan, and you don't need me for your plan, why were you looking for me?"

"Well, I *was* looking for you earlier to help me form a plan, but then I found Bertina and Conora in the library, and they helped instead."

The hairs on the back of her neck rose. "What did the three of you talk about?"

Kennard rubbed the back of his own neck—never a good sign—and paused before answering, "Keep in mind, I didn't tell them anything about training."

"Ken... What did you tell them?"

"With our good health, Bertina had already assumed we had Healed one another, and she and Conora had me cornered. I tried lying, but apparently, I'm terrible at it now."

Odelia reeled. A bitter, acrid taste burned at her throat. She covered her mouth.

"You should have heard them interrogating me. They were relentless."

"What have you done?" she asked in a low, hollow voice.

Kennard took her by the shoulders and stooped to meet her eye level. "They won't say anything, Lia. They're trying to help. It turns out that Bertina's actually pretty protective of you, and I don't think my sister is any more likely to turn on us than your brother."

Odelia squeezed her eyes shut, stuffing down the raw sensation, the urge to go to pieces. "You knew I had everything at stake, and you told the first people who asked you?"

"I didn't tell them the important part, just enough to make them stop prying."

"But even that much put you dangerously close to it, didn't it? How do you know you haven't whetted their appetites for more?"

"Bertina asked me not to tell her how I injured myself and assured me that they wouldn't tell anyone or ask any more about it. It was her idea to lead Father away from the notion."

Odelia shook her head. "You have no idea what you've done." Or what she'd almost done. Thinking of the conversation she'd wanted to have, of the secret she'd almost given him, only deepened the betrayal.

He squeezed her shoulders. "*Lia.* My father doesn't know, and no one is going to tell him. If nothing else, Bertina and Conora taught me to be on my guard. I won't let it happen a second time, and certainly not with someone who isn't a friend."

"Of course it won't happen again," Odelia said flatly.

Kennard gave a relieved smile and let her go. "I'm so glad you understand."

"Because I'm leaving." The words came without a second thought, cold and bitter.

His expression fell. "Leaving? What do you mean? Leaving where?"

"Eaund."

"Owned what?"

"No, the grandrion of Eaund. Grandilady Wilmarie is supposed to hire me at her manor in some capacity."

He furrowed his brows, his breathing heavy. "In some capacity? You're leaving, and you don't even know what for— I've never seen you speak with the grandilady, so where is this coming from?"

"Queen Melaine summoned me after the dinner with Lord Jibiam and offered to help me find suitors at the court in Eaund."

Kennard scoffed. "My mother doesn't know the definition of helping. Why would you trust her?"

"I don't, but I'm not in a position to refuse her, and Eaund has a very fine court." After a short time there, she could find a reason to move on to Iverish quite easily if needed. In light of her future, it wasn't the wisest plan, but it was an option.

His eyes grew wide as he raked his hands through his hair. "If you leave, you'll put both of us at risk."

Odelia put up her hands. "You think I don't know that? Or perhaps you're just upset because the consequences hit you as well this time."

He sighed and hung his head. "I honestly didn't think you were interested in marriage to anyone, or at least not the kind a nobleman needs, what with—"

"That's not what we're discussing now!" she snapped, shocking herself with how harshly it came out.

Kennard stared back pointedly.

"I'm sorry," she said softly, "I can't— You're not entirely wrong, but you're missing the point."

"Which is?"

"I've been asked to leave."

"And are willing to go, it would seem," he said, defeat evident in his eyes and palpable in his voice.

Odelia clenched her fists. Great Giver, Kennard was thick today. "It's not a matter of will. It's a matter of means. Without a better offer, I have no means to refuse a queen."

Hope lit up his eyes. "And if you had the means to stay?"

"I would never leave."

He reached out and pulled her into a bear hug. "I can't let you go. Just tell me what you need to stay."

Odelia couldn't breathe, and not just because Kennard was crushing her. Was he really willing to do what was needed? He'd broken her trust, but given another opportunity, could he be there for her?

She pulled away and took his hands in hers. "Being your friend isn't enough to justify my presence here. I need something more...official."

"Something more official..." His pensive scowl lightened into a bright smile. "It's so obvious; I feel like a fool for not realizing it sooner..."

Odelia's heart swelled. At a loss for words, she smiled back.

"I mean, Bertina and I just talked about this idea."

Wait—what? "You did?"

"Well, it was originally her idea. We were speaking more in general terms, not about who I would choose, but you would be a perfect first choice. You're intelligent, and I know you'd work hard."

Odelia tilted her head. That was an odd way to put it, but sure. "Well, I can't accept if you don't ask me first."

"Oh, right." A touch of pink passed over his cheeks. "Ahem. Lia, would you do me the honor of becoming the first member of my retinue as my private secretary?"

"Yes!" Odelia smiled so hard it hurt. "Absolutely." How could she possibly be happier? Kennard had asked her to be his— "Wait. Did you say, 'secretary'?"

"Um, yes. What did you think I said?" He whispered, "I didn't mumble, did I?"

Warmth crept up from her chest. How could she have gotten that so completely wrong? It was too late to tell him what she'd expected now. "No, you didn't mumble. I'm just so excited to stay that I wasn't listening very well."

Ken had a small window of time in which to meet Father before the ambassador returned. If he missed that, he might not get another chance before Mother and Grandilady Wilmarie set more plans for Lia in motion. As soon as the door to Father's study opened, Ken bounded in and bowed quickly.

Father nodded in acknowledgment. "In a hurry, Son?"

"As a matter of fact, yes. As you pointed out, my time is short, and I'd like to make the most of it."

Father leaned back in his armchair, propped up his feet, and motioned for Ken to continue.

"Appearances matter at court, and right now, it appears that you have no confidence in me—I understand that you do, and I don't object—but I want to improve the way I'm seen."

Father yawned. "And how does this help you make the most of your time?"

"You don't believe I can inherit, so let me serve our people now. Give me duties and responsibilities. Surely you have a project or two that you have no time for."

"Anything else?"

"I can hire a retinue to follow me as well. Having staff of my own will give me allies and power to serve and represent you, and if I do live to inherit, I'll have experienced people around me, as well as experience of my own."

Ken waited as Father stared him down. He hadn't had time to perfect his argument, and he was certain it showed.

Father slowly smiled. "I'm glad you're being sensible about this. I can have your first tasks readied over the next few days. I won't stand for you not completing them, and I expect whoever you hire to pull their weight. I won't be paying any of them until they prove themselves first."

Ken clasped his hands together. "Thank you, Father, but you want me to find people to work for nothing?"

"No, you will pay the first month for whomever you hire."

"Of course, gladly." It would be worth every coin from his own allowance.

"Do you have a man in mind for your first hire?"

Ken chuckled nervously. "More of a woman, actually."

Father pinched the bridge of his nose. "Please, tell me it isn't the DiOrto girl."

"Odelia has as much schooling as I do and works even harder. She'll make a fine private secretary."

"You allow her too close to you."

"Perfect," Ken said. "Then she's already prepared for the job."

Father looked at the tall clock near the door and scribbled onto a piece of paper on his desk. "I don't have time to argue about this right now, but it's your money to waste for the next month. When she isn't up to the task, you can find someone else. Now, if that's all?"

Ken bowed. "Thank you, Father."

"Oh, and one last thing."

"Yes?"

Father handed him the paper. "Before you start anything, take this to the captain of the guard."

Back in the hall, Ken read the contents. It was an order to assign two guards to him indefinitely. He smiled. Father was still being protective, but if he wanted to assign personal guards, it must have been to compensate for other freedoms. Ken couldn't wait to try them.

Lia ran up and took hold of his arm. "What did he say?" she whispered.

He grabbed her with his free hand and grinned. "When can you start, Mistress Secretary?"

Her eyes lit up, a vibrant green, even in the darkened hall. "Thank you so much. Now I just have to face the queen."

"I could come with you." He and Conora were immune to Mother's Allure, and it didn't seem fair to send Lia alone at such a disadvantage.

"Thank you, but I should probably tell her myself." Lia stepped away. "I can't have you fight all of my battles for me."

"What if I don't speak? With her influence, someone in the room needs a level head, or she might talk you into leaving again."

Lia put a hand on her hip and narrowed her eyes. "All right, but please, don't interfere unless her Allure gets the better of me."

"Whatever you say." He waved her forward. "Lead on."

Mother's rooms weren't far, and to his surprise, they were invited into her sitting room without delay. He waited for Lia to enter first.

Mother's voice trailed out of the room, oozing with charm, "Ah, Miss DiOrto, finished with your preparations already? I'm impressed."

Lia curtsied shakily and walked deeper inside, out of his view from the doorway. "Thank you for your generosity, Your Majesty, but regretfully, I must decline your offer."

"Don't be foolish. Whatever is holding you back, I'm sure I can take care of it." Mother coated her words in syrup, but Ken could hear the threatening edge underneath.

"I-I've been offered a position here at the Cedar Palace."

"I have heard no such thing. What position, pray tell, would that be?"

56

Lia didn't answer right away. Mother must have been forcing her Allure. Did he need to step in already?

"His Majesty is allowing Prince Kennard to appoint people to his service—"

Mother snickered. "That doesn't include you. Finish preparing for Eaund. When Grandilady Wilmarie leaves, you will not keep her waiting."

"But I've already been—"

"Clearly, you misunderstood. I am finished speaking to you. That was a dismissal. Go."

Lia backed up and turned toward the door.

Time to intervene. Ken twirled his finger and pointed to the front of the room.

Her eyes widened, but she slowly pivoted back and faced Mother. She clenched the sides of her skirt, breathing deeply, though not yet speaking or moving forward.

Backing her up from the shadows wasn't enough. She needed help. Ken stepped up beside Lia, urging her forward with a hand on her back. He mimicked the saccharine expression Mother used to force her Allure. "Mother, perhaps you should let *Mistress Odelia* finish speaking before you dismiss her."

Mother huffed. "This is none of your concern, Kennard."

"It is if you're trying to send a member of my retinue packing. Did you think I wouldn't notice her absence?"

"And what is her supposed role?"

"My private secretary."

Mother pursed her lips and shook her head. "Your father will never approve the appointment."

Ken shrugged. "Funny, that's not what he told me a few minutes ago."

"You're lying. There isn't a chance he'd have any confidence in someone like her."

He couldn't resist a smirk. "He doesn't need to. As long as I pay the wages, he doesn't care whom I hire."

"Why are you wasting everyone's time Kennard? You've convinced her to give up a good opportunity for a job she's ill-equipped for." She motioned to Lia. "The girl couldn't even tell me herself, and she hasn't spoken a word since you entered."

"A conversation with you is hardly representative of her capabilities, especially when you're using your Gift to your advantage." Ken turned to Lia and whispered loudly, "You can jump in here if you'd like."

Lia's face grew bright red. "There wasn't a pause, and I didn't want to interrupt," she said.

Ken smiled. "See? She was just being polite. She'll do fine. So, unless you have more rude things to say, we have work to do."

"Very well." Mother shook her head and waved them off. As they turned to leave, she laughed.

Ken and Lia looked at each other. Her confused expression matched his thoughts.

"What's so funny?" he asked.

Mother smirked. "I'm just picturing her in the court official's uniform. I'm sure she'll look lovely."

The uniform looked much like the one the guards wore but with the colors reversed: a bright blue jacket with the Elgathan crest and long gray pants tucked into brown boots. Women rarely occupied such positions, so an alternate version did not exist as it did for the general palace staff. And with Lia's small Vistan stature, a uniform meant for an Elgathan man would be huge.

Ken scowled. "When I asked if you wanted to be rude, that was meant to be sarcasm."

"What? You didn't think you could just give out a position without a proper uniform, did you?"

Lia stood up straighter. "Then it's a good thing I know the best seamstress in the palace."

Mother stopped laughing, her eyes bulging as she did a double-take.

Ken grinned and stifled a laugh of his own. "Oh, she is perfect for this job."

Odelia examined herself in the workshop mirror and scowled. The jacket was somehow both boxy *and* lumpy on her. She sighed. "Well, it's only appropriate that I look as stupid as I feel."

Mom gave her a scolding stare. "Clothes are easy to fix, and I don't want to hear you call yourself stupid. We both know that's not remotely true."

"He hasn't even given me a ribbon of intent. Why did I think he'd jump straight to an engagement?"

"It's normal to get carried away by excitement when the heart is involved. I forgot my manners more than a few times with your dad."

"I forgot the entire tradition of courtship!"

Mom pulled the jacket off Odelia and turned it inside out. "He doesn't know that, and with your new position, you'll have plenty of time and opportunity to draw his attention properly." She held out the garment for Odelia to put her arms through it.

"It's a pity that the officials' and guards' uniforms aren't switched. Valerzan has the eyes to pull off Elgathan blue near his face." The color just made hers look muddy. Then again, the gray fabric pleated around her waist wouldn't do much for her on top either.

"Your brother prefers to blend in anyway. And just be thankful it's not yellow. At least blue looks nice with blonde."

Odelia tugged at a strand of hair, comparing the gold hue to her jacket. Mom was right. It was a pleasing combination.

Mom circled Odelia, tucking the jacket and pinning it in place. She stepped back to examine her work, resting her index finger on her lips. She shook her head. "No, it's still not right... Wait. Take it off." Mom ducked into a cupboard and pulled out a sturdy bust bodice. "Try this underneath it."

Odelia looked down at her current undergarment. Over her chemise, a strip of nettle cloth stretched across her back, widening into overlapping triangles at the front and ending in ribbons that wrapped completely around her to tie in the front. For added security, two more ribbons ties behind her neck. "What's wrong with the one I'm wearing?"

"It's worn-out. You have a nice figure under there. We want to show it off, not wrap it up like a bundle of fresh game."

True. Even with the jacket off, it flattened her. She unfastened the ties, then shimmied out of it and into the new band. This one extended a little farther down her rib cage. A series of gussets molded the top to her, and stiff rushes reinforced the fabric. Instead of pulling ribbons around her body, it was fastened with crisscrossing laces down the center of her bosom. As Mom tightened up the laces, Odelia reached in and adjusted her chest. She checked the mirror again and marveled at the improvement. "Wow. I'm sorry, Mom, but I don't think I can give this back to you now."

She laughed. "Then it's a good thing I made it for you. It might not be as freeing during your more clandestine activities, but not strapping down your breasts will do wonders for the fit of your clothes."

Odelia slipped the jacket back on. "If you had this already made, why didn't you give it to me before?"

Mom resumed pinning. "I'd actually planned on taking a little longer to make it, but I rushed to finish when you told me you wanted to pursue the prince."

Although Mom had more than enough work to do already, here she was, giving Odelia more than she'd ever asked for.

Odelia smiled, the edges of her vision watery. "Thank you, Mom. If I weren't covered in pins, I'd hug you."

One corner of her mouth lifted in a sly smile. "You can thank me by catching him." She pivoted Odelia to face the mirror again, revealing a tight silhouette punctuated with tucks and darts. "And when I'm done with your clothes, he may just have to compete to catch *you*."

Ken flipped a dagger in his hand, then flung it at a target across the room, missing the center by inches. With Val on duty as one of his new personal guards, he didn't fear any unexpected visitors. Father had been as thrilled with the appointment as he had been with Lia's, but the choice had been left to Ken. For balance, he paired Val with Herman, a veteran guard who, fortunately, did not object to his orders not to intrude.

Ken glanced at his sitting room clock. Lia should've been here twenty minutes ago. He picked up another dagger from the table beside him and readied his aim. As he let it fly, the door opened with a soft click. "Oh, good. You're here. Now Herman can stop worrying," he said, choosing another dagger and aiming.

Lia laughed. "Sorry I'm so late. Mom insisted on fixing the hem."

Ken turned his head for a peek at the offending garment and froze.

She was wearing an official's uniform, but she looked nothing like any official he'd ever seen. A knee-length skirt replaced the pants, flaring out over her hips just below the jacket, which had been heavily altered. It opened much lower at the neck than he remembered—he couldn't normally see the lacy white neckline of a shirt underneath—and the tailoring tightly hugged curves that hadn't existed yesterday. A silver-embroidered fox head glared from the cobalt jacket. Had the Elgathan crest always been so prominent in the center of the bosom—er, chest?

The knife slipped out of his hand, landing with a thunk, and he struggled to close his now gaping mouth. "It's fine," he squeaked. He cleared his throat. "It was clearly worth the effort." Ken bent down to pick up the dagger, and heat rushed to his face. Did he really just say that? "I mean, Hortensia is an excellent seamstress." Why couldn't he shut up? This was Lia. He didn't flirt with her. Good-natured ribbing, friendly banter, or gentle teasing, yes—but not flirting.

She smiled. "Yes, she really is. Are you done with target practice, or can I join you for a few rounds?"

"Sure, if you can throw in that..." He fumbled for the word for a moment, then gave up and gestured in a crude circle between them.

"Almost." She unbuttoned the jacket, and his heart raced. Underneath, a blue vest clung as closely as the jacket had, but in a thinner fabric. Lace spilled out around the deep V formed by the vest, drawing his eyes back to her lovely pair of— Really? Where had she been hiding those? He couldn't unsee them now.

Giver help him; the uniforms weren't meant to invoke this kind of reaction.

Lia laid the jacket over a chair. "Much better. It looks like I'll need to retrieve what you've thrown. Hold, please."

"Yes, of course." Ken waved her on. She walked past him and headed for the target, giving him a view of her shapely, rounded backside and shattering the last chance of returning to his innocuous image of her. He inhaled sharply. That just wasn't fair.

THE BIRTHDAY GIFT
NOBODY ASKED FOR

O delia had chosen the wrong path.

The young man delivering Kennard's lunch to his study was wriggling his eyebrows at her suggestively as he put his gloves back on, and Kennard hadn't noticed a thing. Odelia gave the man an apologetic smile and shook her head. Even if she hadn't had her sights set on Kennard, she would never have been interested in a fling. It wasn't worth the risk—especially not for a man who hadn't included her lunch on the tray he'd carried up.

For five months, she'd been working with Kennard, and despite the new attention of many male servants, he himself seemed no more inclined to offer her a ribbon than before he hired her. Odelia thought she'd flustered him when she first unveiled her uniform, but clearly, she'd read too much into it, because he hadn't attempted to flirt with her since then—or at least, nothing that qualified as flirting for him. His involvement in her destiny was shaping up to be wishful thinking.

Worse, helping Kennard serve King Gonfrid was demonstrating the need for Odelia to claim the Vistan throne. They were assigned to "manage" the Vistan nobility who came to court. On the surface, it seemed a surprisingly large responsibility to entrust Kennard with—half of the nobility were Vistan, after all—but most of them never bothered to travel to Meria. It was no wonder why. The policies King Gonfrid had laid out for Kennard to follow made it nearly impossible for a Vistan leader to gain an audience with the king. He imposed a maximum project budget, and anything expected to cost more than that was to be rejected before it reached him. It was a pitifully low amount, and no one had yet presented them with a project that fit.

For disputes between nobles, only those between Vistans and Elgathans were brought to King Gonfrid. Kennard was expected to mediate the Vistan-only disputes. This turned out to be somewhat of an improvement as the king didn't hear disputes between Vistans at all before.

However, being pawned off on the prince instead of meeting the king did little to appease them.

Odelia often wondered if her position was approved by King Gonfrid because he expected her presence to temper the frustration of her fellow Vistans. Having not been allowed into that particular meeting, she couldn't know for sure, but she was still Kennard's secretary, and that seemed as good a reason as any for why she still held the position.

Kennard scowled at the stack of documents on his desk and slid them away from his food. "Just once, I'd like to find a project I don't have to reject."

"What about that repeal request?" Odelia asked, not bothering to contain the hope in her tone. Vistan women were currently forbidden from carrying or wielding arms, and several noblemen and women had banded together to draft the request.

Kennard smiled. "Of course, you'd be interested in that one."

"Ken, you of all people should appreciate that one as well. You know what it's like to hide your weaponry. It's preposterous that I cannot legally arm and defend myself."

"I agree, but—"

"But what? Look at me. If I hadn't trained, you could easily overpower me without trying."

He blushed. "Well, I certainly won't be trying—to overpower you, I mean—I will try to present this to Father, but I worry it won't work. I doubt he'll see the merits of arming you."

"You're clever. He hates me, but you convinced him to make my position permanent anyway. I'm sure you can come up with a benefit to him for protecting us."

Kennard rubbed the back of his neck. "Listen to you, trying flattery on me. Maybe you should present the idea," he joked.

"I would if I could."

"I don't want you to get your hopes up when there's such a high chance I'll fail, but go ahead and schedule a meeting."

Odelia nodded and made a note in her book.

Kennard picked up his spoon. "I really will try my best, Lia."

She didn't doubt he would. She knew full well that the cause was likely to fail, but if he was willing to advocate for Vistans, there was hope he could choose to stand by her side if destiny forced her hand. And if Kennard somehow succeeded, even better.

"Mm," Kennard said, swallowing a spoonful of stew, "you've got to try this—wait. Where's your bowl?"

She shrugged. "I guess they forgot. It's fine. I'll visit the kitchen later." It was a frequent mistake but one she didn't make a fuss about. She had more important concerns than the respect of the kitchen staff.

Kennard rolled his eyes and held out the spoon to her. "No, you won't. What they gave me could feed an army. Are you going to share with me or let me make a moose's ass of myself eating in front of you?"

Odelia reached across the tray and picked up the extra spoon the kitchen always sent with a meal in case one was dropped. "Since you insist..." She dug in. The hot broth, potatoes, corn, and venison had been perfectly salted, and they only whetted her appetite.

Kennard dabbed at his mouth. "I swear, that's the second time this week. I'll talk to the kitchen—"

"Don't you dare. Most of them are Elgathans who resent me for outranking them. I probably earn enough spit in my food without directly antagonizing them." Not to mention that his constant intervention on her behalf made her feel like a sponge. She couldn't speak to King Gonfrid or Queen Melaine on her own, but speaking to other servants was well within her capabilities and the scope of her duties.

"Suit yourself, but if you begin to starve because of it, I reserve the right to say, 'I told you so.'"

Odelia smiled cheekily and whispered, "Why would I starve if I can steal your food?"

Kennard narrowed his eyes. "I'm watching you," he said as he pretended to pull the bowl away, then laughed and put it back.

Odelia laughed with him and tentatively reached for the cornbread.

Kennard smiled and waved her on. "Are you excited for your day off tomorrow?"

"What day off?" She had no idea what he was talking about. Her calendar was full.

"Well, you didn't think I'd make you work on your birthday did you? I may look like my father, but I like to think I treat my staff a little better."

"I doubt your father would ever share a bowl of stew, so you can put your mind at ease there. But it's also your birthday tomorrow, which means I'll have twice as much work to do." Odelia opened her notebook. "Let's see... You have a meeting with the king first thing, then meetings with each of the grandilords, starting with Grandilord Doneron of Oulley—"

"Oulley? But that's in Elgatha."

"Yes, I know. Like I said, you're meeting with all four of the grandilords."

Kennard scrunched his face up in confusion. "What business would I have with them? Doivrie and Yophiex I get, but why Oulley and Eaund?"

Odelia fished for a bit of meat with her spoon. "I don't know. Norty only gave me the instructions to arrange the meetings. The king didn't specifically authorize him to tell me more, so he wouldn't say." The king's secretary could be frustratingly pedantic.

Kennard scoffed. "Of course. He never tells you anything. It's a wonder you accomplish anything working with him."

"That's the one perk of nothing making it past you. I never have to initiate a conversation with him. It's always a request from the king's office." It by no means made up for having to witness Kennard crushing the spirits of her people as gently as he could, but she would take whatever upside she could get.

Kennard set down his spoon. "If tomorrow is so busy, maybe we should get some extra target practice or sparring in today."

"It'll have to be an extremely short session. You aren't exactly free today either."

"You know, I think I liked you much better before you ran my schedule," Kennard teased. "There's never time for anything fun."

"You could always send me to Eaund like the queen intended."

He smiled. "Ah, but then, who would I share my stew with?"

"Happy birthday," Father said perfunctorily.

Ken bowed. "Thank you. Nice to see you bubbling with festivity."

Father ignored the sarcasm. "You're nineteen now, and you've done well enough with the assignment I gave you, so I'm giving you a new, even more important one. Consider it a birthday present."

"Thank you?" After the untold joy of rejecting Vistan requests, Ken wasn't sure if he wanted a more important responsibility. What kind of dirty work might that entail?

"I'm sending you on a tour of the kingdom to report on the state of the kingdom and act as my representative."

Ken couldn't believe it. After years of restrictions... "You're letting me leave the palace?"

"Yes, but I expect you to adhere to the same rules at the other courts that you follow here."

Ken nodded. He was still restricted, but at least he would have a little breathing room. He glanced over at Lia, who was standing silently near the door with Norty. A tiny smile showed just enough to dimple her cheek.

"How long will I be gone?" Ken asked.

"Eleven months. That should give you about twelve weeks in each grandrion. You may choose to visit a few arions in each for more local information, but I wouldn't waste more than a day on any of the pettrions. It will be more efficient to have the pettilords visit you, and it will keep them from overstepping their lords and grandilords."

Ken grinned. All these new places to see!

"I will have a set a guards scouting ahead of you. Your secretary will keep them apprised of your schedule, and if they determine that any location is unsafe for you, you will be delayed or redirected to the next one."

And there was the catch. With Father's restrictions, how many places would be approved? "Yes, Father. Are there any specific tasks for me before I make arrangements with the grandilords, or shall I wait quietly in a cage until the nobles hand me information?"

Father Transformed into a wolf and uttered a low growl but, thankfully, did not berate him for the outburst.

Ken bowed and apologized. He knew better than to make his wisecracks to Father's face.

"As it happens, I do have an additional task for you. By the time you return to Meria, you will be engaged to be married."

Ken balked. Now Father was just being unreasonable. "Engaged? To whom?"

"A young noblewoman, I would assume. You should meet plenty over the next several months."

"How will I do this if I'm also working?"

Father gave a wolfy smile. "If your secretary is doing her job, she can make time for you to accomplish everything. I'll also be sending Conora with you. Since she claims she doesn't want the throne, she can help you get one step closer to creating an heir to replace her."

Even for Ken's birthday, Father couldn't abandon his cold, logical control. No wonder he was loosening his grip on Ken; it was all in service to ultimately replacing him. Had the protections ever come from fatherly instinct, or was he nothing more than an asset to guard? Today was not the day he wanted to find out.

"When would you like us to leave?" Ken put as little emotion into his voice as possible.

"Two weeks should be enough time to prepare. Go over any other details with the grandilords. You are dismissed."

Ken bowed and left, taking long strides down the hall. He needed to return to the comfort of his own rooms before engaging in another meeting.

Lia's footsteps skittered across the hardwood as she nearly ran to keep up with him. As soon as they reached his door, she said, "He picked a rotten day to spring that on you."

"I'm not going to let it bother me," Ken insisted, but the slam of the door as he closed it betrayed him.

She unbuttoned her jacket. "Lucky for you, I have just the cure to keep it from bothering you." She flung the jacket over a chair and opened their equipment chest. "Just imagine his face on this." With a grin, she produced the throwing target.

Ken couldn't resist a chuckle. "That sounds a bit treasonous if you ask me...but I love it." He reached in for the throwing knives while she set the target up. "You might be a bit of a liar too. I thought you said we wouldn't have time for practice."

"*We* don't have time, but since the king ended sooner than expected, there's just enough time for you to sneak in a couple rounds. I'll keep an eye on the clock. You throw that frustration away."

Ken smiled. He could never find a better friend than Lia. He took a breath and aimed. As he released the knife, he felt lighter already.

Odelia shushed Kennard. He always laughed like a fool when they snuck out into the garden. After making a yearly habit of it, she was a little surprised no one bothered to head them off as they left after the first dance started.

In the center of the garden, walls of spruce trees formed a winding circle that, from above, resembled a wreath. It wasn't maze-like enough to get lost in, but the inconvenience of meandering into the middle kept most people from visiting the small cedar pavilion there. It had been one of their favorite places since they were children.

Kennard staked out a bench and leaned across it until he was lying on his back with his feet on the ground. "Finally, some peace and quiet."

Odelia took the bench nearest to his head in the ring and looked down at him. "Enjoy it while we're still here. I doubt any of those grandilords will give you a moment's rest when we're in their courts."

Kennard ran his hands over his face. "Oh frog nuggets, the first ten weeks with Grandilord Doneron? I'm tempted to tell Father to pick a bride for me at random if it means I don't have to go there."

Odelia stifled a laugh. "Oh, come on. It won't be that bad. He's friendly to you."

"Lia, the man can't go one sentence without throwing in a 'Your Highness' or 'My Liege.' If he kisses my butt any harder, he might just learn to Heal."

"Ken!" Odelia sucked a breath and pursed her lips, willing herself not to laugh. She shouldn't encourage him—even if he was right.

"Look, I don't trust a man who tries that hard to be friendly. Nothing about him is genuine."

"Then don't. Nobody said you have to trust the nobility. You just have to work with them." She knelt down near Kennard and rested her elbows near his head. "You'll probably have your hands full anyway. There isn't a single woman in Meriveria who wouldn't kill for your attention." Shameless, she gave him a flirty, crooked smile.

Kennard put a hand over hers. "I'm so glad you're coming with me. I can't imagine trying to choose one without you." The words stuck in her heart as true as one of his throwing knives.

Odelia turned so he couldn't see her face and took a ragged breath. "I'm happy to help," she said cheerfully, then stood up. She couldn't linger on the moment for another second. "We should probably head back. With the extra attention this year, I don't think abandoning the party was the best idea."

"You can go back. I'm going to enjoy this for a few more minutes."

Odelia returned to the feast and kept up a smiling facade as she passed through the great hall. But the minute she reached her bedroom, it cracked. Then, it shattered. Tears crept down her face as she sat down on her bed. She covered her mouth but couldn't dam the river flowing from her.

Mom walked in and put a hand on her back. "Odelia, what's wrong?" she asked softly.

When Odelia opened her mouth to speak, the tears came harder. "I can't do it."

Mom wrapped both arms around her. "It's all right," she said, stroking her back.

It wasn't going to be all right. Everything was wrong.

"Just let it out first. You can tell me later. Just let it out."

Odelia took a deep breath and wiped her eyes. Another deep breath. "I chose wrong. I followed my heart, but my heart was stupid. I can't change my future."

"I don't believe that. What happened?"

"The king is sending Kennard on a tour of the grandrions, and he wants him to return with a bride..." Her eyes welled up again. "And I'm supposed to help him..."

"Is that all? Odelia..." Mom squeezed her shoulder. "It's not that bad."

"Not that bad? Mom, he thanked me for helping him. I don't even occur to him as an option."

"Exactly. Help him. Away from the prying eyes of his parents, maybe he'll be more receptive. It isn't over until he proposes to someone. Are you really ready to give up before you've truly tried?"

"I haven't tried? I practically threw myself at him when the queen tried to send me to Eaund, and—"

Mom shook her head. "Look at it from his perspective. Courting you is not a choice he can make lightly in any way. He'd risk your friendship, his family, his reputation, and possibly his throne. The most loving thing you can show him is patience."

Odelia sniffled. "How can I help him meet other women and pretend it isn't killing me?"

Mom tsked softly. "You're not getting it. You've been tasked with helping him find his bride, so *help him find his bride.*"

Sluggish and aching from crying, Odelia's mind spun trying to making sense of the circular statement. Then it sank in. It was so simple. She put her head in her hands. "I feel so foolish," she moaned. "Why didn't I think of that?"

"Because you weren't thinking. You let your emotions get the better of you. It's important to follow your heart, but you mustn't leave your mind behind in the process."

HIDING IN PLAIN SIGHT

Odelia checked her room one last time. Valerzan had already loaded their trunks into the cart, but she wanted to make sure she hadn't forgotten anything important. It wasn't likely. She'd only packed one trunk for herself, but other than her bed sheets, a washbasin, and a lamp, the tiny room had been stripped down to the furniture. Strangely, the sight stirred no emotions, just an urgency to move along.

Dad walked in, holding a scroll. "I think you'll want this, just in case." With a wink, he handed it to her.

She unrolled the top few inches. It was her copy of the Vistan royal line. She held it away as if it were on fire. "I can't take this with me! Who knows how many people will handle my things as we travel. What if someone finds it?"

Dad put one hand up in a *wait* gesture and pulled a small cedar box from behind his back with the other. It had no obvious lid or hinges, and the top was inlaid with a variety of woods, both stained and bleached. Under a pink sunrise, a snow-capped blue mountain rose over a lush green forest.

Odelia gasped. "A puzzle box." She ran her fingers over the textured trees. "This must have taken forever to make." Dad carved wood while he waited for visions, but she hadn't seen him work on this piece. She hadn't even seen many puzzle boxes since they left Iverish.

He smiled. "Let me show you how to open it." With a press on the mountain summit, he slid the second tree from the left down. Another press on a ray of sunlight, and the front of the box popped ajar. He pulled the miniature drawer open, took the scroll from her, and tucked it inside. "There. Now, no one can find it by accident. If anyone asks, the box is just a token of your heritage."

Odelia hugged him. "I promise I'll write home."

Dad pulled back. "I know you will. Now, go before those boys lose their patience."

Odelia took the box and hurried down to the palace entrance. Kennard and Conora waited just outside the door, watching Valerzan and Herman secure their luggage inside a large moose-drawn cart. The guards lashed a woven cedar-bark tarp over top, then hopped down. Herman called out to the driver, who issued a quiet lowing grunt to the pair of moose. With a shake of their antlers, the beasts pulled the cart away.

"I hope that was everything," Valerzan said. "The luggage cart's full."

"I have what I need," Odelia said.

A smaller cart awaited the travelers, this one pulled by a dozen malamutes. Behind the driver were two short benches.

Conora slid into the front bench and beckoned for them to join her. "The dogs are getting restless."

"What? No fanfare?" Kennard joked.

The king had demanded a quiet send-off. He didn't want crowds from the city to form around them. Odelia, Valerzan, and Herman had all exchanged their court official's and guards' uniforms for plain clothes to keep from drawing attention on the road.

Kennard hopped into the backseat and motioned for Odelia to sit beside him.

"I guess that puts me with you," Valerzan said to Conora.

Odelia settled in. "Where's Herman riding?"

"I'm running ahead to scout the road," Herman said. "I prefer not to sit with my legs cramped anyway."

Kennard shifted in his seat. "I don't blame him. And he can make it to Oulley and back by the time we get there."

Herman tapped on the side of the cart and, using his Speed, ran to the edge of the islet and across the southern bridge in a blink. The driver barked, and the dogs barked back, pulling the cart after Herman.

In Meria proper, wooden walkways lined the main road, connecting the buildings just above the dusty street, which would be muddy any other time of the year. The gates of Meria opened ahead, allowing them to continue onto the South Road without stopping. Outside the city walls, acres of colorful grasses circled the walls in a sea of green, white, red, and yellow. Past that, huge firs and red-cedars grew around a thick undergrowth of dark salal and bright ferns. The cool shade of the forest offset the summer heat. Odelia inhaled deeply, embracing the fresh, damp woodland scent.

"What's that?" Kennard asked, his voice pulling her back into the cart.

"What's what?"

"The fancy box you're holding."

"Oh, this?" she said nonchalantly, holding up the puzzle box. "It's just a late birthday present from Dad. He wanted to make sure I got it before we left."

"But what is it?"

Odelia mentally kicked herself for not hiding it under her skirt. "It's just a puzzle box." She handed it to him, hoping that treating the box as mundane might lessen the appeal.

He turned the box over in his hands, gingerly running a finger over the inlay. "It's beautiful. I didn't know Abhenric could do such intricate work." Kennard turned it a few more times. "How do you open it?"

"Well, it wouldn't be much of a puzzle if I told you, now would it?" she teased.

He furrowed his brow and started pressing various locations on the box.

Odelia panicked and took it back. "That wasn't an invitation to try."

"Sorry. That was rude. I should let you solve it." Kennard smiled eagerly.

She set the box back in her lap.

"Don't you want to know what's inside?"

"I can open it later."

He huffed. "It's a long ride to Oulley. What better time could there be?"

Odelia got an idea. "Okay, but I wouldn't expect much to be inside." She pretended to try different pressure points and slides before pressing the mountaintop and sliding the correct tree. As she touched the ray of sunlight, she turned the box upside down and pretended to try more places. Using her arm to cover, she opened the drawer just far enough for the scroll to drop into the folds of her skirt on the opposite side from Kennard. She turned the box right-side-up with one hand and used the other to cover the scroll under more of her skirt.

Kennard frowned. "It's empty? What do you do with it now that you've solved it? Is it a challenge to solve again?"

"It's a safe place to keep things. I don't have anything to put in it now, but I might someday."

The dogs barked, and Conora yipped something back to them. Kennard leaned forward. "What was that about?"

Odelia used the distraction to tuck the scroll back into its home.

Conora laughed. "One of the dogs wants to catch Herman!"

A few hours later, Herman appeared in the middle of the road. When they caught up to him, he jogged to keep even with the carts. "There's a small settlement at the crossroads up ahead with an inn where we can lunch. It's on the list of stops approved by the scouts this week."

Ken nodded. "Good idea. How long can we stay?"

"By my guess, we have about an hour or two to spare. We're more than halfway to Oulley by now."

Almost on cue, a small group of cabins came into view, encircling the intersection of the South Road and the Port Road. A post in the middle held signs pointing south to Oulley, north to Meria, east to Cantahn, and west to Viaporta. The cart pulled up to the largest building, where the scout guards already waited, and everyone crawled out. Ken stretched his arms and legs and started toward the inn.

"Your Highness, please, wait," Herman said. "Let me check inside first."

"I thought you said the place was approved."

"I need to check it again anyway. Valerzan, you keep watch out here." He ran inside before Ken could object again and quickly reemerged. "I advise taking your meal outside."

"Why?" Lia asked.

"I heard someone cough."

Ken closed his eyes. He didn't even adhere to Father's rules when he was in the palace. Out here, he was determined to claim his freedom. "It's okay. We can eat inside. One cough won't hurt me."

"It'll draw less attention than staying out here," Lia pointed out.

"But, Your Highness, it's my duty to keep you safe, and this is the most basic rule I have been given to follow for it."

Ken sighed. *Your Highness.* Grandilord Doneron would be repeating that for weeks. Until now, Herman had been a silent shadow. If he couldn't be that anymore, he could at least not add to Ken's annoyances, or this was going to be a very long tour. Ken put his hands together. "Look, Herman. It seems we're all going to spend the next several months a bit closer than we've been before, so I have a few rules of my own."

Herman nodded. "Yes, Your Highness?"

"That's the first one. Constant honorifics are going to drive me batty. Val and Lia call me Ken, but if you're uncomfortable with that, Kennard will do just fine. Can you do that?"

"Yes, Yo—Kennard."

"Second, I understand that it's your duty to guard me from physical threats, but contrary to what my father says, I don't need protection from my Gift."

Lia cleared her throat and stared pointedly.

Ken lowered his voice so the other guards wouldn't hear, "Val, you've spent more time with Herman than any of us. How trustworthy is he?"

Herman started. "I swore an oath to guard you with my own life."

Ken held up a finger. "That wasn't what I asked, and your name isn't Val." He turned back to Val. "Well?"

"He's not a spy," Val said. "We're trained to ignore anything that isn't dangerous. He knows how to be discreet."

Conora piped up, "He's not in danger because Odelia can Heal him. Can we eat inside now?"

Lia glared at her.

"Really, Sis? Here I am, trying to be somewhat delicate about the matter, and you just blurt it out?"

Conora put a hand on her hip. "It's not that crazy of a concept. You were taking forever to get there, and I'm hungry. I don't know about you, but I'm going inside." She walked into the inn.

Herman, being his usual stoic guard self, kept whatever he was thinking to himself. Thankfully, he also didn't stop Ken from following his sister inside. Now, who had coughed...?

Lia took hold of his arm and whispered, "I know what you're thinking. Herman let you come inside, but don't press your luck."

Ken scoffed. "How do you know what I'm thinking?"

"Because I'm thinking it too. It's instinct."

She was right. An ailing person called to the urge to Heal like the smell of cooking called to hunger. Ken scanned the room. In the corner, a boy stopped clearing a table and coughed into his sleeve. He couldn't have been more than ten years old. Ken took a step forward.

Lia loosened her grip on his sleeve. "Better me than you. Keep Valerzan and Herman distracted. I don't want either of them making a fuss." She slipped deeper into the dining room, winding between the tables.

She needed to be inconspicuous. If the patrons found out, not only would the queue never end, but word would inevitably reach Father that Ken had flouted his protections.

"Where's Odelia going?" Val asked.

"She's looking for a table," Ken pointed to the bar on the opposite side. "You should order some food."

Val nodded and headed toward the bar, while Herman stayed put, scowling, with his arms across his chest.

Ken clapped a hand to his back. "Herman! Don't look so glum." He gently turned the guard away from Lia.

She was leaning close to the boy, speaking quickly.

Ken led Herman after Val. "You still have work to do. I'm sure there will be plenty of danger for you to protect me from in Oulley. Maybe more in Vist?"

The boy grinned and hugged Lia, seemingly putting him cheek to cheek with her and giving her a perfect moment to quickly Heal him without alerting the entire inn.

Ken smiled at the intractable Herman. "You're not much for humor, are you?"

"I don't find your safety to be a laughing matter," he said sternly.

"Oh look, Odelia's found a table." Conora headed for the table where Lia sat. The boy had scampered off.

Herman showed the barest hint of a smile. "She picked a corner. Good. At least one of you is mindful of defense."

Val turned around. "It's a bit crowded for all of us up here. Why don't you both join them? I can carry our order back myself."

At the table, Lia was talking to Conora. "Please, be more careful about who you blurt that out to. Nobles like Grandilord Doneron would do anything to win the king's favor, and that kind of information would be irresistible."

"But Herman wouldn't tell anyone, would you Herman?" Conora said.

Herman cleared his throat and shifted his shoulders as he took his seat. The poor man hadn't been paid this much attention in the entire time he'd guarded Ken. "No. Like Valerzan said, we're trained to ignore anything you do that doesn't compromise your safety."

Ken's curiosity got the better of him. "May I ask why? I'm not complaining, mind you, but that's a very interesting policy."

"Because if I report everything you do, you're going to hide from me, which is going to make my job much more difficult."

Val joined the table with a bottle of raspberry wine, a pitcher of water, and a stack of wooden cups on one arm. The other held two serving bowls full of corn chowder and a stack of smaller bowls. He gracefully set both trays down in the center of the table and began ladling into the smaller bowls while Lia poured the wine.

Herman pointed to the second serving bowl. "Is that one mine?"

"Yeah," Val said. "Is that going to be enough for you?"

Herman nodded, completely serious. "It'll hold me over until we reach Oulley. Thank you."

An hour later, they were back on the South Road. Ken slouched down in his seat and closed his eyes. With a full belly, the movement of the cart, and the warm sunlight, he'd be asleep already if the seat didn't force him upright. As it was, he was deeply relaxed when a familiar and distinctive tingling sensation on his cheek jolted him.

Ken opened one eye and looked at Lia, who folded her hands in her lap as if she hadn't just kissed him. "What was that for?" he asked, keeping his voice low.

She mimed a cough.

"But you're the one who..."

"I know, but we ate at that table. I'm just being cautious." She blushed, and he found himself wanting to return the favor.

Not an urge to Heal. No. He wanted to feel the pink softness of her cheek. After months of trying not to be distracted by the cut of her uniform, why was this the thing that so tempted him now? He couldn't let the fleeting thought lead him astray. Instead, he lifted one of her small hands, cradling it in his own, and kissed it. He lingered a second longer than he intended, and her blush deepened.

They had Healed each other countless times. Why was it becoming more awkward lately?

Lia didn't take her hand back but grasped his fingers for a moment instead. "Thank you."

Silence stretched between them as neither of them moved. Ken needed to break it. "Back at the inn, when you said, 'Better me than you,' what did you mean?"

She shrugged. "Just that the consequences were greater for you. If I were caught, we'd be inconvenienced by the locals, but if you were caught, the king would lock you away forever and fire Herman, just to start."

"That was all?"

"Yeah, why? What did you think I was talking about?"

"With Herman's talk of protecting me with his life, I worried that you might think the same way, that your life is somehow worth less than mine. Mother and Father try to make everyone think that, but it's not true." Ken shifted to face her. "I know I don't always act like it, but you matter to me, Lia. You know that, right?"

She smiled sweetly. "Thank you, Ken. It's nice to hear it said. But don't worry about me. You can rest assured that I'm well aware of my worth."

The dogs slowed as they passed a large market flanking both sides of the road. Past it, small cabins dotted a grassy field, and at the end was a manor that looked much like the Cedar Palace, but roughly a quarter of the size. The cart pulled in front of the entrance, where Grandilord Doneron stood with several royal guards and what had to be the entire household.

Val hopped to the ground before they fully stopped. As he turned to help Conora, Ken stepped out of the cart, then extended a hand to Lia. Whispers rippled through the crowd. Well, this was an excitable bunch. Who knew politeness was such a novelty?

Doneron bowed deeply, and the rest of his people followed. "Crown Prince Kennard, Princess Conora! Welcome to Oulley, Your Highnesses. I assure you, we aren't ruffians out here. We have servants who can help your...guest. A prince need not trouble himself with such matters."

Wow. Ken plastered on a smile. "Thank you for your warm welcome, Your Grace. We look forward to your generous hospitality. And not to worry, I don't think I'll break from the strain of assisting Mistress Odelia."

Doneron eyed her with suspicion. "I'm sorry. I'm not sure we were expecting you, Miss DiOrto."

How could he not be expecting her? Ken had specified that he would be traveling with his sister, his secretary, and two personal guards, as well as several rotating guards. He'd accounted for everyone.

Lia didn't shrink from Doneron as she would with Mother or Father. She pulled herself to her full height—short though it was—and looked the grandilord in the eyes before bobbing a brief curtsy. "I am Mistress Odelia DiOrto, Private Secretary to Crown Prince Kennard. We met at the Cedar Palace when you made these arrangements with him."

Doneron stammered for a second. "A thousand apologies, Mistress Secretary, but I did not realize you were— When His Highness told me his secretary would be traveling, I thought he was referring to..."

Lia crossed her arms. "A man?"

"I fear my preparations are now inappropriate."

"A room is a room, isn't it?" Ken said. "What difference does it make who you thought she was?"

"I provided Your Highness a suite with three bedrooms: one for you, one for your guards to share, and one for your secretary. But she cannot stay there, and all of the suites with other women in them are full. She might be able to stay in the village for the night until I can rearrange the rooms—"

"Absolutely not." Ken refused to navigate this court without her. The grandilord's need to put propriety over practicality was getting on his nerves. "If she has her own bedroom, the current suite will suffice."

Doneron's eyes bugged out in shock, and more whispers rippled through the household.

Lia cleared her throat. "What the prince means to say is that my brother is one of his guards. With Valerzan around, I won't be getting into any kind of trouble."

Doneron stared at her but didn't speak.

"So, um, where should I take these?" Val asked, a trunk in each arm.

Ken stared daggers at Doneron. "I believe the Grandilord was just going to show us." He silently dared him to object again.

"Of course, Your Highness." Doneron smiled as though the argument had never happened. "Right this way."

They followed him in silence all the way inside the manor and up to the second floor. Conora was escorted to her own room partway to the suite. After showing Lia and the men to theirs, Doneron finally said, "Dinner will be downstairs in an hour. I'll leave you to unpack."

Ken thanked him and closed the door. He turned to Lia and smirked, trying to hold back a laugh. "I don't think I've ever heard you call me 'the prince' before."

She gagged. "That *toad*! I couldn't think of any more titles to throw at him. It's the only thing he responds to." She put a hand to her forehead, eyes wide. "No wonder he kept asking me to fetch him food and drink at our meeting. He must have thought I was your maidservant."

Ken laughed. "Well, he knows the difference now."

OULLEY

For the first time in months, Odelia felt acutely aware of her uniform. She had changed into it for dinner and followed Kennard, Conora, Valerzan, and Herman into the dining hall. There, young women and their noble fathers mingled among the tables, all finely dressed, their skin glowing golden in the candlelight. How could Odelia compete with any of them?

She wanted to run back to the room and just hand Kennard the scroll, but her parents' warnings stayed her. If telling him was a mistake, he couldn't be untold.

Kennard stood at the entrance to the room, wide-eyed. "Why are there so many of them?"

Odelia chuckled nervously. "The grandilord did say all the rooms were full."

"I think he could use a smaller manor."

"You don't have to talk to them all at once. Remember, I'm here."

He let out a big breath and smiled. "I can do this—but don't you dare leave my side."

She patted his arm and smiled back. "Never."

The next morning, Kennard met with the Lord of Viaporta's daughter, Sylvia. Odelia watched silently as he smiled and laughed at all of Lady Sylvia's flirtations and high-pitched giggling.

"You know, I've heard rumors about your Gift." Lady Sylvia winked. "Maybe you could show me sometime."

Maybe Odelia could punch her in the face and give her a reason to need some Healing.

Kennard laughed halfheartedly. "Well, aren't you...saucy?" He cleared his throat and leaned back, away from the lady's overreaching hand, which was creeping up his arm. "Mistress Odelia, don't we have another meeting soon?"

Odelia checked her notebook. "Yes, with the Lady Hilda." The meeting wasn't for another hour.

He snapped his fingers and grimaced. "That's too bad. Maybe another time, Lady Sylvia? Mistress Odelia might be able to schedule something after I've had a chance to meet with the others."

Lady Sylvia pouted and sighed. "If I must." She smiled slyly as she left. "I look forward to next time."

The door clicked shut behind her.

Kennard flopped back against the couch. "For the love of all that is good, strike her off the list." He paused. "Then burn the list."

Odelia laughed. "What? I thought she was just delightful," she said facetiously.

He rolled his eyes. "Was it the shrill laugh or the constant winking that won you over?"

"I think it was the way she asked me to leave."

"Thank you for ignoring that. I'm pretty sure she would have tried to climb right on top of me, given the chance. Please, tell me the others aren't all like her."

If only. Odelia would have nothing to fear then. "Thankfully, no. The others appear to be perfectly normal people as far as I can tell."

Kennard stood and shook himself. "I'm serious about striking her from the list. That woman makes me uncomfortable. By the way, when is that next meeting?"

"Not for another hour," Odelia admitted.

He grinned. "Have I ever told you that you're amazing?"

Whether from his smile or the compliment, her whole body filled with warmth. "And don't you forget that," she teased.

Odelia held onto that feeling as she tracked down Lady Sylvia before the next meeting.

The lady smirked as Odelia entered her room. "Ready to schedule me already?" She tossed her dark hair over her shoulder. "I guess the prince is smitten!"

Odelia curtsied. "I'm sorry, but, no. His Highness wishes to inform you that you will no longer need to consider his presence for your plans. Your time in Oulley is now free."

Lady Sylvia sneered. "What did you say? Your accent is so difficult to understand."

"Then it's fortunate that His Highness has declined interest in pursuing you. It would be terrible for you to marry a man with an accent like mine—and yours."

Lady Sylvia narrowed her eyes. Her face turned red. "Who do you think you are to tell me this? I am a lady, and I will not be dismissed by a *Vistan* whore."

Odelia did not flinch or blink but held her chin up and returned a stony gaze. "That is Mistress Odelia or Mistress Secretary to you, *Lady* Sylvia."

"I fail to see the difference."

Taking a deep breath, Odelia forced a saccharine smile. "Well, since you have so much trouble understanding, let me be blunt. His Highness wants nothing to do with you, and"—she put a hand to her chest—"*I* am informing you because that is my duty as his private secretary. If you find my adherence to protocol offensive, I would advise you to take your complaint to my employer, the crown prince." She held up her pencil, poised to write in her notebook. "Now, how would you like to word your complaint?"

Lady Sylvia stared, dumbfounded.

"No, then?" Odelia put the writing implements down. "Good-day, Lady Sylvia." Odelia curtsied before leaving. Good riddance. If Kennard hadn't already made his decision, the lady's behavior now would've sealed it. As it was, Odelia wouldn't bother him with the details. He'd feel the need to step in, and she'd handled the situation just fine on her own.

Odelia arrived back in time to facilitate Kennard's next meeting. Lady Hilda was a striking beauty, with raven hair cascading down her back in perfect ringlets and flawless olive skin. Polite and demure, she was the ideal Elgathan lady. No wonder Kennard ended up meeting with her five times over the next two weeks.

Even as Odelia envied Lady Hilda, she couldn't bring herself to hate her. It wasn't Allure like with Queen Melaine—Lady Hilda had Speech—but that she was genuinely too nice to dislike. She never gossiped or sneered at Odelia or doused people with honorifics, just displayed a warm smile and caring eyes when other people spoke.

So Odelia was surprised when Kennard ended a meeting with Lady Hilda early one day.

He turned away from the door the lady had left through. "You can take her off the list. Not as forcefully as Lady Sylvia, of course, but I'm still not interested."

Odelia had reported Kennard's progress back to Meria as required. He had rejected all but one woman in Oulley in the first week and a half. This morning, King Gonfrid had sent a reply of deep displeasure with Kennard's lack of effort and Odelia's "incompetence." With the addition of Lady Hilda, he'd officially dismissed a quarter of the women he'd been expected to court over the course of a year—in less than three weeks. If she couldn't get him to a make a show of caring, the king would have her replaced with someone he trusted.

"May I ask what was wrong?" Odelia asked.

"She was too quiet. I was bored to tears."

"If it's excitement you're after, I can always reschedule you with Lady Sylvia."

"Very funny. How did she manage to be the first in line anyway?"

Valerzan walked in, and Kennard tilted his head in acknowledgment.

"She's Grandilord Doneron's favorite niece"—Odelia put a hand on her hip—"but we were talking about Lady Hilda. Boredom isn't exactly a valid reason to reject someone. Is that really all it takes to turn you away?" If Kennard was going to be so picky, what hope did Odelia have?

"You rejected Lady Hilda?" Valerzan asked.

"Why do you both seem so surprised?" Kennard asked.

Valerzan's eyes went wide. "Because she's the most beautiful woman here."

"Don't exaggerate, Val. She's not the most beautiful woman here, and if I wanted to hold conversations where I do all the talking, I would speak to my mirror, not marry Lady Hilda. Since you're back, I assume Herman has everything ready?"

"Yes, finally. For someone so fast, he takes forever to check a canoe."

"Good. I need some fresh air. Are you sure there isn't room for one more? Lia's been stuck in here all day too."

Odelia waved him off. "It's fine. I have work to do anyway. I can join you another time."

Kennard shook his head. "You say that, but other than traveling here, I don't think you've been on a single outing all summer. The season's going to pass you by."

"One of your upcoming meetings is a picnic, and I'll be there."

"As an observer. What great fun!" He rolled his eyes.

"I don't have the luxury of leisure time anymore, Ken. I'm grateful to you for this position, but to justify keeping it, I have to do my duty. That's the price of keeping me around."

Kennard smirked. "Okay then, schedule a three-hour meeting for Conora and us at the lakeside tomorrow. We can pretend to discuss court matters while we go for a hike."

By tradition, a couple needed privacy for a ribbon of intent to be given—or as close to it as someone like Kennard could get—because it allowed the woman to reject an offer without embarrassing either person. With Conora along, there wasn't a chance Kennard meant for the lakeside outing to be a romantic one. And after shunning the last of the court, his every move would be under scrutiny until they left for Eaund. Odelia would draw more of the king's ire without getting any closer to her goal.

"You're going to get me in trouble," she said.

"Nonsense," he said with an aloof wave of his hand. "You're my secretary, which means you work for me. I'm giving you an order, so I expect you to do it."

Odelia froze, agape. They'd known each other for over a decade, but that was the first time he'd ever talked down to her as an inferior. And he'd done it with ease.

"Of course, Your Highness," she said, her voice barely above a whisper.

Realization played in his eyes, too late to take it back. "Lia—"

"Herman's waiting."

He took a step toward her. "Lia, I—"

She bowed. "I'll see you at dinner...Your Highness." Pivoting on her heel, she marched straight to her bedroom door.

Kennard called after her, "I didn't mean—"

She closed the door.

So much for him not believing in his superiority. There was more of his father in him than either of them thought.

Ken followed Val out the back door of the manor and down a long slope to where Herman stood on the lake shore. Next to him, a small red-cedar dugout canoe rested halfway in the water. Val held the canoe as the others stepped in, then pushed the craft forward and jumped into the moving boat.

Herman turned his head back to look at Ken as they drifted. "You're being strangely quiet."

Val grabbed a paddle. "He and Odelia got into an argument."

"What about?"

Ken sighed and picked up his paddle. "Ever since I hired her, I've missed the fun we used to have. She's been so focused on her duties that she can't relax for even a few hours. I thought I found a clever workaround by ordering her to schedule time with me, but it made everything worse."

Herman swung his leg over the bench seat to sit backward, furrowing his brow. "I don't get it."

"He decided to emphasize that it was an order and remind her of her place," Val said.

Herman raised an eyebrow. "So what? She is your secretary, and you're supposed to give her orders. You give me orders all the time. I fail to see the problem."

"You haven't been my best friend for ten years." Ken shook his head. "It was a mistake. I wanted my friend back, and I should have treated her like one, not talked to her like a servant— Let's take a left around that rock."

Herman spun back around and dunked his paddle to the right with the others.

Ken continued, "I just know I don't want to make that mistake again. It's not who I am or who I want to be. I don't know what's wrong with me lately."

Val chuckled. "I'll say. I could've told you there was something wrong with you when you rejected Lady Hilda."

Herman turned around again, blurring fast this time. "What? I must've heard that wrong. It sounded like Val said that you've rejected Lady Hilda."

Ken pulled his paddle across his lap. "You too? I don't see what the big deal is."

Herman tilted his head. "Have you lost your mind? She's the most attractive lady in Oulley."

Ken laughed. "What is with you two and your obsession with Lady Hilda? Was there some official ranking of the ladies that I missed?"

"Of course not," Val said, "but you'd have to be blind not to notice her."

Herman nodded in agreement. "She's gorgeous."

Ken shrugged and stuck his paddle back in the water. "You're both crazy. She's pretty, but not more than every single woman at court. I'd argue there are some prettier."

Val scoffed. "Name one."

"Your sister, for a start."

Herman snorted. "Nice. You set him up for that one Valerzan." He looked at Ken. "Oh, wait. You're serious?"

"Yes...?" Ken answered. Why wouldn't he be?

"You think *Odelia* is more beautiful than Lady Hilda?" Herman said.

"You say that like you're surprised," Ken said.

Val frowned and shook his head. "I don't like where this is going."

Ken put up one hand in surrender. "I'm just acknowledging that your sister happens to be a very lovely woman. Also, *you* brought it up."

Herman laughed. "Besides, I think you gave up the right to defend her honor around the time you started playing sentry for her trysts."

Ken and Val turned on him at the same time. "What!"

"Oh, please. Ken, you aren't as sneaky as you think. She's alone with you often, and I can hear noises, not to mention how sweaty and disheveled I've seen the two of you get."

No wonder Herman hadn't asked questions. The idea hadn't occurred to Ken. He and Lia had started training at a more innocent age, and by the time he was old enough to entertain bawdy notions, their sessions had become routine.

Ken and Val started snickering, quickly erupting into full belly laughs. Val put a hand on Herman's shoulder. "Oh...y-you couldn't be more wro-ong..."

Ken clicked his tongue. "Really, Herman, I had no idea your mind was so foul. Surely, a guard would think of another activity first..."

"Since that would be highly illegal, and you admit you find her attractive, I think my conclusion was pretty logical."

Val poked Herman with his paddle. "Hey. Don't go giving him ideas."

Ken laughed. "Well, that would be one way to get closer to her, and she is so very pretty." It was too much fun to mess with Val.

Val leaned forward. "I've had about enough of this talk about my sister. Keep it up, and I'm going to throw somebody out of this boat."

Ken looked up and stretched his arms out wide, soaking in the summer sun. "I'll take my chances. I think I'd enjoy a good swim right about now."

"Relax, Valerzan. It's not like he's going to ask for your sister's hand. He's looking for a noble bride."

Val's face was red now. "That makes it worse! He's just ogling her without intentions and flaunting it in my face."

Ken smirked. "I don't ogle. I merely admire. There's a difference."

"That's it!" Val dropped his paddle, grabbed Ken by the back of his shirt and held him aloft. The boat wobbled precariously. "Care to apologize?"

"Sorry that you aren't as pretty as your sister?"

Odelia finished her latest report to King Gonfrid and set down her quill. She leaned back in her chair and rubbed her temples. He'd be upset no matter how positive she tried to make the situation seem, but she had to make an effort. If she lost her title, not only would she not continue at Kennard's side, but depending on the king's orders, she might not be able to return to Meria either. Oulley was a nice enough place, but Odelia didn't fancy remaining here for the foreseeable future.

The sound of squelching footsteps carried into her bedroom from the shared sitting room, interrupting her thoughts. A loud slopping sound was followed by an even louder plop.

"What are you *doing*?" Valerzan's voice boomed clearly through the thick door.

"It was chafing," Kennard said.

"Your bedroom is just two more yards that way."

"There's nobody in—"

Odelia's curiosity got the better of her. She opened the door to find Kennard, Valerzan, and Herman standing in the middle of the room, dripping from head to toe. Kennard's shirt lay in a tangled mess on the floor, and his hands were on the waistband of his pants.

Raising one eyebrow, Odelia crossed her arms and leaned against the door frame.

Kennard bolted upright and smiled. "Ah...hahaha...Lia...I thought you'd be at dinner by now."

She pulled her lips in, trying in vain not to smile back. She was still angry with him, but his goofy grin and shenanigans had a way of getting to her. "Do I even want to know?"

"Why are you looking at me?" Ken pointed at Valerzan. "He's the one who threw us all in the lake."

"Maybe because you're the one who's half-naked right now," Valerzan said.

Odelia stole another look at Kennard. Without time for a good sparring session, it had been a while since she'd seen him without a shirt. His bronze chest glistened with lake water, highlighting lean muscles. He flexed his biceps and gave her a crooked smile. "I don't think Lia minds."

Valerzan scowled. "You don't know when to stop, do you?"

"All right, Ken, what did you do?" Odelia asked.

"I told you. It was Val."

"What did *you* do to make Val throw you in the lake?"

Kennard called over his shoulder as he strode off to his bedroom. "Ask Val. I'm going to change my clothes before these wet pants give me a rash."

"Me too," Herman said and disappeared in a blink.

Odelia turned to Valerzan and put her hands on her hips. "Well?"

"I didn't like the conversation," he said, then followed Herman to their room.

It wasn't until bedtime that Odelia got an opportunity to corner Valerzan for more information. She pulled him into her room as he tried to turn in for the night. "Can we talk about what happened on the lake?"

He groaned. "Why do you care?"

"Because it's my job to know what Kennard's up to, and the three of you have made this too deliciously mysterious. I need to know what happened."

Valerzan closed the door. "Fine."

"You said you didn't like the conversation."

"Yeah."

"Okay. What was the conversation about?"

Valerzan crossed his arms. "It wasn't appropriate."

"Valerzan..." she scolded. He could be such a pain when he didn't want to cooperate.

"They were talking about you. Are you happy now?"

"Me?" Odelia was taken aback. So that's why he didn't want to tell her. "What about?"

He glared at her.

"Stop being evasive, or we'll be here all night." She could be far more stubborn than him if pressed.

"We were discussing court beauties, and your name came up."

If her name was anywhere near a list of court beauties, she had to be doing something right. She waited for him to elaborate but got nothing. "Oh, come on. You can't do that. What did they say?"

"One of them finds you more attractive than he should."

The lying jerk. So she hadn't imagined his reaction to her uniform. If he could admit it to Valerzan, why would he hide it from her? "Wha—"

"I'm not telling you because it doesn't matter. Between age and rank, neither of them is an appropriate suitor, so they had no business talking about you that way."

Odelia closed her eyes and put her hand to her forehead. "Please, tell me you didn't tell them that."

"Of course, I did."

Flaming crusted frog nuggets. He might have ruined everything.

She sighed. "If Kennard takes an interest in me, you should be encouraging him, not shooing him away," she whispered forcefully.

Valerzan scoffed. "I will do nothing of the sort."

Odelia gritted her teeth. Dad should've been the one to tell him the secret, but she needed an ally, and who knew how much more damage Valerzan could do to her chances in the time it would take for Dad to do it. She locked the door and indicated for Valerzan to take the desk chair.

"And I never said it was Kennard," he added as he sat.

"Uh-huh. So it wasn't the one you threw out of the boat and refused to speak to all night?"

"Leave it alone, Odelia."

"I can't. I also need to tell *you* something."

Valerzan sighed. "Tell me what?"

She took the puzzle box from her trunk and held in both hands. "I'm about to share a family secret with you—one I only recently learned about myself—and I need you to promise that you won't make a big commotion. Herman and Kennard absolutely cannot know about this. Nobody outside our family can."

Valerzan eyed her warily. "Okay..."

Odelia unlocked the box and opened the drawer toward Valerzan.

He took the scroll inside and unrolled it, then shrugged. "It's our family tree." As he looked over it, his eyes widened. "Great Giver... Does this mean Dad's the King of Vist?"

"No. He's abdicating. If and when the throne is reclaimed, he'll do so officially."

Valerzan grinned. "So, that means I am, right? I'm the only son."

Odelia rolled her eyes. "No, Valerzan. That's how the Elgathan monarchy works. We're Vistans. Didn't you pay attention during our history lessons?"

"Then who's the king?"

"Nobody. You have a *queen*." Odelia held her head up and gestured to herself. "We pass the crown to the firstborn, not the first son."

Valerzan closed his eyes and nodded as if to say, *It figures.* "How long have you known?"

"Since a few days before Kennard hired me. Dad's known since long before we were born, but he kept it from us. The only reason I found out was that Queen Melaine told me to look up our tree."

"Dad doesn't surprise me. Everything's cryptic with him, but why didn't you tell me?"

"I'm telling you now."

Valerzan clenched his fists. "You're telling me our parents let me become a guard, knowing that I'm—what—a prince?"

"As I recall they tried to stop you, but you were so eager that you signed up the day you turned sixteen. Dad probably Saw that it was inevitable for you." Odelia sat on the bed. "And yes, that makes you a prince. So will you help me?"

"That depends." Valerzan leaned back in his seat.

"On?"

"What it is you're planning to do with this information."

Odelia clasped her hands together, rubbing at her palm with her thumb. Every time she thought she had a plan, Kennard seemed to change. While news of his attraction was good, she couldn't forget all the signs he'd displayed to the contrary. Patience. She had to be patient with him. Until she had proof that her path was wrong, she needed to stay on it. "I want to make Meriveria whole. Not this fake unity we have now. A truly unified kingdom as our ancestors intended. I think Kennard and I could make that happen if he's willing to stand by my side."

Valerzan crossed his arms with a distasteful scowl. "So you're just using him in your plans to take the kingdom?"

Odelia shook her head vehemently. "No. My plan isn't about taking power. I'm destined to take the throne, but I can't hurt him. Valerzan...I love him. And if I'm being honest, I have for a long time. I tried to hide it, but Queen Melaine could see it. That's why she was so eager to get rid of me."

"Then why are you fighting with him and pushing him away? Earlier, when he asked you to schedule time with him, I'd think you would've been jumping at the opportunity, not snapping at him."

"It's not that simple. The Elgathan king and queen have eyes and ears everywhere. If it gets back to them that I'm vying for his affection, I'll never get to find out his true feelings."

Valerzan snorted. "He established that well enough to get himself thrown in the lake."

"Thinking I'm pretty doesn't mean he loves me."

"He's already courting women he doesn't even like. Why not just tell him that you're what he's looking for? If he knew the situation, he'd probably marry you in a heartbeat and thank you for saving him the trouble."

Odelia smiled sadly. It was such a nice thought. "He might, but there's also a chance he might endanger us. Our existence is a threat to Elgathan rule. Accepting my claim would mean delegitimizing their dominion over Vist. What do you think the Elgathan king would do to our family if Kennard told him he was marrying the long-lost Queen of Vist?"

Valerzan passed a hand over his throat. "He wouldn't tell him."

"Wouldn't he? I didn't think so either until he told Conora and Bertina, and then Herman, that I was Healing him."

Valerzan gave a sheepish grin. "He may have told Herman about your sparring too when we were on the lake."

"Frog nuggets. You're kidding me." Odelia raked her fingers through her hair. At this rate, Kennard might get her killed anyway. "This is why we can't tell him. Now, are you going to help me?"

Valerzan nodded. "Just don't expect me to ever call you Your Majesty."

9

ASCAYMPA

Odelia and the rest of Kennard's retinue were on the road again, though not to leave Oulley quite yet. Kennard's grandfather ruled Ascaympa, an arion in the northwest of the grandrion. Queen Melaine had arranged the detour two weeks prior, and Odelia was intrigued by the idea of meeting the queen's father. She'd never been allowed to be in his presence on the rare times he'd visited the Cedar Palace.

Everyone in the dogcart had their hood up against the constant drizzle of the journey. The prospect of dry clothes and a warm dinner made Odelia nearly jump with excitement at the sight of a village and manor ahead. Unlike their last arrival, nobody waited outside, save for the rotating royal guards who had arrived ahead and a lone, miserable-looking manservant, who opened the door for them.

They scurried inside and waited as the servant fetched his lord. Kennard ruffled his hands through the front of his hair, the dark curls dripping water down his face. He flicked his wet fingers at Conora, who squealed and backed away.

"Don't make me sic Valerzan on you," Conora teased.

"I know he's faithful, but he's not a dog," Kennard said. "Also, he's *my* personal guard. You should have hired your own if you wanted one."

"He can still keep you in line."

Valerzan chuckled. "I don't really care what he does with his wet self as long as he doesn't start stripping again."

Conora's eyes went wide. "Again? As in, he's done that before?"

Odelia couldn't hold back a laugh.

Kennard wiggled his eyebrows. "Hoping for a repeat performance, Lia?"

She was, in fact, though she obviously couldn't admit to it. Her cheeks burned.

Echoing footsteps approached. Kennard and Conora went quiet and stood up straight. Even King Gonfrid and Queen Melaine didn't elicit such a quick response from them.

A very tall and dour man appeared through a door in the hallway. His clothes were finely woven but lacked any adornment or color. If his deep olive skin hadn't broken up the gray of his hair and clothing, he could've been mistaken for a statue. He held his arms out stiffly. "Kennard. Conora. It has been a long time. Come. Give me a hug."

"We've missed you too," Conora said as she and Kennard took turns exchanging with their grandfather the most perfunctory hugs ever witnessed.

The grandfather looked Odelia up and down. "Kennard, please, tell me that isn't your bride."

Odelia was dumbfounded. Queen Melaine's open hostility was nothing compared to her father's. At least the queen didn't usually speak about her as if she weren't there.

Kennard frowned and cleared his throat. "Grandfather, allow me to introduce my private secretary, Mistress Odelia DiOrto. Mistress Odelia, this is Lord Wystan."

Odelia curtsied with a cold smile. "A pleasure to meet you, Lord Wystan, and thank you for your hospitality."

Lord Wystan sneered. "A secretary isn't much better. Why would you hire a—"

"Grandfather." Kennard clapped his hands and smiled. "I would love nothing more than a fresh change of clothes. Where might we all do that?"

Lord Wystan instructed a servant to lead them to their rooms; then he spun on his heels and walked away without a salutation of any kind.

The servant led them upstairs to the end of a long hallway and gestured to two doors across from each other. "His Highness to the left. Her Highness to the right. The rest of you can follow me to the servants' quarters."

"Valerzan and I will need to remain close by to guard the prince," Herman said.

The servant shrugged disinterestedly. "There are two trundle beds in there." He turned to Odelia. "Then I guess it's just you. Follow me, girl."

"Wait," Conora said. "Are there any in my room?"

"Yes, Your Highness."

Conora smiled. "Then we won't waste your time. She can stay with me."

The servant grumbled, "If the lord finds out, tell him I did my job. I'll be back in twenty minutes to escort you to dinner." He bowed and slunk away.

Odelia followed Conora into her room. "You didn't have to do that. Thank you."

Conora opened her trunk. "Oh, no, you're doing me a favor. I expect it to be rather lonely here with old Stone-Skin."

"Ah." The Gift of Stone-skin made people resilient, as though they naturally wore armor, but at the cost of their physical and emotional sensitivity. It didn't explain whatever prejudices Lord Wystan had, but it did explain his complete lack of reservation in expressing them. Odelia pulled her uniform out of her luggage. "Not looking forward to time with your grandfather?"

Conora inspected a gown before tossing it on the bed. "Ha. It wouldn't be so bad if my cousins were here."

They were visiting friends in Cantahn with Conora's uncle and aunt and wouldn't be back in time to see them.

Odelia waited for Conora to step behind a partition before peeling off her own wet clothes. "I couldn't help but notice that your grandfather doesn't seem to like..." She wasn't actually sure what. Was it her sex? Her origins? Her class?

"Anybody?" Conora finished. "Don't take anything he says personally. He could find fault with the Giver himself."

What a miserable man.

Odelia buttoned and tucked her fresh shirt in, then buttoned her skirt. "There isn't anything he likes?"

"Flattery. You have to lay it on thick to get under his Stone-Skin, but he enjoys it as much as Mother does."

Odelia could do that. She fastened her vest and slipped into her jacket. "I'm ready when you are."

"Um...about that..." Conora stepped out from the partition. Her gown transitioned from gold at the hem to deep wine at the top, like a sunset. The back billowed free, and she held a wide ocean-blue ribbon in one hand. "Could you help fasten me?"

Odelia took the ribbon from her and deftly laced the back of the dress. She had helped Mom with the final construction of this dress, and she remembered where everything threaded through to create a diagonal of lacing from the left shoulder to the right hip. "Probably wasn't the best gown choice for a trip without a maidservant," she pointed out.

"I don't need one for the grandilords' manors. They all provide one for me. Either my aunt must have taken hers with her, or Grandfather forgot to send one up."

Odelia tied off the ribbon in long, flowing bow. "Ah, so that's why you wanted me in your room."

Conora gasped. "Oh, no. I didn't—"

Odelia chuckled. "I was just teasing. I don't mind helping. Do you need your hair fixed too?"

Conora scrunched up in an anxious grin. "Would you?"

"Of course, but don't expect anything fancy. I'm starving."

Conora raced to the vanity to sit with her arms resting in front of the bowl. Odelia fetched a comb and a handful of pins from Conora's trunk. She wouldn't object to a chance to play with the lovely waves of maple silk. They cooperated so nicely into a loose, thick braid, which Odelia rolled up and pinned to Conora's nape, then finished off with the gold comb.

It only took a few minutes, but Conora looked impressed. "You always make it look so easy."

Odelia waved off the compliment. "Compared to my hair, it is easy. Yours seems to want to curl into the braid. The pins slip out of mine, so I'd have to fight to get mine to do that." She looked in the mirror at her disheveled blonde braid. "Speaking of which, I had no idea mine was such a mess." Untying the end of her braid, she raked her fingers through from her scalp to comb it out, then sectioned out a piece at the front of her part to rebraid it.

"It looks pretty that way," Conora said. "You should leave it."

The braid had left an imprint in Odelia's hair, and it formed an S-pattern from her crown to the bottom of her breasts. "I look unkempt."

"But in the best way. I bet if you wore your hair like that more often, you'd have your own queue of suitors at the other manors."

Odelia laughed. "Well, I'm not impressing anyone here, but if you insist..." Maybe it would get Kennard's attention.

Someone knocked on the door.

"Coming!" Odelia called. She and Conora opened the door and joined the men in the hallway.

"Took you long enough," Valerzan said.

Kennard looked at Odelia and smiled, then looked away. "I don't think they made us wait for nothing."

Herman pressed a hand on Kennard's back. "Let's not dawdle, then."

They followed Lord Wystan's reluctant servant down to the dining room, where a small table sat in front of the fire, laden with platters of food and surrounded by eight chairs. Lord Wystan seated himself at the head and motioned for Kennard to sit at his right and Conora at his left. Kennard held the chair next to him out for Odelia, earning a scowl from Lord Wystan.

"The servants are eating in the kitchen in an hour," he said.

Kennard gripped the back of the chair, then put on a smile. "For tonight, may my people please sit with us? It's been a long day, and an hour is a long time to wait for food."

Lord Wystan stared at him for a moment, as though not fully understanding the request.

"I promise they're housebroken. At least, Herman is."

Lord Wystan furrowed his brows.

Kennard huffed. "I'm kidding. Lia and Val both received a formal education alongside Conora and me, and Herman has served in the elite guard for many years. No one in my retinue will scandalize you with their manners."

"That you would suggest such a thing makes me question the effectiveness of that formal education."

"It is never ill-mannered to show kindness," Kennard said solemnly.

Lord Wystan put his hands up in defeat. "Fine, if it will keep you from blathering on about kindness, the rabble may sit."

Odelia curtsied deeply and tried to sound sincere as she said, "I humbly thank you for your generosity, Lord Wystan," then sat as gracefully as she could.

Valerzan and Herman bowed as well before taking seats next to Odelia and Conora. For a while, everyone ate in relative silence, save for the crackle of the hearth and the clatter of cutlery against plates.

It was strange to think that anyone as warm and friendly as Kennard and Conora had descended from the callous man at the head of the table. If Odelia ever did marry Kennard, like it or not, Lord Wystan would be her family as well. She was unlikely to ever win over such a hateful man, but she could try to soften him a little.

"Lord Wystan," she said, "from what I've seen so far, your manor is magnificent. The other lords in Oulley must be jealous."

He studied her for a moment before the corners of his mouth twitched. "Yes, the king keeps me almost as grand as a grandilord. Marrying him was the one thing my daughter did right."

She smiled brightly. "Surely, something so clever was your idea, wasn't it?"

He sniffed. "Of course, it was."

"Perhaps she should listen to you more often, then."

Lord Wystan finally cracked half a smile. "Yes, she should."

The two weeks in Ascaympa went by painfully slow. Without any noble daughters to meet or nobles to discuss politics with, the manor had nothing for Odelia to do in the way of official court business. She used the opportunity to catch up on training with Kennard and do some research on Vist. Before they'd left Meria, she'd found a few books on Vistan history, culture, and law in the palace library, and since she could only spar so much without drawing attention, she was glad to have them.

Lord Wystan wasn't much for company, but he nevertheless spent time with Kennard and Conora every day, usually to play cards. He tolerated Odelia's company as well, provided that she continued to ply him with compliments. Once or twice, he even gave her a real, full smile.

On their last night there, Lord Wystan approached Odelia after dinner. "May I have a word with you alone, girl?"

She was wary of what he might want but followed him into his study.

He motioned for her to sit by the fire and closed the door. "When you first arrived, I sent a letter to Melaine, inquiring about you."

"I see." Odelia kept her face expressionless despite the knot forming in her stomach.

Lord Wystan leaned against his desk. "As I'm sure you could guess, she did not have the most flattering things to say about you. She even asked that I inform her of your behavior here."

Odelia nodded. That wasn't surprising.

"I've noted that you've been professional and, at times, maybe even pleasant for one of your kind." He leaned forward, boring into her with cold, dark eyes. "But you have also demonstrated far too much interest in my grandson."

"Lord Wystan, I would never presume to—"

"Don't play the fool. It doesn't suit you. I admire the effort you've put in to flatter me, but I can see the ideas churning in your eyes. My daughter was correct when she told me that you're much more shrewd than you attempt to appear."

She wanted to shrink into the armchair but sat up straighter instead. "Is the queen ordering me to remain here?"

"No."

She crossed her arms. "Then, what do you want with me?"

"Unlike Melaine, I don't wish you any ill will, so I will tell her nothing...for now."

"You're not that altruistic." Odelia knew there would be a price for his silence, but the thought of what it might be frightened her to her core. Growing up, she couldn't avoid overhearing stories of what young Vistan women paid for attempting to raise their statuses. For many, they would be making deals with Elgathan gentlemen one day, and the next, they were never seen or heard from again. Her proximity to Kennard generally kept Odelia safe, but that didn't guarantee her immunity from every unfortunate situation.

Lord Wystan steepled his fingers together. "You're right. I'm not."

She swallowed hard. She felt like a rabbit being cornered by a fox. Reassured that she still had a knife in her right boot, she grasped the arms of the chair to ground herself. "What is your aim?"

One corner of his mouth twitched. "Finally. Some fear. I was beginning to think you lacked the self-preservation to realize you were in over your head." He put his hands on his knees and leaned closer. "I've heard you speak when you think I'm not there. You are going to cease flirting with Kennard, and you are going to call him by his appropriate title. He is not 'Ken' to you. He is 'Prince Kennard' or 'Your Highness.' You will know your place."

"He won't abide that. He hates honorifics. Even Herman has been asked not to use them."

"Good."

Odelia furrowed her brows. "You said you didn't wish me any ill will."

"I don't."

"Then why are you asking me to sabotage my position? My ability to do my duties well is due in part to the autonomy and trust I receive from him, which comes from a place of dear friendship."

Lord Wystan shook his head. "It's better than the exile Melaine seeks for you."

"No. It's cruel. At least if the queen has her way, I can say goodbye to him on good terms. You're asking me to burn a bridge, then sit in the ruins and watch it crumble. Either way, I lose my friend and my position, but at least her way gives me the opportunity to start somewhere new."

"So you would like me to tell my daughter everything? I'm sure she's dying to hear about how you giggle at his inane attempts at humor or how you sit far too close to him."

Odelia held her chin up. "She failed to get rid of me once. I'll chance it again if I have to."

"You foolish girl, I offer to keep you out of trouble, and you want to run to it. Didn't your parents teach you not to play with fire?"

"Why bother bringing this up now? After tomorrow morning, you won't see me again until Kennard's next visit."

"Because I care about what happens to my grandchildren when they aren't here."

Odelia scoffed. "Now who's playing the fool? You don't care about him when he is here. What is this really about?"

"You know."

She did know. Fear hardened into indignation. "I want you to say it to my face. Not in euphemisms or whispers behind my back. After the things you've already said to me, don't turn coy now. I want you to tell me why you really care, because you and I both know this has nothing to do with grandfatherly concern." She stood and stared up at Wystan, every muscle in her posture challenging him to answer. "What is it, Lord Wystan?"

The lord jerked his arm back, hand open, but Odelia didn't flinch. He leaned away and crossed his arms. "I don't want Kennard to sully the family by creating some half-Vistan bastards."

Odelia knew without asking that it wasn't the bastard part of the idea that displeased him the most. "And there it is. For what it's worth, if he does create any *bastards*, it won't be through me, so unless you have anything more to add, I'm going to turn in for the night." She walked away and opened the door.

"It's nothing personal," he said as she closed it.

10

EAUND

Unlike the Cedar Palace or the manors in Oulley, which were all a natural reddish color from their red-cedar construction, the grand manor of Eaund was painted a fiery red. The patinaed copper roof threw the red into sharp contrast. Many of the larger buildings in the surrounding village had been painted red as well. In front of the entrance to the manor, a yellow canopy had been erected, allowing the grandilord and grandilady, as well as most of their court, to form a welcoming party in spite of the autumn sprinkles.

Ken shifted in his seat as the dogcart passed a pair of garishly dressed guards at the gate. "I can already see why Mother likes it here."

Lia chuckled. "As close as the grandilady is with her, we both need to exercise our best manners here if we don't want more angry letters from the king and queen. Perhaps I should do the formal introductions this time. She may be offended that I chose not to come here, and I'd like to make a better impression here than in Oulley."

He hated doing it himself anyway. "Excellent call, Mistress Secretary. I shall endeavor to behave in a manner appropriate to my princely station."

She smiled and shook her head, causing her hood to slip back a little. "I'm serious."

He waved a hand flippantly. "Well, there is no pleasing you then, for I cannot possibly adopt a more serious manner of speech."

She looked at the crowd as they were pulling up. "I'm ignoring you," she said, but the faint dimple in her cheek told him he'd won his endless game of making Lia crack.

"That is highly impolite," he whispered with feigned shock.

The dimple deepened, and Ken grinned.

The cart stopped under the canopy, allowing them to exit and pull back the hoods from their ponchos. A towering man stepped forward. His rich cobalt jacket and pants were covered in silver embroidery, and his long black hair was pulled back in a thin braid. His wife wore a matching gown, and black, eagle-like wings sprouted from her shoulders.

Lia curtsied. "Your Highness, may I present Grandilord Roderick and Grandilady Wilmarie. Your Graces, may I humbly present His Royal Highness, Crown Prince Kennard, and Her Royal Highness, Princess Conora. They thank you for your generous hospitality."

The noble couple bowed and curtsied, and their courtiers followed suit.

"The pleasure is all ours, Your Highnesses," Grandilord Roderick said. "We are honored that you grace us with your presence. Our staff will take your things and have them arranged in your rooms while we show you the manor."

No one else seemed to notice the look of panic that crossed Lia's face. "Thank you, Your Grace."

Grandilady Wilmarie smiled. "Please, come inside."

Ken waited until the nobles turned toward the entrance before leaning down and whispering to Lia, "Everything okay?"

"I don't like people going through my things," she whispered back as they followed their hosts inside.

She was as cagey as she'd been about the puzzle box a few months prior. When had she become so secretive with him? And what could she have to hide?

Grandilady Wilmarie opened a set of double doors into an opulent sitting room for Conora and Odelia. "Here we are. A maidservant should be up shortly to help Your Highness dress for dinner."

"Thank you, Your Grace," Odelia said.

Conora wasted no time finding the bedroom with her trunk.

"May I have a word with you, Mistress Odelia?" Grandilady Wilmarie ducked into the other bedroom and motioned for Odelia to follow.

Odelia nodded. "Of course."

The grandilady closed the door behind them. "As I'm sure you've surmised, the queen expects me to watch you closely." She kept her tone light and polite as though discussing the rain instead of a royal threat.

Odelia matched her tone. "Naturally."

"Although you declined my help before, I would like to extend it again. I promised the queen I would after all."

No help from Queen Melaine could be good for Odelia. "What would that entail, if I may ask?"

"I'm going to find you a suitable husband. Two months is a little less time than I envisioned before, but I already have a few suitors lined up for you to meet tonight."

So soon? Odelia did her best to reign in her shock. "Thank you, Your Grace, but I must decline. I don't plan to— I'm content with my current position."

Grandilady Wilmarie smiled. "Ah, but what if you found the right man? You don't expect to serve the prince forever, do you? The longer you wait, the more damage this situation will do to your reputation, and honestly, you won't find a court more open to your circumstance than this one."

Odelia frowned in confusion. "And what circumstance would that be?"

"Don't think I didn't notice that the prince summoned you to join him in his suite before dinner."

"In an official capacity, I assure you."

Grandilady Wilmarie put a patronizing hand on her shoulder. "It's okay, dear. There's no need to lie about such things here. As long as the prince finds his bride, any pleasures the two of you share need not make it back to the queen."

Odelia balled her fists behind her back. This was the second time in as many days that the implication had been made. What exactly was Queen Melaine—no, she was tired of giving her that power—what was Melaine telling everyone? "I am not, nor will I be, any man's mistress. Whatever you may have heard to the contrary is nothing but lies and slander."

"But reputations are built and destroyed by such things. What you do is irrelevant to what is told about you in terms of your social standing."

"I cannot control what others say about me," Odelia said.

"No, but you can distract them. If you act the model of propriety and demonstrate an interest in someone other than the prince in your spare time, you can build a new image for yourself."

Odelia shook her head. "I don't have the luxury of free time. When I'm not working directly with him, I'm corresponding with Meria or researching things."

Grandilady Wilmarie laughed. "I see that the prince is getting his money's worth with you. Stop worrying so much. Allow me to help with the matchmaking. I know everyone in this court and all of their reputations. And, unlike Doneron, I know how to throw a proper gathering. You can party en masse instead of holding all those little meetings like you did in Oulley." She walked to the door. "Consider my offer while you change your clothes. We can speak again at dinner."

Grandilady Wilmarie was gone before Odelia could reply. She sat in a nearby armchair and put a hand to her forehead. What had just happened? And what did she mean that *Kennard* was getting his money's worth? Odelia was an official member of the royal court...wasn't she?

Ken slammed the lid of his trunk. Why was he so angry? He'd enjoyed the convenience of having Lia close at hand in Oulley, but it was proper that her suite with Conora was on the other side of the manor. It was something else. Lia had been growing distant ever since he appointed her, but especially so today. If he could find out what was bothering her, perhaps that would settle his own mood.

Ken slid on clean boots and stalked out the door and across the sitting room.

"Dinner's not for another hour," Herman said.

"I know," Ken clipped.

"Where are you off to in such a fine mood?" Val asked.

"I need to talk to Lia."

Herman looked confused. "I thought she was coming here."

Ken put his hand on the door. "I don't feel like waiting." He marched out, leaving his bodyguards to scramble after him. The halls were mostly empty as other guests readied themselves in their rooms and servants prepared the banquet downstairs. A pair of guards who stood sentry outside Conora's suite bowed as he approached. He rapped on the door.

No one answered.

He pounded on the door.

Finally, a startled maidservant opened the door. "Your Highness!" She bobbed a curtsy and stood aside.

Conora stepped out of her room. "Goodness, Brother. What did our door do to offend you?"

Ken pointed to the other bedroom. "Is that Lia's?"

"Yes, she's been in there for a while now."

He knocked on her door, more politely this time.

Lia popped her head and one bare shoulder out the door a few moments later, looking flustered. She'd pulled her hair out of its braid, and it fell around her face in tousled, rippled strands of gold. "I'll be just a few more minutes. I'm not decent."

Ken pulled at the edges of his jacket as the room suddenly got a little warmer. "You've had twice as much time to get ready as I have. You should be more than decent by now—fine, even."

She shot him an annoyed look. "I'll explain later, but for now, you can have a seat." She shut the door in his face.

He huffed, then plopped into the nearest armchair.

"What is your problem?" Conora asked.

"I just want to speak to my friend. Why is everybody else making it a problem?"

"Maybe because you're being weirdly aggressive about it?"

Ken took a breath and closed his eyes. Conora was right. He didn't have a decent explanation for why things were so tense—yet.

"I'm going to finish getting ready," Conora said. "Try to refrain from knocking my door down, please." She returned to her room.

Ken waited for what felt like forever. He looked over at Val and Herman, who eyed him warily. Ken stood up. "What's taking so long? She has to be dressed by now. What is she doing in there, playing solitaire?" He went to the door, put his hand on the knob, and knocked as he turned the handle. "Lia? Is everything okay?"

She didn't object, so he opened the door. Inside, she had every article of clothing she owned—save for the white shirt and gray skirt she was wearing—strewn across the bed. The desk was spread with books and papers. Darting across the room, she rummaged through things and muttered curses between heavy breaths. She looked up at Ken, her eyes wide with horror. "It's gone."

"What is?"

"My puzzle box. It was in my trunk. This is why I didn't want people going through my things. I—"

Ken gently grasped her shoulders and looked her in the eyes. "It's okay. We'll get it back. I'm sure if you tell the grandilady—"

She tensed. "No!"

Val stepped in. "What's wrong?"

"Her puzzle box is missing," Ken said calmly, determined not to escalate her panic.

Val's eyes nearly popped out of his head. "What!"

Ken put a hand up. "It'll be fine. I'm sure—"

"I'll take care of this," Val told Lia, then hurried out of the room.

Ken ushered Lia toward a nearby chair. "What's so special about that box that has you both so worried?"

Lia shook her head and looked at her feet. "Please, Ken. This is a family matter. There are just some things I can't tell you."

Ken scowled. "See, this, right here—this is what I came to talk to you about." He closed the door.

She jumped up. "Ken! What are you doing? This isn't home. You can't close a bedroom door." She moved to open it.

He put a hand in front of her. "I want a private conversation, Lia. You haven't been open with me in months, and I'd like us to talk without Herman or Val for a change."

A knock sounded at the door, and Ken moved out of the way so Lia could answer. It was Herman. "Are you all right? I saw the door close."

"We'll be fine, Herman. Thank you. Ken would like you to wait outside, please." Her voice sounded tired.

Herman said gruffly, "Without Val here, this isn't a good time for one of your *games*." That was his word for their sparring sessions.

"Don't worry, we're not. I know how this looks. You and Val can cluck over me like mother hens about it later." Lia closed the door, then turned back to Ken and crossed her arms. "I'll give you ten minutes. Any more than that, and you might as well feed rumors to the grandilady yourself."

"What's changed? You used to tell me everything. Now you tell me nothing."

"What do you want to know—besides what's in the box?"

"What have I done wrong?" Ken asked quietly.

Lia frowned. "I don't understand."

"You've been pushing me away. I feel like you're always cross with me. What did I do to sour our friendship so?"

Lia covered her mouth with both hands, and her green eyes shone a little brighter. The expression pained him. She lowered her hands over her chest. "Nothing. You've done nothing wrong. I just have so many conflicting things to handle lately. Things that are my responsibility. And I don't feel like I'm doing any of it right. And now you're getting caught in the middle of my problems because I've let everything spill over. It's not fair to you, I know, but it's the truth."

He took one of her hands in his. "Then tell me what you can. With everything you do for me, it's only right that I share your burdens too. I want to know what you're dealing with."

106

"I don't even know where to start."

"Then start with the most recent."

Lia exhaled sharply. "While you were dressing, Grandilady Wilmarie spoke with me. She already has suitors lined up at dinner tonight for me." Lia put her hand over her stomach as though she might be sick. "She promised the queen to have me matched before we leave Eaund."

"What did you tell her?" Ken asked.

"Nothing. She didn't give me a chance to say no, but I can't be matched with a nobleman. I can't..."

It was a thought neither of them could ever complete aloud. They shared the same Gift, but as a woman, it could cost Lia more. No nobleman would marry her without expecting heirs, and childbirth could be risky for any woman, but according to Bertina, no woman with Healing had ever survived it. Wilmarie's promise to Mother was a death sentence for Lia.

Ken squeezed her hand. "You are not going to be. It doesn't matter what she promised Mother."

"What if I'm dismissed for being uncooperative? The king already thinks I'm incompetent. It's a wonder he hasn't—" She stared at him, eyes wide.

"That won't happen."

"No, it won't, will it? I thought Grandilady Wilmarie was mistaken when— The king never approved my appointment, did he?"

Ken looked away, guilty. "No, he didn't. Your wages are still coming from my allowance."

He hated the hurt in her eyes. It was the same look she'd given him when he'd told her secret to Conora and Bertina. Full of emotion but only one word: *Why?*

"You work hard," he said, "and you're good at it. Father is just being stubborn and spiteful. I didn't say anything because you seemed so proud of what you do. I didn't want to take that from you. If I had known it would cause you so much worry, I would have told you ages ago. "

Lia gave him a cautious smile. "I can't believe you've been paying all this time. 'Thank you' feels inadequate."

"I'll settle for a hug." Ken smiled and opened his arms. "I would pay everything I have if I needed to."

She wrapped her own arms around his middle, falling naturally into the embrace.

"Especially since you're the one keeping me alive and healthy," he teased.

Lia buried her face into his chest as she laughed, her bosom shaking against him in a pleasant way. A little too pleasant. Oh no. He hoped she wouldn't notice, but that was unlikely with the evidence poking her in what was most likely...her womb? Great Giver, that was not helping! An apology would probably be best, but for once, he had no words. She looked up, drawing his gaze to her softly sculptured lips. What would they taste like?

No! He came here to repair their friendship, not destroy it. It was his urge to Heal confusing him. Their talk hadn't healed all of her emotional wounds, and his instincts mistook his desire to repair them for an urge to Heal. That had to be it.

Then again, the urge to Heal had never made him want to kiss someone on the mouth before...or excited him...

Ken slowly opened his arms and leaned back. Lia lingered for a moment before pulling away herself. He decided to pretend nothing had happened. As long as she didn't mention it, he wouldn't either.

Lia smiled. "Thank you. I didn't realize just how badly I needed to get that off my chest."

Given the circumstances, Ken had to bite his cheek to keep from snickering at her choice of words as he sat on her bed. However, she must have picked up on it herself, because a touch of pink bloomed on her cheeks.

"I still need to decide what to tell the grandilady at dinner," Lia said. "I doubt she'll be pleased."

"And you're still worrying." Ken shook his head. "Lia, when I gave you this position, I did it to set you free, not burden you. I know you won't tell me everything that's bothering you, but whoever and whatever is weighing on you, I want to you forget about them all for a moment. Forget about your duty to me. What do you want to do?"

"I..." Lia's eyes searched his as though the answer could be found there. Her breathing grew heavier. "I need to find that box."

"Lia!" He rolled his eyes. "Don't worry about that right now. Val's looking for it. Now, what were you going to say before you distracted yourself?"

"But I—" She put her hands on her hips and took a deep breath. "Never mind."

"Do you need me to talk to the grandilady for you?" Ken offered. "Because you only need to ask."

She gave him a shaky smile. "I think I can manage it."

Grandilady Wilmarie was inspecting table arrangements in the dining hall before the other guests had arrived for dinner. Odelia curtsied. "Your Grace, I must speak with you about your offer."

The grandilady winked. "So eager, are we?"

Odelia stood up straight. "I appreciate the generosity, and the effort you must have gone to already, but I'm afraid I must decline again."

The grandilady raised an eyebrow. "May I ask why?"

"I would not make a suitable wife for any of your lords or pettilords."

She looked around, took Odelia by the arm, then led her out and down the hallway to an office, where she shut the door. "Is this about the prince?"

Odelia scoffed. "What? No. Why would it be?"

"Powerful men can get a little jealous when their favorites must find another bed, but—"

Odelia groaned. "Oh, for pity's sake, I am not his mistress. I thought I made that clear before. My objection is for myself and my Healing."

Grandilady Wilmarie crossed her arms. "Any of your suitors would see your Gift as an asset, especially if the stories about how Healing feels are true."

"And because of it, I will die trying to produce an heir if I marry one of them," Odelia blurted out. Not thinking about it made it easier to say.

Grandilady Wilmarie gaped. "Is that true for every Healer?"

Odelia clasped her hands in front of her, forcing her posture and voice to be as academic as she could. "According to what I've read, it is for women. No Healer has survived childbirth before." Yet. If anyone could save her from it, it was Kennard, but not if she were separated from him. It was a large *if*, but it was all she had to keep the thought from terrifying her.

Grandilady Wilmarie laughed.

Odelia's eyes narrowed. "I don't find this funny in the least, Your Grace."

The grandilady sighed. "Oh, dear, I'm not laughing at you. It's that the queen has been wasting her time worrying about you. Obviously, the reason she wants to marry you off is to keep you from seducing the prince to distraction, but—" She cracked up again.

Odelia let out a breath and smiled, praying that Grandilady Wilmarie would not suspect the same loophole she had thought of. "Exactly. The queen has nothing to worry about. Does that mean I'm free to work in peace here? Despite all the rumors about what I actually do, I care about doing my job well."

Grandilady Wilmarie put a hand on Odelia's shoulder. "If all you say is true, I pity you, for you will never experience the most enjoyable part of life. Do as you like in my court."

Ken and Herman found Val just outside the dining hall. "Any luck?" Ken asked.

Val shook his head. "No one will tell me anything. I don't know if nobody's seen it or if they just don't want to speak to me."

"We can help you look again after dinner," Ken said. "Everyone else should be coming down any minute, and I wanted to speak with Grandilady Wilmarie before the hall is crowded."

They entered the hall, and Ken approached Wilmarie near the head of the table. She stood and curtsied before returning to her seat. "Your Highness, I hope your rooms are to your liking so far. Please, have a seat here." She motioned to the empty chair on her right.

Ken sat down. "It's been more than satisfactory so far, thank you. Though I must admit, I haven't spent much time in there yet. Have you spoken with Mistress Odelia recently?"

She chuckled. "Well, you do get to the point, don't you?"

"She was quite distressed about the prospect of suitors being arranged for her."

Wilmarie patted his hand. "Not to worry, Your Highness. We've already spoken, and I'll let the men know I was mistaken. Had I known the curse she was under, I never would've made the arrangements in the first place."

Ken scowled. "Curse?"

"Well, that's what I would call it. I knew the cost of Healing was steep, but I didn't realize it extended that far. It sounds miserable."

"It's a Gift, just like any other. It has its drawbacks, but I wouldn't consider myself or Mistress Odelia miserable for it."

As she reached for the cup in front of her, Wilmarie smirked. "You reveal your innocence, Your Highness. You wouldn't be so quick to declare that if you knew what she was giving up."

Ken's cheeks warmed. His inexperience was none of her concern. He never thought he'd miss the quiet pretentiousness of Oulley. Clearing his throat, he changed the subject. "I was wondering if anyone in your court has found a puzzle box..."

Ken, Herman, and Val were on their way out the door the next morning when Grandilord Roderick approached them. "Your Highness, I was just looking for you. May we have a word?"

"Will it take long?" Ken asked. "We were on our way to escort my sister to breakfast."

"It will be but a moment, but I think it best that we speak privately. Shall we?" Roderick motioned back to the room they'd left.

"Of course, Your Grace." Ken waited until they were in the sitting room before continuing. "What is the matter?"

Roderick held out a large bag. "I fear I may have some bad news about your secretary. One of my servants found this in her trunk. We'd hoped to ascertain where she'd stolen it from before alerting you; then my wife told me last night that you were looking for it."

Lia, a thief? That didn't sound like her at all. Ken reached into the bag and pulled out the puzzle box. "Oh, thank the Giver. Mistress Odelia has been worried sick about this. She was tearing her room apart looking for it. I'll return it to her right away."

Roderick blinked. "It's hers?"

Ken raised an eyebrow. "It's clearly of Vistan design, with an image of Vist on the top, and was found in the trunk of one of the only two Vistans in the manor. Who else could it belong to—other than Valerzan here? And frankly, it looks a little delicate for his taste."

Roderick shrugged. "It's of finer quality than I would expect someone of her station to own."

Ken clenched his jaw. "Her position doesn't preclude her right to own nice things. If you must know, her father made it. I could've told you that if you'd asked. Next time you want to accuse one of my people of stealing, I suggest that you bring the matter to me before you steal from her." He turned to the door. "Now, if you'll excuse me, I need to return this, and I expect you to find a fitting punishment for the servant who *did* steal it."

Without waiting for a response from Roderick, he headed straight for Conora and Lia's rooms. As much as Ken had complained about Doneron's hollow honorifics and rigid adherence to propriety, he would rather return to Oulley for the rest of the year than stay in Eaund.

He ran a hand through his hair to clear his head as he neared the door. It opened before he could knock, and a maidservant emerged and curtsied before going on her way. Inside the sitting room, Lia was writing in her notebook, facing away from the door. He approached her quietly and peered over her shoulder, then whispered, "Good morning."

She instinctively threw her elbow back toward his head, which he deftly avoided.

Ken laughed. "You missed."

Lia turned around to kneel on the chair with her arms across the back. She smiled. "I didn't miss. I was aiming for the air in front of your face."

Ken grinned. There was the Lia he'd missed. "I have something for you." He held up the puzzle box.

She gasped. "Where was it?"

Val sneered. "One of the servants thought you stole it."

"Well, it's back now," Ken said, "and I already admonished the grandilord for it."

Lia took the box, inspecting it thoroughly. "Ken, may I speak to you alone?"

"Are you sure?" Val asked somberly.

Lia gave Val a stern nod. "Conora already left, so if you would wait outside with Herman..."

Clearly, Val knew something that Ken didn't, but if so, why was Lia sending him out to wait with Herman? It was strange, but he preferred this cheerful strangeness to the tense mystery of before.

Lia ran her hands over the puzzle box. "You have no idea how important this is to me. Thank you for bringing it back."

The way she smiled at him recalled the feelings he'd had yesterday, and heat rose from his chest to his hairline.

Ken cleared his throat. "Before you say whatever it is you wanted to talk about, there's something I feel I should say."

Lia pressed a portion of the box. "Oh?"

"I was too embarrassed to mention it at the time, but I feel the need to apologize for what happened in your bedroom yesterday evening. I didn't mean to make you uncomfortable... I— It just...happened."

Her cheeks turned pink, but she took his hand in hers. "It's okay, Ken. It didn't bother me."

He took his hand back and shook his head. "I don't want you to make the wrong assumptions. I don't— It wasn't that kind of— I don't really feel that way."

As she took a step toward him, her eyes met his, so bright and deep. "You don't or don't want to?" It sounded more like a challenge than a question.

"Lia..." he warned. What was she doing? This was a dangerous road to follow. It led to the one line he couldn't cross. He'd put her at too much risk already; he couldn't invite more of Father's ire upon her. And he certainly couldn't take advantage of her feelings while he looked for someone to marry. Lia deserved better than to be used and tossed away.

She slid a panel of the box. "You told me yesterday to think about what I wanted, to forget everything else."

Ken put a hand up between them. "That was different."

"How?" she asked softly as she pressed the box one more time until it clicked.

"You have me to overrule the demands others place on you. I don't. My obligations stay with me."

Lia looked at him earnestly. "It's a simple question. Have you really never considered it?"

The longer he looked at her, the more tempted he was to say or do something he'd regret. He could lie and break her heart, or he could give her false hope. He took a step back. "No good can come from asking that kind of question, Lia. Either answer can only hurt both of us."

As they had been talking, Lia had solved the box and reached inside. Without looking away from him, she slid the drawer closed and set it on the arm of her chair. She folded her hands in front of her. "Thank you again for returning my box. I have a letter to write, and then I'll meet you downstairs."

Ken furrowed his brow. "I thought you wanted to talk. Isn't that why you sent Val and Herman out?"

Lia's gaze turned impassive. "It doesn't matter now."

After passing her letters to a messenger, Odelia took her seat at breakfast as far away from Kennard as she could without abandoning the rest of the retinue. She wanted nothing to do with his cowardice this morning. If he couldn't even reject her outright, how could he be expected to stand by her side as she claimed her throne?

Hopefully, Dad could send her the information she would need in Vist before they left Eaund. Without Kennard's cooperation, she would need to focus on Vist to find a solution to her destiny. Revolutions didn't spring from nothing. People there were prepared to fight, and if she found them quickly, she might be able to steer them to a more peaceful route.

A well-dressed man sat down next to her, his light brown hair neatly trimmed and a winsome smile reaching his striking blue eyes. "Mistress Odelia, I don't believe we had the pleasure of meeting last night. My name is Rhonwin, and my father is the Lord of Atmos."

Odelia smiled politely. "That's nice." Had Grandilady Wilmarie forgotten to speak to all of the suitors? Or maybe this Rhonwin thought he stood a better chance to win her over—and by extension gain access to Kennard—because he had a drop of Vistan blood somewhere in his line.

Rhonwin held up a hand, palm away from her, and wiggled his fingers, displaying a shiny gold wedding ring. "I actually wanted to speak to you about a school that *my wife* and I have started in Losuno."

Odelia smiled for real. Thank the Giver. Finally, someone wanted to talk about business. Was his wife here to talk as well?

He pointed to a tall, elegant beauty further down the table, who smiled sweetly at him and waved back with her fingertips. "That's my Moira. Isn't she lovely? We'll have been married for two months tomorrow."

"Congratulations. You seem very happy." Her smile faltered. If only Odelia could have that kind of happiness. She wished he would get on with whatever business he had instead of rubbing it in her face.

"The school we're running is for training newly acquired Gifts. Nobles have tutors, but not the commoners, and too many preventable accidents have occurred from young people who don't know what to do with their Gifts."

A good idea, but what did this have to do with Odelia?

"Atmos is able to fund the school, but we are in need of teachers. Since you're traveling around the kingdom, we thought you might help spread the word for us, especially since your position allows you to mingle with both noble and common alike."

True, but they'd already visited Oulley. Would they want teachers from Vist? A lord with a drop of Vistan blood was not the same as flooding the school with full-Vistan teachers.

"I don't care where the teachers come from. Losuno is at the edge of Atmos, close to Vist. It would do our students good to have more positive interactions with our neighbors."

And those positive interactions might be just what she needed to keep Vist from pushing her into a full-fledged rebellion.

"Yes, they might," Rhonwin said.

The hair on the back of Odelia's neck stood on end. Was he Listening to her thoughts?

He sighed. "And I was doing so well... Yes, I have Listening. I usually try not to pry, but you've been rather loud since you walked in here,"—he leaned close and lowered his voice to the quietest whisper—"Your Majesty."

Odelia dropped her fork. She gripped the arms of her chair to keep from shaking. Flaming frog nuggets! How could she be so stupid? Decades of secrecy ruined because she couldn't remember not to think about it in a crowded room full of unidentified Gifts. She had never met a Listener before, but that didn't mean she shouldn't have been on guard against one.

Rhonwin smiled as though the conversation hadn't just taken a horrifying turn. "Don't place all the blame on yourself. You see, Moira has the same Gift as your father, and she has some fascinating thoughts about you."

He could have outed her by now. What did he want?

He beckoned Moira with his hand as he said to Odelia, "I think it best that we continue this conversation somewhere more private, don't you?"

Odelia turned to Conora. "I have some business to attend to. Would you please inform His Highness that I'll find him later?"

"But you've hardly touched your breakfast."

"It's all right. I'm not that hungry."

Conora shrugged.

Odelia curtsied to her, then followed Rhonwin and Moira, who walked arm-in-arm up to their room. Instead of a suite like Kennard or Conora's, theirs was simply a bedroom, though a well-furnished one.

Moira closed the door, then turned and curtsied. "It's a pleasure to meet you, Your Majesty."

Odelia panicked, instinctively curtsying back. Were they blackmailing her? What did they want?

"Not at all," Rhonwin said. "We wish to offer our support."

"I don't mean to sound ungrateful, but why?" Odelia asked.

"I've Seen what is coming," Moira said. "We want to stand with the victors."

That didn't make sense for a pair of Elgathans. "But, if I claim the throne, you'll be left on the wrong side of the border for me to help you. You'll be branded as traitors."

"Will we?" Moira asked. "There is more than one way to claim a throne. And who's to say that the borders will stay as they are now? Atmos is adjacent to Vist. It would be simple enough to annex, especially with the cooperation of its leaders."

Odelia shook her head. "I'm not looking for a fight with Gonfrid. Breaking Meriveria will weaken all of us. If I could just give Vistans a voice, I might not need to."

"A fight with Gonfrid is inevitable," Moira said. "What you need to decide is where and how."

Rhonwin nodded. "And when you do, all you need for our help is to ask."

For the next few weeks, Ken met with the local lords to discuss trade in the mornings while Wilmarie held gatherings in the dining hall in the afternoons. Lia took note of the women he saw potential in and scheduled a few private meetings here and there. Much as either of them hated to admit it, Wilmarie's method was easier than what they had done in Oulley. At first, meeting everyone at once was daunting, but after a few days, Ken appreciated it when he realized that he wouldn't have to be alone with the women he didn't want to see. It also deflected some attention away from him, as many young noblemen also came to the manor to find brides. Most of them were more than happy to shower attention on the women who had failed to earn Ken's favor.

At one such gathering, near the end of their stay, Ken noticed a group of three young noblemen standing in a corner of the dining hall and laughing raucously. He hadn't laughed like that in the entire time he'd been in Eaund. After all, he'd been on his best behavior for weeks. What was so funny? He needed to join them and find out. Excusing himself from a pair of young women, Ken wove his way across the room until he was a few feet behind the group of men.

"...heard a new one yesterday," one of them said.

"Go on," said a second. He and a third man nodded, grinning.

"All right." The first man cleared his throat and recited:

There once was a woman from Vist
Who Healed all the men whom she kissed.
    The prince got a shock
    When she puckered his cock,
So he gave her a post for the tryst.

He had barely finished the last line when the other two roared with laughter.

Ken's nails dug into his palms, and he clenched his jaw so tight, it ached. The nearby fireplace now burned too hot. He wasn't even sure upon whose behalf he was angrier, his own or Lia's. But he saw red.

"You really think her lips tingle?" the third man whispered loudly.

The second one smirked. "Why? You hoping to find out?"

They laughed again. The sound grated, making Ken's skin crawl. "You vile pricks!" he spat.

The men sobered, and the room began to quiet.

"How dare you, you degenerate parasites! Are your minds so feeble and foul that only scandalous slander can fill the sewers that are your souls? Your lice-ridden carcasses would wither into dust if you tried to work half as hard as she does, you slug-licking mongrels. You spend so much time waist-deep in lies, you wouldn't know the truth if it bit you on your hairy, dung-covered, over-sat-upon—"

"That's enough." Lia's voice radiated calm as she laid a dainty hand on his arm.

Ken inhaled deeply through his nose, clenching his jaw. Only the roar of the fireplace broke the silence of the hall.

Lia curtsied to the men and smiled politely. "You'll have to forgive His Highness. It's been a long day. If you'll excuse us, I have a meeting to get him to." She put one hand over his arm and the other on his back, then led him to the door.

As Ken let her pull him along, he continued glaring at the men, who gaped back at him in frozen horror. When they'd exited the hall, Lia gripped his arm and quickened her pace, letting her smile drop away.

Ken shook his arm free. "Did you hear what they—?"

"Not another word," she said through clenched teeth. She put both her hands on his back and shoved him toward the foot of stairs. They climbed up, then walked in tense silence back to his suite. Lia waited for Val and Herman, then closed the door behind them. She planted her hands on her hips. "Have you lost your mind?"

"But they—"

"Do you have any idea how much boot licking I'm going to need to do now? For the love of— Two of those men are future lords, and one is a pettilord. You will need their loyalty someday."

Ken scoffed. "You already apologized on my behalf. That's more than they deserve."

She groaned. "What they deserve is irrelevant. It's foolish to burn bridges before you've built them. After your tirade, an apology won't be enough. I've spent the last week rebuffing Pettilord Baldovin's advances. Now, I'll need to accept his offer of a private dinner and pray he keeps his hands to himself. I don't even know how I—"

"No." The idea was nauseating. "You will not apologize for me again. I won't give you that authority."

"Ken!"

"You didn't hear what they said."

She crossed her arms. "Nothing I haven't heard before, I'm sure."

"Lia, it was a foul poem about you and me." Just thinking about it again made his blood boil.

She shrugged. "I'm all too familiar with dirty court poetry. Which one was it this time?"

"I think it's the most recent one," Herman chimed in.

"Oh," Lia said, mildly amused, "the one that rhymes Vist, kissed, and tryst? That's one of the better ones. At least the rhymes make sense this time."

Ken's jaw dropped. He couldn't believe how casually they talked about this. "You've heard *more* of these? And they don't bother you? How many are there?"

"They've been going around for years," Val said. "You just never noticed because people in Meria have the decency to recite them where you can't hear them."

Ken looked at Lia. "How does this not bother you?"

She shrugged again. "I've had worse directed at me. When I have to inform women that you are uninterested, most are gracious, but more than a couple have called me a whore. One particularly creative lady called me a pasty harlot." She snorted. "At least that one was original."

"How can you be so flippant about this? These lies are malicious."

She glared. "If I seem flippant, it's because it's better than crying over it. I can't keep these rumors from spreading. All I can control is my reaction to them. Most people grow bored of taunting me if I play along or refuse to give them the satisfaction of a response. But what you did tonight—"

Ken shook his head. "You would rather I not speak up for you? Fine. Just remember, yours was not the only name dragged through the mud. I have the right to defend my own reputation as well."

Lia's face turned red, and her eyes narrowed. "Yes, Giver forbid you wallow in the mud with me. How could you live with yourself if people thought you'd taken up with someone like me?"

How could she think that? He had always seen her as his friend and his equal. "I was defending your honor."

"You were fanning the flames." She stepped closer to him, then had to look up to meet his gaze. "Your passionate display likely convinced many people that we are, in fact, lovers. For a man who doesn't want me in his bed, you've done a fine job giving me the social status that comes with it. All I'm missing is the actual experience."

Ken grabbed her shoulders. "Is that what you want? You think it doesn't matter?" He turned her toward his bedroom and pointed. "The bed's right there. We could get it over with now. I could use you for a little while, then go back to finding my bride in the morning. Is that what you want?" He didn't mean a word of it, but he couldn't seem to stop.

Val put a hand between them. "Prince or not, you need to back off. Now."

Lia pulled away from Ken, red and shaking. "You've always told me that you have nothing in common with your father. But right now..." She took a step back and opened the door. "You have never been more like him."

DOIVRIE

The remaining time in Eaund passed quietly. Neither Kennard nor Odelia wanted to bring up their fight. They went through the motions of court business, polite but more distant than usual. Pettilord Baldovin and his friends made themselves scarce whenever they saw Kennard, but everyone else took to whispering whenever he was near Odelia.

Just like in Oulley, Kennard failed to find a bride. It should've made Odelia happy. But what did it matter that he rejected others if he'd never choose her anyway? Gonfrid and Melaine would be furious. Kennard had at least made a show of trying up until the last day in Eaund, but he'd also rejected the last of the Elgathan brides.

Six days before they were scheduled to leave, reports came in of a Tehazian raid on a village in the north of Eaund, near the river and dangerously close to the route they'd planned to take to Doivrie, the next grandrion on their tour. It couldn't have been a coincidence that the bridge intended for trade and diplomacy with Tehazy had recently been finished. Hopefully, it wouldn't become a pattern. Within a day, Odelia had new arrangements planned for the detour and everyone's bags packed. After everything that had happened in Eaund, nobody objected to the early departure.

"Finally," Kennard said as they pulled away from Eaund, "I'll get to see Vist. Do you know how long I've wanted to go there?"

"Don't get too excited," Odelia said. "The alternate route takes us through the flooding in the valley. It's going to take about three days to get to Doivrie—and that's if the river isn't too frozen near Iverish."

His face lit up. "Iverish? We get to see your hometown? That's even better. Val, you've got to be excited too."

Valerzan shrugged. "I was seven we left. It's hardly home for me."

Odelia had been almost nine. Over half of her life had been spent in Meria. Ancestral home or not, Iverish no longer called to her as it had when they'd first moved. "We'll just be stopping there for the night. You won't get to see much."

Kennard sighed. "Couldn't we spend just one extra day there? I've wanted to see it for years."

"Grandilord Patricius will be expecting us," Odelia said.

"Three days travel still puts us ahead of when we planned to get there originally. We can spare one day."

"There really isn't much to see in Iverish, but if you're so determined, I can plan a long stop there when we pass by again on our way to Yophiex in a few months."

He grinned. "I'm going to hold you to that."

After a short day of travel, they stopped for the night in Losuno, where Rhonwin and Moira were living while they worked on their school. Moira's father, Pettilord Niven was happy to offer them warm lodgings in his relatively humble manor. He apologized profusely for the condition of his guest rooms, which, though finely furnished, were showing their age. "If I'd had more time to plan, I would have bought some new bedding for Your Highnesses."

"They're perfect as they are," Kennard said.

"You're too gracious, Your Highness," Niven said, then left the retinue in the guest hall to settle themselves.

"Lia, I'm amazed you set this up so quickly," Kennard said.

Was that a compliment or an insult? "Thank you?"

"I mean, I've never met Pettilord Niven before, but you seemed to arrange things so easily."

"His daughter and son-in-law were at the grand manor with us several weeks ago. Moira and Rhonwin?"

Kennard tilted his head and pursed his lips, then shook his head. "No, I don't remember meeting them either."

"I do," Conora said. "She had a meeting with them after breakfast on the first morning we were there."

Kennard looked confused. "You had a meeting without me?"

"They wanted to talk to me about finding teachers in Vist for their school." Odelia chuckled. "Not everything concerns you, Ken." She turned in to her room before he could ask any more questions, content to let him think she was annoyed if necessary.

By the middle of the next day, they caught a riverboat in Ormoint. The wide flatboat was fitted with two long benches facing each other in the middle. A series of smaller seats lined the outside, each with a Strongman wielding a paddle. Normally, the benches would be stuffed with passengers, but only the five of them were riding today.

As the boat picked up speed, trees blurred past, and the icy wind bit through the thick dog wool of Odelia's poncho, causing her to shiver.

The boat captain looked over at her and guffawed. "What kind of Vistan shivers? We laugh at the cold."

"The kind who's spent the last ten years in Meria," Odelia said through chattering teeth.

"Val, are you able to open my trunk? I have an extra poncho in there," Kennard offered.

Odelia hung her head in shame as the wind stung her eyes. They had been in Vist for a matter of minutes, and she'd already proven herself to be an outsider to her own people. How was she supposed to be their queen? Logically, enduring the climate had no bearing on her leadership potential, but perception mattered. When they reached Doivrie, she would re-immerse herself in the culture. She needed to get back to her roots.

Valerzan handed Kennard the requested garment. The captain shook his head as Kennard crossed the boat, poncho in hand, to sit beside her. He draped it over her head and huddled up close. "What good is your Vistan pride if you freeze? I'll need you to have all your fingers and toes when you make my introductions in Doivrie."

In Vist, they traveled by dogsled instead of dogcart, and Herman wore a pair of snowshoes. Ken was in awe of the glittering white landscape. He had seen snow in Meria for a few days each year, but never this much at one time. It wasn't slush; it was a fine, soft powder that covered everything in sight. As beautiful as it was, Ken was glad to see the grand manor of Doivrie rise in the distance. Set into the mountainside, only the log structure of the entrance was visible from the road.

Nobody came to greet them here, but someone must have been watching from inside because the large double doors opened as soon as they hopped out of the sled. A short but slender, pale man with a shock of deep red hair stepped into the entryway. His yellow jacket and dark green pants were finely tailored and embroidered with a delicate white floral pattern, simpler than those of the Elgathan grandilords. He smiled and bowed. "Grandilord Patricius, at your service. Welcome to Doivrie, Your Highnesses. Please, come warm yourselves by the fire. We have hot cider and spiced mead and wine if you'll follow me."

Ken grinned as they all followed Grandilord Patricius through the entryway to a large hall with a blazing fire. The walls reminded him of the Cedar Palace. Though not as ornate, the wood had been polished into the same warm sheen.

"Come, have a seat, everyone." Patricius motioned for a servant to pass around mugs full of hot drinks. "Even you, my good men," he said to Val and Herman, smiling and patting Valerzan on the back, then turned to Lia and looked her in the eyes. "It's a pleasure to see you again Mistress Odelia," he said in a respectful tone that was almost reverent.

Ken had never heard someone speak to Lia in such a way before. It was a little odd, but refreshing. He could relax for once, instead of waiting to see if he needed to speak up for her—not that she had appreciated it lately.

As everyone else settled into their chairs, only Herman seemed tense.

"Relax, Herman," Ken said. "After all the miles you've run, you can take a seat."

Herman leaned down and whispered, "I don't trust the grandilord. He's hiding something."

Ken raised an eyebrow. They'd been here for a few minutes, and Herman was already suspicious? "Really?"

"I don't know what, but that man has secrets."

Ken rolled his eyes. None of the Elgathan gradilords had earned such distrust, even when they'd stolen from them. This was already his favorite place so far, and he wasn't going to let Herman's prejudices ruin it for him.

For the first time since the start of the tour, Odelia had a room entirely to herself—and it was grander than the one she had at home! The cozy bedroom had a thick, soft bed with room to lie spread-out if she wanted to, and it even had a tiny sitting room with two armchairs in front. But better than all of that was the privacy. With a room between her things and the shared hall, her secrets felt safer than they had been in ages.

She smiled and was running a hand over the fluffy down comforter when someone knocked on the door of her suite. Odelia closed the bedroom door before answering in the sitting room.

Grandilord Patricius looked around before stepping inside and motioning for her to close it.

She curtsied. "Good evening, Your Grace."

He shook his head. "You need never to curtsy to me when the Elgathans aren't watching, Your Majesty."

Somebody else who knew? At this rate, her secret wouldn't last long. "How do you know who I am?"

"I've known your father since before you were born. When he was younger, Abhenric thought to start a revolution himself. He approached me with his secret, and I helped him come up with a few plans."

Odelia laughed. "Dad wanted to start a revolution? Ha. He told me he's spent twenty years trying to prevent it."

Grandilord Patricius nodded and sat down. "True, but before you were born, he was a different man. Our plans didn't get far. When Hortensia became pregnant with you, Abhenric abandoned everything and returned to that little cabin in Iverish. When I heard he'd been hired by Gonfrid, I knew he was up to something. I didn't think that it would take another decade for it to come to fruition."

Odelia took the other chair. She should've guessed the grandilord was a separatist. Between the colors and the dogwood pattern, his clothing had all the elements of a Vistan flag. "Are you looking for me to take up your plans?"

"Yes and no. I talk to Abhenric when I visit Meria—discreetly of course—and he's told me about his visions and your most recent plan. How is that working for you, by the way?"

Odelia looked down at her unadorned hands. "Poorly, I'm afraid."

Grandilord Patricius cocked his head. "Huh. That's surprising. With as many glances at you as the Elgathan prince steals, I would think he's either in love or trying to paint your picture."

She laughed bitterly. "Someone should tell him that. He's too afraid to admit to it."

"Have you tried asking him directly?"

"Yes, twice—although, we were in the middle of an argument the second time, so that probably didn't help."

Grandilord Patricius laughed. "Well, no, I should think not. You need to try again."

"That's a little difficult when he's focused on meeting any woman but me."

He smirked. "What if you were the only one?"

"What are you saying?"

He shrugged. "I'm afraid none of my nobles are interested in marrying off their daughters to the House of Elgatha—or at least, I don't think they'd be if I'd asked."

Odelia gasped. "If Gonfrid and Melaine found out..."

"Why would they? Are you going to tell them? And why should they care? They don't really want him to find anyone here anyway. It's all an act to show that they've included Vist, but everyone knows they want an Elgathan girl."

"And what if that still doesn't work? What if he's not ready for any of this?" Odelia wasn't sure she wanted to hear the answer.

"Then you need to do what you were made for. Say goodbye to your prince, take up your crown, and raise your army. Vist will not wait for much longer. The more time you take, the more Elgathan blood they may demand in the uprising."

Lia marched into Ken's sitting room, wielding her notebook like a shield. "I have some good news and some bad news."

"What's the bad news?" Ken asked. Better to get that out of the way first.

"The bad news is that the grandilord hasn't found any young women for you to meet here, but the good news is that you'll have more time to focus on the real work we have in Vist, like that petition to repeal the ban on weapons."

Ken laughed. "That all sounds like good news to me."

"I thought you'd say that."

Lia seemed in better spirits already without the added strain that the search for a bride had put on their friendship.

Behind her, a messenger zipped down the hallway, then backtracked and stopped just inside the doorway, which he knocked on. Lia turned around and took a letter from him, and the man zoomed away.

She looked at Ken, worried. A messenger in enough of a hurry to come directly to his room instead of relaying to a servant at the door couldn't bring anything but bad news. Lia broke the royal guard's seal. Reading the letter, she swore under her breath. She looked back to Ken and handed it to him. "There's been another Tehazian raid, in Doivrie this time, not far from Fort Solace. We're to go back to Meria immediately."

Ken scanned the short letter and confirmed what she said. "I can't believe this. We've barely settled in here." He looked back up.

Lia looked shaken.

Ken took her hand. "I'm sure we can return once these attacks are taken care of."

"I think destiny may be rallying against me," she said softly.

"What do you mean?"

She shook her head and forced a smile. "Just that I wish we could stay."

The explanation rang false, but Ken sensed that it was all he was going to get from her.

12

A RIBBON OF INTENT

K en didn't even have time to change from his travel clothes before he was called in to meet with Father. Lia followed him in and waited near the door.

Inside with Father and Mother, a young woman waited for them. She had long black, wavy hair and a thin scar running down the side of her nose. Though the light in the office was strangely dim, he could tell that the purple gown she wore was as fine as anything Mother owned.

Father put his hand on Ken's back. "This is my son, Crown Prince Kennard. Son, meet Queen Barbenia of Uskev."

The hand pressed him forward, and Ken bowed. "A pleasure to meet you, Your Majesty."

Barbenia flashed a pretty smile, then said with a heavy accent, "And you as well, Your Highness."

Father motioned for Ken to sit. "As you have been having trouble on your tour, your mother and I have decided to help you search for a bride."

No. They did not just call him home from his new favorite place just to change the rules on him again.

Father continued, "Queen Barbenia happens to be looking for a consort. Between the two of you, the shared lands of Meriveria and Uskev could make a formidable kingdom someday."

Ken doubted that. Uskev was an island and not even the closest one to Meriveria. Baythroas sat between them.

"We'll leave the two of you alone to talk," Mother said before she and Father walked out the door.

Ken chuckled. "Well, it would've been nice if they'd told me to change my clothes first, wouldn't it? I'm sure you weren't expecting the crown prince to look like such a mess. I certainly wasn't expecting you...at all."

Barbenia laughed. "It is quite all right. Truth be told..." She cleared her throat. "Father was a fisherman."

"I see." He didn't know what else to say. He wasn't prepared for any part of this.

Ken looked to Lia, who was staring daggers at Barbenia and gripping her notebook so hard her knuckles turned white. So much for help from her.

Ken bowed to Barbenia. "Will you excuse me, please? If you don't mind, I'd like a chance to change into more appropriate attire and try this again. Perhaps we can talk at dinner?"

She smiled and nodded. "Of course."

Kennard went to his rooms, with Odelia trailing silently behind him. Scarcely had he closed the door before Odelia dropped her notebook on his table.

"I resign," she said.

Kennard looked like he'd been punched in the gut. "What?"

"I resign."

"Why?"

"What will happen if you marry someone like Queen Barbenia?"

Kennard shrugged. "I'll have to move to Uskev, I guess?"

Odelia put her hands out. "Then, I don't have a job anyway."

Kennard scoffed. "Nonsense. You'd come with me."

She shook her head. "I can't."

"What do you mean, you can't? Lia, I need you with me, and you need me."

She closed her eyes and sighed. "I can't leave."

He rounded on her. "You're jealous of her, is that it?"

"I would be lying if I said that the thought standing by your side as you marry someone else doesn't kill me. But that isn't why I can't stay. To be honest, even if you had picked someone on the tour, she would have wanted me dismissed as soon as possible. What woman would want me around to kiss her husband? And even if she did, I *still* couldn't stay."

Kennard sank into a chair. "That's it. You would just leave me? To die? To let yourself die? Why would you—why?"

Tears filled her eyes. "There are things more important than myself. I wish I could tell you more, but not if you go through with this."

"Lia, I was caught just as unawares as you were. I don't know how much of this they've planned out, but I may not have much of a choice."

"I asked you before what you would do if you didn't have any obligations—"

He stood up. "Lia, don't do this again. I told you, I can't answer that."

She stood toe to toe with him and looked up into his deep brown eyes. They held pain, and she wanted to make it go away, but the only way to do that was to make it worse first. Odelia put a hand over his heart. "I don't care if it hurts me, Ken. I don't care if it kills me. I need you to tell me."

He stared back at her for what felt like an eternity. Odelia thought her heart would beat right out of her chest. He tried to look away, but she reached up and gently guided him back.

Please, just answer.

Kennard brushed the back of his hand against her cheek and tucked a strand of hair behind her ear.

Please, please, answer.

His fingers circled back along her jaw, then softly tipped her chin up higher. She closed her eyes as his lips pressed against hers. A warm tingling sensation enveloped her lips and slowly spread through her from head to toe. His fingers raked through her hair as he held the back of her head with one hand. The other slid to the small of her back, pressing her against him and making her yearn for more. She stood on tiptoe and wrapped her arms around his neck.

Odelia broke the kiss and gasped for air. She looked deep into the warmth of Kennard's eyes.

"Lia," he breathed as he dove back into the kiss.

She never wanted it to end. Not the way his strong arms held her, nor the beat of his heart next to hers, nor the sweet, tingling taste of his lips against hers. The power of his Healing flowing through her was refreshing and intoxicating. As he broke away, she ached to pull him closer. They held each other's gaze, breathing heavily.

He tried to move in one more time, but Odelia seized a moment of clarity and put a hand on his chest. "I have something to show you," she said softly.

Kennard touched his forehead to hers and smiled. "Can't it wait?"

She pulled out of the embrace and took his hand in both of hers. "Trust me, Ken. You'll want to see this."

Lia led Ken by the hand down the hallway. He hadn't expected an ultimatum, but he couldn't complain about the outcome. After a kiss like that, he would've followed her anywhere. Into her family apartment they went, and she continued on to her bedroom. Ken pulled her back, and she spun on her heel toward him, bringing her lips deliciously close again. "If I go in there right now..."

She frowned in confusion. "I just need to fetch something from my trunk. You didn't think..."

His face warmed, and hers turned pink.

"Never mind. I'll be right back." She dropped his hand and stepped into the room.

Ken exhaled and ran a hand through his hair. She was so much better than anything he'd imagined.

Lia came back out with her hands behind her back. "I've wanted to show you this for so long, but I needed to know how you felt first." She presented her puzzle box on the palms of her hands.

Ken raised one eyebrow. "Um...I've seen that before."

She giggled. "No, it's not the box. It's what's inside. Hold down the mountaintop."

He did as she asked.

"Now, slide down this tree here, and press on that ray of sunlight."

He did, and a drawer popped out the front. Inside sat a scroll. Had that been in there the whole time? "What's on it?"

"Just read it," she said eagerly. Her hand trembled slightly as she put a hand on his arm.

Ken unrolled the scroll slowly. At the top was the seal of authentication used by wise women. "Lineage papers?" He held the scroll out to her. "Lia, I think we're past this point. It doesn't matter to me."

She pushed it back to him. "Please. It matters to me."

He took back the scroll to humor her. The first few lines were as he had expected, but then, he had to read it twice. "King Uldrio?"

Lia nodded nervously, biting her lip, her eyes intense under worried brows.

"But that would mean you're...you're..."

"The rightful Queen of Vist."

Impossible. The evidence was there, but he didn't understand it. "How? The Vistan royal family all died of some plague."

"Massacred, actually, via poison—but that's not the point. Two of my ancestors had eloped, so when the poisoners killed the husband, they didn't realize they'd missed his wife. As far as anyone knew, all of my ancestors were dead. The secret was hiding in plain sight with the wise women, but nobody bothered to check because who checks a dead family tree? That's where I ended up finding out. Dad didn't even tell me until I confronted him about it."

"Wait. Slow down." There was so much to take in. "You said they were poisoned. Who poisoned them?" A knot in the pit of his stomach told him he didn't want to know the answer.

She shook her head. "That doesn't matter. What our ancestors have done is beyond our control."

The knot grew. "Our ancestors? It was mine, wasn't it?"

She didn't deny it.

He felt sick. "My ancestors massacred yours." An entire palace full of people, and they'd killed every last one. He knew the past rulers in his family—and even the current one—had done unsavory things, but this was beyond that. It wasn't an act of war against an enemy kingdom. It was cold-blooded murder of their friends and allies.

If Father knew the truth, he would do anything to keep it buried—including burying Lia. And after all the times Ken had betrayed her trust... "No wonder you couldn't tell me. Why tell me now?"

"Because I love you, and I don't want to hide from you anymore. But I also need your help. Vist is getting restless, and frankly, having you abandon the tour there didn't help. They are going to demand a rightful ruler, and I have to answer. I don't want a civil war, but your father isn't going to let me reclaim Vist without a fight—not on my own, anyway. But if you're willing, you and I could set things right together."

He held her hand. What could he say? Hearing her say she loved him, he wanted to promise her everything, but the weight of it all was overwhelming.

"I know it's too much to ask of you all at once. Take your time to decide what to do. I only ask you to promise one thing."

Ken kissed her hand. "Anything."

"Tell no one, especially not your parents."

He held her hand to his heart. "I promise." With his free hand, he dug into his pocket. "And if I'm contemplating such matters, it's only right that I do this properly." Ken pulled out a long piece of deep raspberry satin ribbon and wrapped it twice around her wrist. He tied it off in a wide bow, the ends dangling a few inches over her hand.

Lia laughed. "If you were truly proper, you would've given me that before you kissed me—and would've waited for me to tie it on."

He brushed his hand against her cheek, softly cupping her face. "I can take it back if you want."

She brought her lips within inches of his. "You wouldn't dare."

He kissed her softly, the tickle of it making a delightful shiver run down his spine.

Someone cleared their throat, startling both of them out of the kiss. Abhenric stood in the doorway, arms crossed and eyebrows raised. "Valerzan didn't tell me your tour was so successful."

Ken's cheeks grew warm.

Lia ran to Abhenric and hugged him. "I missed you. We have so much to talk about."

Hortensia walked in and immediately lifted Lia's beribboned wrist, then grinned and embraced her.

Ken was half-surprised Val didn't show up as well, but he and Herman were reporting to the captain of the guard and likely had no idea that Ken wasn't in his room for a bath and a change of clothes as planned.

Abhenric slowly plucked the scroll from Ken's hand. "I see you know our family secret now." He was weirdly calm for a father who had just caught a man in an intimate moment with his daughter.

Lia gripped Ken's arm anxiously. "Has anything changed, Dad?"

"Maybe, but I don't know yet if it's for better or worse. All I know is that you've managed to unsettle this vision far more than I ever could."

"What vision?" Ken asked.

Abhenric turned to Lia. "You didn't tell him about the vision?"

Her face turned pink. "I was getting there..."

He gave her a disapproving look, then turned back to Ken. "She's destined to claim the throne of Vist, but we're hoping to avoid the civil war that comes with it. Since the vision has only just now changed, I can assume that your involvement is the reason."

Lia laced her fingers through Ken's. "I know you want to be the best possible king for Meriveria someday. What better way to do that than to help me keep it whole?"

He couldn't think of one, but how was he going to do it without provoking Father against her?

Ken adjusted his circlet and smoothed out his jacket before stepping into the dining hall. If he was going to upset his parents, the least he could do was give them less fuel for their anger. He'd warned Lia to stay far away as well. He wasn't foolish enough to reject his parents' plans and spring his newfound love on them in the same night, and her presence would draw their blame too quickly.

Mother was already pouting by the time Ken reached the table. "Queen Barbenia tells me you didn't speak with her for long. I hope you'll be remedying that now."

Ken slowly took his seat. "About that..."

"No, Kennard. You are not going to reject her as you have already done to all the respectable women in Meriveria."

Ken resisted the urge to roll his eyes. "I didn't even meet them all, Mother. I was pulled away halfway through the tour."

She waved it off. "You met all the ones who matter."

"And haven't rejected all the ones I have met. That's why I need you to call off whatever you have planned."

Mother's eyes widened with interest as she tugged on Father's sleeve, pulling him into the conversation. "Why didn't you tell us you found someone? I should have known that secretary of yours couldn't be trusted to send accurate reports."

"There was nothing wrong with Mistress Odelia's reports. She didn't know before. But yes, I have given someone a ribbon of intent, and I would like the chance to honor that."

"Who is she? Why didn't you tell us?" Father asked.

Ken chuckled nervously. "It's only a ribbon for now. I haven't given her a ring yet. I want to woo her for a little longer before I subject her to the scrutiny of the entire court—especially the two of you."

Father shook his head. "You should have told us. Now we have plans with Queen Barbenia, and it will look very bad for us to end them so abruptly."

"And you could've asked me before you made plans for my life," Ken said.

"How long do you plan to woo this girl for?" Mother asked.

Ken needed time to plan with Lia. "I'd hoped for a month."

"I'll give you two weeks," Father said. "You will present her to us at the Midwinter Feast."

Ken prayed that Lia had a plan in place already.

"And you will be the one to break the news to Queen Barbenia," Mother added. "Now."

Ken found Barbenia in a dark corner of the dining hall, absentmindedly running a small, gauzy cloth between her fingers.

He bowed deeply. "My apologies for keeping you waiting, Your Majesty."

She smiled. "It is fine. I am glad to make you more comfortable."

Ken rubbed his neck. "There's really no easy way to say this, but—"

"You have a beloved already."

Ken was taken aback. "How did you know?"

Barbenia laughed. "You did not notice me in the shadows, but I saw her lead you by the hand. Why is she not here now?"

"My parents...they're not exactly fond of her."

She nodded. "Ah. I see. Then it is good that I have not told anyone. When will you tell them?"

"I have two weeks."

Barbenia put a hand on his shoulder with a conspiratorial smile. "If you need to run, Uskevis have a soft spot for disparate lovers."

Ken hoped to the Giver that they didn't need to.

Odelia contacted Grandilord Patricius and Rhonwin and Moira via Flight messenger in the city of Meria. With only two weeks to prepare, she couldn't wait for a Speed messenger on foot, and she couldn't trust a royal messenger to not ask questions or tell someone whom she was contacting. In the likely event that things went poorly with Gonfrid and Melaine at the Midwinter Feast, she needed to have a plan to flee.

Patricius offered sanctuary and the means to an elopement. Rhonwin and Moira offered safe and discreet travel through Atmos to get to Doivrie. They just needed to make it out of the palace. Valerzan suggested to Odelia that they skip the feast and take Patricius up on his offer right away, but she wouldn't hear of it. Kennard wanted to present her at the feast as promised, and she had to give him the chance to try. He also hadn't yet officially proposed marriage. The ribbon of intent only marked her as his sweetheart; it signaled romantic intentions, not lasting ones. If she ran, he was not guaranteed to follow.

Besides, if and when they fled to Doivrie, Gonfrid was sure to send soldiers to Patricius's doorstep. Odelia had to seize the opportunity to try to avoid a military confrontation. Once that started, there was no telling when it would stop.

She decided to check the library for any laws or traditions that might help as well. Deep in the history section, Odelia found an unexpected but familiar face.

"Bertina? What are you doing here? I thought Conora was done with her studies when she went on the tour with us."

Bertina nodded. "She was. But after a few weeks of looking for a new post, the king asked me to work here in the library. He said he believed the prince might need some review classes and wanted me close by."

"Review classes? Why?" Kennard had learned everything he needed to know.

"It was so silly. He heard he was hiking and canoeing in Oulley."

Odelia laughed. "Well, I think Kennard and I could probably teach *you* about Healing by now."

"True. How has your little experiment gone?"

Odelia looked around. The library was empty, but she whispered anyway, "I think we can create a loop—like with Fire and Ice—but in a good way."

Bertina shook her head sadly. "I can guess at how you found that out. What are you doing, Odelia? I've heard rumors, but I thought you were smarter than that."

"I thought you lived for new knowledge."

"Not when it comes at the expense of my students' safety."

Odelia smiled innocently and waved the comment off. "It was perfectly safe. We already knew we could Heal each other."

"That's not the kind of safety I was talking about."

Odelia knew that perfectly well. It was what she'd been planning for this past year. "All I have for you are discoveries. If you're not interested in them, I know of a teaching post in Losuno that might be perfect for you."

With Bertina there, Odelia could not only repay her allies but get her former tutor as far from this court as possible.

"Losuno, you say?"

"Yes, the school serves all of Atmos." An arion which happened to contain Ormoint.

Bertina smiled. "I do miss home..."

The morning of the feast, Odelia awoke to a surprise. Mom's dress form stood at the foot of her bed, with a beautiful gown hanging from it. The lustrous raspberry wine fabric fell to the floor in waves and gathers. The light beadwork around the neckline was perfect.

A note had been pinned to the neck of the form, reading:

> For my dearest Lia,
> I cannot wait to see all the heads you will turn at tonight's feast.
>
> All my love,
> Ken

She put a hand over her mouth to stifle a squeak of excitement. Carefully unpinning the note, she tucked the first written declaration of his affections into her puzzle box for safekeeping.

Mom stepped into Odelia's bedroom. "I take it you like it?"

"Oh, Mom," Odelia gushed, "it's gorgeous. Is it ready to try on?"

"That's why I set it out now instead of this evening. I figured I could make any adjustments before the feast since I couldn't let you try it on as I made it."

Odelia hurried to put on the proper undergarments, then slipped into the gown with Mom's help. She examined her figure in the mirror and sighed. "I wish I could wear this all day."

Ken paced in his sitting room, going over the sequence of events he had planned for that night in his head. He had to shake these nervous jitters. Hoping that a little knife practice might soothe his mind, he walked over to the dagger chest. But it wasn't there. He searched the room frantically. Hopefully, a servant had simply moved it to scrub the floor. But, no. It was nowhere to be found. He sat down and ran both hands through his hair.

Someone knocked on the door.

"Come in," he announced, not bothering to move from the chair.

Father stalked in. "Where is your secretary? Has Mistress Odelia finally fallen ill, or is she just too lazy to ready you with your schedule in the morning?"

This was not a good mood for him to start with, especially today.

Ken stood up and bowed. "I'm letting her enjoy the holiday."

Father shook his head. "You give her too much leeway. Are you ready to tell me about this mystery woman of yours?"

"We agreed that I would tell you at the feast. I won't have you scaring her off before then."

Father snapped into a wolf, hackles raised. "Must you defy me at every turn?"

"How am I defying you? I'm following exactly what we agreed upon. Why are you changing the terms now?"

Father growled. "You will tell me before you present her tonight, and if you do not, I will announce your engagement to a lady I have already chosen." He headed back for the door. "By the way, are you missing something?"

Ken froze. If Father found his weapons...

"We will discuss that subject later tonight as well," Father said, then popped back into a man and marched out of the room.

"Flaming crusted frog nuggets!" All the Transformations had finally cracked Father's mind. For the first time in his life, Ken truly feared him.

A few hours, a bath, and a change of clothes later, Ken finally regained his composure. He was going to celebrate this feast with Lia, and Father's threats were not going to ruin it.

Ken had chosen not to check Hortensia's progress on the dress he'd commissioned, even going so far as to not read the list of materials he'd agreed to purchase. The gown would be as much of a surprise for him as it was for Lia.

He adjusted the circlet in the mirror. For once, he didn't mind wearing it. Not only that, but he cared that his jacket and pants lay right. He fluffed his shirt collar and checked to make sure his cuffs peeked out just so.

Enough. This was Lia he was going to see.

How many times had she seen him at his worst? He'd seen the way she looked at him when he was a sweaty mess. He laughed. Clearly, the woman had low standards.

Ken made his way down the corridors, with Herman and Val at his heels, trying to picture what Lia might look like, but he couldn't do it. It had been a year since he'd seen her wear anything but her official uniform or plain traveling clothes, and before that, even her long gowns weren't made to be impressive. He had no idea what a regal gown would look like on her.

He knocked on the DiOrtos' door, and Abhenric answered. "Right on time. She just finished getting ready."

Ken joined him in the common room.

"Go on. He's waiting for you," Hortensia said from Lia's room.

Lia walked out gingerly, like a deer entering an open meadow, and she took his breath away. The deep red satin hugged her curves so well, he found himself jealous of the fabric. The neckline was deeper than he had ever seen on her before, and if the straps had been set any wider, they would have fallen off her shoulders. The ribbon he had given her matched the dress perfectly, and she had woven it through her light golden hair, which had been curled and pinned up, leaving teasing little tendrils around her face and neck.

She smiled and blushed. "Please, say something."

Ken held out his hand. "I think we'll be the envy of everyone at the feast."

Lia put and on her hip and pouted. "We?"

"Yes, all the ladies will envy your beauty,"—he took her hand and put it through his arm—"and all the men will envy me for walking in with you on my arm." Ken winked.

Lia pulled in close and laughed softly. "Considering the circumstances, I'm pretty sure it's the other way around, but thank you just the same."

"Well, I had no idea the ladies envied my handsome face," he teased.

She broke into a deep-dimpled smile. If her parents weren't watching, he would've kissed her then. They waved goodbye, and he led her out into the corridor and toward the stairs, where he'd asked the men to wait.

He covered her hand with his. "You really are beautiful."

"Wait. Where are we going? The dining hall is the other way."

"I know. We'll go to the feast soon. I wanted to go somewhere else first."

Kennard had dressed in finery for many things before, but he'd always had an unkempt edge, as though he'd dressed in a hurry without checking a mirror—and often he actually had. But tonight, everything about his appearance was polished. His teal jacket was properly buttoned and showing off his broad shoulders, and his brown curls, though not completely tame, were shiny and defined and not fighting with his circlet.

Odelia let go of Kennard's arm as they climbed the narrow stairs to the balcony overlooking the dining hall. He took her hand and led her as he had when they were children exploring the nooks and spare rooms of the palace. When they reached the alcove at the top, he turned around and wrapped his other arm around her waist—a newer gesture that she hoped to grow just as familiar with.

"I meant what I said. No one down there can compare with you tonight."

Odelia smiled. "The dress helps."

Kennard smiled back and shook his head. "You look beautiful in anything, even that uniform. You know, I almost lost a few toes, dropping that knife, the first time I saw you in it."

"I wasn't even sure you noticed."

His smile became a sly grin. "Oh, I noticed all right. Do you have any idea how much willpower it's taken me to turn my focus away from you?"

Odelia took a step out of the alcove toward the balcony, but Kennard curled his arm tighter and pulled her close again. He brushed his lips close to her ear. "I just want you to myself for right now. Just for a few minutes longer."

Her insides quaked, and she let out a little sigh. He was so dashing and put-together tonight; he could've had the attention of anyone downstairs, and yet this was what he wanted.

He pulled back to meet her gaze and played with a loose strand of hair near her ear. "I've been such a fool and a coward. We could've been here so long ago if I hadn't fought this. I've loved you for years, Lia. I thought it was the love of dear friendship, but it's so much more. I love you the way a man loves a woman, and someday soon, I want to love you the way a husband loves his wife."

Odelia's heart raced. She couldn't speak. She could hardly even breathe.

Kennard knelt before her, head low, as though swearing fealty, and reached into his pocket. "When I am king, I want you to be the queen by my side, to rule as my equal." He tipped his head up and looked into her eyes as he took both her hands in one of his and held up a tiny ring with the other. "I want to honor our ancestors' treaty, Queen Odelia of Vist."

Odelia pulled him to his feet. She still couldn't speak. She had no words to match the beauty of his.

So she did the next best thing.

She kissed him so hard, they both nearly toppled over. He lifted her off the ground and held her tight. She clung to his neck and reveled in his kiss and his touch.

He slowly set her back down and took a breath. "I'm going to assume that's a yes," he whispered as he opened his eyes.

"You didn't actually ask a question," Odelia said, out of breath and smiling dreamily.

He leaned down to kiss her again. "It was implied."

"As was my answer," she said just before their lips met for a brief kiss.

Kennard slipped the ring onto her finger, then lifted her hand up for her to see. A trio of rose gold dogwood blossoms lined the braided gold band, and three little blue sapphires sat inside the flowers.

He beamed. "It was in the treasury, with the Vistan collection. I know it's yours by rights anyway, but it just looked like it was made for your hand."

Odelia gasped. "I think it might have been." She'd seen a sketch of this ring in a Vistan history book, and Tasia's journals mentioned missing it in her rush to collect family heirlooms. "It looks like the Meriverian Unity ring that King Uldrio had made for the couple who unites the kingdoms."

Kennard wrapped his arms around her. "I guess we should prove old Uldrio right then, shouldn't we?"

13

A DECLARATION OF WAR

Ken took in the sight of his betrothed before taking her hand once more and leading her down the stairs. Soon the entire kingdom would know of their love. Once he presented her as his bride at the feast, Father would be unable to object without appearing to lose control of him.

At the foot of the stairs, Lia grinned and wiggled her ring finger at Val.

He nodded. "Does this mean we can leave now?"

She shoved Val's arm. "Be nice."

"Aww, I love you too, Brother," Ken said facetiously, continuing to lead them down the hall to the next stairwell.

Ahead of them, Conora hurried up the hallway. "There you are. I've been looking for you. Mother and Father are wondering— Odelia! You look amazing. Where did you get that dress?"

"I commissioned Hortensia to make it," Ken said.

Conora looked the dress up and down. "I should get her to make one like that for me and— What are you both grinning about? Father is livid with you right now."

Ken held up Lia's hand. "I just asked Lia to marry me."

Conora's eyes lit up. "Congratulations! I see my brother's finally seen what's good for him for once." She took Lia's hand and inspected the ring. "Such a lovely design. I don't think I've seen one like it before."

"It's a combination of Vistan and Elgathan symbols," Lia said. "The dogwood flowers are from the Vistan crest, and the sapphires are Elgathan blue."

Conora hugged her. "We're going to be sisters," she squeaked, then turned to Ken. "What are you still doing here? Go, talk to Father."

"May I have my future bride back first?" he asked.

The color drained from Conora's face. "You're not going to tell him about this right now, are you?"

"Yes... I intend to present her at the feast."

Conora shook her head. "Have you seen the mood he's in today? You need to wait until he cools off."

"I can't. If I don't make my announcement, he's going to make his own, with a lady he's chosen."

Lia furrowed her brow. "You didn't tell me that."

"He only told me this morning, and I didn't think that the middle of a proposal was the right moment to bring it up. Would it have changed your decision if you knew?"

"No, but if you knew he wasn't amenable today... Was there anything else?"

He rubbed the back of his neck. "My equipment trunk is missing, and I think he might have it."

Lia gripped his arm tightly with both hands, eyes wide with fear. "Ken, if I need to run—I have an escape route and allies in place, but it won't matter if I can't get out of the palace."

Val stepped in, speaking low. "If we move now, I can have us out of Meria unseen and on the road within an hour."

Ken grumbled. This wasn't how things were supposed to go. He wanted to make his stand, not run. But protecting Lia was more important than proving himself. "Fine. We'll need to change our clothes first. Conora, I hate to get you involved, but can you keep Father away from my rooms for a while?"

Conora crossed her arms. "That's not a good idea. The anger at your engagement will be nothing compared to what will happen if you elope. She'd be safer running without you for now."

Allies or not, how could Ken abandon Lia to reach her first destination alone? Traveling north meant bringing her closer to the raids they'd canceled the tour for. "No. We need to go together. If she leaves first, Father will keep me from following her later."

"Please, Conora," Lia said, "I need Kennard. I know it doesn't make any sense, and I wish I had time to explain, but something worse than the king's anger could happen if I do this alone."

"I very much doubt that," Conora said. "Father's been more unstable than usual lately. I wouldn't put anything past him right now."

Ken put his arm around Lia. "I'll just have to go in what I'm wearing then. Goodbye, Conora." He hurried them down the hall in the direction of the DiOrto apartment. They needed to pass by the stairs that would lead to the dining hall, but that was unavoidable.

They made it past and were halfway there when they heard an eerie, blood-chilling shriek. A cougar scream.

Ken turned around, praying that the sound came from somewhere else.

Father stalked them from the top of the stairs, going from cougar to bear as he neared. "Where are you going, Kennard?"

Ken laughed nervously and pulled his arm tighter around Lia's shoulder. "We were on our way to the feast, but it's so cold, I insisted we go back and get a shawl for Mistress Odelia."

Lia trembled, and Ken made a show of rubbing her bare arm.

Father turned into a man. "She should have gone back by herself, and she should be in her uniform. Now, tell me who you gave a ribbon to."

Ken smiled innocently. "If we head down now, you can find out with everyone else."

Father glared. "You think you're being clever, don't you? You don't control me, Son. You answer to me. I know what you're trying to do. I'm not letting you go out there unless I am satisfied with the announcement you're making. And the only reason you would have for stalling is that you know I won't be."

He turned his gaze to Lia. She swallowed hard and hid her hands behind her back.

Father smiled wolfishly. "What a particular color choice." He reached over and flicked the ribbon in her hair.

Lia flinched, and Ken involuntarily clasped her closer.

"I know it's you," Father taunted quietly. He clicked his tongue. "You are not suitable to be queen."

"You're wrong," Ken said.

Lia shifted uncomfortably, her breath coming faster. He rubbed her shoulder in what he hoped was a reassuring gesture.

"I am not an idiot," Father said. "You think I don't know you favor her? You think I don't recognize a ribbon of intent?"

Ken shook his head. "You're wrong to think she's unsuitable. She's intelligent and educated and well-versed in courtly manners. I couldn't ask for a finer woman to stand by my side."

Father sighed. "I understand a man's need for certain tastes, and I've indulged you in this one for long enough. While you looked for better, I didn't mind what you partook of on the side. I thought if you had your fill of it, you might settle down."

Ken didn't bother to hide the disgust rising in him. A sliver of guilt reminded him of the moment he'd implied the same to Lia in Eaund. He'd been bluffing to prove a point, but Father was as serious as could be.

"But it's all about defiance with you," Father continued, "and this little ploy is pure defiance. A commoner and a Vistan. How could you resist? The same way you couldn't resist this…"

From inside his jacket, he retrieved a dagger, testing its balance on the ends of his fingers. "When you were so secretive about your little sweetheart, I grew curious about what else you might be hiding. I thought the chest in your room might hold some love letters or other clues. Imagine my surprise to find it full of weapons."

Ken held his chin up. "Learning to defend myself has only made me safer."

Father pointed the dagger at Ken's face. "Well, since you insisted on learning this skill, you're going to put it to use. You want to fight my protection and guidance? You're going to find out what it's like without them."

"Are you banishing me?" Considering that Ken was planning to run away anyway, it would be a relatively easy punishment.

"Worse."

Dread gnawed at Ken. "What are you saying?"

"There was word of a third raid on our northern border while you were on your way back from Doivrie. I sent Ambassador Felix to Tehazy to inquire about the matter." Father's face grew grim. "A chest was delivered to me this morning—with his head inside."

"You're declaring war," Lia said bluntly.

Father nodded but kept his eyes on Ken. "You're going to Fort Solace as soon as preparations can be made. The infirmary will need your Healing. We'll see how brave you are when you're covered in blood and don't have your pet to fawn over you. You won't need a secretary where you're going."

Lia took a shaky breath and exhaled sharply. "Send me too."

Panic slammed Ken in the heart. "No. What are you doing?"

She blinked hard. "I volunteer my Gift as Healer. I'm the reason Ken's still healthy. I can protect him and Heal your soldiers."

"Father, no! You can't. She's defenseless." Ken would tell whatever lie he needed to keep her from going too.

Father put his hand up. "I'm not going to turn away a Healer. I thought it fitting that you would have to mend the Vistans, since you like them so much, but I think leaving her with her own kind will be even better. She can go to Fort Solace, and you're going to Fort Vigil with me."

Father started to walk away, then turned back again. "And lest you think you can get around your separation, there will be no travel between forts for you. If either of you breaks that, she will be arrested for desertion. If you think to sneak in a wedding before you leave, she will be arrested for treason. Besides, unlike you, I keep my word, which means I'm going downstairs to make an announcement about your more appropriate engagement."

Ken clenched his fists. "No, you won't."

"It wasn't a question, Kennard."

"If you make that announcement, you'll be made to look like a fool because I won't go through with it." He stood tall and stared down Father. "Make all the threats you like. You've already wished death upon my love. Let Conora be my heir because you won't get one from me that way."

Father sneered. "It won't matter anyway. Alone and unguarded with all those Vistan men, your girl won't survive the fort—not untouched, at least. And when she's gone, you're going to take whomever I give you." Apparently satisfied with the power he now held over them, he became a wolf and stalked away.

Odelia held her composure until Kennard pulled her into her family's now empty common room. The moment the door closed, the floodgates opened. She struggled to breathe as she choked on her own tears. He silently wrapped his arms around her, and she buried her face in his chest. A drop fell on the top of her head. He kissed her forehead softly, and the warmth of his power soothed her.

"We should run to our allies," he whispered.

She shook her head. "It's too late now."

"Don't worry about his threats. Claiming your throne will earn you treason with him anyway. You'll have an army to protect you."

Odelia looked up at him and wiped her eyes. "If we run now, with war freshly declared, we'll be branded as cowards. That's not a trait that will inspire a kingdom to follow us."

"But we're not running from the war. We're picking up the fight in Vist."

"We can't start a civil war in the middle of a defensive one. It makes Elgatha more vulnerable for us, but it also weakens Vist. Neither one alone is strong enough to hold back Tehazy. Meriveria needs to be whole."

Kennard wiped her cheek with his thumb. "You would just give up?" The pain in his eyes broke her heart.

"Never. We just have to be patient." She was trying to reassure herself as much as him. "If the war and his Transformation really are making Gonfrid unstable, then it's only a matter of time before he leaves us an opportunity to take his power from him or gets himself killed."

"Without each other to mitigate the cost of our Gift—" Kennard choked up.

Odelia looked at her ring. "Destiny is determined to put me on the throne, and if this ring means anything, it wants us together as well. I waited a long time for your love. I can wait even longer for destiny if I must."

"So, we do nothing?"

"Not nothing. While we wait for your father to make a mistake, you need to get him to let his guard down. Flatter him. Show deference and obedience. If you try too hard, you'll make him suspicious, but give him just enough to make him believe he's starting to break you."

"What about you?" Kennard swallowed and blinked. "Alone in Fort Solace..."

She put her hand to his cheek and met his gaze. "I am the Queen of Vist. Fort Solace is in my domain and, more specifically, Doivrie. I'll talk to Grandilord Patricius. He's bound to have trusted men in that fort. You and I cannot be together for a while, but we will not be alone."

14

VIGIL AND SOLACE

"How much farther to Fort Vigil?" Ken whispered.

They had traveled by dogcart from Meria to Vanderin, amassing troops behind them along the way. It was now their third day of travel, having left Vanderin on foot, and despite trudging through mud for hours that day, there was no fort in sight. The only structures they'd seen were the broken husks of raided homes.

Ken tried again. "I can see the Norlach River up ahead. Are you sure we haven't veered off course?"

Father, who liked to travel in moose form, changed into a man and looked up into the trees. "Not at all. In fact, we're here."

Ken followed his gaze upward. To his surprise, a suspension bridge stretched above his head, barely visible between branches. Contrary to its name, the security of Fort Vigil came not from fortification, but from concealment. The fort was in the trees, high enough above the lowest branches to remain unnoticed from the ground but still low enough to stay out of view from above as well. "How do we get up there?"

Father walked over to a five-yard-wide spruce. It was hard to see at first through the bark camouflaging them, but stairs spiraled around the trunk forty yards up to the middle of the tree to meet the bridge. A rope, nailed to the tree in intervals, was the only handhold.

"Go ahead, Son."

Ken climbed carefully around the tree. With every step he took and every person who climbed behind him, the tree swayed ever so slightly—until he reached a platform at the top. There, the movement was more pronounced, though at least it had a railing.

Two soldiers bowed and parted to allow him passage to the suspension bridge. On the other side, an enclosed structure wrapped around and between three trees that had grown close together. From there, more bridges linked between the other trees and enclosed structures. He opened the first one and found hammocks and packs strung everywhere in tidy rows. Several of the hammocks held sleeping soldiers. Ken closed the door quietly.

"Take the bridge to the left," Father said.

Ken followed the narrower bridge to a smaller enclosure than the first. Inside, a table and several stools filled much of the room. On the left, a ladder led upward to a loft, where three hammocks hung.

Father motioned for him to move deeper inside. "You and your guards will stay here. Leave your packs, and report to the infirmary. It's just over the next bridge." He turned and walked back the way they'd come.

Ken climbed up to the loft and hung his pack on a hook near the middle hammock. A soft light filtered in through a window by the ladder, illuminating the cramped space. He chuckled. "Well, this is...cozy."

Val and Herman hung their packs without a word. Herman had always fallen into stoicism easily, but Val's silence was spiteful. He blamed Ken for their current situation, for choosing a grand gesture instead of running in the days leading up to the feast—and he was right.

"Right, anyway..." Ken continued as if the conversation were not a one-person affair, "let's check the infirmary, shall we?" He descended the ladder and headed across another bridge. A gust of wind rocked it, and Ken grabbed the rail to right himself. The unstable footing would take some getting used to.

The infirmary enclosure was almost as large as the first barracks, though it held far fewer beds. The hammocks were more structured: the feet were tied to posts around the room instead of both ends against the wall, allowing for a range of movement around both sides of any given bed. At the back of the room, a tiny brazier was being used to boil a pot of water. It was the only fire he'd seen in the fort. None of the barracks had a place for it. Since smoke was a good way to find someone in the forest, it made sense that there'd be as little as possible here. Still, Ken was thankful that he'd packed warm clothes and an extra blanket. A stretcher hung from a pulley over a trapdoor in the middle of the floor. Of course. That explained how the injured could get up there. Those stairs at the entrance were hard enough for a healthy man to climb. How many other ladders and pulleys were scattered around the fort?

A young Vistan in one of the hammocks groaned. His leg had been wrapped in gauze from the knee down, and a red streak stained his wrappings down the side of his calf.

Ken approached him. "May I?"

He didn't respond.

Ken put two fingers to the man's wrist. His Vitality undulated in strange patterns on top of its slight weakness. Someone had given the man a strong dosage of herbs to dull the pain. Ken quickly brushed his lips against the young man's knuckle. After years of practice, that was all he needed—and this was not a place to use more than he needed.

The man bolted upright. "What did you do?"

Ken shrugged. "I just Healed you. You can return to the barracks."

The man's eyes went wide. "You have Healing? Are you—?

"Crown Prince Kennard, I presume?" An extremely tall Elgathan man with thick glasses walked in. Near-Sight?

"Yes. I'm assuming you must be the surgeon?"

He bowed. "Call me Esmond, Your Highness."

"Well, Esmond, would you mind if I made one very small request for the infirmary?" Ken indicated how small with his thumb and forefinger, scrunching his face.

"Certainly, Your Highness. What is your request?"

Ken cringed. "Okay, make that two requests. One: No 'Your Highnesses' in the infirmary. It wears on my nerves after the second repeat, and too much formality will be a liability when there are injured men in need of our attention. Two: I understand the importance of relieving their pain. However, it makes Healing more difficult for me. The power I expend Healing one man from the herbs you give him could be better saved for the next man. So, please, check with me first before administering any more now that I'm here. You can save them for the ones I cannot Heal or those who would do just fine without my help."

Esmond nodded. "That sounds sensible to me. I look forward to seeing what you can do for these men."

Odelia sat in bed, hugging her knees. Grandilord Patricius had been kind enough to board her in the same room as before while she waited to join the recruits on their way to Fort Solace. The last time she'd visited, she'd reveled in the privacy, but now she just felt alone. It was by design, of course. Even Dad had been sent to Fort Vigil when he volunteered. The Elgathan King hadn't been satisfied with separating her from Kennard; he didn't want her near anyone she loved.

Mom had seen her off from Meria, enduring the noisome docks as Odelia boarded a riverboat to Iverish. From there, she'd paid for a sled ride into Doivrie rather than going with the men who were set to march through Iverish from Yophiex. She needed time to talk to Patricius, and, truth be told, it was a convenient excuse to procrastinate joining the ranks.

It was one thing to volunteer at Kennard's side. It was another to walk alone into a company of strange men who had no reason to believe she wasn't physically defenseless.

Patricius wanted her to declare herself the rightful queen now—to turn the troops already gathering on Elgatha. But Odelia wouldn't leave the Tehazian border unguarded, nor would she march against the Elgathan King while he was surrounded by her fiancé, her brother, and her father. They considered a compromise: Odelia would seize command of the Vistan army and continue the fight at the border, then bide her time for the opportunity to turn the fight westward. But she didn't trust such a plan to stay secret for long—especially when communications with the Elgathans would be necessary. With everyone she loved either in Meria or Fort Vigil, there was too much leverage against her to succeed without the element of surprise.

They'd talked in circles for two days, and Odelia was running out of time to come up with a better plan than to stay the course.

A drum banged outside, signaling the approaching army. Patricius would host the men overnight before they began the two-day march to the fort.

Odelia sighed. Time had run out.

She threw a poncho on over the shirt and fitted coral vest she wore for traveling. Patricius kept his manor plenty warm, but the thinner jacket she normally wore indoors had been tailored like her court uniform, and male attentions were the last thing she wanted right now. The shapeless layer was unlikely to protect her, but it made her feel better.

Downstairs, Odelia joined Patricius to wait for the sergeant.

"It's not too late," Patricius said. "I can present you to these men as you really are."

"No, thank you, Your Grace."

A servant shouted from above, and another opened the entrance. Odelia smiled as a familiar face came into view, bowing to Patricius. "Sergeant Rhonwin, requesting quarter for my division and two others."

Patricius nodded. "Welcome to you and your men."

Rhonwin took two steps back and signaled outside, then followed Odelia and Patricius to the grandilord's private office.

"It's so good to see you again," Odelia said. "We missed you when we stopped at your father-in-law's manor a few weeks ago."

Rhonwin smiled apologetically. "We were at my father's home, and were supposed to meet you there, but Moira wasn't feeling well."

Odelia gasped. "Oh, no. Is she better now?" If he'd have told them, they could have stopped to help.

Rhonwin laughed. "Well, she's certainly bigger now. And I appreciate the thought, but I doubt there's anything you could have done for her."

Bigger? Was she expecting?

Rhonwin grinned proudly.

"Congratulations! Why did you not say in your letters?"

"I didn't think you'd find it relevant."

Odelia put a hand on her hip. "Of course it's relevant. You're one of the only friends I have out here— Wait. Why would you enlist with a baby on the way?"

"Moira Saw that I needed to. I didn't know why, but now I'm guessing it was to bring me here. What is your plan?"

Patricius pursed his lips, and Odelia was about to answer when Rhonwin said, "Not on my watch, Your Grace."

Odelia cleared her throat.

Rhonwin put a hand up. "Sorry, Your Majesty. He was thinking that you're going to get yourself killed at Fort Solace. But I'm sergeant of the intelligence division there, and I'll do whatever I can to keep you safe."

Patricius put a hand on his chin. "Are you able to add any men directly to your division?"

"Yes, within reason. They need to have Gifts I can use. Listeners are too rare to have a second of when other forts need one. I have Hearers and Speakers, but I can take more if that's all you have. If you have any Seers or Invisibles, you will be my favorite person in the world."

Odelia sighed. "My dad could've been helpful if he hadn't been called to Fort Vigil."

Patricius smiled. "Perfect. I have a loyal man with Hearing. He has no family to leave behind, so we should be able to enlist him right away. I know it will be a bit of a waste for your other purposes, but I want him to guard her."

"He'll have to be very discreet," Odelia said. "We can't let people notice his men lurking around the infirmary all the time."

Rhonwin smiled. "That's easy. You're a valuable asset. Regardless of your true title, your Gift makes you too rare and useful. A few untoward thoughts from our men are all I need to request guards on you."

Odelia sank into a chair. "You have no idea how relieved I am to hear that."

Night had already fallen when they reached Fort Solace. Like Patricius' manor, the fort had been built into the mountain, but the front facings were stone instead of logs. From the high altitude, Odelia could see over the foothills and across the river into Tehazy, where a tall stone tower watched them.

A sentry approached them silently, motioning for them to stop as the cave door of the fort opened. The sentry gestured for them to approach the entrance in threes.

Inside, a passageway turned sharply right before opening into a large cavern. Wooden partitions had been erected, creating smaller rooms, some of them with flat roofs and ladders. A smaller passageway to the left of the cavern had a white sign over top with INFIRMARY painted in red letters. Odelia headed straight inside. It was smaller than the main cavern, but still a decent size. Two dozen beds lined the room in three rows. Two bunk beds flanked the entrance, with trunks and cabinets on either side. One small partition, barely large enough to cover a man to his shoulder stood against the wall—the only privacy she would get here.

A man stirred from one of the bunk beds. "Is someone hurt? What— Oh, a woman. You must be the Healer. Throw your belongings on a bunk, and get to Healing. You can rest when you're done. I'm going back to sleep." He rolled over and tucked his blanket under his chin.

A lovely introduction. Was that the surgeon assigned here? Odelia didn't even get his name. Well, she could always ask him in the morning—assuming she'd be able to tell morning in here.

Only five cots were filled, and none of them looked serious. Within fifteen minutes, she Healed them all, then explained to them as a group that they'd been Healed and sent them on their way.

Odelia had pulled back the blankets from her bunk, prepared for sleep, when Rhonwin dashed into the infirmary. "I had no idea your Gift would be such a problem," he said.

"What do mean?"

"I Listened to those men you just Healed. I'll need to talk to the fort captain first thing in the morning, but for now, I'm guarding you myself."

"Don't you have your own barracks to sleep in?"

Rhonwin shook his head. "Trust me. Word about how effective your Healing is and the way it feels are going to spread quickly. Don't be surprised if they start injuring themselves on purpose—because they're certainly thinking about it."

Raucous voices pulled Odelia into consciousness. When she opened her eyes, a crowd of men loomed over her bunk. She scrambled back against the wall. "Flaming frog nuggets!"

Some of them jeered and guffawed, and a few shoved each other. Then, a loud whistle pierced the air, and they all fell quiet. The crowd parted as Rhonwin pushed his way through, followed by a stocky man with dirty blond hair.

"I don't care if your arms are falling off," the stocky man said. "If you don't form an orderly line, nobody is getting Healed." He grabbed the whistle hanging from his neck and blew.

The men hustled into a line down the length of the infirmary, curving slightly to the left as they reached the back wall. Rhonwin motioned for Odelia to get up and join him next to the man, who faced the line.

"Since all of your legs appear to be working," he continued, "you can run forty laps around the main cavern. Return here when you are finished. Go!"

The men ran single file out the door, and the stocky officer turned to Odelia and shook his head. "The only woman in my fort... You must be the infamous Odelia DiOrto. One night here, and you're already causing a commotion. Your Healing had better be miraculously good to be worth the trouble."

Odelia curtsied and guessed at his rank from his possessive claim on the fort. "I'm sorry, Captain. My Gift is powerful, but I'm afraid its method of application is limited."

The captain crossed his arms. "Rhonwin, I know it's beyond the scope of intelligence, but I need you to requisition a small squad of guards for her. I'd pick the watch to do it, but I trust, with your Gift, it shouldn't take you long. Miss, you are going to stay in this infirmary. You aren't leaving, even for meals. Word about what you do here is already getting enough attention without you prancing around and turning their heads out there too."

The infirmary began to feel much smaller. The lack of daylight hadn't fully sunk in yet, let alone confinement to a single room. Odelia wrapped her arms around her middle, self-conscious of her fitted travel clothes. She'd have to check the cabinets later for a uniform and an apron.

The captain harrumphed. "And what are we going to do with all these men? I can't have half the fort rotating through here, and I can't ban them from medical attention."

Odelia held up a finger. "I can help with that. My Gift will tell me if they're faking it."

He laughed. "I don't think they'll care if you know as long as they get what they came for."

She shook her head. "I don't think you understand. I don't have to kiss them. All I have to do is feel their pulse to check. In the time it takes to write down their names, I could have all of them reported to you."

The captain nodded. "Do that. If you suspect a self-inflicted injury, report it to Rhonwin. You'll need to be diligent. You're guarded for now, but only minimally so, and if we lose men, I won't have any to spare."

"Yes, Captain," Odelia said.

There was a groaning yawn behind her, and she turned to see the surgeon she had met last night sitting up in his bunk.

"Nice of you to join us, Milo," Rhonwin said.

Milo stretched. "I don't see any patients."

"They're out running laps," the captain said. "You'll both have your hands full when they get back. Goodbye, Miss, I trust you'll see to it that I don't have reason to come back here again."

Ken took his place in line for food. Though—as Herman frequently pointed out—Ken could have used his station to his advantage and walked straight to the front, he preferred it this way. Did he really need to get his food five minutes before everyone else? Besides, it gave him a chance to mingle with the soldiers for a short while. At first, they'd fallen silent every time Ken approached, but after several months, they'd grown used to his presence, and now, they didn't pay him any mind.

Two Elgathans standing just in front of Ken were laughing. One slapped the other on the back. "What about you?"

"Nah. It's too much work to coax them. I'll take a girl who doesn't care and have her a few times by then."

The first man shook his head. "Oh no. You don't know what you're missing. It's so much easier. You can just get straight to the good part because they don't know the difference, and it's not like they're enjoying it either way."

"You still have to get them in bed." The second man handed two cards through the window.

The first man scoffed. "Once they see what's in my pants, they're too impressed to object."

"Really?" The second took a basket from the window.

"Oh yeah. My favorite, she laid right back for me, and I took her so hard and fast that she was screaming like mad. I've never finished so quick."

Both of the men started laughing again.

Herman put a hand on Ken's shoulder. "A bit distracted, Kennard?"

"What?"

"I said Valerzan has our food."

Ken looked over at Val, who held up a basket as the other men wandered off. "Sorry, I was listening to those men."

Herman shook his head and scowled. "Those poor women."

"I know," Val said. "The women in Meria won't look twice at me, but they'll sleep with those two ugly fools."

Herman led the way back to their quarters. "Don't pay them any mind."

Ken shrugged. "I was curious."

Herman sighed. "Of course, you were, but they are not the men to listen to. No woman deserves to be taken so carelessly. For all their exploits, I guarantee that neither of them has ever truly made love."

"I take it you have better advice," Ken said.

"Yes."

Val groaned. "No, no, no. You are not going to tell him how to make love to my sister."

"I'm going to marry her first," Ken pointed out.

Val shook his head with a grimace. "Nope. That doesn't make it any better to hear." He removed some food from the basket, then shoved it into Ken's arms. "I'll eat somewhere else. Consider this the end of my shift." With that, he stormed off toward the barracks.

Ken turned back to Herman. "So, about that advice?"

"For starters, assume the opposite of everything they just said." Herman opened the door to their quarters. "It matters how you treat her the first time, and women are not stupid, especially Odelia. Even without experience, she'll know." He took the basket from Ken and set the table in a few seconds.

Ken grabbed a chunk of cornbread. "What makes you such an expert? I've never even seen you flirt before."

Herman smiled wistfully. "Eda and I were about your age when we married. She had the most beautiful smile."

Had. Past tense. "What happened to her?" Ken asked softly.

Herman picked up an apple and turned it over in his hands. "We were married almost two years when she died in childbirth."

The blood drained from Ken's face, and the room went cold. "I'm so sorry. That's awful. But you're a father? I had no idea."

"Was. For an hour."

Ken covered his mouth. "I didn't mean to— I shouldn't have pried into something so personal."

"It was a long time ago." Herman's voice was quiet but steady. "I've made peace with it."

Ken set down his food and pushed it away, his appetite gone. "Do you think— You know what could happen to Lia if I— You lived through it. Do you think I'm making a mistake, marrying her?"

"What do you think?"

"The thought of life without her, of losing her in any way is too painful to bear."

"Then, no."

"But she might end up like—"

"She might not, and without you, her Gift will eventually kill her anyway. Look, I miss Eda more than you could possibly know, but I don't regret loving her. Marriage is a partnership, one that Eda and I entered into *together*. She chose to marry me. She chose to love me. To take all the blame for myself or say that it was a mistake is to dishonor her part in our marriage." Herman pushed Ken's food back in front of him. "I've seen the way Odelia looks at you, and it's the same look Eda gave me. If you think I'm telling you to walk away, then you're missing the point. I'm telling you all this because the idea of you treating her like those idiots..." He shook his head. "When you love a woman like that, you cherish her."

"Herman, I do cherish her. That's why I wanted to know what to do."

He took a calming breath. "Be gentle and attentive. If you force yourself inside before she's ready, you'll hurt her."

Ken smiled. "If her kisses are any indication, she's very eager."

"That's not—" Herman exhaled. "Women need foreplay."

Ken nodded. "Of course."

"You have no idea what that actually entails, do you?"

Ken grimaced. "I've heard of it. Does that count?"

Herman chuckled. "You have two hands and, more importantly in your case, a mouth, and what you do with them is important..."

Odelia handed Milo another stack of bandages and plopped down onto her bunk with a sigh. "That should be plenty for a while, right?"

Milo shrugged. "Well, that's all we can fit in this cabinet anyway." He shuffled over to his bunk and lay down.

She'd come to accept that he didn't like to talk to anyone, but as one of the only people she'd seen in months who was neither writhing in pain nor leering at her, the dour surgeon had grown on her. For the past month, the infirmary had been even more isolating as the captain pulled her guards away to make up for lost men. When messengers became more scarce, non-official correspondence was lost as well. She hoped Mom wasn't too worried that she couldn't write home.

It would soon get even quieter. Rhonwin had said that the Flight, Speed, and Animal Speech divisions were transferring to Fort Vigil tonight. Speed alone would account for a large number of men. It didn't seem possible that they could spare any more, but the orders had come straight from the Elgathan King.

She prayed the fort could hold with the men they had. Without correspondence, Odelia would have a difficult time coordinating an escape to join her Vistan grandilords. And even if she could make it out, the loss of Solace would quickly lead to the fall of Doivrie.

Was it malice or neglect? Gonfrid wasn't forgetful. He knew she was here, and he still wanted her dead. Would he really risk a whole grandrion to do it? That seemed unlikely, given his desire for power. No, he probably expected the strong stone fort to hold on its own, the lost Vistan occupants of little consequence—mostly. He'd be apathetic to all the deaths but one.

Odelia shook her head. Dark thoughts came so easily now that she lived in a cave. She reached into the neckline of her gray tunic, pulling out her engagement ring, which was tied around her neck with the ribbon of intent. The memory of Kennard's ridiculous grin and his warm brown eyes were the brightest thing she had to hold onto in her months without daylight.

Shouts echoed down the corridor. It seemed that someone had already run into trouble with the transfer.

A muscular, red-headed man carried in another with bright orange hair. The orange one's leg twisted at a sickening angle, his shin bone sticking out.

The Strongman set him down on a cot. "He stepped in a hole just outside the entrance." He turned the injured man and scolded, "That's why you don't use Speed until you're further away."

The Speeder screamed. "What do you know, you brute? You move like a slug."

Odelia checked his wrist, his Vitality was weakened but stable, just what she'd expect for a broken leg. "I can Heal you, but I need to set your leg first so my Gift can work better." Healing would knit the bone and tissue back together, but it didn't pay any heed to proper form; it simply worked around crooked bones or foreign objects in wounds. She nodded to the Strongman. "Can you hold him down, please?"

The Strongman shook his head. "Sorry, I'm needed on duty." He took off before she could ask again.

"I've never been in here before," the Speeder said.

Odelia smiled and nodded. "Good for you. Milo, can you help me with this?"

Milo moved to the man's foot while she took hold of the knee. She counted to three; then they jammed the poor man's bone back into position as he howled and arched his back. Milo inspected the placement while Odelia took the man's hand, keeping two fingers on his Vitality.

"Sorry," she said. "I know that hurts, but you'll be Healed soon."

The Speeder sighed with relief, and his Vitality took on a slight waver. Odelia looked over at Milo, who was spreading an ointment over the break. He handed the Speeder a tincture.

She scowled. "I just said I was going to Heal him."

Milo waved her off. "I'm tired, he's squirmy, and you're going to bed after this anyway."

"You're pretty," the Speeder said.

Odelia rolled her eyes. "How much did you give him?"

Milo raised one eyebrow. "Not enough to make him loopy."

Sure enough, the waver in the Speeder's Vitality was less than what a single cup of ale would produce.

"Are you finished yet?" she asked. She didn't want this man in here any longer than was necessary.

"All set. Heal away." Milo turned back toward their bunks.

Odelia leaned down to kiss the Speeder's hand, but he yanked it, pulling her across him as he sat up. With his other hand, he grabbed her hair and kissed her roughly. It was like being kissed by a sponge, sloppy and siphoning.

She tried to pull away, but he tightened his grip. Pinching his ear, she yanked hard until he released her; then she turned and elbowed him in the groin and hopped away from the cot. "You can Heal that yourself."

The Speeder doubled over in new pain, but his leg was completely mended.

Odelia wiped her mouth on her sleeve and pointed to the door. "Get out of my infirmary. I don't deal with self-inflicted injuries. Captain's orders."

Ken returned to his quarters after a relatively quiet day at the infirmary. After three months, he'd become adept at gauging how far he could push himself and still be useful the next day. At first, he'd Healed as many men as he could before he passed out, and the method quickly proved to be inefficient. It pained him to leave men behind each day, but Esmond had them stable and dulled their pain. By making them wait, he could ultimately help more of them.

Val had left ahead of him, and sat at the table, rifling through a small pile of letters. He slid two across the table. "These are yours."

Ken knew without looking who they would be from. Conora wrote every week, keeping him apprised of both herself and the court. The second was from Hortensia, sending him the love that Lia could not. She passed along news about her daughter, reminding him not to lose hope.

He climbed into the loft. Reaching into his pack, he pulled out the most cherished object inside: a Vistan puzzle box. He pressed the mountain, slid the tree, then touched the sunlight. With a satisfying click, the drawer opened. The former contents had been left with Hortensia. Inside, he kept all the letters he'd received. But none of them were from the one person he wanted most to hear from.

Ken ran his thumb over the scenic inlay. At least he had this. She'd been so insistent that he take it. On the day they'd parted, he'd stolen a moment alone with her, just to say goodbye. Ken had brushed his fingers against Lia's cheek, memorizing the soft texture of her creamy skin. As he ran his hands through her hair, he kissed her softly, trying to immerse himself in the taste and feel of her lips on his. They only had a minute, but he tried to convince his heart that that minute was really an hour.

She put her hand on his chest, eyes shining. "I have your ribbon and your ring, but I want you to have something of mine."

He shook his head as he held the box out to him. "I can't take this. Abhenric made it for you."

"That's why I want you to promise you'll bring it back to me."

Ken took the box and leaned down for one last fleeting kiss. "I love you, Lia," he'd said before he walked away. He hadn't wanted to make a promise he might not be able to keep.

With the most recent letter from Hortensia, he began to wonder if his promise was the one he needed to worry about. She hadn't heard from Lia lately. Whether she was too busy to write or it was too dangerous to send a letter, neither boded well.

Val climbed to the top of the ladder. "Did you get a letter from Mom too?"

Ken ran a hand over his face and nodded.

"Have we received any word about Fort Solace?" Val asked. "She's safe within the fort, right? We would have heard if the fort had fallen, wouldn't we?"

Herman rolled over in his hammock. It was about time for his shift to start. "Why don't we find out? You'll both lose your minds if you don't."

Ken opened Conora's letter. She was unlikely to know more than they did, but he didn't want to miss it if she did.

More bad news. Mother was conducting a bridal search in his absence, and Conora was unable to dissuade her. Telling Mother that he was already engaged would do more harm than good. Knowing how she felt about Lia, the knowledge would only make her more determined to interfere.

Ken sighed. Was it too much to ask that everyone leave the subject of his marrying alone? Apparently, yes. "I think it's time to speak to my father. Are the two of you ready?"

Herman rubbed his eyes and yawned. "Can we eat first? I'm starving."

Of course! He could bring Father his dinner. Surely, a good meal would put him in an easier mood. "You're a genius, Herman."

Ken left their quarters, followed closely by Val and Herman. They moved deeper into the middle of the fort, to an enclosure surrounded on all sides with bridges, like the spokes of a wheel. A tan man with blond hair stood at one of the windows. Ken handed him a wooden card, painted with a small Elgathan crest and three dots in white, yellow, and red. "Rations for all three, and I'd like to bring the king's if no one else has done so yet."

The man looked over the card, then bowed. "Yes, Your Highness." He took a basket and filled it with three pieces of smoked meat of various sizes, three different sized pieces of cornbread, and seven apples. Val took the basket while the man retrieved a wooden tray with a lid and handed it to Ken. They thanked the man, then headed back through the network of bridges to the king's quarters. Ken knocked on the door, and a guard answered.

"I come bearing food!" Ken announced.

"Oh, good," Father called from inside. "I'm famished. Come in, Son. I haven't seen you in days. I trust that means you've been working hard."

Ken entered and bowed, then set the tray on the table in front of Father. "I do my best. Although, I wish I could do more." He waved Val forward with the basket. "Do you mind if my men and I join you?"

Father nodded. "Go ahead."

Ken took an apple and the smallest portions of meat and cornbread, leaving the rest for Val and Herman. Even at full use of his Gift, he didn't need as much as they did.

"Have you heard news from the other forts?" Ken hoped that if he kept the question more general, Father might not pounce upon his intention as harshly.

Father shrugged and lifted the lid from his tray. "Vigil and Solace are taking the brunt of it so far. The lull for the last two days has been nice, though."

The soldiers here had taken a beating in nearby battles. Ken had a few shirts that would forever be covered in stains that could attest to that, and their numbers were dwindling, but Fort Vigil itself stayed safe. He didn't know how long that would last.

"I hope Solace is doing better than we are," Ken said.

"The fort is holding." Father picked up his knife and fork and began cutting his salmon steak.

"What about the soldiers?"

Father smirked. "Do you really care about the soldiers, or are you asking about someone else?"

Ken set down his food. "Both. We've already lost too many here. I've seen it myself. But yes, I also want to know that Lia is well. I know you're punishing me, but Val and the rest of her family don't deserve to be in the dark."

Father clicked his tongue. "Your little sweetheart is alive, but I'm not sure you'd want to know the rest."

Val started. "Is she hurt? ...Your Majesty."

Father took a bite and chewed before answering, "No, not as far as I know."

He was goading him, but Ken wouldn't rise to it this time. Whatever rumors he was trying to put into his head were not going to work.

"Have you heard anything from Mother?" Ken asked.

"Of course."

"Then has she told you about her most recent project?"

Father shook his head. "You'll have to let that one go."

Ken took a deep, calming breath. "I meant what I said before. You cannot force me to marry. Mother is wasting her time."

Father leaned back in his chair and dabbed at his mouth. "I wouldn't be so sure of that. I doubt you'd be so loyal to your lover if you knew what she was up to."

"You have nothing but rumors, Father. She is doing the same thing I'm doing, and if Solace is as bad as here, she's as exhausted as I am, as well."

Father gave a malicious grin. "What? You don't want to hear about all the soldiers who line up for her kisses? Half the fort passes in and out of her quarters like ships in the harbor. And she's especially close with one of the sergeants there."

Ken crossed his arms. It was the dirty poem all over again. But Father was trying too hard. There wasn't a chance in the world that Lia would sleep with that many men. It wasn't even a matter of trust or fidelity. The risk was just too stupid for her to consider. Ken decided to call his bluff. "And this sergeant, does he have a name?"

"Rhonwin, I believe. His father is the Lord of Atmos."

Ken was taken aback for a second. Father actually had a name? But it was familiar. Where had Ken heard that name? Wasn't he... Ken hid the smile that threatened to creep up. It made perfect sense that Lia would be close to that sergeant. She wasn't having an affair; she was plotting treason—a preferable scenario to Ken, though he doubted Father would agree.

Father must have been getting desperate. He had forbidden them from wedding, separated them, sent them to the worst forts in the kingdom, and cut off their communication. And yet he still feared Lia.

Ken shook his head. "I still stand by my decision. Mother would be better served focusing on Conora."

Father ran a hand over his face. "You're a fool, but you may be right. If this fort falls, it won't matter who she has picked for you. That's why we're attacking the bridge in two days."

Ken nearly choked on his bread. The new bridge between Tehazy and Meriveria was the heart of the war front. The closer to the bridge that battles had been fought, the more casualties they'd suffered. "Are you trying to lose the fort?"

Father pounded his fist on the table. "Nothing will end as long as that bridge stands. I am not a coward who will run from it."

"We don't have the men for that." Anyone with eyes could notice the dwindling population of the fort.

"I'm bringing in men from Fort Gale and Fort Solace."

"Fort Solace cannot afford to spare them either. You're going to leave them vulnerable."

Father sneered. "I hear enough anxious talk from my generals, Kennard. You haven't been in the field and are not qualified to hold such an opinion."

Ken scoffed. "I've seen enough from where I am. It's only been in the last few days that I've finally begun to clear out the infirmary. Every time I empty a bed, someone new fills it. Last week, we had half the men on the floor."

"But if you're doing your job, all those men are ready to fight again."

Ken clenched his fists under the table. "And where there are injuries, there are deaths. For every man I Heal, how many more do I not get to see?"

Father held up a finger. "That is an excellent point. Clearly, I'm not using you to your full potential. You can have men fighting right away if you Heal them on the battlefield."

Ken shook his head, eyes wide. That was a horrible plan.

Herman cleared his throat. "Your Majesty, if I may..."

Father nodded.

"I do not believe His Highness is capable of such a task. Having watched him use his Gift, I can see how it tires him. It's not uncommon for him to collapse from the exertion. If he is Healing men in the field, he will not have the strength or stamina to defend himself at the same time."

Father folded his hands. "That is what the two of you were hired for." He turned to Ken. "You should go now. You'll need to talk to the quartermaster and the tactician to prepare."

Ken stumbled outside, numb. He hadn't thought Father could lose any more of his mind. In a matter of months, he'd swung from overprotective to reckless.

Abhenric ran up the bridge, eyes wide with fear. "I just Saw a vision." He grabbed Ken by the shoulders, his fingers digging in, like a drowning man would grasp at flotsam. "What have you done?"

15

GOODBYE, FAIR PRINCE

K en adjusted the mail over his torso and began strapping knives to his boots.

"Are you sure you don't want plate?" Herman asked him again.

"I won't be able to move right in it." Ken added a harness over his shoulders for more daggers. "Agility and stealth are my greatest asset with these. Stealth won't be on my side. I can't squander agility. Besides, you're both in mail."

Val slung a four-foot-long sword over his back. "You trained against my sister, not soldiers. You're going to get yourself killed."

Ken sighed. "I didn't ask for this, Val. Any sane man would know I was trying to talk him out of the battle entirely, not join it. But I don't exactly have a choice now, do I?" He tucked two daggers into the harness and another two into scabbards on his hips. "I don't want to kill anyone today. I'd rather save lives than take them. But if someone gets past the two of you, he'll get a knife in his throat." Ken added a deep green poncho, concealing most of his arsenal.

Abhenric walked in, dark circles under his eyes. "No good will come of this. Please, Kennard, you must try again to convince your father to change his orders. He will not listen to me."

Ken shook his head. "He won't listen to me either. Talking to him is what got me dressing for battle. If I try again, he'll have me on the front lines, waving a flag and doing a dance to entice the Tehazians."

"You have to try. I See death surrounding you."

"Tehazian deaths if we're lucky," Ken said.

"Your presence is going to kill more Meriverians than you can save out there."

Ken ran his hand through his hair. For the sake of the men, he had to try. They deserved that much. "Follow me."

Across the maze of platforms and bridges, Father was readying himself for battle as well. With his Transformation, armor wasn't particularly useful if it didn't fit the form he was using. In the same way that his clothing stayed with his human form, his animal forms kept whatever was worn. Before a fight, he had to choose what forms he expected to use and have a servant put armor on each one.

When Ken and the others walked in, it was grizzly bear armor. It wasn't a lot: just a helmet and plate fitted over the middle of his back and chest. The pieces may have disappeared between forms, but their weight would not. He was likely pushing his limits by choosing multiple large forms with equally large breastplates.

"Are you ready?" Father asked.

Ken nodded. "Almost. I have my arms and armor, but I still need medical supplies."

"Then what are you doing here?"

Arguing had gotten Ken nowhere. It was time for a different tactic. Instead, he genuflected. "On behalf of our men, I must humbly ask that you consider Abhenric's vision. He has never been wrong before."

Father harrumphed. "You have until I finish dressing."

Abhrenic bowed. "Your Majesty, I see many Meriverian deaths if you send His Highness into the field."

Father became a cougar. "It's a battle. Death is to be expected. Your vision means nothing."

The servant began fitting a breastplate.

Ken pleaded, "Father, he has Seeing. If you ignore him, the blood of those men is on your hands."

"The blood of my army is always on my hands," Father said. "This battle is no different."

"What about your son's blood?" Abhenric asked coolly. "Are you willing to have that on your hands?"

Ken went cold. The entire room fell silent.

Father's feline eyes narrowed. "Is that a threat, Seer?"

Abhenric met Father's gaze. "If he walks onto that field, men will die protecting him. And if he stays out there, none of these three"—he pointed to where Ken, Val, and Herman stood together—"will make it back alive."

Father tipped his head up for his helmet. "I see. You're just trying to get your son out of the battle."

Abhenric took a deep breath and closed his eyes. "I am trying to protect both our sons from certain death."

Father became a man clad in mail and crossed his arms. "My son has lived with certain death for almost eight years. My order stands."

Ken clutched his stomach as he stepped outside. He couldn't seem to get enough air. How could Father send him on a suicide mission? Was he really that far gone?

Nobody spoke a word as they walked to the infirmary. There, Ken gathered dressings, bandages, and tourniquets, stuffing them into satchels. Doomed or not, he'd still save the men around him. When he had what he needed, he sat on the stretcher over the trapdoor between Herman and Val, who used the pulley to lower them down.

All around them, soldiers in mail descended from the fort via ropes, which snaked back up into the trees as they dropped the last yard into a foot of standing water, where the swollen river and endless rain had flooded the valley.

The muddy water sloshed against Ken's boots as he dropped from the platform. Val slipped in the muck behind him and had to catch himself on the stretcher.

"Careful," Ken said. "We can't have you braining yourself before the Tehazians get their turn."

Val laughed. "Either way, I won't have to go to your wedding."

Herman chuckled. "I'm surprised you'd want to get out of it, Valerzan. You know the alternate shift is night duty."

Val gagged, and Ken and Herman snickered.

A soldier trudged past them, scowling, and the moment of levity dissipated as swiftly as it had arisen.

They joined the gathering army at the northwest corner under Fort Vigil. Soldiers split into their divisions and formed square squadrons for each. Speed, Strength, and Stone-Skin formed the front squads, followed by Fire and Ice, which were split by Animal Speech, with soldiers mounted on bears and moose. Water and Flight stood separate, ready to take their own paths to the battlefield. Ken, Val, and Herman joined the back of the main formation.

A general flew overhead, inspecting their formation. He gave a signal, and the main group began marching northwest. The water division headed due north, and the Flight division took to the air.

For half an hour, they marched, no one speaking. Ken focused on the squelching of their boots in the mud, the rustle of undergrowth as they passed. He couldn't dwell on what would happen. Even thinking of Lia didn't help; it only made him think of what might happen to her if Abhenric was right. What if Ken's death made her into the cruel, cold woman she'd tried not to become? He wished he'd had the foresight to write her a letter before they left the fort.

They halted as the general flew back down in front of the formation. Men readied their weapons. Val held his massive sword in one hand, a shield in the other. Ken unsheathed a dagger. Though he wouldn't attack like the others, he wanted his weapon ready for defense. Herman altered his stance from holding his quarterstaff like a walking stick to gripping one end across his body with both hands.

Due north, peeking through the trees, the tents of the Tehazian army covered a wide bridge—the cedar of the beams and planks still looked freshly cut—and more tents straddled both sides of the river. The main Meriverian formation would attack head-on while the Water-Breathing division swam up and attacked from the river on the east side, and Flight descended from above.

They inched forward, following the general, treading lightly. Ken tried to breathe as quietly as his racing heart would allow. His every hair stood on end.

They halted, waiting for the signal to attack.

Screams rang out to the southwest.

Ken cringed and spun to his left.

Flames rose from the forest. A flurry of wings filled the air as Flyers joined the fight. Speeders blurred through the formation to reach the new front. But the Strongmen and Stone-Skinned couldn't move so easily and were stuck at the back, with mounted Animal Speakers in their way.

More screams came from above.

A Vistan with green wings fell with a splash at Ken's feet, a deep cut in one of his wings. Scarcely had Ken checked his Vitality and kissed his forehead when another with blue wings appeared with a gaping head wound, red oozing from his bashed in skull. The green one flew away as Ken checked the blue. His Vitality was too weak. Ken would black out if he tried. The Vitality faded more. "I'm so sorry," Ken said helplessly as the man fell face first into the swamp. Many men had died in the infirmary, but never like that. The worst injuries never made it that far.

Swallowing down nausea, Ken moved on to the next men who landed in front of him, Healing whoever he could. Gashes, puncture wounds, head trauma, broken bones, missing hands... The pain was never-ending, and it was more than he could Heal. He lost track of how many he'd seen—and how many he'd lost. He was flagging, but he couldn't turn away.

Herman grabbed his shoulder. "Kennard, we have to move. The Tehazians have spotted you."

170

Sure enough, several enemy soldiers headed their way, eyes fixed on Ken. But several more men languished right next to him.

"I can save one more," Ken said.

Herman gripped the front of Ken's poncho and dragged him back a hundred feet. "Not if you're dead, you can't. I'm not letting Abhenric's vision come true."

Val ran to meet them. "This ambush is a mess. We have to retreat. Ken, we can't stop. They've seen what you're doing, and they're coming for you."

Ken pulled a throwing knife from his boot and struck an approaching Tehazian in the eye. The man screamed, and Val turned and took off his head with a single blow from his sword.

"Impressive," Herman said, "but the longer we stay, the more impossible our retreat becomes."

Val held his sword up. "We have to take these ones out first. We can't have them following us."

Herman grumbled and twisted his quarterstaff toward the enemies. Ken grabbed three more knives, feeding them with his left hand and throwing with his right in quick succession. They hit an arm, a leg, and a shoulder. None of the wounds were lethal, but it slowed the Tehazians down. Ken pulled out his hip daggers and waited for the distance to close. Herman darted forward, whirling his quarterstaff like the wings of a hummingbird—a deadly hummingbird. He aimed for the man with the knife in his shoulder and jabbed him in the stomach with the end of his staff, then swung around and broke his neck as he doubled over.

Val hung back near Ken, sword in front of them. Two more enemies bypassed Herman's fight to charge at Ken. As they neared, Ken ducked down to his knees and drove his blades into their thighs, letting Val cut them down.

"I think that was the last of those ones," Val said.

"Good. Let's get Herman." Ken looked over to where he'd been fighting. He wasn't there. "Where did he go?"

"I don't know. He was just right—"

Herman appeared in front of Ken, eyes wide. "*No!*" He leaped between Ken and Val, bashing in a Tehazian's head.

Ken turned to Val.

His eyes were wide. A blade protruded from his chest, spreading a carmine stain through his shirt. Ken couldn't breathe. He rushed to Val's side, steadying him as he stumbled to the ground. Ken had to save him. If he could just remove the sword, he could undo this. He had to undo this. It might be his last Healing for the day, but he would do it. He put two fingers to Val's neck.

His Vitality was almost unreadable.

Ken felt as though the blade had pierced him too. Even if he gave him everything... "I can't—" He choked. "I have nothing left. I've failed you, Brother."

Val tried to speak, but blood burbled up instead of words.

Herman grabbed Ken by the shoulder. "More are coming. We have to go."

Ken gripped Val's hand. "We can't leave him here." Not Lia's brother. He couldn't let him die alone.

"We don't have a choice," Herman growled, grabbing Ken's shoulder.

"No!" Ken fought him off and held onto Val.

But Herman was stronger and faster and yanked Ken to his feet. Val slipped halfway under the muddy, bloodstained water.

Ken cried out as a sharp pain ripped through his right thigh. An arrow protruded from his leg, aligned to have hit his chest if Herman hadn't moved him.

"Dammit." Herman bent down and hoisted Ken across his shoulders. "Hold on."

He ran faster than any sled or cart Ken had ever ridden. Ken squeezed his eyes shut. The arrow scraped against Herman's back, jamming deeper into Ken's thigh. Between the pain, the grief, and the vertigo, Ken thought he would be sick, but the trip was mercifully short. Within a few minutes, Herman was calling down the infirmary platform.

"We have to go back," Ken insisted as the platform reached them.

"No." Herman shoved him onto the stretcher and pinned him down with one knee.

"But—"

Herman grabbed Ken's face with both hands, forcing them eye-to-eye. Pain and anger reflected back like a mirror of horror. "Valerzan is dead."

Ken's vision blurred, his eyes stinging. He closed them and surrendered until Herman slowly let go.

Inside, Esmond and Herman helped Ken off the stretcher and onto a nearby hammock. Ken left his right leg hanging off the edge and took deep breaths to dull the pain. Herman helped Esmond cut the fabric away from Ken's pant leg. Esmond offered him a pain-easing tincture.

Ken shook his head. "No. I need to stay clear. There are more men coming."

"You've done enough," Herman said. "No one could ask more of you."

Tears threatened to spill over. "No, I haven't. Val is out there dying—or already dead."

Herman crossed his arms. "Fine. Punish yourself. But if you start screaming, I'm shoving that concoction down your throat."

Esmond took a heavy pair of serrated shears and cut the fletching end off the arrow, then handed the severed end to Ken. They'd worked together long enough that Ken knew what he wanted him to do with it. He stuffed the wooden piece between his teeth. As Esmond grasped the arrowhead and pulled the rest of the shaft through, it slithered sharply through the hole in his leg, and Ken grunted and bit down hard.

Next, scalding water and alcohol were poured through. Ken clawed at the hammock and bit harder, but willed himself not to scream, though his breathing was getting intense.

Esmond held up a jar of ointment.

Oh, Giver, yes. Ken nodded vigorously.

The cool, oily medicine worked quickly. Ken sighed and spat out the arrow shaft as his leg numbed.

Esmond dressed and bandaged the wound, then patted him on the shoulder. "There was a lot of mud, but I think it's clean now. You were lucky to miss the artery and the bone."

Ken struggled to sit up.

Esmond tried to push him back down. "Hey now. You need to rest and keep that leg up. You missed the artery, but with your condition, you're still at risk of bleeding out."

Ken groaned. "There are too many wounded coming. I saw them. Herman, if I stay in the hammock, will you bring patients to me?"

Herman nodded solemnly.

For the next hour, Ken worked in his reclined position, Healing as much as he could. He was too weak to do as much as he wanted, but he was determined to use up what energy he had to give. With another Healing or two, he would black out.

Gonfrid stormed into the infirmary as a man. "What are you doing here? My orders were for you to Heal men in the field."

Ken's blood boiled. "Your orders? Your *orders*? Your orders got a good man killed today! I did as you ordered. I saved countless men before the

Tehazians realized what I was doing. If Herman hadn't carried my wounded carcass here, they would've killed the two of us as well."

The rage strengthened Ken, and he pulled himself upright. "Do you see this wound? It would have gone through my ribcage if Herman hadn't forced me to retreat. I had to watch my friend suffer in my arms, knowing he was going to die, because you wouldn't listen to reason. Valerzan is *dead*, Father, and I had to leave him to die alone. We can't even give him a proper burial because—thanks to your failed plan—our retreat was too hasty to remember where we left him."

The infirmary fell silent, all eyes watching Father and Ken.

"I know that Valerzan's loss affects you deeply. You two have known each other since you were boys. But what of the men you Healed out there? Are their lives worth less than his?"

Ken ground his jaw. "Not one of the men I Healed today couldn't have made it to the fort. My Gift is not unlimited. Those too weak to survive the trip here are too far gone for my help anyway. I am a liability in the field. Valerzan died because he was more focused on defending me than watching his own back."

Father sighed. "He was a guard, Kennard. Defending you was his duty."

"No. Defending me from unavoidable threats was his duty. Your orders today were avoidable. I hold you accountable for his death." Ken grabbed a cloth and wiped his hands, cleaning off the blood of who knew how many, then turned to Esmond. "I need fresh air and food. I'll be back when I'm finished."

Esmond shook his head. "What you need is rest. I would advise you not to take long."

Ken threw the bloody cloth at Father. "Perhaps you'd like to survey the results of your failed plans," he spat.

Father said nothing as Ken limped out the door. It was the closest he could ever come to admitting he was wrong.

Herman showed up at his side, offering his quarterstaff as a crutch. "Why don't you wait at our quarters? I can get food by the time you get there."

Ken nodded. He actually felt too sick to eat, but it was the first excuse he'd thought of to leave the infirmary. As Herman zipped away, Ken leaned on the staff, taking deep breaths and focusing on his destination as he limped toward his quarters. By the time he reached the door, beads of sweat poured down his brow. At the table, he stopped to catch his breath, then slowly and shakily eased himself onto a stool. He rested his head on the cool wood of the table.

"Kennard?" Abhenric's concerned tone cut deeper than Ken's arrow wound.

Ken looked up. His head was so heavy.

"Where is my son?" Abhenric's voice was barely audible, his face contorted.

Ken swallowed the lump in his throat. "I'm so, so sorry..." His eyes stung. "I couldn't save him. I wanted to. I tried, but—"

Abhenric, quiet, serene Abhenric, screamed from the depth of his lungs, a vengeful, sorrowful wail.

Ken couldn't look. The sound brought him back to the field, and hot tears spilled over. He tried to move to comfort Abhenric but found himself meeting the floor.

Herman darted inside. "Kennard? Help me get him up. We need you to stay with us so we can get you in your bunk..."

Ken blinked.

When he opened his eyes, he was laying in his hammock, but the room was at a strange angle. He lifted his head just enough to look left and right. They had shoved the table to a corner of the room and restrung his hammock in its place.

Ken still felt weak. He put a hand to his wrist. His Vitality had grown weaker. Something wasn't right. Had he lost too much blood?

He tried to sit up to check his dressing.

"Feeling better?" Abhenric asked. "Your dinner's ice cold by now."

"Abhenric, why are you here? I didn't save Val."

Abhenric stood up and moved where Ken could see him. His eyes were red, but he didn't look angry. "Herman told me what happened. It's not your fault, Kennard. I don't blame you."

But that didn't stop Ken from blaming himself. He wiped his forehead, the heat of the room creeping up on him. "Can you dowse the fire?"

Abhenric furrowed his brow. "What are you talking about? This is Fort Vigil. There's nowhere to light one."

Ken panted. "There isn't?" He knew that, didn't he? But it was so warm...

Abhenric touched the back of his hand to Ken's forehead. "You're feverish."

That wasn't good. "What color is my leg?"

Abhenric unwrapped the bandage and lifted the dressing. Ken winced as the cloth stuck to him.

"It's not bleeding much, but the opening is turning yellow."

"Flaming crusted frog nuggets." An infection. This was how he would die.

16

MIDNIGHT RUN

Odelia looked over the logbook, ready to scratch in a revised number. "You forgot to add in the broken leg from the other night."

Milo scoffed. "I forget nothing. I chose not to put him in."

"Why would you choose not to record a patient?"

"Because then we can deny he was here. Or do you want to explain to the captain why you punched a patient in the jewels? That seems like more trouble than it's worth to me."

Odelia shook her head and revised the number. "I'm not afraid of the captain. I'm allowed to defend myself. Besides, the man's not going to say anything anyway. What soldier would admit to getting—"

Someone Speeded in, skidding to a stop in front of Odelia.

She dropped the pencil and tilted her head. "Herman? Is Kennard with you?"

He shook his head, panting.

Odelia's heart caught in her throat. Why would he be here without Kennard? Dread pricked at her, and she clutched her hands to her chest. "No." She shook her head. This couldn't happen...

Herman put up his hands. "Just breathe. He's alive, but he needs you."

She exhaled, tearing up with relief. "Where is he?"

"Still at Fort Vigil. He took an arrow to his leg, and it's infected. The surgeon says it's beyond what he can treat."

Forget the Elgathan King's threats. "How do I get there?"

"You're small. If you can hold on tight, I can run you there faster than a dogcart. It's dangerous territory, so make sure you're prepared."

Odelia nodded. "I'm always prepared." With no guards around, she always kept a few weapons hidden on herself, in case a well-thrown elbow wasn't enough.

"You aren't supposed to leave the infirmary," Milo warned.

"Then, don't tell anyone I'm gone," Odelia said.

Herman crossed his arms. "I can move quickly enough through the caves to keep you from being seen, but we'll need help getting past the entrance to the fort."

Milo put up his hands. "Don't look at me. I can keep my mouth shut, but I'm not getting involved in any desertion plans."

Rhonwin...! Odelia singsonged in her head as hard as she could. If he were nearby, it would get his attention without alerting anyone else.

Herman scowled and turned to Odelia. "Do you know someone else who—"

She held up one finger. *Help, Rhonwin!*

Footsteps echoed up the corridor.

Odelia smiled. "Yes, as a matter of fact, I do."

"What are you shouting about?" Rhonwin asked.

"I need your help," Odelia said.

Rhonwin looked at her, then at Herman. He nodded. "I can take care of that, but I have a better idea. Mistress Odelia, keep your hood up and your head down. Both of you, come with me."

They followed him into the main cavern, where he immediately turned into a side corridor. It opened up into a small room with sleds, carts and other equipment.

Rhonwin flagged down a soldier. "I'm leading an urgent mission. I need the smallest cart you have. No harnesses. Just a rope."

The man requisitioned the items without question, too absorbed in completing his task quickly to pay any mind to Odelia.

Rhonwin nodded. "Good. Now, I need you to run ahead and let the watch know to open the door. I'll be right behind." He clapped his hands. "Go."

"Yes, sergeant." The man hustled out.

"I should've known you'd make friends with someone in power," Herman said.

"Not that much power," Rhonwin said. "You'll still have to hide to get past the guards. Don't dawdle. He'll have that door open soon."

Herman tied the rope through the front of the cart, then crossed the other end over his chest. Odelia hopped in the tiny cart. It had no seat, being designed for small cargo, and there was barely enough room for her to fold her body into the bottom so Rhonwin could throw a blanket over her.

The cart creaked as Herman pulled her through the fort. The reinforced door groaned open, and a blast of cold air shot under the blanket. Slushy mud squelched as they rolled outside. He ran straight for a good while, then turned, whipping her around the corner. The cart tipped precariously. Odelia gasped and braced for a rough fall, but the cart landed back on its wheels.

Herman slowed down, then stopped the cart with his hands, and pulled back the blanket, revealing a night sky. "You okay?"

Odelia nodded. "A little shaken but not hurt. What happened? Did you have to swerve around something?"

"No, it was just a normal turn, but this cart isn't designed for my Speed." He held out his hand. "Get up. This thing will kill you if I run at my best, and we don't have time to slow down."

Odelia let him help her to her feet and wrapped the blanket around herself. Herman tied the rope into a makeshift harness, then crouched down. She climbed up on his back, wrapping her arms around his neck, and he fastened the rope around them. He bounced up and down a few times, then bolted forward. It took conscious effort for Odelia not to choke Herman as she held tight against the strong icy wind he generated.

He ran that way for about half an hour before the slope of the ground tapered off, and the forest grew swampier. He stopped and untied the rope, then eased her to the ground. "We're about halfway there." Arching his back, he twisted right, then left. "You can stretch your legs if you need to. No more than five minutes. Keep your eyes open. We aren't too far from the river."

Odelia nodded. She shook her legs out and reached up high, then bent to touch her toes, relishing the pull along the back of her thighs and calves.

Something snapped behind Herman.

Odelia slid her hands up to the top of her boots and removed throwing knives. She carried the motion up, pretending to continue into a long stretch up.

Just to the right behind Herman, someone approached, disguised in dark greens and browns. But the glint of his eyes gave him away.

Odelia settled on a spot just between and below the eyes. With a flick of her wrist, the man was clutching at his throat and gurgling. She readied the second knife and spun around, looking for another.

Herman darted around her a few times, then yanked the knife from the man and wiped it on his shirt. "Let's not wait for his friends." He handed her the knife. "I don't know how many of these you have, but you probably want to keep it."

Odelia nodded grimly. "Thank you." She tucked both knives back into place and wrapped the blanket around her shoulders, hardly feeling the difference as she pulled it tighter. Between the night and the undergrowth, she couldn't see the man she'd killed anymore, but she couldn't take her eyes off the spot.

Herman helped her back into place. "First kill?"

She swallowed. "First one I've caused."

He tightened the rope. "Just don't get sick on me. This is a hard enough run without doing it covered in vomit."

"I won't." She didn't feel sick at all. Just cold. "Herman, what I just did—if anyone knew—"

He nodded. "I saw nothing." Herman looked around, then ran.

Odelia closed her eyes. Was it wrong that she didn't feel remorse? On the way to save a life, and she had snuffed one out. Whoever he was, she had traded his life for her love's and would do it again if she had to. Was this the cruelty and coldness Dad had feared? What would she do if Herman couldn't reach Kennard in time? If she could kill for his sake...

No.

She had spent too long in that cave. She would only be as dark as she let herself become. Kennard would never want that for her—not on his behalf. And she didn't want that for herself.

But an act of defense was not going to tip her over the edge. Not tonight. Tonight, she needed to save Kennard.

Herman slowed his pace, splashing through swampland to stop between two giant spruces. He untied the rope.

"Herman, are you okay? Why are you stopping? I thought we were almost there by now." Odelia tried to check his Vitality.

He ducked away and tugged a thin rope hanging down from one of the trees, then pointed up. "I had to ring the bell."

Odelia followed his finger to the canopy above, where a platform descended toward them. It stopped a couple feet above the water, bringing its stretcher level with her chest. She jumped and hoisted herself onto the platform while Herman climbed up the other side. Once they were both seated, the platform rose, passing through the outstretched branches around them.

At the top, they stepped into a room full of bandaged men in hammocks.

"Where is he?" Odelia asked. "I don't see him." She fought the rising panic.

"He's in his quarters," Herman said. "I didn't want the guards to stop us at the front entrance, and from a distance, being carried on my back should've made it look like I was bringing you here for treatment."

He led her to the door, where a tall, bespectacled man almost ran into them.

"How is he?" Herman asked.

The man ran a hand over his face. "He's more feverish. I can't even make him comfortable anymore."

Herman grabbed his arm. "Have you told the king?"

The man shook his head. "You said you needed time, and I've given it to you. But I can't keep him in the dark much longer. He should be with his son for his final moments."

"I have another Healer, Esmond," Herman said. "If she fails, you can tell His Majesty, but he's too stubborn to let her try, so please, continue to keep your silence."

Esmond gripped Odelia's hand, meeting her gaze with sad, soft brown eyes. "Giver be with you."

Herman pressed Odelia from behind. "Time to go."

She followed him across rope bridges until he pointed to a small building formed around a tree. She ran to the door, but when she opened it, Dad barred her path.

"I need to get through," she snapped.

"No. You shouldn't be here."

She shoved against him. "Get out of my way."

"If he's too far gone—"

"Don't you dare. If anyone determines the limits of my Gift, it will be me."

His lip trembled. Red-rimmed eyes bored into her. "I can't lose you. Not you, Odelia. His life isn't worth—"

Herman pulled Dad out of her way, glaring at him. "Not now. Let her do what I brought her for."

Dad clenched his fists. "But if she—"

"She already took the risk to come here. How far she takes it is her decision." Herman turned to Odelia. "Go."

She couldn't think about whatever had turned Dad against Kennard. They could talk about that later. Odelia pushed past them into the room.

As the reek of sweat, pus, and vomit assaulted her, she gagged involuntarily. Kennard lay sprawled on a hammock, blankets twisted around him as he moaned and writhed lethargically. The slickness of his sallow brow reflected in the lantern light. Someone had stripped him down to his drawers, revealing the sickly color of the rest of his body. Around his bandaged leg, green and yellow oozed through the edges of the bloodstains. Dark veins spiderwebbed around the dressing.

Odelia closed the door, then knelt by his side and took his hand. He grimaced. She brushed a damp curl from his face, cradling his stubbled cheek in her palm. "I'm here now, love," she crooned. With the edge of her sleeve, she wiped some of the moisture from his mouth and took a deep breath, careful not to inhale through her nose. Sweeping her hand down to his neck, she checked his Vitality.

It was dull and fragile as if it could fade away at any moment.

Tears fell as she removed her boots. She gingerly climbed into the hammock, curling up against his good side. She had never tried this much Healing, and it was bound to knock her unconscious...if it didn't— No. She wasn't going to think about that. She would black out, and she didn't need to bash her own head in the process.

Odelia kissed him, gently at first, then with more force as she poured her power into him. She would give him everything she had. She *did* give him everything she had. The world grew fuzzy and gray, fading and pulling away from her, but still, she gave. Tears mixed in, salty and wet, and a creeping numbness enveloped her limbs.

And then Kennard's lips pressed back.

His arms circled her, and he held her close. The darkness receded, and her senses revived. Power looped through her, letting her share more with him again. Able to move, she broke the kiss. Odelia opened her eyes and met Kennard's dark ones, losing herself in their depth.

He raked his fingers through her hair. "Lia?" He let out a shaky breath. "I've missed you so much."

As he clutched her to himself, she rested her head on his chest. "I missed you too."

"I don't know what frightens me more: that I'm so far gone that I'm hallucinating you or that you're in the most dangerous place you could be."

She pulled her head up to look him in the eyes. "Nothing could stop me from coming the moment I heard you needed me."

He caressed her cheek. "I always need you."

More tears spilled over. "I was so afraid I wouldn't make it here in time."

"But you did."

"Please, don't scare me like that again." She held his face with both hands. "I need you too."

He smiled. "It's all right. I'm alive and Healed, and you did it without fainting—which I have to say is beyond impressive. I've ended up passed out on the floor for less."

She chuckled and wiped her eyes. "So have I."

"How did you do it?"

"I don't know. I thought I was going to, and I almost did. But then...I think I borrowed some of your Healing."

He smirked. "Well, then, you can borrow my Healing anytime." He tipped her chin up and kissed her. A deep kiss this time. One not meant for Healing.

Herman opened the door, and Dad peeked inside.

Odelia's face felt on fire as she pulled away, and Kennard's was red. The impropriety of her nearness to his almost naked body suddenly became apparent, and she scrambled out of the hammock. The rocking motion sent Kennard tumbling. He swung his feet to the floor, steadying himself on her arm, then stood upright.

Herman put his arm around Dad and pulled him in. "She's okay. It worked."

Dad scowled. "You put her in danger while deliberately withholding information that she deserved to know before she made her choice."

"She couldn't be distracted from what she needed to do," Herman said.

Odelia looked to Kennard. "Do you know what they're talking about?"

The color drained from his face. "You didn't tell her?"

"Tell me what?" What could have ever possibly distracted her from this? She looked back and forth between Kennard and Herman and Father and... "Where is Valerzan?" The sinking pit in her stomach told her she didn't want to know.

Kennard laid a gentle hand on her shoulder, his eyes haunted and his other hand covering his mouth.

"We never should've been on that field," Herman said quietly. "Abhenric warned the king that there was death out there. Nothing went right, and Valerzan—he was cut down defending Kennard."

"Where is he?" Odelia's voice didn't sound like her own. It was like someone was speaking for her. "Will we be able to...?" So many couldn't be sent home.

"We retreated too quickly," Herman said.

She barely heard Kennard say, "He died alone."

"They recovered the fallen an hour ago." Dad's hand trembled. "I identified him."

"I need to see him," Odelia said.

Dad walked to a back corner of the room, where he pulled back a blanket covering a long pine box. "They Iced him for return to Iverish. They weren't going to until I told them who he was." He laughed bitterly. "The very position that got him killed is what earned him a proper burial—or part of one. Hortensia's the only one who can do it, and I don't even know how to tell her."

Odelia took a step forward, but Kennard tightened his grasp on her shoulder. "Are you sure? I was there. It's an ugly sight."

She swallowed. "I've seen a lot of ugliness in the past few months."

He tipped her chin up to meet his gaze, his eyes full of pain. "So have I, but this isn't the same."

It didn't matter. She needed to see for herself. Her annoying little brother, too strong and proud to call her his queen, he couldn't be gone. Not until she saw him.

As Odelia moved toward the box, Kennard took her hand, lacing his fingers in hers and lending her his fortitude. Herman took Dad's place by the box and lifted the lid. She closed her eyes and took a few deep breaths, then looked down to see her brother one last time.

The body was broken, muddy, and bloodstained. It had his strawberry blond waves and strong muscles. His rounded nose and stubborn jaw. On instinct, she put on her finger to his cold wrist, but his familiar Vitality wasn't there. It wasn't Valerzan she saw. Just an empty shell. Her brother was gone.

Odelia turned away and clung to Kennard. He folded his arms around her as she shook with anger and pain.

17

A VISTAN SUNRISE

K en limped his way to Father's quarters. He'd scrubbed the sickly smell off himself and wrapped a fresh bandage around his perfectly fine leg, careful to stain it with blood to make it look more authentic. If Father found out Lia had Healed him, it wouldn't matter that she'd saved his life. She would be arrested for desertion.

They had only been reunited an hour ago, but as much as Ken longed to comfort her, keeping her alive was more important. The longer he waited to seek out Father, the more likely someone was going to seek out Ken and find Lia hiding in his quarters.

Despite the late hour, a guard let Ken into Father's quarters as soon as he arrived.

"Finished pouting?" Father asked without looking up from his desk.

Ken closed his eyes and took a huge breath. He wanted to scream but calmly said, "It is not pouting to mourn the loss of a dear friend and a good soldier. In fact, that's part of why I'm here. I would like permission for Abhenric and me to attend Valerzan's funeral in Iverish."

Father leaned back in his chair, looking Ken up and down. His gaze lingered on the pant leg that had been rolled up to make room for the bandage underneath.

"He died protecting me," Ken said. "By rights, he is owed a hero's burial, laid to rest in his home soil by his family and honored by his liege."

Father crossed his arms. "Iverish is not a short trip. To get there and back will take a few days."

Ken nodded. "True, and we *are* woefully short of men, I know, but we would make the journey as quickly as possible." He had never been good at this, but if ever there was a time to learn manipulation, it was now. For once, he hoped he'd inherited something from Mother.

Father frowned in thought. "We are in need of recruits, and the Vistans haven't been sending me the numbers I would like. I need them put in their place."

"Of course." It might actually have been working.

"You may both go to Iverish, but you will bring back Vistan troops with you. You will have two weeks."

Ken bowed. "Gladly. Thank you, Father. May I make one more request?"

"Perhaps."

Ken clasped his hands together and proceeded carefully. "If you want me to manage the Vistans as I have before, I will be much more effective with the help of my secretary. The Vistans are more amenable when she is with me, and by rights, she should be at Valerzan's funeral anyway."

Father's eyes narrowed. "You can talk to the Vistans without her."

Ken hung his head. "I'm embarrassed to admit this, but my leg is not doing well. There isn't anything more that Esmond can do for me. I thought if I could get myself Healed, I wouldn't need to worry you, but it's much worse than I let on in the infirmary. This injury will kill me. I've already lost so much blood..."

Father closed his eyes and held up one hand. "Kennard, if this is some game—"

"It's not." He gripped the chair for effect. "When have I ever acknowledged the cost of my Gift? This is one thing I never say lightly."

Father blinked and cleared his throat. "She may help you, but as soon as she is done, she will go back to Fort Solace." He held up a finger. "Ask for one more thing, and I'll take it all back."

Ken let out a breath and smiled. All that was left was to get Lia back to Solace unseen before anyone there noticed her absence, and she would be safe. "Thank you again. I won't ask for anything more."

After writing a short note, Father signed and sealed it, then handed it to Ken. "Give this to the captain there. You may have one moose cart from here and add a dogcart from Solace."

Careful to maintain his limp, Ken bowed and turned for the door.

"One last thing," Father said as Ken reached the threshold. "My previous ban still stands. If you try to run away with the girl, I will find her, and she will hang."

Ken suppressed a shiver. "Of course," he said, then limped away.

He wanted to run back to his quarters, but the ruse needed to be maintained. As soon as his door was safely shut, Lia poked her head out from the loft. "What happened?"

Smiling, Ken held up the letter. "I have a message to deliver to Fort Solace as soon as possible. Let's not keep them waiting."

Lia climbed down, asking questions in quick succession. "Is there a funeral? Am I safe to go to it? Will I have time to meet with Patricius?"

Ken gently grasped her shoulders. "Yes to all of it, especially the recruitment idea. He jumped on that."

"How long do we have?"

"Two weeks. Are we ready to go?"

She nodded. "Herman has all your things packed. He's packing Dad's things now while he sends the letter to Mom."

Though Lia held herself together, Ken could tell she wasn't okay. Her stoic facade faltered around her eyes, barely hiding the pain. It was a look he had willfully ignored for years, but this time, the pain was even deeper. Like any pain, he longed to Heal it away. Pulling her closer, he kissed her forehead and wrapped his arms around her. It was wholly inadequate. "We'll leave as soon as they're ready."

Lia stepped back and grabbed a blanket off Ken's hammock. "They'll be back any minute. You should start wrapping me up now."

They each took two corners and laid the blanket on the floor. Lia sat in the center, hugging her knees. Ken took the corners and pulled them all over her head, knotting the opposite ends together. With some rope, he tied a handle on the top, then tentatively lifted her off the ground. She didn't make a sound. He set her back down and peeked inside one of the folds. "Can you breathe in there?"

"It's a little stuffy, but I should be fine. I can make myself a nice opening when the cart moves. How far do we have to go to get to one? I noticed the flooding's too deep for a dogcart here."

"Not that far. There's another trapdoor a couple trees away from the infirmary that lowers right into a moose shed. But we only get one cart, so it's going to be tight in there."

Her eyes widened. "I hope they don't pile the bags on top of me."

He reached in and tucked her mussed up hair behind her ear. "Don't worry. You may be baggage, but you're royal baggage. I'll make sure you ride in my lap."

Lia gasped and turned red. "My *father* will be sitting right next to you."

"He won't object to me keeping you safe." Ken smiled. "Besides, are you afraid he'll demand that I marry you to make it right?"

She chuckled. "He could tell me not to marry you."

Ken scoffed. "Never. He knows we're destined for one another."

Lia's smile faded. "He might. When I first got here, he asked me not to try to save you if you were too far gone."

"Lia, I knew how bad my Vitality was when I was still lucid." Ken shuddered. "It could only have been worse when you Healed me. I was on death's door, and I could've just as easily taken you with me. He must have been terrified for you. I would've been if I'd known what you were doing."

"I just worry that he blames you for not saving Valerzan."

Ken shook his head. "No, he doesn't, though he has every right to. He stayed by my side through the infection. That much I do remember from my fever."

There was a short knock before Abhenric and Herman walked in. Abhenric had a bag slung over his shoulder.

"Perfect timing," Ken said. "Abhenric, Lia's worried that you'll withdraw your approval for our engagement."

Abhenric set down his bag and knelt next to Ken in front of Lia. He widened the opening to reveal her better. "Never." Abhenric put a hand on Ken's back. "You've made a fine choice, one that's changed your fate for the better. I wouldn't try to take that from you."

She scowled. "What about when you said Kennard wasn't worth saving?"

That hurt. Had Abhenric really said such a thing?

Abhenric shook his head. "I didn't say he wasn't worth saving. I was trying to say that he wasn't worth both of my children's lives. Without Valerzan, you are the last of my line. Your future was in flux again. I was afraid that it was because you would die saving Kennard, but I realize now that letting him die is what would have changed your future."

"For what it's worth, I agree with him," Ken said. "Val's life for mine is already one too many."

Herman cleared his throat. "Speaking of Valerzan, let's get him loaded into the cart. Since Odelia's bundled up, I assume all plans are in place?"

Ken nodded. "We have one cart here, and we can get a second in Solace."

Herman said, "I'll get two Strongmen to load him. Odelia, they'll have to come in here, so say whatever you need to say quickly. Once I return, you won't be able to speak again for a few hours until we reach Solace." A second later, he was gone.

Abhenric looked at Lia. "Let's be honest. Even if I withdrew my approval, that wouldn't stop you from marrying Kennard, would it?"

She blushed again. "No, but I like having it."

"Anything else before Herman comes back?" Ken asked.

"Just remember that Sergeant Rhonwin has Listening, and he knows to be alert for my return. If we all address our thoughts to him forcefully when we get there, we should be able to get his attention."

Ken laughed. "I was hoping for 'I love you,' but advice works too."

Herman knocked on the door, and Ken jumped into his fake injured stance, shifting his weight to his "good" leg. Two men entered, picked up Val's coffin, and walked him outside. Abhenric picked up his and Ken's bags, and Herman picked up his bag and Lia. Val's belongings had been stuffed across all of their bags, but if anyone asked, it was all in Ken's bag, while Ken's belongings were in the bag containing Lia.

They all followed the coffin out and through the fort. Ken wished he could carry something himself to help, but he needed to maintain his limp. When they reached the trapdoor for the cart, the platform took the coffin down and quickly returned for them. Ken hobbled on behind Herman and Abhenric. As they lowered, instead of going to the bottom, the platform stopped level with the back of a moose cart with Val loaded along the right side. One of the Strongmen took the bags from Abhrenic and stuffed them into the back of the cart. The other attempted to grab Herman's.

"The big one needs to stay with me," Ken said.

"You won't be far from it, and we can pack it more efficiently for you, Your Highness," the man said.

Ken shook his head. "I'm particular about my belongings. I'll let Herman help me, thank you."

The man shrugged. "Of course, Your Highness. You're all set then. Giver protect you."

Abhenric and Herman stepped aside to allow Ken on first. He awkwardly settled himself in the back and motioned for Herman to bring Lia to him. "Careful of my leg," he warned.

Herman lightly set her between Ken's legs, where she sat a little too upright for a bag full of clothes and gear. Ken cradled the bag, then leaned back, letting her fall against him. Judging by the feel of her elbows under his hands and against his abdomen, she was sitting sideways against him.

Abhenric sat next to them, then Herman took the back and signaled to the driver to go.

Ken waited several minutes past the outskirts of the fort before checking in on Lia. He slowly reached a hand inside until he felt her silky braid. Abhenric looked at him anxiously. Her hand grasped Ken's and held on. He nodded, and Abhenric exhaled and relaxed.

In no time at all, both Abhenric and Herman fell asleep, heads on their shoulders. Considering they'd both been up half the night, and Herman had run himself ragged, it was no surprise.

Lia's hold on his hand began to weaken as well. Ken let go and slid his hand to a more comfortable position around her waist. Her breaths came deep and even. Thank the Giver, she didn't snore.

It took Ken much longer, but eventually, the sway of the cart and the warmth of Lia in his arms lulled him as well. He closed his eyes and rested his head on hers. When he opened them again, they were inside a cave, with guards talking to the driver.

"I didn't know about this," one of the guards said.

"Didn't Sergeant Rhonwin say he was expecting someone from Vigil?" another said.

"Then go get him."

Apparently, they didn't need to summon Rhonwin after all. Ken nudged Abhenric awake, who blinked, then turned to do the same to Herman. Lia tensed in Ken's arms.

An approaching voice echoed somewhere ahead of the moose. "I can take them to the captain. The cart can be stowed for now, but don't touch their belongings. I'll fetch whatever they need later. And make sure you bow, men. That's the crown prince."

Lia relaxed. Clearly, she recognized the voice.

Footsteps moved around the cart until the back end opened. An Elgathan man with bright blue eyes smiled and bowed. "Welcome to Fort Solace, Your Highness. My name is Sergeant Rhonwin, and I understand you have a letter for Captain Jonus. I can take you to him now. And I can see that Your Highness is very particular about your *baggage*, but I assure you that if you leave it right there, it will not be disturbed."

Herman and Abhenric disembarked, stretching out their stiff limbs and backs. Ken gave Lia a little protective squeeze before shifting her to lay on her side and dragging himself to the end of the cart.

Rhonwin gave a hand to help Ken down. "That's quite the injury. I'll take you straight to the infirmary as soon as we talk to the captain. Will you need help getting there?"

Ken shook his head as Herman handed him his quarterstaff. "I can manage, thank you."

They followed the sergeant down a passageway to a huge cavern filled with wooden partitions and closed rooms. Toward the back, one row of rooms had a set of stairs built into the side, leading up to an enclosed second story. Rhonwin led them up the stairs, where Ken pretended to struggle his way up. Rhonwin backtracked and slipped his shoulder under Ken's arm. "Good show," he whispered. "The slower you go, the more time you buy her."

Ken slowed his pace more, trying to relive his earlier leg pain, but if he overdid it, they might send him to the infirmary earlier.

When they reached the door, Rhonwin let go and knocked on the open door. "We have a royal visitor. Prince Kennard, this is Captain Jonus."

A sturdy blond Vistan stood up from behind a plain desk laden with paperwork. He walked in front of it, then bowed. "To what do I owe this visit, Your Highness?"

Ken dug into his jacket and pulled out Father's letter. "I have a message for you, as well as a need to borrow the services of Mistress Odelia."

Jonus took the letter. "Need her to Heal your leg?"

Ken nodded. "Yes, but I also bring sad news. She is needed in Iverish to attend her brother's funeral."

Looking over the letter, Jonus frowned. "Two weeks without our Healer? I hope His Majesty isn't planning for us to attack anytime soon."

"No. She'll be helping me recruit more men for you first."

Jonus shrugged. "I can't argue with orders, can I?" He leaned back against his desk and crossed his arms. "I was wondering something about her—if you don't mind my asking."

Ken smiled. "Of course not." He didn't care how impertinent the question might be if talking to the captain a little longer kept him away from the infirmary.

"Given the restrictions on her, one would think she was dangerous, but after the initial hubbub with the men, she hasn't caused any problems. She didn't even object when I confined her to the infirmary."

Taking a calming breath, Ken tried not to raise his voice. "You confined her to the infirmary?"

Jonus smiled grimly. "Her Gift attracted a lot of attention the first morning after she arrived. I decided it was safer for her not to wander the fort. When I had more men, I even posted a few guards with her to keep the more unruly ones in line."

Ken tamped back the rage burning up through him. "You kept her prisoner?"

Shaking his head, Jonus held up his hands. "Her orders already made her a prisoner. I simply made sure she was a live and productive one. But

I'm dying to know what she did to earn her sentence. Sergeant Rhonwin here claims he can't tell me."

"Nothing," Ken said.

Jonus raised an eyebrow. "Nothing at all?"

Ken ran a hand through his hair and sighed. "The only thing she's guilty of is taking my heart, and that was freely given."

The captain's eyes widened. "Oh... I see. Rhonwin, you could've told me we were protecting the prince's mistress—"

"She's my"—fiancée was correct but probably unwise—"sweetheart. I have not defiled her."

Jonus bowed. "Apologies, Your Highness. I didn't mean it as an insult. But either way, if she is so dear to you, I will not keep you from her. I'll take you to the infirmary myself so I can let her know she's free to go."

Odelia didn't dare breathe, let alone move. The cart took forever to reach storage, and it took even longer before someone jumped onto the cart. She gripped the hilt of a knife hidden in her boot, praying she wouldn't need it. The stranger lifted her bag off the cart and walked her somewhere.

Panic strangled her. As much as she trusted Rhonwin to help her, she had no way of knowing whether this person was him or one of his men.

Eventually, she was set down on something soft, and the knots above her untied. She blinked at the sudden intrusion of torchlight, and the infirmary came into view. A burly young Vistan smiled at her, his similarity to Valerzan like a stab in her heart. "Rhonwin sent me. You should be safe now."

Odelia smiled back. "Yes, thank you."

"You're welcome," he said, then jogged away.

She hopped off the bed, folded up the blanket and coiled the rope. Both were stuffed into the cabinet she kept her belongings in.

True to his nature, Milo didn't budge from his bed. That man could sleep through anything.

Odelia pulled off her boots and climbed into her cot. It was the most likely place she'd be without any patients to tend to and where she would've ended up if Herman hadn't fetched her.

Moments after she closed her eyes, a hand shook her shoulder. She wasn't supposed to know Kennard was coming, let alone be eager about it, so she squinted her eyes open in a show of reluctance.

But it wasn't Kennard.

It was the Speeder she'd fought with the other night, cradling a bloody arm. He winced. "I need your help again."

Odelia glared. She wanted no part of this game. "Get out," she snapped.

"But I have a gash in my arm!"

"Then have Milo stitch it up. Milo!"

Milo rolled over.

Odelia got up and poked him in the back. "You have a patient."

Milo rubbed his eyes, looking utterly dazed and confused. "Why can't you do it?"

"I don't Heal self-inflicted injuries," she said.

The Speeder gasped. "How dare you? You think I did this to myself?"

Milo moved the Speeder's hand out of the way, exposing the diagonal cut on his left forearm, and nodded.

Odelia put a hand on her hip. "You've avoided the infirmary for months, but now, you've suddenly injured yourself again. And the cut just so happens to have the same angle and location as it would if you'd wielded the blade yourself?" She shook her head. "After what you pulled last time, you're lucky I'm not screaming for someone to haul you away. I'm not touching you with a ten-foot pole."

The Speeder rounded on her, scowling. "I can make you Heal me, and I won't be caught off-guard this time."

She backed toward the doorway, keeping her eyes on him, and pointed. "*Get out!*"

Ken hobbled behind Jonus and Rhonwin, with Abhenric and Herman behind him. None of them spoke as they traversed the main cavern until they reached a tunnel marked with an infirmary sign.

Rhonwin looked back at Ken with a concerned frown. "Did you hear that?"

"Hear what?" Ken asked.

A feminine shout echoed up the tunnel.

Ken's heart stopped. "I heard that."

He lurched forward, but Herman put a hand on his shoulder. "I'll go."

The other men raced ahead, and Ken chased after as quick as he could without dropping his limp. Thankfully, the passageway was short, and he only lagged a few seconds behind.

A bleeding Vistan stood a few feet away from Lia and another man, who both glared death at the injured man with crossed arms.

"What is the problem here?" Jonus asked.

"These two aren't doing their duty," the bleeding man said.

Lia fumed. "He had his chance to get stitched up by Milo, and he refused."

Ken stepped into her line of sight. "Perhaps I can help?"

Her eyes lit up. "Ken?" She rushed over to him, brows furrowed. "You're hurt."

As part of the ruse that he hadn't seen her, Ken let himself get swept up in his first impulse. He embraced her with a full kiss, holding her tight. Then he looked into her green eyes and smiled. "Not anymore."

The bleeding man scoffed. "Are you kidding? She assaulted me when I tried that."

Ken turned on the man, fire coursing through his veins. He grabbed him by the shirt collar and balled up his fist. "You did what?"

Jonus sighed. "You see, Rhonwin? If you had told us she was the prince's sweetheart, this kind of thing wouldn't happen."

What little color the injured man had drained from his face.

"It isn't common knowledge," Rhonwin said. "Given that the king sent her here as punishment, I doubt he wanted us treating her as such."

Ken clenched his jaw. "I don't care whether you knew that she was spoken for. Her refusal stands on its own."

Lia wrapped her hands around his fist. "I haven't seen you in so long. Let's not waste any more of our time on him. The captain is capable of dealing with him now, and I already made him pay for his first transgression. Although, if he needs a reminder..."

The man flinched and covered his groin. "Please, no."

Ken knew how hard Lia could hit when she was trying not to cause pain and aiming for less sensitive areas. That had to have been excruciating. Why would he come back after that? Unless it was for revenge...

The rage burned again, but Jonus stepped behind the man and grabbed him by the back of his shirt. "I'll take care of this." Jonus yanked him away and pushed him toward the exit, then turned back to Lia. "Forgive me. I almost forgot why I came down here. Mistress Odelia, you have been granted two weeks leave in the company of His Highness. I'll leave the explanations to him."

Ken wrapped his arms around Lia. "We did it," he whispered.

She let out a breath. "For now. We'll need to contact Patricius on the way to Iverish. Rhonwin, do you think you could convince the captain to let you join us?"

He shook his head. "Not a chance. He's annoyed enough losing the rarest Gift in the fort. He's not going to let the second rarest go as well. But if you send for Moira, she can speak for both of us. Truth be told, with her Seeing, she's the better planner anyway."

"She had trouble making it to Losuno, are you sure she can meet us in Doivrie or Iverish?" Lia asked.

Rhonwin shrugged. "She hasn't felt sick for months now, but she does say she's waddling like a duck. That tutor you sent has been wonderful, though, so at the very least, she won't be worried about leaving the school."

Ken rubbed the back of his neck. Rhonwin and Lia had lost him.

"My wife is heavily pregnant," Rhonwin said.

"Oh. Congratulations," Ken said. That still didn't explain half of what they were planning, but with Milo and Herman in the room, the details were probably best left vague.

Rhonwin looked at Ken and nodded.

Ken suppressed a shudder. He wasn't sure that having someone Listen to his thoughts was something he could ever get used to.

"Do you need help packing?" Herman asked Lia.

She shook her head. "No, thank you. I don't have much, and I prefer not to have you sifting through my undergarments."

Ken smirked. "Can I volunteer to help?"

Abhenric cleared his throat loudly.

Lia laughed. "I think I'll take you up on that offer *after* our wedding." She turned to a set of cabinets behind her, passing Milo, who stood dumbfounded. "Something wrong?" she asked.

"Your fiancé is the crown prince?"

She cocked her head and blinked. "Yes...I told you that."

"You say a lot of things that I don't listen to," Milo said.

Herman chuckled. "You didn't think it was odd when I took her away to save Kennard?"

Milo shrugged. "It could've been another Kennard. I'm not that familiar with Elgathan names."

Lia rolled her eyes. "Milo, why don't you go get yourself breakfast?"

"Right, good idea." Milo bowed to Ken. "It was nice to meet you, Your Highness." He sauntered out of the infirmary.

Ken scratched his head. "How did someone that apathetic become a surgeon?"

Lia sighed as she started packing. "I don't know, but I must say, he makes for a cheery partner in here."

Ken looked around the cavern. The torches provided enough light to work by, but the dark walls and ceiling made everything smaller and dimmer. Even with room for all the beds, it wasn't a large space to be confined in for months. It didn't even have windows, being too deep inside the caves.

He hadn't noticed how pale she'd become. Vistans were always light, but the soldiers inside Solace were lighter than usual, and Lia could get lost in the snow outside. If he hadn't just kissed her, the pallor would make him worry for her health.

Lia held up a full bag and Ken's blanket. "Let's go."

The dogcart with Ken and Lia pulled ahead of the moose cart, which Abhenric insisted on riding in. Despite the shortness of his nap on the way to Solace, Herman ran ahead to contact Patricius and relay a letter to Moira via messenger in Doivrie.

The sky was lightening, and soon, the sun would rise. Ken tucked his blanket tighter around himself and Lia, and she snuggled up to him. He brushed the backs of his fingers against her pallid cheek. "Lia, when was the last time you saw the sun?" he asked softly.

"Two days after we last parted." Her voice was quiet and detached.

His heart broke. Even prisoners were given windows. "Did you really never leave that infirmary?"

She shook her head. "The captain was trying to keep me separated from the men. That man you almost punched was far from the only one of his kind."

"He should've allowed you to get a little fresh air every once in a while."

"That was your father's doing. His orders were to not let me set one foot outside the fort or anywhere near the exit."

Ken closed his eyes. He'd brought her so much pain. How was she so often the one to pay for his mistakes? "I'm sorry."

She reached up and turned his head to face her. Her eyes, the color of the trees around them, looked deep into his. "Your father is the one who is cruel and spiteful, not you. I knew that facing him was a risk when I pursued you, so if you're to blame for his opposition, then so am I."

Lia was right. Father was cruel and spiteful. Separating them should have been satisfactory if all he was after was keeping them from marrying. He didn't need to trap her in a dark hole. And unlike with Val, Ken couldn't tell himself that it might have been a mistake, that Father didn't really believe it would happen. He knew full well what Fort Solace was like and had gone out of his way to add the order beyond standard placement.

Behind Lia, a rose and violet blush began to tint the sky just above the dark green treeline. Even the snow on the peak above them looked like pink dust in the soft light.

Ken smiled and tilted his head up. "Look."

She turned and gasped. "It's so beautiful," she choked.

"It is."

Lia chuckled, then sniffed and wiped her eyes. "I feel so silly crying about the sun."

Ken kissed her temple. "There's nothing silly about it."

She broke down into a sob.

He pulled her to his chest, stroking her hair. "That's okay, love. You cry all you need." He needed to make her pain go away. If only his Gift worked that way. But more surprisingly, he realized he wanted to make the source of her pain go away as well: Father.

IVERISH

It was late afternoon, and Odelia stood at the river dock with Kennard and Dad. Kennard had insisted that Herman rest at the inn while Patricius, whom they'd picked up on the way to Iverish, took over the funeral arrangements in town. While Kennard's height made him stand out in the former Vistan capital, he wasn't easily recognizable with his head down and his hood pulled low. Odelia had told him he could stay back with Herman, but he refused to leave her side, holding her hand as they waited.

When the next riverboat docked, it was hard to tell who was disembarking because everyone was bundled up for the ride. Two women approached them, one much taller than the other. The shorter one, who was hauling a large bag, pulled back her hood as they neared. It was Mom. Dad didn't say a word as he embraced her, teary-eyed, and held her close.

The taller woman walked up to Kennard and hugged him. "I missed you," she said.

"Conora?" Kennard and Odelia asked.

Conora stepped back. "I was in Hortensia's workshop when she got the news. I couldn't not come."

"I'm surprised Mother let you," Kennard said.

"She didn't object when I told her I wanted to see my brother."

Dad put a hand on Odelia's back. "We should go. We should get to the burial woods before dark, and I need to talk to Herman and Conora before they can attend."

"Oh." Conora furrowed her brow in curious concern. "Is there something different about Vistan funeral rites that we need to be prepared for?"

"Yes and no. But it will have to wait until I can speak to you both privately."

Dad led the way back to the inn, keeping his arm around Mom. Inside, he took Conora up to Herman's room. Mom gave Odelia and Kennard clothes she had brought from the Cedar Palace, then met them downstairs after they'd changed. They found a table and ordered a round of ciders, which the three of them stared at for a long while.

Odelia picked at the skirt of her dark gray dress. The long fabric suffocated her. Kennard looked equally uncomfortable in his gray pants and jacket.

Mom finally broke the silence. "He was assigned to guard you. Were you with him at the end?"

Odelia shook her head. "Mom, that's not—"

"I was standing right next to him when it happened." Kennard didn't look up from his drink, his voice hollow. "I would have Healed him if I could but..."

It wasn't the whole truth, but it was what Mom needed to hear. Valerzan was Odelia's brother, and it was hard for her to find out what had happened, but he was Mom's baby. It was enough that she had to bury her child. She didn't need to know that he'd died alone in the mud.

With tears in her eyes, Mom reached across the table and took Kennard's hand. "Thank you for trying."

Patricius walked in with a pine cone and a lantern and joined their table. "It's good to see you again, Hortensia. I wish it were under any other circumstances."

"Is everything ready?" Odelia asked.

Patricius nodded. "We can start the procession as soon as everyone is here."

Odelia stood up. "I'll tell them." Anything to get away from this table. Being near Mom, feeling the pain radiating from her, was too much. Odelia couldn't stand being helpless to fix it.

Upstairs, she knocked on Herman's door, then opened it slowly. Herman and Conora stared back at her, eyes wide.

"Patricius has everything ready," Odelia said. "You can come downstairs when you're done."

Dad nodded solemnly. "I've said all that I need to." He walked out.

Herman blinked, shook his head, then followed him.

Conora hugged Odelia. "You and I are going to have a very long talk about princess things later."

"Of course," Odelia said, then chased after Dad. She caught him at the bottom of the stairs. "You told them the secret?"

He put a hand on her shoulder. "It was time. Valerzan deserves a burial worthy of what he truly was." He motioned to the table to get up and join him, then led everyone outside.

Patricius handed the lantern to Dad and the pine cone to Mom. "Do you remember the route to the burial woods from here?"

Dad nodded and took Mom's hand, then set off toward Lake Iver. Patricius lined everyone up in order behind them: Odelia, Kennard and Conora, himself, and then Herman. Behind them, four Vistan Strongmen carried Valerzan's coffin. No one spoke as they walked along the lake, leading him to his rest. When they reached the eastern edge, they continued on toward the forest and the walled-off ghost of the former Vistan palace. A thicker grove of trees grew just north of the palace, and the procession walked straight into it.

Within the burial woods, huge stones stood in front of even larger trees, all bearing names. On the south side, nearest the old palace, the Vistan crest was engraved as well. Mom and Dad had taken Odelia and Valerzan here when they were very young children—so young that Valerzan likely wouldn't have remembered, as Odelia barely did herself—though she hadn't noticed the difference between the stones back then. Now that she knew the truth, it was obvious which ones were royal.

A fresh hole had been dug among the royal graves, and a wooden marker stood in front of it, with "Prince Valerzan DiOrto" painted on the side away from the grave. Dad placed the lantern next to the temporary grave marker as everyone else gathered around the hole. The Strongmen set the pine box down over a pair of ropes nearby and moved several yards away.

Mom and Dad each kissed their fingertips, then laid them on the top of the coffin. Odelia kissed her fingers, wishing she could feel the tingle of her own Gift. When she touched the coffin, she couldn't transfer that power. There was nothing but rough pine under her hand and a cold wind blowing through the trees. Kennard put a warm hand on Odelia's back and gave Valerzan his goodbye kiss, then gently pressed her until she remembered to move on her own again.

As each person took their turn, Patricius passed them a shovel. The Strongmen used the ropes to lower the coffin into the ground, then bowed and walked away.

Dad dropped the first shovelful of dirt onto the box. The clay-heavy soil thudded on the wood. When Odelia's turn came, she sliced her shovel into the earth, and she couldn't help but shudder at the way it mirrored the wound she'd seen in her brother's chest.

After everyone had shoveled once, Herman and Kennard removed their jackets, then stood near the head and foot of the grave and began shoveling in earnest. After a while, Herman stepped aside for Patricius. Then Conora. Then Mom. Odelia took over a few minutes after her, but Kennard didn't stop. Not until Dad put a hand on his shoulder.

When the hole was filled, Dad picked up the lantern. "My son, you deserved a full royal procession, your name chanted through the streets of Iverish. We cannot give you that." He cleared his throat. "But we've buried you with our ancestors, and pray you find rest with the Giver. Eighteen..." He closed his eyes and took a deep breath as tears fell. "Eighteen years was not enough. I Saw the great warrior prince you could've become, that the world will never see."

Dad stepped over the grave and opened the lantern, exposing the flame inside. Mom held the pine cone over it, turning it back and forth until the resin dripped from it, and its scales began to open. She pressed the cone into the freshly turned soil.

"May a tree grow here, as Strong as you were in life," Dad said. "Rest well and find peace, Prince Valerzan."

Back at the inn, Patricius ordered food and drink. Though Odelia ate and drank while everyone swapped stories, she tasted nothing. Everything she'd avoided thinking about while she was running and fighting bubbled up and washed all her senses in funeral gray. Soon, she would have to bury these feelings again if she were to successfully make use of her time to plan with Kennard and Patricius. An early night's rest might make everything brighter in the morning.

Odelia said her good-nights and retired to her room. Though she'd fallen asleep so easily on the road back to Solace, she could only toss and turn now. She rolled from anger to numbness to pain and back. Shutting her eyes brought her no peace.

Before she could think through her actions, she was pulling a skirt and jacket on over her sleeveless chemise. In her bare feet, she snuck down the hallway to Kennard's room. Candlelight shone under his door. Odelia knocked softly.

She looked down at her half-dressed state. What was she doing? She started to turn back.

Kennard opened the door a crack and tilted his head. "Lia?"

Were there footsteps coming up the stairs? Odelia moved toward Kennard, and he stepped back to let her in, quickly closing the door behind her. He was barefoot and bare-chested, wearing only a pair of loose pants.

She looked away, then hugged her arms around herself and took a deep breath. "I couldn't sleep. I don't know why I came here, but I couldn't stay in my room."

He put his arm around her and led her toward the bed. "Why don't we just sit down?" He sat and pulled her down with him. "You were so quiet at dinner. Maybe you haven't said what you need to."

She gripped her skirt. "It's all so dark. And when I let myself feel, it's mostly anger. I'm angry at Tehazy. I'm angry at Gonfrid. I'm angry—" Odelia swallowed "—I'm angry at myself."

Kennard rubbed her back, concern etched over his face. "What do you mean?"

"Valerzan wanted me to run to Doivrie as soon as I told you the truth, and I wanted to give you more time, which was bad enough, but I should've run with you when Gonfrid threatened me. Maybe if we'd left, Valerzan would still be alive."

"Don't." Tipping her chin up, Kennard looked into Odelia's eyes. "Don't do this to yourself, love. I already have, and it doesn't help."

"Is that why you couldn't stop digging?"

"Yes."

"I want this all to end." Odelia looked at her skirt, smoothing the folds over her legs. "I have two weeks of access to Patricius and all my other followers, and I can't waste any more time." Taking a breath, she looked back up at Kennard. "If I claimed my throne now, would you stand by my side?"

He put his hand to her cheek, his dark eyes shining. "I will always stand by your side."

Her pulse quickened. "I'm asking you to overthrow your father."

Kennard held his gaze on her. "I know."

"This is treason."

"I can live with that."

Odelia couldn't look away from his beautiful face. There wasn't an ounce of hesitation in him. His devotion lightened the gray cloud over her.

He tucked her hair behind her ear. "What do you need me to do?"

Every word he said felt like a ray of sunlight from that morning's dawn.

"The troops Gonfrid sent you to gather are Vistan. We can turn them against him. If we don't let on what we're doing, he'll trust that the men are his, and it should be easy to surround him and demand surrender. And if Fort Vigil is anything like Solace, I doubt you'll have much resistance from the men already posted."

Kennard nodded. "I can do that. What else?"

"We need to strengthen our claim to the throne"—warmth crept up Odelia's cheeks—"which means we need to marry before you lead those men."

He furrowed his brows. "What happens if he finds out we've eloped before the coup?"

She leaned in close. "I guess we'll have to get good at hiding, but I can't sit back any longer. If I don't want any more blood on my hands, I have to take advantage of this opportunity to make Gonfrid surrender. I might not get another one."

"We," Kennard said. "We might not get another one."

Odelia smiled as tears spilled over. The hope and love he'd given her helped, but the pain and anger were still there. "I just keep expecting Valerzan to walk in here and tell us about his part of the plan."

Kennard laughed bitterly. "One of the last things he said to me was that he wouldn't have to go to our wedding if the Tehazian's got him." He teared up and shook his head. "Curse him for being right."

Odelia gasped. "Are we dishonoring his memory? Would he not—"

He put a finger to her lips. "Stop worrying. He made a joke. I couldn't help but taunt him all the time, and he always returned the favor. Val told us to run before. He'd be the first in favor of securing this plan."

Odelia sighed and laughed. "He was such a pain sometimes." Her laughter turned to crying again.

Kennard wiped her tears with his thumbs.

She looked up into his gentle, caring eyes. Food and drink and sleep had done nothing for her. Talking to him was the only thing that had made her feel anything good. Odelia needed to feel, to crawl out of her cave and be alive. Leaning closer to him, she pulled his face to hers and kissed him slowly, half expecting him to make her stop, to tell her it was wrong.

But he deepened the kiss, digging his fingers into her hair. With his eager lips, there was something desperate in his embrace that she'd never felt from him before. He slid his hand inside her jacket and around her waist, sending a delicious shiver up her spine as his touch warmed her through the thin fabric of her chemise. Giving into the passion of her own desperation, she buried her fingers in his soft curls and ran her hands over the hardened muscles of his torso. He pressed his body and his lips against her until she felt the bed under her back. His hands explored upward, caressing her breasts. It was more even more sensual than she'd expected, and as his fingers brushed over her with so little material between them, she let out a soft gasp. She wanted more.

His hand brushed down her side, lingering to caress her hip before working along her thigh to grasp the bare knee just under her skirt. She trailed her fingers down his back, curiosity taking hold as she hooked one under his waistband.

Kennard tensed, then scrambled off the bed, attempting to cover his arousal with one hand. His face was crimson. He ran his other hand through his hair and rubbed the back of this neck. "Lia, we can't."

Humiliation oozed over her, burning and sick. She took a shaky breath and covered her face with her hands.

He knelt by the side of the bed and took her hand. "I love you, and Giver knows how much I want you right now. I mean you're beautiful and half-dressed, and your hair is doing that messy, wavy thing that—" Eyes closed, he shook his head and cleared his throat. "I have regrets, Lia, and I don't want the first time we make love to be one of them. Taking advantage of your grief, that's not how I want to become one with you."

Odelia sniffed, holding back tears. Everything he said was rational, but it still felt like a rejection. She sat up and let him pull her up from the bed. "I'm sorry. I shouldn't have left my room."

Kennard put his arm around her shoulders. "Let me take you back." He opened the door and checked down the hallway, then escorted her into her room. He stepped inside and quietly closed her door.

Confused, she furrowed her brows. "I thought you didn't want to bed me."

He smirked. "Oh, I very much want to. I said I wasn't going to. But you came to me because you couldn't sleep, and I was thinking about how easily you fell asleep in the moose cart. I assume that's what you were wanting. If you can keep your hands to yourself, maybe I can help you sleep."

"I would like that," Odelia said softly. She began removing her jacket, keenly aware of his eyes following her movements. Between the bare shoulders and thin fabric, she was giving him quite the view. "Maybe you should turn around?"

He raised one eyebrow. "Says the woman who was going to take my pants off."

She turned her back to him. The chemise ended a little above her knees, but the front dipped low. Her covered bottom was preferable to flashing her bosom as she bent to shimmy out of the skirt.

Kennard laughed. "Looks like I got to see some of your undergarments today after all."

Pivoting back to glare at him, she realized he had, in fact, turned around as well. Odelia climbed into bed and pulled up the comforter. "I'm covered."

He sat next to her, wrapping his arms around her. With a gentle hand, he pressed her head to his chest and stroked her hair.

She sighed at the soothing movement. "If I were a cat, I think I'd be purring."

He chuckled. "If you start, I'll have to make Conora translate."

Odelia laughed and closed her eyes. It seemed like no time at all before consciousness slipped away.

All morning at breakfast, Ken had expected someone to call him out for the events of last night, but instead, Lia's parents had summoned them to their room. Though Ken had taken more liberties with Lia than he should've, he'd also been careful to check the hallway before he'd snuck back to his room once she'd fallen asleep. No one seemed suspicious of him, yet it still made him nervous. It was a good thing Lia wanted to elope soon. Ken wasn't sure he could hold out for thirteen more days. Stopping her from undressing him had taken all the willpower he had.

Ken held Lia's hand, lacing his fingers through hers as they stepped into Abhenric and Hortensia's room. Inside, Patricius and Conora were making small talk. Herman pointed to a large sack in center of the room. "What's in there?"

"A wedding dress—among other things," Abhenric said bluntly.

Lia put her free hand on her hip. "You knew. Mom wouldn't bring that unless you told her, which means you already knew when I was worrying about you withdrawing your approval. Why didn't you say so?"

Abhenric held out his hands apologetically. "You needed to get there on your own. I honestly thought it would take you a few more days, but your mom told me about the decision last night."

Ken and Lia tightened the grip on their handhold.

Frog nuggets. They had been caught. Ken's heart thudded. How much had Hortensia Heard? More importantly, how much had she told Abhenric? She hadn't tried to stop them or even said a word about it all morning.

Conora crossed her arms. "You're actually eloping this time?"

Ken smiled. "I think it's only half an elopement since the bride's parents are clearly involved."

Conora rolled her eyes. "Unless Father's changed his mind, he will hang Odelia."

"If things go according to plan, he won't be able to hang her or anyone else," Ken said.

Conora gaped. "Oh great Giver... Kennard, tell me you aren't talking about a coup. You've always rebelled against him, but that? For all his faults, he's still our father and—"

"And a cruel and callous king. He sent Val to his death. If Herman and Lia hadn't defied him, I'd be dead too." Ken shook his head in disgust.

"We all know Gonfrid's not stable," Lia said quietly. "You may not care about the plight of Vist, but he isn't even good for Elgatha anymore. This may be our only chance to do this peacefully."

Patricius scowled. "Why are the Elgathans even in the room for this discussion—with the exception of His Highness, of course?"

"I stand with Kennard," Herman said solemnly. "Like he said, I've already defied orders in an effort to save him. And I owe Odelia."

Abhenric nodded. "We had a long talk while we watched over Kennard the other day. As long as the prince is involved, Herman will be too."

Patricius crossed his arms. "And the princess? Who could be more inclined to warn the king than his own daughter?"

Ken raised his hand. "Um... I'm his son, and more involved than anyone."

"You're also madly in love with our queen," Patricius pointed out.

Ken put a hand on his sister's shoulder. "Father and Grandfather have threatened Lia. Mother hates her. Conora, you are the only family I trust to share in our wedding. Please, don't make me do this alone."

Conora pulled away and shook her head. "What kind of choice are you presenting me with? Either you and Odelia die as traitors, or I help you kill Father."

Lia reached for her, eyes wide. "No, no, no. We aren't trying to kill him. The plan is to capture him."

Sighing, Conora closed her eyes. "I love you both, and truly do want to see you happy together, but I can't participate in a coup—"

How could she do this to them again? Ken held up his hand and opened his mouth.

"—which is why I don't want to know anything more than wedding details. Tell me when it is and if there are things like dresses or flowers that I can help with, but I don't want to know anything else."

Ken hugged her. "Thank you. That's all I wanted."

Hortensia put a hand on Conora's back. "Let's go to your room." She picked up the bag on the floor. "You can give me your opinion on these wedding clothes."

Conora nodded and followed her out.

"What is the plan, Your Majesty?" Patricius asked.

Lia laid out her plan to use the Vistan troops to force a surrender, then bring Father back to Meria to stand before a gathering of the nobility. "The most important thing is formalizing our union. The sooner, the better."

Ken put his arm around her. "I'm ready to marry tonight if we have someone who can perform the ceremony."

Lia's eyes lit up. "Dad, since we haven't claimed the throne yet, you haven't officially abdicated. You have the power to marry us."

Abhenric smiled and nodded. "I can't think of anything better for my first, last, and only act as king."

Patricius shook his head. "This is a royal wedding. This inn is hardly fitting, and more witnesses can validate your claim. I can call a meeting of the Vistan nobility in Doivrie in ten days and give you a proper ceremony."

"More witnesses means more wagging tongues," Herman said.

"And make it that much harder for the Elgathan king to silence them and declare the marriage invalid."

Lia crossed her arms. "I'm not willing to wait that long. With the time to get the troops to Vigil, Kennard and I would have to leave the morning after the wedding."

"How long can you wait?" Patricius asked.

Lia reached up and scratched her neck as if in thought, but two of her fingers lingered near her vein. She was checking her Vitality. "Four days."

Ken's breath caught in his throat. Women's Vitalities cycled. It was too subtle to interpret from touching someone once, but after years of daily checking, Lia had internalized her rhythm. Even Ken was familiar enough with it to tell if he paid attention, and he'd run his fingers over her pulse points enough last night to know where she was.

Patricius furrowed his brow. "I can get you to Doivrie and send for Grandilord Straton and my own lords and pettilords, but I'm not sure that's enough time to get all of the lords and pettilords from Yophiex there. You need them in attendance to claim your title and solidify your union."

She sighed. "We can hold a meeting with the Vistan nobility after the wedding. There are—" blushing, Lia averted her gaze from Patricius and Abhenric "—more important ways to solidify this union. I won't wait more than four days."

Ken took a calming breath. If he wasn't sure before, Lia was definitely planning their wedding around her fertility. She'd failed to mention that last night. She was putting more trust in his Healing than he had, but he wasn't about to voice his reservations here. An earlier wedding still suited him, and the two of them could discuss this later. "You know, Herman makes a good point about the risk of witnesses," Ken said, desperate to change the subject.

Ignoring him, Patricius said to Lia, "You can always accomplish that later. I'm sure the prince will be very attentive. We need Vist to rise up together—"

Ken took a step toward Patricius. "Your Grace, I am not discussing this subject in front of my future father-in-law. Your opinion has been noted, and we are moving on."

Patricius narrowed his eyes. "I was speaking to Her Majesty."

"And *Her Majesty* has made her will known," Abhenric said.

Clasping his hands together, Patricius took a breath and stepped back. "Apologies, I will send Flight messengers to Yophiex as soon as we're done here."

"Are there any other details we need to establish before the wedding?" Herman asked.

"Until they can rule Meriveria jointly, Kennard will need a Vistan title," Abhenric said.

"Prince consort would be proper," Patricius said.

Lia put her arm around Ken's waist. "King consort."

Patricius pursed his lips, his face turning red.

She sighed. "What is the objection now?"

Patricius steepled his fingers. "There are those who would rather see an independent Vist. They may be a bit reluctant about your union in the first place, but naming him king will be an affront to them. You are simply trading one Elgathan king for another."

Ken shifted uncomfortably.

Lia looked up at him, her brow furrowed in thought, then turned to Patricius. "If he did nothing, he'd already be in line to be the King of Meriveria, but he's risking everything for me. And when he thought I was common, he was willing to raise me to his level. I cannot do less for him."

Ken couldn't resist a smile. He tucked a golden strand behind her ear. "Thank you, love, but it's just a title. You know it doesn't mean anything to me."

She put her hand to his chest. "But it's what it represents. Like you said, you and I are in this together, and your status should reflect that."

"What if you tell the Vistans about Kennard when you hold your meeting?" Herman suggested. "If you help them understand, maybe they'll be more open to him."

"You should give our people more credit, Patricius," Abhenric said.

"King consort it is," Patricius said. "Anything else?"

Lia nodded. "Make sure you invite Moira, Sergeant Rhonwin's wife. She'll be at the manor in Losuno. The two of them were my first allies, and if we can't keep Meriveria whole, they want to join Vist."

Patricius bowed, then left.

Ken frowned. "He was such a delightful host when I last saw him. Did I do something to offend him?"

"He likes being the one to make the plans," Abhenric said. "You should've seen how upset he was when I decided not to claim the throne. But he'll settle back down as Odelia asserts herself more."

Ken raised an eyebrow. "Are you sure he isn't more interested in an independent Vist?"

Lia shook her head. "Even if he is, he'd be a fool to turn on you, considering that you're integral to our plan."

"On second thought, maybe I should help him send those letters," Abhenric said, then walked out the door.

"Herman, would you mind making sure my things are packed?" Ken asked. "I'll meet you in my room later."

Herman nodded and dashed out.

"We should probably check on Mom and Conora." Lia took a step toward the door.

"It would've been nice if you'd told me about your plans to bear my children," Ken mused.

She pivoted slowly. "What does that mean?"

Ken crossed his arms. "You'll reach peak Vitality in a week, and four days from now gives you a perfect window of time. You want me to impregnate you as soon as possible."

Lia rolled her eyes. "Of course I do. Why do you sound so surprised? That's part and parcel to this marriage. Our heirs will secure the Treaty of Meriveria better than anything."

He took her hand in both of his, so soft and small, and traced the delicate lines of her fingers. "Patricius was right about one thing. We don't need them right away. You won't be safe as long as my father is in power, and I want to protect you from that before I put you in danger again."

She smiled sweetly. "I pulled you from the edge of death, and I trust that you can and will do the same for me. Besides, you're the one who wanted to marry tonight. What were you expecting to happen?"

He felt her wrist, the familiar hum of her Vitality shifting brighter than last night, but not at its brightest. Ken grinned. "I would expect a very fun night and nothing more."

Lia turned pink. "I can't believe you can tell that."

"Why not? I have almost as much practice with it as you do."

"And what were you planning to do later?" She took her hand back and pressed herself closer. "I doubt you'd want to stay away from me for a whole week."

He smiled. "Well, no, I hadn't planned on being intimate that way." Then he wiggled his eyebrows and whispered, "But there are other ways of being intimate, especially with this." He brushed his lips against her ear, counting on the tingling sensation to get his point across.

Backing away, she cleared her throat. "We really should check in on Mom and Conora."

Ken bit back a laugh. "You'll talk about fertility, but intimacy embarrasses you?"

"I'm not embarrassed. I'm suppressing the urge to ask you to show me." Lia put a hand over her mouth, eyes wide.

He laughed harder. "Wow. This is going to be a really long four days, isn't it?"

She nodded vigorously, then scowled in thought. "Our wedding night is set now. Would you really avoid consummating?"

Ken sighed. "Of course not, on the first night. But it still scares me."

"Then don't think of it as dangerous. Think of how it could protect me. Even if we fail to unite the Vistan and Elgathan nobility, Gonfrid couldn't attack me while I carry your heir because it would be his as well."

"It didn't stop him from sending me to that battle."

"He didn't do so publicly, did he?" Lia pointed out. "He can't afford to do that in front of the nobility when his crown is at stake."

"You're going to have an argument for every angle, aren't you?"

She smiled. "You know me too well."

He smiled back. "Not as well as I'd like, but we'll remedy that in a few days."

Lia scoffed. "And I thought I was bad last night. We should go before you succeed in tempting me into trouble."

The door to Conora's room opened before Odelia reached it.

Mom hefted a large bag over her shoulder. "I Heard. Four days." She adjusted her earmuffs and closed the door.

Kennard put a hand on Odelia's back. "How's Conora taking all this?"

"Fine," Mom said. "Once she saw your outfits, she relaxed a bit more and focused on that. She's packing now. I would definitely keep an eye on her, though. I doubt she means any harm, but just in case, I don't think we should let her send any messages without checking them first."

"That's probably for the best." Kennard rubbed the back of his neck. "Is there anything you need to know for your part of the planning?"

Mom shrugged. "No, I could Hear everything through the wall."

Kennard's eyes went wide.

Odelia suppressed a laugh. "What is it, Ken? Are you the one embarrassed by our conversation now?"

"I'm not thinking about the one we just had," he said.

"Oh," Odelia said softly. "I guess you did mention that earlier, didn't you?"

Mom waved it off and shook her head. "What's done is done. I don't want any more details."

"Nothing happened," Kennard insisted.

"You were in and out of each other's rooms, which is something enough," Mom whispered.

Odelia bit her lip. "How much did you tell Dad?"

"Only what he needed to know," Mom said.

Odelia's face was warm. "If you knew what I was trying to do, why didn't you stop me?"

Mom sighed. "You're a grown woman, Odelia. Your choices are your own."

She had raised Odelia to use her head, not give in to impulse, and she didn't need words to show her disappointment. The look in her eyes said everything.

Odelia nodded. "I'm going to get my bag," she said quietly, then returned to her room.

Four days. She only needed to hold back for the next four days.

19

EVERGREEN VOWS

The next four days went by so quickly that they practically strung together in Odelia's head. Mom and Conora kept her busy planning every wedding detail, the three of them sewing all the while. After months in Fort Solace, the wedding dress, made from the same dimensions as her last gown, didn't fit Odelia as closely as designed. And judging by the alterations needed for Kennard's clothes, he had lost weight as well.

Conora lamented the lack of flowers available so early in the spring until she discovered an indoor arboretum on the top floor of the manor. It was filled with dogwood trees, all blooming early from the warmth inside. She deemed them passable, though lacking variety. Odelia decided they were perfect.

Of course, in between all of this, Vistan nobility trickled in, quickly filling all the rooms in the manor. Odelia, Kennard, and Patricius greeted each one, tracking how many soldiers they had coming in their wake.

Despite the exhaustion of getting everything ready in such a short time, Odelia awoke early on her wedding day. While she waited for a hot bath and breakfast, she burned off a little nervous energy with dagger practice. She moved through her forms, her steps light, but not light enough to keep from waking Mom, who leaned against the door frame, arms crossed. She yawned and smiled. "Too excited to sleep?"

Odelia grinned. "Yes. You and Conora were still going over a few things when I went to bed last night. Did you get it all settled?"

"She doesn't know it yet, but yes."

"You're almost as cryptic as Dad."

"You'll see soon, but it sounds like your bath is on its way in first." Mom waved and slipped out the door.

Odelia groaned. That didn't help her excitement at all.

She bathed and ate quickly, eager to get dressed so she could move on to whatever Mom was hinting at. With her chemise, petticoat, and bust bodice on, Odelia began pinning her hair up. Her normally deft fingers fumbled with the silky strands, and after the third pin in a row shot out of her hands to the floor, she pulled everything out and shook her fingers through her hair. Clearly, she needed reinforcements. Opening the door, she found both Mom and Conora in the sitting room. Odelia grimaced. "Help? I'm hopeless with my hair today."

They hopped up from their chairs and into her bedroom. Mom set a decent-sized wooden box on the vanity. Conora twirled a piece of Odelia's hair around her finger. "This could never be hopeless. Do you know how enamored my brother is with your hair?"

"Really? My hair?" She could think of a couple other things he was definitely fond of, but he hadn't said that much about her hair.

Conora smiled. "I wasn't very old then, but I'll never forget the day we met you and Valerzan, because Kennard wouldn't stop talking about your hair." She laughed. "He couldn't decide if it was made of butter or gold, but either way, he wanted to touch it."

That made sense. She hadn't thought about it before, but Kennard always buried his fingers in Odelia's hair when he kissed her. She chuckled. "Now that you say it, I guess he does like to play with my hair."

Conora laughed. "We should do something complicated so he has to work for it."

Mom shook her head. "Simple and elegant is more appropriate. Besides, she already told us what she was going to do, so I'm not going to change it." She twisted a few pieces back from Odelia's left temple, gathering the hair into a loose and piece-y roll, then pinned it in place and copied it on the right. At the back, she braided the rest, then pulled on each loop of hair until the plait doubled in width and shortened.

Conora pursed her lips. "It needs something. Maybe some flowers?"

"Let's get the dress on first." Mom held it out for Odelia to step into, then stepped back to let her shimmy the shoulder straps and waistline into place.

Odelia smoothed out the front of the gown, the pine and moss satin brocade both smooth and textured under her fingers. Conora held the dress closed for Mom, who worked her magic, lacing and tightening ribbons under the narrow panels on Odelia's back, which were designed to pull closed and create an invisible fastening that looked like a normal seam.

"Do you have the flowers?" Mom asked.

Conora nodded. "I'll go get them."

As soon as she was out of the room, Mom led Odelia to the full-length mirror. "Close your eyes."

Odelia did. Behind her, the box opened and closed.

"Open," Mom said.

Odelia gasped.

Mom was lowering a rose gold tiara onto her head. Light salmon gems studded it, melding into the color of the metal but catching the light as it moved. The delicate floral design gave it an air of weightlessness, but it was surprisingly dense as Mom settled it a couple inches back from Odelia's hairline. Mom put her hands around her shoulders and gave a teary smile. "This has been waiting for six generations to be worn. It would've been mine if your dad had gone through with his claim, but I like it better on you."

Odelia covered her bursting heart with her hand. Despite all the talk of the throne and her title, *this* made it real. "I look like a queen," she whispered.

Mom chuckled. "That's the idea."

Used to finery, Ken was dressed and ready long before Patricius and Abhenric came to fetch him. They weren't expecting to start the ceremony for another hour, but Patricius insisted that he needed either him or Lia, and he refused to disturb a bride in the midst of getting ready. They led Ken to the great hall, in front of an assembly of Vistan nobles. In spite of Patricius's reservations about the early date, all of the Vistan nobility had managed to arrive, the last few trickling in through the early morning. Ken wasn't sure whether to be impressed or worried by the grandilord's ability to inspire such a quick response. The lords and pettilords of Doivrie were bound to jump at the word of their liege, but those from Yophiex had no obligation to follow him and much farther to travel.

With a wave of his hand, Patricius gathered the attention of everyone. "For the sake of Vist, what will transpire today is not to leave this room. I don't need to remind any of you what the Treaty of Meriveria says. The Elgathans require us all to keep a copy in our great halls—" he motioned to the document, hanging on the wall behind him "—to remind us, to keep us accepting. But they're the ones who have forgotten what the treaty was made for. Today, two people are going to make that right. I'm going to let Crown Prince Kennard explain."

Ken swallowed hard and whispered, "Shouldn't Lia be here for this?"

Patricius patted him on the back. "You'll do fine. She'll have her turn to address everyone after the wedding."

With a nod, Ken took a deep breath and smiled at the crowd. "By now, you all have met my private secretary, Mistress Odelia DiOrto." He put a hand on Abhenric's shoulder. "Her father, Abhenric is here with us now. Over the past several months I've discovered two things about her. The first is the love she and I share for one another, and the second—which is more important to all of you—is her ancestry."

A murmur rippled through the crowd. Abhenric gave him a solemn nod to continue.

"You will all be witnesses to the unfolding of King Uldrio's most famous vision. If you can't tell, I'm dressed for a wedding—my wedding, and my bride is the heir to the royal Vistan line."

The murmur rose to a rumble.

Ken raised his voice louder. "Vist will have a queen once more."

Patricius clapped until all of the nobles joined in thunderous applause. As he raised his hand, it died back down again. "I cannot emphasize enough that all of this must be kept secret."

Ken nodded. "Many lives are at stake, especially your queen's. If word reaches my father before we're ready to face him...he will kill her."

There were gasps and more murmurs.

Patricius raised his hand again. "Which is why for the next week, none of you will be leaving this manor, and messages out will be watched. Once this union is complete, it cannot be undone. Our queen will forever be joined with him. If anyone has questions, ask them now."

A blond man who looked about Abhenric's age stood up. "What you're promising is too good to be true. How did you find the heir to a dead bloodline? How do we know this isn't a hoax?"

"We have proof." Abhenric held up Lia's authenticated scroll, which Hortensia had brought from Meria. "See for yourself." He unrolled it and motioned for the man to come forward.

The man approached and read the scroll. His eyes widened in disbelief. "It's real..."

"Did you think I would go to this effort for anything less?" Patricius asked. "Does anyone else need to see it?"

Several more nobles came forward to check the scroll for themselves. The last, an older gentleman with white hair, turned to Ken with narrowed eyes. "Why should we trust you? The last time a marriage like this was attempted, our royal family conveniently died and made way for yours. They wouldn't have hidden for this long if they weren't afraid of someone powerful. What's to stop you Elgathans from killing this queen too?"

"He's marrying her in half an hour," Patricius said. "If he wanted to repeat his ancestors' treachery, he's run out of time."

The older man shook his head. "I'm sure he's learned from their mistake. He'd be smarter to wait until after the wedding—or even smarter, after she's given him an heir. There's nothing stopping him from exploiting her and the treaty, then returning to the Elgathan status quo. Only a fool would entrust their treasure to a fox."

Several people murmured in agreement.

Ken recoiled. "What you've just described is my greatest nightmare, not my plan." He put his hand over his heart. "Lia is the love of my life. I would rather kill myself than her. Even if she wasn't, with our Gift, she and I together are each other's only chances at a long life."

"I'm a Seer," Abhenric added. "There's not a chance I would let this happen if I Saw such a thing. This is the best possible future for her and for Vist."

Ken continued, "And let's not forget King Uldrio's vision. Is that enough to put you at ease, or does the Giver himself need to proclaim his approval directly?"

The man furrowed his brows. "You said your father would kill her. What do you think he'll do to the rest of us for participating? How can you protect us all from that?"

"If we all play our parts correctly, my father will not be your king anymore," Ken said.

The man scoffed. "So we should trust your word that we won't hang for treason?"

"Show a little courage," a woman's voice said.

The man scowled and looked behind him, where an Elgathan woman slowly pushed herself to standing, revealing a large belly. She must've have been one of the last to arrive while Ken was getting dressed, because her poncho was draped over one arm. Even without the introduction, that was clearly Rhonwin's wife.

"You cannot hope to change anything without it," Moira said, "and it is time for the current reign to end. I have Seen what Queen Odelia is capable of, which is why the arion of Atmos is offering support and requesting to be annexed if Vist becomes independent."

The older man returned to his seat, a little pink in the face.

Ken smiled at Moira. "Thank you."

She bobbed a short but awkward curtsy and sat back down.

When nobody else rose for a while, Abhenric put his hand on Ken's back. "I'll check on the women and let them know we're ready."

Most of the Vistans talked amongst each other. Ken nervously played with his fingers behind his back. He would've liked to pass the time with a little conversation as well, but Moira was the only one he had anything to say to, and after the suspicions against him, it probably wouldn't be wise to approach the only other Elgathan in the room. Ken adjusted the circlet Hortensia had smuggled in for him amongst his wedding clothes. It seemed like an eternity before Abhenric returned again, smiling, with Hortensia at his side and Herman and Conora behind them.

"They were waiting for me," Abhenric said.

Conora laughed. "Odelia's as eager as you are to get started."

Patricius bowed and took a seat, and Abhenric took his place, facing the center of the room. Ken stood to his left, with Conora and Herman behind him. Hortensia stood a few paces to Abhenric's right. As the drums started, Ken took a deep breath.

Then, the doors opened, and that breath was gone.

As beautiful as Lia had been on the night he proposed, she somehow surpassed it this morning. The evergreen fabric of her gown—a symbol of undying devotion and their new life together—hugged her from her waist to the low sweetheart neckline. The only jewelry she wore was a delicate tiara that he'd never seen before. His mother and sister always wore more heavily jeweled and robust tiaras, but this dainty one on his bride suited her. In her hands, she carried a cedar branch, woven into a circle and dotted with dogwood flowers. She walked gracefully past the gathered nobles and stood before him. She put her hands through the tiny wreath and took his. Her smile lit up his soul. The green of her dress matched her eyes, and when her gaze met his, he couldn't look away.

He was vaguely aware that Abhenric had begun speaking. Ken smiled at Lia, his best friend, his beloved, his bride, his soulmate... This was finally happening!

A crease formed between her perfect eyebrows. "Ken?" she whispered anxiously.

Oh no.

Abhenric had stopped talking. Ken was supposed to say something. But what? Was it "I do"? He had to say *something*—now even Abhenric was looking at him strangely. "I do," Ken said, projecting confidence but hoping he wasn't mucking everything up.

Lia let out a breath and smiled again.

"How do you pledge your devotion?" Abhenric asked.

Ken took the ring off her finger and moved it to her other hand. "This ring is my pledge, the offer of my heart."

Abhenric said, "And do you, Crown Princess Odelia DiOrto of Vist, accept Crown Prince Kennard of Elgatha as your husband?"

"I do!" She beamed and squeezed Ken's hands.

"How do you pledge your devotion?"

Lia untied a thick gold band, set with an emerald and a sapphire, from the bottom of the wreath and slid it onto Ken's finger. "This ring is my pledge, the offer of my heart."

Abhenric smiled softly. "Under my power as the King of Vist, I declare you wed. You may now seal your vow with a kiss."

Ken nearly burst with happiness. He cupped Lia's face with both hands and leaned down. One of her hands rested on his chest as she stood on tiptoe to meet him. Though the kiss was brief—relatively speaking—the soft touch of her lips filled his whole body with warmth.

The witnesses applauded. Ken smiled and took Lia's hand, ready to lead her away, but Abhenric put a hand on his shoulder.

"This next part is important too." Abhenric raised his hand until the room fell silent. "In the interest of maintaining the unity of our peoples and in accordance with the laws of Vist and the Treaty of Meriveria, I hereby renounce my claim to the throne of Vist and leave my title to my heir, Crown Princess Odelia." He took the wreath from Lia, then put Ken and Lia's linked hands through it and raised them high. "I now present to you Their Majesties, Queen Odelia and King Kennard of Vist. Long live the queen and king!"

After the documents had been signed for the marriage and abdication, Patricius brought out chairs for Odelia and Kennard and led all of the nobility in expressing congratulations and declarations of loyalty—one-by-one. When that was finished, a feast was served, and as they ate, each noble once again visited with them personally. At first, Kennard seemed content with putting a hand on Odelia's knee under the table as they ate, but as more and more well-wishers joined them, his hand had snuck a few inches up her thigh.

"I think he's the last one," Odelia whispered as the Lord of Embit walked back to his seat.

Kennard stood and offered his hand. "I think it's about time we leave everyone else to eat in peace. Don't you?"

She grinned. "How thoughtful." She took his hand and let him pull her up, thankful for the help in her heavy gown.

As they crept through the door, hand-in-hand, someone called out, "Lllong lllive the Queen an' King o' Vissst!" and a round of cheers erupted.

Odelia giggled. "I think Patricius might've been a bit free with the mead."

"Why? Are you afraid you partook of too much?" Kennard teased. He let go of her hand and slipped his arm around her waist.

"Well, considering the effects of your kisses"—she walked her fingers up his chest—"I don't think that's possible."

He pulled her into a rough kiss. The power behind it was overwhelming, and she involuntarily pressed closer. As they broke, he stared back at her hungrily.

"We should get to your room quickly," she said breathlessly.

He took her hand again, and they silently raced up the stairs, down the hallway, and through his sitting room as fast as Odelia's skirts would allow, pausing only to close the doors. As the second one clicked shut, her stomach fluttered. For all her desire, this was new territory, and being outside of a heated moment, being planned and expected added a surprising level of anxiety.

Kennard exhaled. "So much for a quick ceremony. I thought that feast would never end." He pulled off his boots and dropped them by the door.

Odelia backed deeper into the room, edging away from the bed. "Well, it's over now."

He crossed the room in three steps and swept her into an embrace. She jumped ever so slightly and stiffened. With a frown, he tucked a stray hair behind her ear, his eyes soft with concern. "What's wrong, love?"

"I'm sorry. I wasn't this nervous the other night."

He gave her a crooked smile that meant he was trying his hardest not to laugh. "This was your idea, and you were very adamant that we do this tonight."

The blood drained from her face. "I know," she squeaked.

Kennard's eyes lit up. "Oh...I see. I'm quite familiar with this problem."

Eyes wide, Odelia gasped. "You are? But I thought— You never told me you'd done this before." She thought she'd been privy to all his secrets.

He laughed. "What? No. I meant this." He gently lifted the tiara off her head. "These crowns are so uncomfortable, it's hard to think with that on your head." He set the tiara on a table. "Let's see...ah." Still using a gentle touch, he started pulling pins out of her hair, combing his fingers through it until it fell around her shoulders, then raking them over her scalp. The light massage was relaxing, and she closed her eyes and let out a soft moan.

"There's my Lia," Kennard cooed.

Odelia chuckled. "My body is yours now, and the first thing you fondle is my hair."

Grinning mischievously, he slid his hands down her back and squeezed her bottom. "Is that better?"

"Yes." She tipped her head up to kiss him, but a glint of gold caught her eye. Running her fingers through his soft brown curls, she grasped his circlet. "I should make you more comfortable too." She turned and set it on the table next to her tiara.

He wrapped his arm around her stomach and swept her hair over her shoulder. She gasped as his kisses on her neck sent tingles down her spine and flooded her body with warmth. Wanting to give him the same, she reached up and dug her fingers into his hair, pulling him to her mouth. He spun her to face him. Her pulse raced. His hands ran up and down her back with searching fingers. She slid his jacket off without releasing from the kiss, relishing the feel of his strong arms underneath her hands. In one fluid motion, he pulled away and removed his shirt.

Odelia let out a ragged breath and ran her hands over his bronze chest. "I can't believe you're mine. How am I so lucky?"

Kennard chuckled. "You might change your mind if this dress defeats me. Turn around." He pivoted her on her toes. His fingers moved up and down her back, poking along the seams. "How does this work?"

She felt behind her for his hand and slid it down past the small of her back. "There should be a bow or a knot under one of the skirt pleats if you reach down a little farther."

After some honest fumbling and a few unsubtle gropes, she felt a tug, and the dress expanded with her next inhale. A familiar whooshing sound meant he was pulling the laces out of the holes. When he reached the end, the back fell open, and she stepped out. He raised one eyebrow. "A dress under your dress?"

She shrugged and pulled off the petticoat, then reached for the lacing on her bust bodice.

He put his hand over hers. "Allow me. This one looks too fun." He pulled slowly on the ribbon until it popped loose, then hooked his finger through the loops and pulled until the whole thing fell off, leaving her chemise underneath. Kennard groaned. "For Giver's sake, Lia, how many layers are you wearing?"

Odelia laughed. "This is the last one, I promise. You can feel for yourself." Guiding his hands back to her body, she could feel his warm hands through the thin fabric, exploring her, making her ache for more.

He kissed her again, trailing his lips down until the neckline of her chemise blocked his path. "It's still too much." He yanked the offending garment over her head. Moving back a step to look at her, he let out a shuddering sigh and grinned.

She kissed him deeply, not letting go as she unbuttoned his pants. He lifted her off the ground and pulled her legs around his waist. Wrapping his arms around her, he started walking. His ability to do so while kissing her was impressive—until her back hit a bedpost. He mumbled an apology into her lips, then fell down on the bed with her in his arms.

Odelia giggled. "I don't think I'll ever be able to forget our wedding night now."

Kennard ran his hand up her leg. "Let's see if I can give you something better to remember."

Flashing a mischievous smile, he pressed his lips to her inner thigh, and the jolt of it, the power coursing straight through her, tensed, then relaxed her entire body in the course of an instant. He repeated it on the other side, forcing a whimper of pleasure from her. Again and again, he kissed her, moving his lips and his fingers a little closer each time. The tingling was so strong now that she trembled. She whimpered once more as he found her center, the shock turning the tremble into a quake.

"Wait," she panted.

He lifted his head, brows knit together. "Is it too much? Am I doing it wrong?"

She brushed back a curl that had fallen into his eyes and smiled. "No...I...just..." She forced herself to take a slower, deeper breath. "I want to see you first."

Kennard exhaled and smiled back. "I thought it might be easier for you if I waited until afterward. I don't want you to get nervous again."

Odelia chuckled. "Well, now you're just boasting. You aren't a small man. I already assumed that if it's as well proportioned as the rest of you..." She raised one eyebrow and took hold of the waistband of his drawers, smirking at the visible strain on them. "I'm more afraid you might rip this seam." As she pulled them down, he sprang free, proving himself as proportional as expected.

He bit back a laugh. "You just went pale."

"No, I didn't. I'm always this color."

He brushed her cheek. "It's all right, love. I'll go back to what I was doing. You seemed to enjoy that."

Just thinking about it brought a smile to her face. "It's not exactly what we're expected to do, though, is it?"

Tracing his fingers over her breasts, he met her gaze. "It is. I've heard that it's better if I...make you ready. That if I do it right, I'm not supposed to hurt you." He looked away and chuckled nervously. "The problem is I heard a lot more about *what* I'm supposed to do than *how much*."

Her silly anxiety was making him worry now. She shook her head. "We're overthinking this." Pushing his hand back down, she encouraged his fingers back into the position she'd interrupted him from. "This is...mmm...it's good...but there's another way...one that only you can do." She gasped and turned his head, his eyes hungry as they met hers. "A faster way."

He nodded vigorously.

Odelia pushed Kennard onto his back, then rolled over to sit astride his waist. She pulled up onto her knees and inched back. "I know you won't hurt me."

He smiled. "Never."

"That's why I'm going to be the one to do it."

His eyes widened, but he couldn't stop her. She sat hard, crying out as the pain ripped into her.

"Lia?" He grabbed her shoulders and pulled her down into a kiss.

The pain disappeared, replaced with the most exquisite sensation of simultaneous satiation and yearning. With her maidenhead gone and the tearing Healed, the results of Kennard's careful ministrations could be fully appreciated, allowing her to slide smoothly.

He frowned. "Why? I would've been gentle."

Odelia thrust her hips, eliciting a moan from him. "That's why. Now the rest of the night is ours to share without holding back."

Kennard put his hands around her waist and looked up at her, concerned. "I'm not still hurting you, am I?"

A giggle turned into a squeal of pleasure. "This is anything but pain."

With a grin, he pressed her hips down and guided her into a faster rhythm. "Then, hold tight."

She obliged, squeezing her legs as he bucked and rolled them both over. Now in control, he strengthened the rhythm as he leaned forward, his body bearing heavily on hers. His pace quickened more, years of untapped longing fueling his ardor as much as hers. Rapturous desire built with each heartbeat, and she lifted her head to kiss him, sending a tingling warmth to mingle with the sensuous swells surging through her, crescendoing in a seizing shudder that forced her to cry out as loudly as before—but this time in sweet, violent ecstasy. Every part of her clasped to him; she arched her back, desperate not to lose his touch. More tingles swept her as he covered her mouth with his until he tautened with a grunt, quivering inside her and filling her. When he pulled away, for the briefest moment, she mourned the severing of their physical connection.

Odelia laid her head back on the bed and blew a limp golden strand from her face. It only moved an inch before clinging to a damp cheek. She panted as Kennard tucked the stubborn hair behind her ear. He bent closer and kissed her forehead. His dark eyes sparkled with mischief. "Again?"

She smiled and let out a weak laugh. "Yes!"

Ken awoke the next morning to a knock on the door. He looked down at his wife, still asleep under his arm, with her back against his chest, her golden hair spilling wildly across his pillow. His wife. How long before he got used to thinking that? He could scarcely believe the events of yesterday were real—especially what had transpired last night.

He eased himself out of bed, careful not to wake Lia, and pulled the covers over her shoulder. The shock of cold air on his bare skin made him shiver. Searching the sea of discarded clothing, he hoped to find a blanket or something warm, but another knock sounded at the door, and he didn't want to disturb Lia. Ken opened the door a crack, keeping as much of himself behind it as possible.

"There's a messenger for you downstairs," Herman said.

"Can't you take the message for me?"

"It's from your father, and he wants it delivered personally."

Ken groaned. "Okay, let me get some clothes on."

Herman shoved a bottle of mead in his face. "You'll want to drink this."

Ken raised an eyebrow. "Why?"

"I told him you were nursing a hangover after a long night of drinking away your sorrows."

Ken was not awake enough for this game. "Again, why?"

Herman cleared his throat. "I didn't have many good excuses to work with. It's almost noon, and you're still in bed. Would you rather I told him you were up all night deflowering your wife?"

Ken sighed. "Fair enough." He took a large swig, then dipped his finger in and rubbed some on his neck.

"Speaking of which: how is she? You were rather...loud..."

Ken put his hands up. "The only bad sound was not my fault, okay? She fell asleep smiling." He dabbed a little more on. "Who's with the messenger now?"

"Abhenric and Patricius." Herman sniffed. "You're gonna need more than that. You smell like a rutting elk."

Ken wrinkled his nose. "How do you know what a rutting elk smells like— On second thought, I'd rather not know." He splashed some more on. "Is that enough?"

Herman took a whiff. "You smell like an alcoholic beehive."

"Perfect." Ken closed the door, then went to his bag and pulled out a rugged pair of pants and a plain shirt. He dressed quickly and sloppily, leaving his shirt mostly untucked and askew. As he left, he smiled at Lia's sleeping form and gently shut the door. "Where's the messenger?"

"Patricius's office."

"Okay. Is there someone else to guard Lia? If he has someone with him or ends up wandering, I don't want anyone to see her leaving our room."

Herman nodded. "There are two Vistan Strongmen just outside now."

Ken smiled and clapped a hand to his back.

Shuffling his way down the stairs, Ken squinted groggily and made his gait uneven. Thanks to his Healing, alcohol took a long time to pass through him. If he really had drunk enough to completely reek and pass out all morning, he'd still be hammered by now. If he played the belligerent drunk more than a normal hangover, maybe he could annoy the messenger into leaving quickly. Patricius's door was already open a crack, and Ken launched himself into it, slamming it open. "I'm here. Wadda ya want?"

A large Elgathan man with black wings jumped back, then bowed. "I have a message for you from His Majesty, Your Highness," he said quietly.

Ken reeled. "Ssshhhhhhhh... Not ssso loud..." He rubbed his temples. He put a hand on the messenger's shoulder and leaned in, making sure to breathe in the poor man's face. "Whatsa message?"

The messenger wrinkled his nose and blinked. "His Majesty has heard that Vistan nobles were traveling here. He's impressed by your efficiency and is ordering your return now."

Ken shook his head. "Thasss no good. Got noblesss, but no men."

"What do you mean, no men?"

"If I may?" Patricius smiled and held up a hand. "What His Highness is trying to say is that the troops are still en route. Even with all the nobility requesting them as quickly as possible, it takes time for a large group to move."

"How much time do you need?" the messenger asked.

"Two more days," Abhenric said. "If we leave in two days, we can all get there four days from now. That's still much earlier that His Majesty originally asked for, and it's as fast as the men will be able to move."

The messenger huffed. "I can tell him and have his answer back by tonight, but you should have your bags ready. Also, I have this for you." He stretched his arm out and handed Ken two letters. "Do you have any other messages for His Majesty?"

Ken frowned, brooding as hard as he could. "Tell 'im he wasss right. I'm not—" he gagged "—not pursssuing Mistress Odelia anymore."

With a bow, the messenger left. Nobody spoke as his footsteps echoed down the hallway. They watched through the window as he flew away outside.

Ken exhaled. "Thank the Giver that's over. Lia should probably stay out of sight until he comes back."

"Was the lie really necessary?" Abhenric asked.

Ken shrugged. "It wasn't a complete lie. I don't need to pursue Lia because she's already mine. Besides, a little capitulation is what got us out here in the first place. If he thinks he's won that battle, he might be more inclined to give us those extra two days."

"What's in the letters?" Patricius asked.

"I'll open them with Lia. We can discuss this further after I let her know what's happening." Ken bounded out of the room before they could object. The interruption was bad enough. He didn't want anyone to keep him from her longer.

Fingers ran down Odelia's back and around her waist. A soft kiss tingled her shoulder. She shivered and let out a low hum.

"Good morning, Wife."

She smiled and rolled over. "Good morning, Husband."

Kennard was sitting on the bed behind her, haphazardly dressed and giving her a crooked grin. She sat up to give him a kiss, but an olfactory assault stopped her a few inches short. "Why do you smell like a drunkard?"

He laughed. "It was Herman's idea. Father sent a Flight messenger, who insisted on seeing me personally. Herman had to explain why I was still in bed, and the truth—that it's because the most beautiful woman in Meriveria is there—was out of the question."

"You don't have to try so hard, man," Herman called out through the ajar door. "She already married you."

Kennard blushed. "I thought I closed that." He walked over to the door. "Nobody asked for your opinion, Herman," he said, then closed it.

Odelia stretched and caught a whiff of herself. She was pretty rank as well. "We should call for baths."

Kennard crawled onto the bed beside her. "Already done. I asked for one on the way back from Patricius's office." He grinned. "I was hoping we could share it."

She chuckled. "We could, but we have to actually bathe. I want nothing more than to stay in here with you, but if we don't do some planning soon, we might not have much time left together."

He snuggled close and slid his hand down her stomach, sending little flutters through it. "I thought you were interested in another type of planning."

"I am." She gasped as his hand found its mark. "Tonight..."

"I'm going to hold you to that."

"I'd be disappointed if you didn't."

Someone knocked on the door, and Kennard and Odelia both pulled up the covers.

Two servants wheeled in a steaming tub of water and left a bar of soap and a small stack of towels next to their crowns on the table. They bowed and left quickly, shutting the door firmly behind themselves.

Odelia tiptoed across the cold floor and slipped into the hot water with a sigh. Kennard took off his shirt and picked up the soap. Kneeling behind her, he drew her hair over her shoulder and kissed her exposed neck, then dipped the soap in the water and scrubbed her back. The pressure of his strong hands and the heat of the water would drive her to distraction if she let them. She took a deep breath. "What was the message?"

"Message?"

"The one you doused yourself in mead for."

He cleared his throat. "Father wants me to head back to Fort Vigil right away."

Her heart stopped. She gripped the edge of the tub. "What?"

He put a hand on her shoulder. "It'll be okay. Abhenric and Patricius told the messenger we need two more days for the soldiers to arrive here."

"That's still cutting things close."

"I know."

Odelia scowled. "You didn't think that would be important to tell me before you started seducing me?"

"Well, the messenger will be coming back with Father's reply sometime before tonight, so—"

"So you wanted to take me while you could, in case he says no." She couldn't object to his reasoning there.

Kennard started scrubbing again. "Something like that."

"Was there anything else?"

"Here." He handed her the soap and stepped away. "He gave me these letters, but I haven't opened them yet."

"Who are they from?"

"My parents..." He opened a letter. "Father wants me to return to Meria after I deliver the troops. That's why he wants me back early."

Odelia leaned forward. "If he doesn't say, then I'm guessing this is Melaine's doing. That doesn't bode well. Do you think Conora's betrayed us?"

Kennard shook his head. "She hasn't had the opportunity." He opened the second letter. Eyebrows raised, he burst into laughter. "Mother...she..." He looked at Odelia and doubled over.

His laughter was infectious, and Odelia joined him. "What?"

He sighed. "Oh, she's going to be so disappointed. The thing I'm supposed to return to Meria for? It's a wedding!"

Odelia's eyes widened. "You're joking. I guess it's good I claimed you yesterday while I still could."

Kennard looked over the letter again. "She's gathering the Elgathan nobility for the ceremony and wants me to send the Vistans to join them."

Odelia gasped. Their next step after capturing Gonfrid was to gather the nobility to put him on trial. "She's bringing together everyone we need when we need them? Either she knows something, or the Giver is smiling on us."

He shook his head. "She started this a while ago."

"If that's what you're heading back for, do you think Gonfrid will grant you the time we need to gather troops? Our plan requires them."

He moved behind her. "I hope so. We have eleven days to get to Meria, and they're not even expecting me to march there from Vigil, so it should be plenty of time."

Odelia sighed. "And if he doesn't, we may have to hold our ground and declare Vistan independence."

Kennard pressed the soap into her back. "Scooch up." She slid forward, and he climbed in, wrapping his arms and legs around her. "See, I knew there was room in here." He pulled her back against his chest and kissed her cheek. "We'll do what we must. If that means independence, I am with you."

"Even if we leave in two days, we're cutting into our other plans. Would you be too shy to make love in a tent?"

"When have I ever been shy?"

Odelia smiled. "True. I should have known better."

"Speaking of which..." Kennard held her tighter. "I've been thinking. Carrying our child is going to be dangerous for you. I know it's necessary, and I can accept it in spite of my fear. But I want to protect you, and facing my father feels like a needless risk. And with his change of orders, I'm scared of what will happen to you if he changes his mind again."

"We can't avoid confronting him," she said quietly.

"I could go alone. Knowing you're waiting here safely will put me at ease."

"Absolutely not." She turned around to kneel between his legs, her hands on his shoulders, eyes locked with his. "We are stronger together. Right now, our best allies are Vistans, and their loyalty to you is on my behalf. I'm sure a few of them would have no qualms about letting things fall apart with Gonfrid to force Vist to separate. But as the last heir to the Vistan throne, they're less inclined to let harm come to me. For all your worry about protecting me, right now, I'm the one who needs to protect you."

"And here, I thought I owed you for saving me already."

Odelia leaned closer and smiled. "If you do your duty as consort soon enough, you can return the favor in nine months."

He chuckled. "That's what I've been trying to do. And if you're willing to be quick, I think we could try now *and* tonight."

Her whole body warmed. "Show me what you had in mind."

20

A CAGED MONARCH

When the messenger returned four hours later, Ken had him sent to his sitting room, leaving the bedroom door open a crack so Lia could listen. Herman stood sentry in front of it. If the message from Father wasn't favorable, she could step out and deliver a message of her own.

Patricius accompanied the messenger, who bowed.

"What is the word from my father?" Ken asked.

"His Majesty was greatly displeased to hear of the state Your Highness was in before, but you seem much better now." The messenger looked at him curiously, eyes narrowed.

Ken needed to throw off the suspicion. He gave a lecherous smirk. "Well, in spite of the circumstances, Mistress Odelia is still good for a Healing, isn't she?"

Patricius didn't hide his frown of disgust as the messenger nodded. He was a good actor. Ken caught himself worrying that Patricius actually believed him.

"What did he say about returning?" Ken asked.

The messenger clasped his hands in front of him. "In light of your recent cooperation, you may have the extra two days you requested. His Majesty requires news of your progress. Expect to see the occasional scout as you make your way to Fort Vigil."

Ken smiled. "Thank you. Send my appreciation to my father as well."

With a bow, the messenger left, escorted by Herman.

Patricius shook his head. "I don't like this sneaking around or hearing you speak of our queen that way. Our time to rise up can't come soon enough."

"I don't like it either," Ken said, "but it's only a matter of days at this point."

Lia stepped out of the bedroom. "With the scouts, I'm either going to spend another few days in a bag or come up with a good disguise."

Herman returned in a blur.

Patricius crossed his arms. "It would be safer if you stayed here."

233

Sighing, Ken put up his hands. "That's what I said."

Lia put her hands on her hips. "I will not abandon my husband. The matter is not up for discussion."

Ken smiled, glad to be on the same side as the woman who wore such a determined expression.

"Why go at all?" Patricius asked. "We have more men than are stationed at Fort Vigil. We can easily overpower Gonfrid. Even if the scouts report your absence, he won't have time to ready himself without dropping his defenses against Tehazy."

"Knowing Father, he might just do that," Ken said. "We risk losing ground to Tehazy as well as whatever men are at Vigil now."

"And even with better numbers on our side," Herman said, "the fort gives the king enough of an advantage to draw out the fight. We need his guard down if Their Majesties want to accomplish this peacefully."

"It's better to lose some Elgathan soldiers than the Queen of Vist," Patricius said.

"Those Elgathan soldiers are your countrymen," Lia said. "We are all Meriverians, and I aim to keep it that way. If I cared only for Vist, I could've claimed this throne a year ago. And don't forget, the same marriage that makes Kennard your king also makes me Crown Princess of Elgatha. He and I are duty-bound to serve *all* our people."

Ken put his arm around her in silent solidarity. She'd already said everything he was thinking.

Patricius punched his palm. "Then, just assassinate Gonfrid and be done with it."

Closing her eyes, Lia took a deep breath. "Please, don't—I have as much reason to want that as anyone—but what Kennard and I do, we do as one. I cannot ask him to kill his own father."

Clearly, she didn't understand how far Ken would go for her. "Lia, you wouldn't have to ask. After what he's done and what he's threatened to do, I—"

She took his hand with a teary smile. "I know you would do anything for me, but I love you too much to take advantage of that." Blinking, she shook her head. "Besides, killing us is what Gonfrid would do. We need to be better rulers than him."

"What will you do about the scouts?" Patricius asked. "I doubt a disguise will be sufficient."

"He's right," Ken admitted. "You're too short to pass for a man—even a Vistan one—and assuming you can get past that, your, um...shape will be much harder to hide." Even when she was more tightly bound for sparring, her bosom was noticeable. A smile crept up at the thought.

Lia shrugged. "So I hide."

"Where?" Patricius asked.

"The cage for Gonfrid will be ready by then," Lia said. "With the tarp over it, it's designed to hide it's occupant anyway."

When covered, it would look like any other supply wagon, which they already had three of.

Ken recoiled. "You were just trapped in a cave for months, and you want me to imprison you?"

She chuckled. "I'm not asking you to lock it. Two days is nothing, and I'll be spending nights in your tent anyway. That alone makes it infinitely better than the cave."

"And if anybody does look inside," Herman added, "you can claim to have imprisoned her for betraying you. It's a legitimate reason for her presence, which is more than can be said for any other disguise or place she could hide."

"Won't they wonder why I didn't send word about it?" Ken asked.

"Say that you wanted to surprise the king," Lia said. "As much as he hates me, seeing you turn on me would be the kind of present that you'd insist on witnessing his reaction to first-hand."

Ken relaxed. "That should work. Patricius, if you can gather the necessary leaders, we're ready to get into the details of coordinating the troops for Vigil and Solace."

Patricius looked to Lia, who nodded. He bowed and left.

Tucking a loose strand behind Lia's ear, Ken kissed her forehead. "I will do everything I can to keep you safe in there. I just wish you were a little less brave."

She gave him a dimpled smile. "If you can be brave, then so can I."

The other leaders proved much more amenable than Patricius, leaving enough time after planning all day for Ken and Lia to revel in their newlywed status every night. Abhenric and Moira were especially useful, steering plans toward favorable outcomes. No Seer ever knew the whole future, so having both of them filled in gaps. He Saw more of Lia's path and Fort Vigil, while Moira Saw more of Fort Solace and a bit of Conora's path.

True to their nature, they didn't give many details, but both stressed patience and stealth. The safest course of action was to appear as cooperative as possible for as long as possible.

When the troops arrived in Doivrie, a third of them continued north to Solace, carrying messages from Lia and Moira. The fort would be claimed by Vist, and if Captain Jonus cooperated as Moira expected, Rhonwin would follow new orders to join her, Hortensia, Conora, and the Vistan nobles in Doivrie. Ken, Lia, Herman, and Abhenric joined the remaining two-thirds of the troops to travel northwest to Vigil.

Ken walked behind the moose-drawn cage Lia traveled in. The back tarp was left rolled up, allowing them to interact through the bars. The scouts would appear from in front of them, and their own Flyers would give them warning to drop the tarp when someone approached. In between, there was no reason to keep Lia isolated.

After the first several hours of marching in the misty rain, sliding down the muddy mountainside at points, Ken hopped onto the back ledge of the cage and wrapped his arms around the bars to hold on. He tucked his head in and sighed at the welcome dryness. "Oh, that's nice." Ken chuckled. "I'm onto your plot, woman. You get to sit back and ride under cover."

Lia stood up from the large wooden chest she'd been using as a seat and picked her way to the back, gripping the bars along the right side as the wagon went over bumps. "Not a pleasant day for a march, is it?" Her warm hands clasped his, and she kissed him through the bars, sending heat all the way down to his toes.

He smiled. "That makes it a little better."

A call came from above. "Scout!"

"Sorry, love." Ken untied the rope holding the tarp up and jumped off the back, landing with a squelch.

A blue-winged man touched down beside him. "A black Flyer, coming from the northwest."

That sounded like Father's messenger. Ken nodded. "It's a good time to break for lunch anyway. Let the front know to halt."

The blue Flyer bowed and lifted off. A few minutes later, everyone stopped, and he returned. "The Flyer is gone. He got close enough for us to show our crests, then turned back toward Vigil."

"That was too easy," Lia called out, slightly muffled by the tarp.

Herman stretched his arms and leaned against the cage. "Gonfrid has no reason to search us. That means everyone in Doivrie is keeping their mouth shut for now."

"Or that he already knows and is luring us into a trap," Lia said.

"I doubt it," Ken said. "If he knew, he'd taunt us. His messages have been straightforward, and like Herman said, he would definitely search us. For one, just to demonstrate that he could, and for two, to gather information he could use against us in a trap."

"What did the other Flyer look like?" Herman asked. "Did he look like he was watching us intently?"

The blue Flyer shook his head. "He looked tired and bored."

"That bodes well. I think we can breathe a little easier, but all the same, we should stay cautious." Ken peeked behind the tarp from the back of the cage. "What do you think? You're the one trapped in there."

Lia crossed her arms. "Even if it weren't drier in here, I'd rather stay put. Gonfrid might not suspect anything, but that doesn't mean the scout can't circle back."

A drop rolled off the tarp and hit Ken in the eye. He blinked it away, then opened the cage.

"What are you doing?" she asked.

"Getting dry." The drizzle was turning into showers. He stepped inside and pulled back his hood. "I'll eat lunch in here with you, then go back out for the rest of today's march."

She offered him a seat on the chest. "I just hope a harder rain doesn't slow us down."

Ken nodded. "So do I. We're in so deep, most of our plan is in the Giver's hands now."

"Then let's hope we're right about him being on our side."

That night, their tent was set directly behind the wagon, giving Odelia the minimum amount of space to cross between them. It would've been more practical to sleep inside the cage, but considering what the end use of the cage was, it seemed wrong. As soon as the tarps had been stretched around the pyramid frame, she ducked inside and began laying down a reed floor mat and setting up a cot. It was only a little wider than a normal cot—roughly the size of one and a half put together—but it would work fine for the night.

As she finished tucking a pillow into place, Kennard entered, carrying a basket of food. He handed her the basket, then stripped off his wet outerwear and pants. Without a word, he sat next to her on the bed, and they shared a quiet meal of cornbread, smoked salmon, and dried berries.

Outside, the sounds of soldiers passed through their tent, the conversations growing bawdier over the course of dinner. Kennard turned red. If Odelia didn't act soon, he'd lose either his nerve or his temper—likely both. She set down her food and stood in front of him, slowly unbuttoning her vest.

His eyes grew wide. "Don't you hear them?" he mouthed.

She grinned and held up one finger. "*Oh, the maiden of Vist, so lovely and fair,*" she sang out, "*known far and wide for her shining hair...*"

Several men continued the verse, "*What man alive wouldn't give his heart for the Giver's own little work of art...*"

Odelia dropped the vest and leaned her hands on Kennard's knees until she was nose to nose with him, staring into his dark brown eyes, and whispered, "If they're singing, they're not listening."

"That's one song."

She laughed. "'The Maiden of Vist' has over thirty verses."

Kennard smiled and kissed her. "You're a genius," he said huskily, pulling her onto his lap.

The second day was full of fog and mist. Lia stayed in the wagon again until they halted a mile from Fort Vigil. There, Ken sent word to Father, requesting that he inspect the troops before they entered. After all, one couldn't be too sure about a group of Vistans, and Ken lacked Father's honed discernment about such things.

As he stood between Herman and Abhenric and waited for the reply, Ken wanted to hold Lia's hand, to share in her strength, but she needed to stay hidden until they were sure Father was coming—and without reinforcements. Instead, he found himself humming the tune to "The Maiden of Vist."

Herman groaned. "Not you too. That was the longest song I've ever heard in my life."

Ken grinned. "It's my new favorite song."

Herman chuckled. "Of course. Why wouldn't you love a song about your own Vistan maiden?"

"It is fitting," Ken said, "but I doubt it was written with Lia in mind. With all the added verses, that song must be at least a hundred years old."

"Three hundred," Abhenric said. "Old enough to predate Uldrio's vision. But for you, it really is about Odelia. My maiden of Vist is Hortensia. The song's about every Vistan woman. As they say, Wretched are those who've never known such beauty," he finished in a pitch-perfect tenor.

Herman raised an eyebrow. "You sang last night too?"

Ken turned his head slowly and stared at his father-in-law. "You know how to sing?" In all the years he'd known Abhenric, he'd never heard him sing—not once.

Abhenric shrugged. "Of course, I sing. I've just haven't felt a reason to in a long while."

Ken tilted his head. "And you've picked now...?"

The blue Flyer from yesterday fluttered through the trees and landed in front of them. "His Majesty approaches with ten guards, Your Majesty."

"How far?"

"Passing through the front lines. He's a wolf."

Hopefully, the stink of an army of men who hadn't washed in days would overwhelm his canine nose before he got close to Lia. Ken nodded, and the Flyer bowed and rose into the trees.

The moment of betrayal had arrived. In truth, the decision had already been made when he'd married Lia, but his focus had been on love then. This was about Father.

Ken unsheathed his dagger and held it behind his back. He had more than enough men for protection, but it made him feel better.

Ahead, a group of Elgathans moved toward them. Vistans filled in the space behind them, subtly bringing their weapons at the ready. The Elgathan guards spread out, and Father came forward, stopping in front of Ken and turning into a man.

"Hello, Father," Ken said coolly.

Father glared. "Have you all forgotten how to bow?"

"No." Ken gave the signal, and the Vistans closed ranks. Speeders jumped the Elgathan guards and had them pinned them to the ground by the time they realized they were not allies.

Several Vistans trained their weapons on Father, who started. "What is this?"

They began disarming and tying up the guards.

Ken took a deep breath. "As the King of Vist, I am returning you to Meria, where you will stand trial for crimes against the kingdom of Vist and defend the competency of your rule of Elgatha."

"How dare you!" Father roared, becoming a grizzly bear.

Ken gripped his dagger between them but held his ground. "You are outnumbered and surrounded."

Father growled. "By what right do you name yourself King of Vist?"

"Technically, the title is king consort," Ken admitted.

Eyes wide, Father shrank back into a man. "What have you done?"

Two Vistans cuffed and chained him before he could move or Transform again.

"He married me." Lia stepped out of the cage, still dressed in her traveling clothes but adorned with her tiara. She held her head high. "Five days ago, I reclaimed Vist as it's rightful heir."

"You." Father seethed. "I don't need a rope or an executioner for you. I'll rip your throat out with my teeth, you traitorous little bitch."

Ken lunged forward. The hilt of his dagger connected with the side of Father's face. He pulled back his fist for another strike. "You will not threaten her again."

Father spat blood. "This is a sham. There is no Vistan queen."

"Enough!" Grabbing his chains, Ken yanked him toward the cage. "Denial won't free you."

"Don't you see, Son? This is all her scheme. She poisoned you against me, then whored herself to you to steal your crown."

"You will not sully what Queen Odelia and I share." Ken shoved him inside. "Don't blame her for your faults. You've brought this upon yourself."

Two Strong soldiers removed large stones from the chest in the cage and attached them to Father's chains. If they had chained him to the floor of the wagon, the shackles would be part of his surroundings and easier to get out of, but detached, the cuffs would Transform with him like his armor or his clothes, keeping his forelimbs locked together even if the chains were not visible. The weight of the stones would prevent him from moving in a smaller form and slipping through the cage bars.

Lia took Ken's hand. "Let's leave him be."

He glared at Father. "I won't let him speak so ill of you."

She put a hand on Ken's chest and stood in front of him until he looked down into her eyes, so gentle and green and calm. "Words are all he has now."

Ken nodded. If she could ignore Father's insults and threats, so could he. He took a step back, then let her lead him away, paying little heed to the string of profanity Father promptly unleashed.

Lia stowed her tiara in a satchel at her side; then together, they walked to Fort Vigil, taking Herman, Abhenric, and half of the Vistans with them. The other half were ordered to make camp where they were and guard the wagon. Having expected Ken to bring reinforcements, none of the guards in Vigil questioned their arrival. While the Vistans filled the fort occupying positions at each bridge and the entrance of each enclosure, Father's guards were taken to the stockade. Ken, Lia, Herman, and Abhenric went straight to Father's quarters. Lia organized the war correspondence and maps as Ken and Abhenric gathered Father's personal belongings by the door, and Herman fetched officers and a number of new Vistan soldiers.

When Herman returned with them, Ken stood hand-in-hand with Lia behind Father's—their—desk.

"Everyone's here," Herman said.

Ken cleared his throat. "Good evening. We've called you all here to share important news and establish some changes. First, I present my wife, Queen Odelia of Vist."

Several officers looked at each other, confused.

"Thank you." Lia squeezed his hand. "This fort is now under our rule and will conduct only vital communication with Elgathan forts until King Kennard or I command otherwise."

The captain of Vigil crossed his arms and looked at Ken. "Why are you in charge? What's happened to King Gonfrid?"

"He is under arrest," Lia said. "Vist is no longer under his command, including this fort. In a few days, he will lose Elgatha as well."

The captain scowled at Lia, then turned back to Ken. "Your Highness, I don't know where you found this woman, but the two of you are committing multiple acts of treason and sedition."

Ken sighed. "Yes. That is the inevitable consequence of deposing a tyrant, but I find it's a necessary step in restoring the rightful ruler of Vist."

The captain's eyes grew wide. "So your plan is to tear the kingdom in half? The Tehazians will devour us."

Lia lifted Ken's hand. "We're married, in accordance with the Treaty of Meriveria. To rule both sides together, all we need now is to secure his claim on Elgatha."

"She and I are going to put an end to this war," Ken said. "Don't forget, I was there when we were ambushed at the bridge. I remember how many men we lost—I was almost one of them. How many of you advised against that battle?"

Several officers nodded grimly.

"It's still treason," the captain said.

"Your loyalty is truly commendable," Lia said with utmost sincerity. "Is anyone else concerned?"

A young man stepped forward. "We pledged to serve the king."

There was a long pause as they waited for others, but the captain and the young man stood alone. A murmur moved through the crowd, and officers shook their heads.

Lia nodded. "Thank you for your courage. You are both stripped of your posts." She motioned to the Vistan soldiers, who surrounded them. "Put them in the stockade and do not let them send any messages out, but keep them well-fed and otherwise unpunished."

The men looked to Ken, eyes wide with fear.

He nodded. It was unfortunate but necessary. The dissenters were going to be a liability until the trial in Meria. As they were hauled away, Ken put a hand to Abhenric's back. "Lastly, since we will need to go to Meria, Abhenric DiOrto will act here in our stead. The plan is to hold fast until we return. If he has a vision that changes that plan, he is authorized to do so. Thank you all for your cooperation. You are dismissed."

Ken slept poorly that night, and judging by her tossing and turning, Lia did too. Father couldn't escape from his cage, but that didn't stop Ken from holding her more tightly every time he heard an animal in the forest below.

He wouldn't let the threat against her become real.

Gingerly, he slipped out of bed and wrapped a blanket around himself, then padded to the door. Four Vistans stood sentry outside.

"It seems quiet," Ken whispered to the nearest guard. "Anything to report out here?"

"There have been a handful of men planning resistance, but their fellow soldiers have been quick to turn them in. Also, a Flight messenger came about an hour ago and left this for you." He handed Ken a letter.

"Good. Just the same, I want four more guards out here."

"Yes, Your Majesty."

"And if any animals try to get past you—whether it's a bear or dog—you kill it."

The guard bowed. "Understood."

Ken went inside and pulled back one of the curtains slightly, letting a sliver of lamplight pour through the window to illuminate the letter. He opened it carefully, trying not to crinkle the paper. It was from Rhonwin. Unlike Vigil, Fort Solace had put up no resistance at all. Captain Jonus had been so relieved to see the Vistan takeover that he'd cried, and the soldiers had cheered both the arrival of reinforcements and the news of their restored leadership. Rhonwin was already on his way to Doivrie via dogcart.

Lia gasped.

Ken turned around.

She sat up and sighed, then gave him a groggy frown. "Ken?"

"I'm right here." He set down the letter and closed the curtain. "I was just reading a message."

She closed her eyes and lay back with a soft groan. "Come back to bed."

Crawling in next to her, he spread the extra blanket over both of them and snuggled close to her soft, warm body. "It was good news." He kissed the curve of her neck, then trailed his lips up to her ear. "Don't you want to hear?"

She groaned again. "I want to sleep. Is it urgent?"

"No, but—"

She rolled over to face him. "Unless we're under attack, I don't care. It's been hard enough to sleep tonight with you squeezing the air out of my lungs. Please... Just let me sleep."

"Sorry." He shifted onto his back and let go of her waist, instead, taking hold of the hand she rested on his chest and running his other hand through her hair.

She sighed. "I'm sorry. That was rude. What was the news?" Her words were half-mumbled.

"Jonus joined us. Solace is ours."

"Mmm... That's good..."

He wasn't sure whether she was reacting to the news or his fingers on her scalp, but either way, he could tell her again in the morning. Soon, her long, even breathing lulled him as well.

The convoy left for Meria first thing in the morning, leaving behind Abhenric and the Vistan soldiers who had entered the fort the night before.

More amenable to news after some rest, Odelia had been delighted by the letter from Fort Solace and sent word to Doivrie that they could leave tomorrow under the expectation of continued silence. Mom and Moira would pay special heed to Conora, who would hopefully be placated by the knowledge that Gonfrid had been captured unharmed and without any collateral bloodshed. Odelia chose to omit the part about Kennard punching him in the face. As utterly satisfying as it had been to witness, it wouldn't win him any favors with his sister.

They kept a dozen guards around Gonfrid's cage. Kennard refused to go anywhere near it and suggested that Odelia do the same. Given the lovely words the Elgathan king had had for her last time, she was inclined to agree.

Thankfully, Odelia and Kennard no longer needed to be cautious of their affections for this leg of the journey. The convoy stayed off the main roads, cutting a straight line through the forest to Meria. Melaine was not expecting an army to be coming her way, and the dense woods covered their approach from anyone who was neither nearby nor looking for them. And even if word did reach Melaine that Kennard had been spotted holding Odelia's hand or putting his arm around her, the army itself would be a much bigger concern.

They marched through mud from the flooded valley to the Elgathan coastal terrace, going uphill much of the way. By sunset on the fourth day, they were several miles short of Meria. With home so close, Kennard and Odelia decided to push the army through the growing darkness, despite the exhaustion of a long day's trek. They were trudging through the night, tired and more than a little cranky, when the walls of Meria came into view.

Kennard spun around—"Look, Lia, we're home!"—and promptly slipped, landing frontward in the mud.

Odelia put her hands to her mouth, trying not to laugh at her husband's misfortune and failing miserably. Nearby soldiers were having trouble holding back their laughter as well. Taking a deep breath to somewhat regain her composure, she offered him a hand up.

Kennard pulled himself upright but didn't let go of her hand, instead, tugging her closer.

Odelia yanked her hand away. "What are you doing?"

With a grin, he put his arms out wide. "I just wanted to give my lovely wife a hug."

She backed up, eyeing him sideways. "Oh ho ho. Don't you dare..."

His longer legs gave him the advantage. He caught up to her in two steps and wrapped his arms around her, squishing mud between them. "Mmm. Isn't that nice?"

With a grimace, she let out a low squeal. "You're awful."

"You love me."

She chortled. "I can't believe I married you. What was I thinking?"

"That I'm irresistibly desirable," he said, low and throaty.

"Not right now you're not."

"And yet, here you are, in my arms."

Odelia laughed and kissed him. Unkingly or not, she cherished his ridiculousness.

Herman cleared his throat. "I don't know about the two of you, but I'm ready for a warm bed, and the gates are right there."

Kennard smiled. "Of course."

He took her hand and led her toward the city gate. Like Fort Vigil, the guards of Meria opened the way for him on status alone. Darkened windows and empty streets indicated a sleeping populace—one that likely wouldn't appreciate waking to an army a few hours before dawn. Word was passed back through the ranks to keep quiet as they moved through the city.

At the bridge to the Cedar Palace, Kennard informed the nearest guards that the Vistans would be camping on the royal islet, between the palace and the wise women's lodge. They crossed the long expanse to the palace and circled to the back door, leading the cage wagon behind them. Herman went in first, disappearing deeper into the palace.

Inside, a servant bowed to Kennard. "I'll send word to Her Majesty."

Kennard shook his head. "There's no need to wake her at this late hour—or early hour—is it considered late night or early morning by now?"

Odelia yawned. "I have no idea anymore. But I do know that you should send word to the servants to have a hot bath sent to His Highness's room."

The servant looked her over. "My condolences, Mistress Odelia. Valerzan was a friend. Should I request a hot bath for you as well? The servants' facilities will be cold by now."

Odelia was taken aback, and she blinked away tears. "No. Thank you for the kind offer, but that won't be necessary."

Kennard smiled. "We only need one."

The servant looked confused until his gaze drifted down to her and Kennard's linked hands. "Oh." He furrowed his brows at Kennard. "Are you excited for the wedding, Your Highness?"

Kennard shrugged. "There won't be one—can't be one, actually."

The servant gasped. "Are you sure you don't want me to fetch the queen? At the very least, someone could tell the bride."

Having been one so recently, Odelia sympathized with the poor girl. "We really should."

Kennard nodded. "If you give me some paper, I can write a note to be left at the door of Lady...um..."

The servant nodded and ducked into a nearby room.

Odelia rolled her eyes. "You don't know her name?"

Kennard put his hands up. "What? It was irrelevant. The wedding was never going to happen."

"It was in Melaine's letter."

"How do you know that?"

Odelia shook her head. "I read all your letters. As your secretary, it was my duty, and as your wife, it's my right—and apparently, still necessary. Her name is Lady Sylvia."

Kennard scratched his head. "Lady Sylvia? Why does that sound so familiar?"

Pawing at Kennard, Odelia giggled forcefully, then said in a high falsetto, "Oh, Your Highness, you're so handsome... I can't wait to get you alone so you can use your Healing on me. Tee-hee!"

He wrinkled his nose. "Her?"

"Yep."

He shuddered. "Please, don't ever do that again. You are disturbingly good at it."

She grinned and continued in the voice, "But I just want to crawl right up in your lap"—she squeezed his cheeks together—"and make kissy faces with you."

"This is payback for the mud, isn't it?"

"Absolutely."

The servant returned with a pen, ink, paper, and a clipboard. "Here you are, and your bath is on its way."

Odelia held the ink while Kennard scratched out a short letter.

Herman zipped up the hallway. "The cell is ready. Do you want to escort him?"

"Only if he's gagged," Kennard said without looking up from the paper.

"I'd prefer to see him put away." Odelia motioned to the servant. "Have him get a clean cloth if you need one."

"No need," Herman said. "One of the guards gagged him back on the second day of travel." He went outside.

Kennard handed the letter to the servant. "Lady Sylvia can read this when she wakes."

The servant nodded. "Of course. Do I need to let anyone know about your prisoner?"

Kennard shook his head. "Don't ask. In fact, let me make sure Herman puts a hood on him too." He walked out the door, leaving Odelia alone with the servant.

"So...just to clarify, so I know what to call you, you and His Highness are..."

"Married, yes."

He nodded. "I guess Mistress Odelia doesn't work anymore. Crown Princess. It's Your Highness now, right?"

Your Majesty, technically, but... "Correct."

Growling and shuffling sounded through the doorway.

"You might want to stay out of the hallway for this," Odelia warned. "He's probably going to lash out."

The servant bowed. "Let me know if there is anything else you need, Your Highness."

"I will, thank you."

The man turned down the hall, and Odelia stepped into an open doorway to make room for the group outside. Soon after, Herman and Kennard marched inside, followed by Gonfrid and a dozen guards. The Elgathan king was still chained and weighted—the stones carried by Strongmen—and a rough bag covered his head.

Kennard held his hand out to Odelia. "This way, love. I'll feel better if I know where you are."

Gonfrid lunged toward them. Odelia clasped onto Kennard. He wrapped his arms around her and spun, shielding her with his body. Gonfrid stopped short with a loud clank, and a guard pulled him back.

Kennard walked Odelia farther down the hallway. "I think it's safe to say he's still angry. Are you okay?"

She nodded. "Let's just get him downstairs."

She didn't want to admit that Gonfrid had rattled her. Doubtless, he really would rip her throat if he ever got out. Reaching into her boot, Odelia unsheathed a dagger.

Kennard kept an arm around her as they continued along the hall and down a flight of steps into a dark underground corridor. It was cold and damp and smelled a bit like low tide. Gonfrid moaned and jerked against his restraints as he joined them.

Kennard pulled off the hood. "Sorry for the smell, Father. It was either this or the cage."

Herman stepped forward. "The cell is this way."

He led them down a few more corridors to a barred door. Inside, prison guards watched them pass from behind a desk. Gonfrid fought harder in front of them, but they made no move to help him.

Herman gestured to an open cell a few doors down from the guard room. It was small but had a large stack of blankets on the cot. Odelia and Kennard stood back, and the guards took Gonfrid inside. They set the stones holding his chains in the far corner, behind the cot and backed away, removing the gag at the last moment before locking him in.

"This is your last chance to avoid tomorrow's trial," Kennard said. "If you abdicate willingly—"

"I will kill all of you, traitors!" Gonfrid turned into a wolf and snarled. "I am your king!"

Kennard tightened his hold on Odelia. "That's enough for me. Let's go."

Gonfrid sniffed, then bared his teeth. "I smell blood. I think it's yours, girl."

Odelia stiffened, but Kennard pulled her away. "Don't listen to him. He'll try anything to taunt us."

Gonfrid laughed. "She knows it's true, and you don't believe me. What is your little courtesan hiding?"

Neither Kennard nor Odelia spoke as he brought her back upstairs and up to his rooms—their rooms. A steaming tub waited for them in the bedroom. Kennard undressed and climbed in first, then held his hand out to Odelia.

She hesitated. Gonfrid hadn't lied. She had noticed a small amount of blood that morning but had kept the disappointing discovery to herself. Odelia couldn't even bring herself to check her Vitality. It was a whole week earlier than expected, and she hadn't seen any more for the rest of the day. If the bleeding didn't come back, it might actually be a good sign. But what if it came back now—in the water with Kennard? She wanted to tell him everything, but he had such torn feelings about the situation. He needed an heir as badly as she did, but he'd also made it clear that the prospect terrified him. Until she had something definitive to tell him, she'd keep it to herself.

Kennard smiled sweetly. "Get in. This water won't stay warm forever."

Odelia took his hand and stepped in. If that morning wasn't a fluke, and she ruined the bath, she would just apologize profusely.

As they scrubbed themselves down, she was relieved to find her fears unwarranted. Afraid of falling asleep there, they didn't linger in the bath and toweled off as soon as they were clean. Odelia shivered in the cool bedroom. Although a fire had been lit, it hadn't had time to penetrate the room. Kennard wrapped a soft robe around her and kissed her cheek.

Odelia braided her hair out of the way and looked down at her discarded muddy clothes. "Great. I just realized that was my last clean shirt. I wonder if any of my spares are still here. Or do you think they were confiscated with your weapons?"

He opened a drawer and removed a stack of clothing. "I'm not sure, but I don't feel like looking either. You can wear one of my nightshirts until we get that sorted out. It's not like I wear them anyway."

She took the proffered garment and pulled the soft fabric over her head and down to her knees. "It's so soft."

Kennard put on loose pants. "And it looks better on you than on me." He uncovered the bed and sighed. "You have no idea how much I've been looking forward to sleeping here tonight."

"I think most people miss their own beds, although in my case, it's not that much of a loss." The hard little bed in her family's apartment was functional but far from comfortable.

He swept her off her feet. "Well, this glorious one is yours now, and frankly, the addition of you is bound to improve the whole thing for me too." With a few steps forward, he tossed her into a pile of pure fluff.

"Mmm. How do you ever get up in the morning?"

He snuggled up next to her and spread the comforter over them. "I'm not having any trouble with it right now."

Laughter shook her whole body. "I said, 'get up,' not..." She dissolved into laughter again.

He snickered. "I know, but it was too easy and completely worth it for that smile."

And it was exactly what she'd needed. She relaxed, laying her head on his chest. "I take back what I said earlier. I know why I married you."

"Of course, you do. I told you. I'm irresistibly desirable."

"Yes, you are." However, the demonstration of how much so would have to wait for morning. Between the exhaustion, the amazingly comfortable bed, and the protective arms cradling her, Odelia couldn't keep her eyes open.

At least, not until the shrieking woke her up.

An argument was happening just outside their bedroom, and Kennard and Odelia both stirred and looked at one another in confusion before realization dawned on them.

"Mother."

"Melaine."

The door burst open, and sure enough, Melaine barged in. "Kennard, you have a lot of explaining to do. Why didn't you tell me you were home, and what is this I hear about—" She gasped and stared at Odelia.

"Excuse me!" Kennard said. "Can't a man sleep in peace? Surely, you know how to knock."

Melaine put a hand on her hip. "Have you no shame, Mistress Odelia? I thought you knew better than this, but here you are—and on the eve of his wedding!"

"Mother, I—"

"And you." She turned her withering gaze on him. "What did you tell Lady Sylvia? Look at her. She's absolutely beside herself."

Behind her, Lady Sylvia stood in the doorway, tear-stained and agape.

Kennard voiced what Odelia was thinking, "Oh, great Giver, what a mess. We should've handled this first." In their exhausted stupor and the scuffle with Gonfrid, they'd overlooked the message for Melaine.

"Explain. Now," Melaine demanded.

Kennard put his arm around Odelia's shoulder. "This wasn't how I pictured this moment happening, but I guess we're stuck with it. Mother, let me introduce you to my wife. You might know her better as Mistress Odelia DiOrto."

Odelia held her breath and gave a timid smile and wave. This wasn't how she'd hoped this would go either.

"That's not funny, Kennard," Melaine said.

"Good, because I don't think so either," Kennard said.

Melaine stared at him.

"He isn't joking, Your Majesty," Odelia said. "We've been married for ten days now. He received your summons to return home the morning after our wedding."

Melaine clutched at her heart. "You eloped? With a commoner!"

"Not that it matters," Kennard said, "but she's anything but common—"

Melaine sighed. "I'm not talking about whatever feelings you have for her—I'm sure she seems special to you—but she has no title beside the one you bestowed upon her in your employ."

Odelia scowled. "He was trying to explain just that. Perhaps if you would let him finish, you would understand—"

Melaine threw her head back and gasped. "Oh, for the love of—" She pinched the bridge of her nose. "Kennard, what have you done? You are a prince. It's expected that you will indulge yourself, but when accidents happen, you don't marry the problem away."

Odelia's jaw dropped. "I beg your pardon!"

"Ten days isn't that long," Melaine continued. "Word likely hasn't gotten far. The child will make things a little more difficult, but—"

"Now you're just being rude," Kennard said. "I tell you the best news of my life, and you start yelling, insulting my wife and falsely impugning her honor. Not to mention, you're interrupting our sleep."

Melaine crossed her arms. "Must you make light of everything?"

Kennard shrugged. "You say that like it's a bad thing."

"I am trying to salvage this situation," Melaine said. "Your father can have this all declared invalid and have you ready to marry in the morning, and Mistress Odelia can go to Eaund. If she can keep quiet, I think Lord Baldovin could be convinced to marry her quickly before he realizes she's already—"

"Enough!" Kennard got out of bed. "Your suggestions are revolting and ultimately pointless. I couldn't have married Lia for that reason because I never slept with her before then. And whether or not I had, the very idea that I can and should abandon my wife in her greatest time of need and disown my unborn child..."

Melaine shook her head. "Kennard, you don't understand—"

"I wasn't finished!" Kennard stared her down. "The idea sickens me. But your plan is irrelevant because this marriage cannot be undone. It was presided over by a king, in view of twenty-eight noble houses, and has been thoroughly consummated. Father couldn't undo that with any decree, even if he could make one, which he can't do right now."

Odelia felt silly sitting there while Kennard confronted his mother. She crawled to the edge of the bed and stood beside him.

"You're lying," Melaine said. "There's no way Gonfrid approves of this marriage, let alone presided over it."

Odelia crossed her arms. "He never said he did. A king did preside, but it wasn't Gonfrid."

Kennard put his arm around Odelia. "You're missing the important question here, Mother. I told you that my wife isn't common, and you haven't asked who she is."

"Because she's no one," Melaine said. "The two of you are making up stories to make me cancel this wedding, and it's not working."

Odelia was done. "Think what you like. It doesn't change the royal blood in my veins or the vows we've pledged to one another."

Melaine glared at Odelia. "You think that by calling this ridiculous affair a marriage, you're suddenly my equal? I am a queen."

Odelia stood on tiptoe and glared back. "So am I. But unlike you, I was born to my title."

"You lying little temptress." Melaine slapped her across the face, the sting bringing tears to Odelia's eyes.

Odelia put a hand to her cheek. Kennard shoved Melaine away and kissed Odelia's forehead, tingling her where his lips touched and soothing the pain away. He rounded back on Melaine. "You've gone too far. Herman!"

Melaine put her hands on her hips. "You don't speak to me—"

"Herman!" Kennard clenched his fists and growled. "Where is he? Why isn't he doing his job?"

Herman darted in, looking flustered. "Sorry, I failed. I—"

"I need you to escort Mother out of here and lock her in her room for assaulting the queen," Kennard said.

Melaine scoffed. "Assaulting the—I am the queen!"

Herman looked at Melaine and turned red, then averted his gaze. "I..."

Melaine must have used her Allure on the poor man to force her way in.

Kennard huffed. "Oh, for Giver's sake, fine. I will escort her out, and you can make sure Lady Sylvia gets to her room. When you're done, find several guards with Stone Skin for Mother and for Lia. We're not repeating this incident."

He grabbed Melaine by the arm and dragged her from the room in spite of her protests.

Lady Sylvia, who had stood still in shock through the whole ordeal, broke down into hysterical sobbing as soon as Herman started to lead her away.

The whole encounter had been surreal. Normally, Melaine had to break her Allure by going too far. But she hadn't broken Odelia. She hadn't felt her Allure at all—not even before Melaine had turned on her. The only way to be immune to Melaine was by blood, and she had been stuck on the idea that Odelia was pregnant. The more Odelia had spoken, the harder Melaine had clung to the idea, and she'd first suggested it after Odelia had defended Kennard...

Kennard returned, red-faced and fuming. He slammed the door. "Herman's dismissed until the meeting tomorrow. I know he's tired, but if I didn't owe him my life..."

Odelia put her arms around his waist. "Go easy on him. Melaine is difficult to handle for those who are not immune to her Allure."

"You seemed to have no problems with it tonight."

"I know. I'm normally a babbling fool around her."

Kennard shrugged. "Maybe you've finally learned to overcome it. You should teach Herman how you did it."

"Kennard..."

"What?"

She looked up into his dark eyes. "I need you to check my Vitality."

He furrowed his brow. "Your Vitality? She didn't hit you that hard, did she? I Healed you."

Odelia smiled. "No, love. I'm fine. I just want you to check it."

He put his hand to the side of her throat. "What am I looking for?"

She licked her lips and took a deep breath. "Is it still bright, or has it dulled?"

He tilted his head. "It's...warmer, richer."

That wasn't part of the normal cycle. She felt her wrist. Warmer and richer really were the best descriptions. It was as if the hum reverberated more, and it filled her with more joy than the Vistan sunrise. Her breath caught, and tears welled up.

Kennard wiped her cheeks. "What's wrong?"

"Nothing." Odelia smiled. "I didn't learn to overcome Allure, but I am immune through blood—your blood. I wasn't sure if I'd be able to tell so soon, but at least one part of our plan has already—"

He kissed her deeply, running his fingers over her neck. It was the kind of kiss that sent waves down her body and weakened her knees, the kind that had to be chased after as it ended too soon.

She panted. "Were you overcome with excitement or just trying to stop me from finishing that sentence?"

He laughed. "Both?"

"I'm pregnant."

"You couldn't let that stay ambiguous?"

"Nope." She grabbed a handful of his shirt and drew him onto the bed. "But it wouldn't hurt to make sure that I am."

He smirked and ran a hand up her leg. "Such powers of seduction. Now that I've had you, how can I say no?"

21

MERIVERIA

The next morning, Ken and Lia wasted no time getting ready. After last night's fiasco, they needed to catch up on the rumors swirling around the court. At least Father was secure. With all the extra Vistan guards, even if someone found out that he was imprisoned, he wasn't getting out.

Lia dove into Ken's wardrobe—their wardrobe—and emerged with a long skirt in deep mossy green and Elgathan blue and a vest to match. She laid them on the bed next to the crowns she'd brought in her satchel last night.

Ken tucked in his shirt. "I didn't know those were in there."

She smiled and stepped into the skirt. "Neither did I, but I'm glad I checked. I'll have to remember to thank Mom later."

As they finished dressing, Ken dropped his circlet into place and reached for the door, but Lia grabbed his hand. "Wait." She stood on tiptoe and motioned for him to crouch. Her graceful fingers combed through his hair, and she kissed his cheek. "There. Now you look dashing."

Two Vistan guards met Ken and Lia in the hallway, along with Grandfather, whom they'd prevented from entering. He bowed. "Good morning, Kennard," he said stiffly. "We need to have a talk."

Ken forced a smile. "Of course. We were on our way to the great hall. Why don't you walk with us?"

"This is a private conversation," Grandfather said.

Ken put his arm around Lia and pivoted back to their sitting room door. "We can go inside if you'll be brief." He opened the door.

Grandfather furrowed his brow. "The girl needs to go to *her* room."

"That's precisely what she's doing."

"What have I told you about jesting with me? Grandilady Wilmarie is waiting to speak to her."

Lia backed a step away from Grandfather and shook her head. "I'm not an idiot. Did you think I'd walk into such an obvious trap?"

Clearly, Mother had not given up. There wasn't a chance Ken was going to let the grandilady try to spirit his wife away on her behalf.

Ken pulled Lia closer. "She's not leaving my side today. You speak to both of us or neither of us."

Grandfather marched into the sitting room and waited for Ken to close the door before saying, "You have brought shame upon this family."

Ken smiled and shook his head. "What particular shame is it? It's impossible to keep track of everything that displeases you."

"I spoke to your mother and Lady Sylvia. The story they told is scandalous and disgraceful. You have very little time to make it right."

Ken scoffed. "Mother was in rare form last night, so this should be interesting." She would need to twist the tale a lot to think she had a prayer of ending his marriage.

"Your mother says you were openly fornicating with your mistress, and according to Lady Sylvia, they found the two of you in a carnal embrace."

Ken rolled his eyes. "She is my legally wedded wife. And for what it's worth, we were fast asleep in our nightclothes. Giver forbid they'd actually witnessed sex. The sight might've stopped their feeble hearts."

Lia pursed her lips, but her dimples gave away her suppressed smile.

"What else?" Ken asked.

Grandfather counted off on his fingers. "You mocked Lady Sylvia for finding you. This girl attacked your mother. And the two of you eloped because you lost control of your urges and are now attempting to legitimize a common half-Vistan bastard as your royal heir."

"None of that is true," Lia said.

Grandfather took a step toward her, jabbing his finger at her face. "You swore to me—and to Grandilady Wilmarie—that you wouldn't bear his children."

Lia huffed and straightened. "I promised no such thing. I said I would neither be a mistress nor bear any bastards."

"And she hasn't." Ken smiled and squeezed Lia's shoulder. "Our marriage is valid."

"Such careful words." Grandfather narrowed his eyes. "If only you were as careful with your seed. You don't deny that you've impregnated her."

Ken held his head high. "No, I don't, but Mother has the cause and effect backward."

Grandfather harrumphed. "The order in which you got there doesn't matter. This situation is unacceptable."

"Unacceptable?" Ken couldn't resist a smirk. "If the outcome truly matters more than the method, then you and Mother should be thrilled. I've exceeded your expectations. I actually managed to *marry up* and have wasted no time in securing an heir."

"Married up?" Grandfather sneered. "You married a Vistan, you fool. Do you have any idea to what lengths my grandfather went to keep her kind out of both the royal family and our own? He was a thorough man. There is no Vistan royalty to marry into. Not only have you violated his wishes and efforts, but you've let this girl play you."

Lia gasped, then said quietly, "He supplied the poisoned honey."

A shiver ran up Ken's spine.

Grandfather started. "How do you know about that? He didn't tell anyone outside of the family how he did it—not even the King of Elgatha."

"Because he wasn't as thorough as he claimed," Lia said matter-of-factly.

"A mistake that can be remedied if you refuse to go quietly," Grandfather said.

Heat rose through Ken. Every muscle in his body tensed. "You have threatened my wife and unborn child. I would advise you to look out the window before you speak another word against the Queen of Vist."

Grandfather eyed them suspiciously as he sidled up to the window, then looked outside.

"That army is at our command," Lia said, backing toward the door, "and this conversation is over. Guards!"

The guards burst in.

"Lord Wystan has threatened my life. Shackle him and bring him to the great hall."

Lia was shaking by the time they neared the great hall. Knowing that Father's office would be empty, Ken pulled her inside as they passed it and shut the door.

"People are already gathering," she insisted. "We need to get in there."

He brushed her hair back from her face and rubbed her shoulders. "You need to calm down first. If you're this worked up already, you won't be able to hold it together in there, and I need you to hold it together in there because you're better at it than I am."

She let out a shaky breath.

"Do you need to talk about what Grandfather said?" Ken swallowed hard. As disturbing and disappointing as the revelation had been, the thought of anything coming between them was worse. "Knowing that even more of my ancestors were a part of that—"

"No." Lia embraced him. "Ken, that changes nothing. You are who you are. So what if they carried out the massacre? We already knew about the ones who ordered it."

He breathed a sigh of relief. "Must everyone I'm descended from be awful? Can't one of them have raised orphaned puppies to give to widows or something?"

She chuckled. "King Rainald signed the Treaty of Meriveria. That's worth something." Despite her smile, her lips trembled.

"Yes, it is." He kissed her forehead, hoping to soothe her with his Gift, yet the tension still radiated from her. "What has you so shaken? I've watched you endure worse insults and threats without flinching."

"They all affect me. I don't let it show—usually—but I'm tired, and I'm scared, and I'm angry."

"You were so confident when we captured Father. Why didn't you tell me what you were really feeling?"

Lia looked away. "I'm a queen. I have to be stronger than that now. You said so yourself."

Ken tipped her chin up until she met his gaze. "No, you don't. You've always been better at keeping calm in public, but why would you think you need to hide from me?"

"Because you were already facing your fear to plan for a child right away." Her eyes were shining. "How could I burden you with more?"

"You are never a burden to me. I don't fear fatherhood. I fear losing you. And I mean that in every sense." He brushed his hand up her cheek. "Now if you need to cry or scream or hit something, then do it. If you just want me to hold you, then tell me. Whatever you need to prepare yourself for this meeting."

Lia buried her face in Ken's chest, and he instinctively curled around her, rubbing her back as the shivers melted away. He had been ready for the coming confrontation before, but now, he was eager for it.

Odelia emerged from the office on Kennard's arm. Herman, who had joined the guards outside, bowed. Kennard ordered him to bring Gonfrid. Herman let out a breath and smiled before running off. Another guard was dispatched to retrieve Melaine. Lord Wystan already stood by the door, bound and surrounded.

As Odelia and Kennard led everyone around the corner of the hallway, the herald who stood in front of the doors to the great hall bowed. Odelia handed him a piece of paper. "Read this as we enter."

The herald scanned the note, then looked at Kennard, eyes wide. "Begging your pardon, Your Highness, but this could be a problem..." He grimaced. "You see, I just announced the arrival of Lady Sylvia, and she was wearing a wedding gown—"

"Fetch her," Kennard said.

The herald flapped his brown wings and flew inside the great hall, reemerging a short while later. He shook his head. "The lady says Her Majesty ordered her to carry on, and she refuses to leave."

Kennard rolled his eyes. "What is she thinking? She knows I can't marry her."

"I guess she and the queen placed a lot of confidence in Lord Wystan and Grandilady Wilmarie's ability to get rid of me," Odelia said.

Kennard shrugged. "We tried. If she thinks her presence will stop us from entering, she's sadly mistaken. She's earned the humiliation that will follow. Read the announcement."

The herald flew inside and hovered above the doorway. As Odelia and Kennard entered the room, he proclaimed, "Presenting Her Majesty, Odelia, Queen Regnant of Vist and Crown Princess of Elgatha and His Majesty, Kennard, King Consort of Vist and Crown Prince of Elgatha."

Everyone in the room bowed or curtsied as the pair made their way to the front, though murmurs rose around them.

Lady Sylvia scowled, her red face contrasting sharply with the deep green of her dress. "What is she still doing here?" she whispered through clenched teeth.

Kennard smiled and said in a low voice, "Interesting. We were just asking that about you." He dropped the smile. "Sit down."

When the lady didn't move, Odelia added, "If you want to avoid further embarrassment, you should sit before he says something that everyone can hear."

Lady Sylvia glared at her but did as she had been requested and sat next to Conora in the front row. More murmurs rose.

Kennard held up his hand until the room fell silent. "We ask all of the grandilords to rise and confirm the presence of all of Meriveria's noble houses."

They would need each and every one of them—down to the pettilords—to conduct a valid trial of the sovereign.

The grandilords, Patricius, Straton, Doneron, and Roderick all stood.

Odelia received confirmation from Grandilords Patricius and Straton, then motioned for the two of them to sit. "Let it be known that all of Vist is represented today."

Kennard took his turn. "Grandilord Doneron, are all of the ruling nobility of Oulley in attendance?"

Grandilord Doneron bowed. "Apologies, Your...Majesty? I didn't realize it would be necessary to count."

"Lords of Oulley, rise."

Two guards brought Lord Wystan to his feet as the other three lords rose. Grandilord Doneron checked with each of them, receiving confirmation from all except Lord Wystan, who had to be difficult, refusing to speak or nod.

Kennard grumbled something under his breath. "Pettilords of Ascaympa, rise."

The two pettilords stood.

"The grandrion of Oulley is accounted for," Grandilord Doneron said.

Kennard nodded and motioned for them to sit before turning to the last man standing. "Grandilord Roderick, are all of the ruling nobility of Eaund in attendance?"

"No, Your Majesty. The Lord of Atmos and the Pettilord of Losuno are not here."

"Have they authorized representatives to act on their behalf?" Kennard asked.

Grandilord Roderick smiled. "Not that I'm aware of."

Of course, Grandilady Wilmarie's husband would try to stall the proceedings.

Rhonwin stood, a piece of paper in hand. "My father has appointed me to speak on behalf of Atmos. And my wife, Moira speaks for Losuno."

Kennard called Rhonwin forward and took the paper from him. Kennard raised an eyebrow as he read it. "This has been signed by Pettilord Niven, Lord Flinor, and yourself, Grandilord Roderick."

The grandilord crossed his arms. "That signature was obtained a week ago. I revoke it."

Kennard shook his head. "It's too late. You cannot claim a revocation now that the meeting has started. Is anyone else missing?"

"No, but—"

"Then, let it be known that all of Elgatha is also represented today."

"Bring in Queen Melaine and King Gonfrid," Odelia announced.

Two Stone-Skin guards led Melaine to the front, where she was given a seat to the left of the dais. The Elgathan king was still in the same chains and gagged, with the same guards from the night before. The crowd was louder now between the jeers from the Vistans and the protests from the Elgathans, but Kennard still managed to regain their attention with a raised hand.

Odelia gripped Kennard's arm and barely kept the tremor out of her voice as she said, "King Gonfrid, as Queen of Vist, I hereby charge you with the unlawful rule of the kingdom of Vist and crimes against its people. By default, your rule over Meriveria is illegitimate."

Kennard added, "And as Crown Prince of Elgatha, I hereby declare you unfit to rule and call for your dethronement."

Melaine stood up. "You fool! You're dismantling the very throne you're supposed to inherit."

The guards pulled her back down. A roar of angry protests rained from the Elgathans. In turn, the Vistans shouted them down. Odelia moved her hand down to hold Kennard's as he blinked against the outburst. He'd been right: she needed to maintain control of this meeting.

She held up her other hand. *"Silence!"*

The power of her own voice over the noise surprised her. It must've surprised the nobles as well because they all stopped and stared at her.

"You will all have your chance to speak when we have finished presenting our petition," she said. "For the first matter at hand, I am directly descended from Prince Idris, the last publicly known heir to the Vistan throne..." Odelia explained the Elgathan massacre of the Vistan palace, Tasia's escape, and her family's decades of hiding. "...but under King Gonfrid, Elgathan rule of Vist has become intolerable, and I cannot keep silent any longer. I have sufficient proof to back my claim. Tasia DiOrto had Memory, and her journal gives a detailed account of what happened in

Iverish. As to my lineage, Grandilord Patricius has several authenticated copies, which he will distribute to you now. If anyone doubts those, I invite you to check the original book in the wise women's library. In a little while, you will be given the opportunity to do so."

Patricius stood up and passed the documents to various Elgathan nobles.

"Unfortunately," Kennard said, "The return of Vist to its rightful queen means that the kingdom of Meriveria is no more. My father is only the King of Elgatha. My marriage to Queen Odelia does fulfill the Treaty of Meriveria, but it cannot take effect until I inherit the throne of Elgatha. To maintain the union of our people, we must have a union of leadership."

"And with our war against Tehazy, that unity is more important than ever," Odelia said. "Yet I cannot in good conscience send my Vistan subjects to die in battles led by King Gonfrid. He doesn't listen to counsel and has never been an amenable or considerate leader. But King Kennard and I can rule as one, working side-by-side for the good of all Meriverians, Vistan and Elgathan alike."

Gonfrid groaned and strained against his chains, glaring at Odelia.

"Thank you for the demonstration, Father," Kennard said. "We will now discuss the competency of your rule. His poor decisions have done great harm to his subjects and led to many unnecessary deaths. He has even gone so far as to gamble with *my* life. Two weeks ago, he was warned that my presence on the battlefield would cause more deaths there, and he sent me out anyway. Valerzan DiOrto died protecting me, and I barely escaped with my life. I was in such dire straits that Healing me was a risk to Queen Odelia's life. I am King Gonfrid's own flesh. If he places so little value on the life of his own heir, imagine how little he values yours, or even less, those of his other subjects. How many of our people must be slaughtered in ill-advised battle plans and grandiose displays of power before we put an end to it?"

Kennard was becoming emotional. Odelia squeezed his hand tightly, and he took a deep breath.

"How many of you has he dismissed or toyed with as a show of power?" Odelia asked. "He cares more about who will flatter him the most than what is best for his people. Lord Egino, how long have you been petitioning for a much-needed road to Cantahn, only for King Gonfrid to refuse to acknowledge you? And Vistans? Most of you have all but given up on appearing in court because you know you will be ignored. This isn't an imagined slight. As a prince, when King Kennard sought to serve his people, he was disheartened that he was given the task of preventing Vistan petitions from ever reaching King Gonfrid."

Gonfrid became a bear and growled.

Kennard looked right at him. "And most importantly, he is losing control of himself. He has abused his Gift of Transformation, and the constant changes are breaking his mind. He is violent and unpredictable. If we do not take this reign from him, I fear what kind of whim might strike him next."

Odelia rubbed the back of Kennard's hand with her thumb. This next part was going to be ugly. "Before we open the floor to hear questions and additional evidence, it is only right that the accused should have a chance to speak for himself."

Gonfrid popped back into human form. A guard removed his gag. No matter what he said, she couldn't let anything show.

He grunted and spat at their feet. "I am the King of Meriveria, and as such, I do not answer to traitorous filth or their overambitious courtesans. I will have your head for this Odelia."

"If all you have to offer are insults and threats, then you will not speak," Kennard said coldly. "I will give you one last opportunity. You are about to lose everything. Do you have anything to say in your own defense?"

Gonfrid rolled his eyes. "We are at war. Men die." He pointed at Odelia. "And so will your pale-skinned whore when this farce is over."

Kennard snapped, "Since you cannot keep a civil tongue or appearance, you will be silent."

The guard gagged Gonfrid. Though her pulse pounded, Odelia kept her face like stone. She shoved the terror down deep inside. Kennard was by her side, and the guards wouldn't let go of Gonfrid. He couldn't follow through with his threats here.

Grandilord Doneron stood up. "You say that the two of you are married, but there has been no royal wedding, and King Gonfrid and Queen Melaine have clearly not consented to such a union. All we have is your word that it occurred. How do we know that your marriage is valid?"

Kennard smiled. "I'm so glad you asked. The wedding was performed by Abhenric DiOrto in his capacity as the King of Vist, moments before he abdicated the throne to his daughter. Would all of our witnesses please stand up?"

Half of the room stood, including Conora. Melaine gasped loudly.

"Thank you. You may take your seats. Grandilord Patricius, did these events happen as I've described?" Kennard asked.

"Yes, Your Majesty. I hosted the wedding in my manor. I have the marriage certificate here, as well as King Abhenric's declaration."

Grandilord Doneron looked over the documents.

Patricius produced a bundle of cloth and began unfurling it. "Do you need proof of consummation? I have that too."

Kennard cleared his throat. "That's...uh...thorough of you..."

Grandilord Doneron turned red and shook his head.

Odelia's cheeks warmed. "Thank you, Grandilord Patricius, but I believe we have sufficient evidence without the sheets. Has your question been answered, Grandilord Doneron?"

"Yes, Your Majesty." Grandilord Doneron sat.

A Vistan pettilord rose. "What happens if King Gonfrid stays in power? What is to keep him from invalidating your marriage in Elgatha or killing our queen?"

"He has no power to do either in Vist," Odelia said. "And he would be unwise to attempt either in Elgatha. This union has been ensured beyond mere consummation. An attack on me would be an attack on King Gonfrid's own blood and heir."

Kennard smiled at her. "She is already carrying my child, the first true heir to all of Meriveria."

Gonfrid became a wolf and snarled. Scattered cheers rang out, including one from Conora, who had otherwise been quiet. Odelia smiled back at her.

"Does anybody need to verify my claim to the Vistan throne?" Odelia asked.

Grandilord Roderick and two of his lords rose. Odelia sent a few guards with them and gave everyone time to talk amongst themselves while they waited. Gonfrid was hauled off into one side room, while Kennard and Odelia took refuge in another.

Just before they closed the door, Conora joined them. "Is it true? You haven't been married long. Did you really conceive that quickly?"

"Well, I wouldn't have announced it if it wasn't, would I?" Kennard said.

Conora wrapped Odelia in a bear hug. "Thank you! I hope you make many, many more."

Odelia laughed. "You don't want to be a queen?"

"I wouldn't mind marrying a king," Conora said, "but no, I really don't want to reign."

"I'm surprised you followed us in here," Kennard said. "I thought you needed to remain neutral."

Conora shrugged. "Well, I've already revealed myself as one of your wedding guests, so thank you for that."

"There were plenty of other witnesses," Odelia said. "You could've just as easily stayed seated."

"Mother knew I was in Vist," Conora said. "With everyone else standing up, she would've suspected me anyway."

Kennard crossed his arms. "If you aren't staying neutral, why aren't you helping? A word of support from you would go a long way with the Elgathan nobles."

Conora shook her head. "This isn't my fight."

Kennard clenched his jaw. "This is everyone's fight. Father and Grandfather have both threatened to kill Lia. How can you be content if they win this trial?"

Conora put her hands on her hips. "I'm not, but I'm also not content with treason."

"So my restoring the rightful ruler of a kingdom and capturing Father without bloodshed is as low as his promise to *rip my wife's throat out with his teeth*?"

Odelia stepped between them, placing her hands on Kennard's heaving chest. "Easy, love. Haven't we estranged enough of your family?"

"How can I take your side when you exaggerate?" Conora asked.

"But he didn't," Odelia said. "That is actually one of the threats King Gonfrid has made on my life in the past few days. Herman and the Vistans who were part of his capture can confirm that."

Conora stared. "That's violent, even for him."

"You've never seen him before a battle," Kennard said.

"What will you do if they don't accept your claim to the throne?" Conora asked. "He certainly won't let you stay here."

"If we're lucky, we'll retreat to Vist, exiled from Elgatha for the rest of King Gonfrid's life." Odelia swallowed. "But I doubt he'll let us go quietly."

Kennard put his arm around her and kissed her temple. "We'll make it to Vist. Our guards are the ones holding him. They'll get us out of the palace, and our army will protect us the rest of the way."

He couldn't be sure of that, but the effort to lie about it was sweet.

Conora pursed her lips, deep in thought.

"Conora," Odelia said, "if our claim fails, we won't see each other again for a very long time. So I want to thank you for your kindness and friendship. I understand it's that kindness that's keeping you from choosing a side. The rest of your family may be spiteful, but I'm glad to call you my sister."

Conora teared up. "You shame me."

"I don't mean to."

"I know." She embraced Odelia. "Your claim had better stand because I've had hardly any time to experience official sisterhood with you."

Kennard's eyes lit up. "Does that mean you'll speak up?"

Conora nodded. "She's talked me into it." She chuckled, then whispered, "That wife of yours is a wily one. You should keep an eye on her."

Kennard laughed. "Well, according to our parents and Grandfather, that's how I ended up married to her."

There was a knock on the door.

Kennard opened the door. "Back already?"

"No, Your Majesty," a guard said. "Queen Melaine is requesting to speak with you."

"Send her in," Odelia said. It wouldn't hurt to give the queen a moment now, especially since her Allure wouldn't work on anyone in the room.

"Are you sure?" Kennard asked. "She struck you last time."

"Whatever she wants, I'd rather find out now than in front of everyone," Odelia said.

The guard escorted Melaine to the room, then shut her in.

"I—" Melaine blinked and swallowed, holding up a document. "I read the lineage paper..."

Kennard waved for her to continue. "And?"

"How long have you known about this?"

"Since the last time we returned home from Doivrie, just before the Midwinter Feast," he said.

Melaine scrunched up her face in thought. "She was the reason you turned Queen Barbenia away?"

"Of course," he said.

Melaine shook the paper. "This is valid. Why didn't you tell me you were marrying a queen?"

Kennard grabbed his hair. "What! But I— What?" He pointed at Odelia. "She told you last night, and you slapped her for it."

Melaine sniffed. "You didn't present proof."

"You never gave me the chance," Odelia said.

"You should've told me months ago," Melaine said. "I understand the need to marry for power. You got yourself a better title and did your part to maintain our hold on Meriveria. I'm still not fond of you carrying on with a Vistan, but I could look past it in light of her usefulness."

Odelia wrinkled her nose. "Oh, thank you. How gracious of you." Giver forbid her mother-in-law ever gave her a real compliment.

Melaine smiled and waved her off.

Kennard raised one eyebrow. "Her usefulness? See, this is why I didn't tell you. You would try to make her your puppet—or worse, get rid of her before we could bring the truth to light."

Melaine sighed. "We're certainly past that now, aren't we? You've played your game well, and I admire your ambition, but this needs to stop. Rescind your attack on your father, and I can convince him to be lenient with you. If the girl can be compliant, her presence will keep Vist under control, and you can wait out the rest of his rule."

Compliant? Odelia scoffed. "You cannot be serious."

Melaine grabbed Kennard's arm. "Son, if you continue with this, you will be exiled to Vist, trapped in those wretched mountains forever."

Kennard pulled away. "It's a lovely place to be trapped, and even if it weren't, it's preferable to your offer."

Melaine gasped. "Conora, do you hear this? Your brother would abandon us without a thought!" She turned her back to him. "Does family mean nothing to you?"

"He's doing this for family," Conora said. "He's protecting the one he's starting with Odelia."

"And if I trust you," Kennard said. "I'll lose that family. Even if you can talk Father down, why would I ever believe you wouldn't kill them yourself?"

Melaine's eyes grew wide. "Why would you believe I would?"

Odelia crossed her arms. "Because you already threatened to, and you used Lord Wystan and Grandilady Wilmarie to try to get rid of me before this meeting."

Melaine shook her head. "The plan was to sequester you, not kill you. You think I'd do that to a woman with child? I'm not a monster. You would've lived comfortably in Eaund with your baby."

Odelia and Kennard exchanged a look.

"Lived comfortably? Mother, sending Lia to Eaund would've resulted in our child being raised as an orphan."

Melaine scoffed. "You expect me to buy the same lie you sold to Wilmarie? If that's true, then her death has been on your hands since the moment you took her as your lover."

Kennard clenched his jaw.

Odelia put her hand on his back. "The risk was mine to choose, and he's a powerful Healer."

"You're trying to twist things," Kennard said. "This is about your plan. If I trusted you—which I don't—the protection for Lia would only last until our child is born."

Melaine shrugged. "Her claim isn't one that can be taken back. Yours is. I'm offering you as much safety as I can."

Kennard opened the door. "I've heard enough. Thank you for your concern, but I heartily decline. Guards, keep her away from the others until the meeting resumes."

"You're making a mistake," Melaine said as they escorted her out.

Kennard turned to Conora. "If you don't mind—"

"Oh, of course not." She hugged him. "Giver grant you favor."

"Thank you." He closed the door behind her and exhaled.

"Do you think she was sincere?" Odelia asked. "Your mother never offers help unless it benefits her."

"You're right. She doesn't. But she will ally with whoever has the most power."

"Even a loathsome Vistan like me? She must be desperate."

Kennard smiled. "She thinks we might succeed."

Grandilord Roderick and the others quietly returned to their seats, avoiding eye contact with everyone.

Kennard chuckled, then whispered to Odelia, "Should we ask him what he found?"

She shook her head. "Not directly. Everyone knows what he found there. No sense in rubbing his nose in it."

He pounded on the table that had been set up on the dais during the recess. The room fell silent. "Does anyone have any more objections to the claims presented?"

Nobody spoke up.

He lifted a document from the table. "Queen Odelia and I have drafted this declaration, formalizing the vow of fealty that some of you have already sworn to us. To sign this is to reject King Gonfrid as your sovereign and accept our rule."

"Twenty-eight of you have sworn to us," Odelia said. "We invite you now to sign. Grandilord Straton..." As he approached, she called up each of his arions, the lord and pettilords coming in groups of three to sign. Doivrie was next, in the same order. When all twenty-six of the original Vistan nobles had signed, she called for Atmos.

People gasped and murmured as Rhonwin helped Moira out of her seat and walked hand-in-hand with her to the dais. A young Elgathan stood and followed them, looking around nervously. Rhonwin finished signing and whispered to the man, who nodded and took the pen from him. He signed as the Pettilord of Ormoint.

Kennard smiled and squeezed Odelia's hand. "We have the support of twenty-nine, including all of Vist. That is more than enough to declare our sovereignty there. As it stands, Vist is now a separate kingdom and annexes the arion of Atmos."

Noise swelled up from the crowd.

Odelia pounded the table. "But Meriverian law demands a three-quarters vote to remove the sovereign. That is thirty-nine signatures. It only takes ten of you to preserve this kingdom. Who will start?"

The Lord of Vanderin stood up.

"*What* are you doing?" Grandilord Roderick asked.

"I won't be surrounded. It's bad enough having Tehazy to the north. If Atmos is Vistan land now, they'll have us to the south and east." The lord walked to the table.

"And the rest of Eaund to your west," Grandilord Roderick warned.

The two pettilords of Vanderin stood up. The older of them said, "Two safe borders is better than one."

Just seven more.

"The eastern half of Eaund stands with us," Kennard said.

The lords and pettilords of the western arions looked to their grandilord, but a stern look rooted them in their seats.

Odelia switched to the southern grandrion, all that was left of Elgatha. "Who will sign from Oulley?"

"No one from Ascaympa will touch that cursed paper," Lord Wystan called out from his seat.

Kennard gave a sardonic smile. "Thank you, Grandfather. Supportive as always."

Grandilord Doneron was the first to rise. He bowed to Kennard and Odelia as he approached the table. "Your Majesties."

Odelia and Kennard looked at each other as he signed.

"You look surprised," he said.

"Well, I wasn't expecting you to be the first after you questioned the validity of our marriage," Kennard admitted.

Doneron shrugged. "I was only being thorough, but if the Treaty of Meriveria is invalid, it must be made legitimate again. It would only be proper." He bowed, then returned to his seat.

Lord Egino of Cantahn strode up to the table, then turned to face Gonfrid. "All I asked was permission to build a road. I didn't even need funds. Perhaps years of being ignored will make the Vistans more receptive than you've been."

The king growled as Lord Egino signed.

Unfortunately, his pettilords did not follow him. Nobody else stood either. Farther from the Tehazian border, those in Oulley hadn't lost as much from King Gonfrid's military failures. They couldn't be counted on to value their borders like their northern compatriots.

Odelia's heart sank. The kingdom of Meriveria was dissolving. She put a hand to her womb, sorry for the broken mess her child would inherit.

Conora rose and placed herself between her father and her brother. She didn't speak at first but simply stared out over the crowd. It wasn't until questioning whispers spread through the room that she finally found her voice. "I never wanted to see my father deposed, and I cannot fault some of you for seeing my brother and his wife as traitors."

Odelia gripped Kennard's arm and hand, determined to anchor him as well as herself.

"But I also never want to see this great kingdom divided, and I also know that my brother is a kind and honorable man, whose instinct is to make things right. He could've killed our father—and most of you would've in his position—but he brought him back here instead. Now, we can talk on and on about loyalty and Vistan territory and Elgathan territory, but the truth is that we are all Meriverians. I am not the only one who will have family on both sides of this split. There is strength in Meriveria, in the trade between the mountains and the sea, in the united forces that hold countries like Tehazy at bay, and in our shared history. If we want to keep the power that gives us, we need to act as one."

Conora knelt in front of Kennard and Odelia.

Gonfrid pulled on his chains.

"No," Melaine said.

"In observance of Your Majesties' sovereign rule, I hereby pledge my loyalty and obedience as a Princess of Elgatha to you, Queen Odelia and King Kennard of Meriveria."

Odelia held back tears as she offered a hand up to Conora. "Thank you. We accept your pledge."

Conora nodded, then signed the document. It wouldn't count as a vote, but it strengthened her support. She returned to her seat, next to a seething Melaine.

Several men came forward, silently and solemnly, to sign the declaration. When they finished, Odelia held her breath. She had lost track of the count. Was it enough?

"Anyone else?" Kennard asked. After no one responded, he picked up the document. "So that both sides will know it is valid, Grandilords Patricius and Roderick, would you please count the signatures? There must be at least thirty-nine for ratification."

Odelia tried not to move, holding tight to Kennard's hand as the grandilords looked over the document.

Grandilord Patricius turned to the crowd. "With the approval of forty Meriverian nobles and one princess, the declaration is official."

Cheers rang out from the Vistans and some of the Elgathans. Kennard put his arms around Odelia, and she melted into his embrace. It was the most intimacy they could appropriately share on such an occasion. He let out a shuddering breath. "You're safe now, love."

Patricius backed up toward them and cleared his throat.

Odelia stepped back and smiled. "Almost." She let Patricius gather everyone's attention, then announced, "King Kennard and I are now the rightful rulers of all of Meriveria. As a demonstration of our goodwill, we offer clemency to anyone who joins us now. This is your final chance to sign your allegiance."

Six more lords and pettilords rose and signed. Grandilord Roderick and Lord Wystan remained in their seats, whispering harshly to those closest to them.

"Do not fear them," Kennard said. "Queen Melaine, Lord Wystan, Grandilord Roderick, and Grandilady Wilmarie will all stand trial for assault and attempted kidnapping of Queen Odelia."

Melaine nearly swooned. Wystan tried to stand but was pressed back into his seat. Guards surrounded Roderick and cuffed him. Two more guards Sped out of the room to fetch Wilmarie.

The four remaining nobles jumped up and signed.

Odelia turned to her father-in-law. "King Gonfrid, you have been declared an unlawful ruler of Vist and an unworthy ruler of Elgatha. You are hereby stripped of all rank, title, and authority."

The color drained from Gonfrid's face.

"By rights, you should be hanged for Prince Valerzan's death alone, not to mention the violent threats you've made against me personally, and I have more than enough reason to want such a sentence carried out."

He was breathing heavily now, sweat beading on his brow.

"However, in honor of the love I have for your son, your life is spared. You will live out your days in a prison here in Meria, which we will build just for you."

Gonfrid furrowed his brow and moaned, pleading with his eyes. Kennard nodded to one of the guards, who loosened the gag.

"Why, Son? How could you do this to me?"

Kennard put a hand on Odelia's shoulder and met his father's gaze. "I will never forget what you said to me on the day of my Gifting Ceremony. You told me that you do what you must to protect what's yours and that someday, I would too. Unfortunately for you, today is that day." He pulled Odelia closer and turned to the guards. "Take him away."

Gonfrid didn't fight as the guards hauled him off but glared death at both of them.

Kennard took Odelia's hand. "There's one more thing we need to do."

He led her to the thrones, where they took their places together. The seats were stiff and unyielding—as expected for flat, solid wood—but nothing could bring her more comfort than uniting their people at his side.

With a grin, Kennard proclaimed, "Long live the queen!"

They still had much to face: bringing peace to their people, seeking justice for Vist, and delivering their heir. And they would do it all as they were meant to—as one.

Odelia smiled back. "Long live the king!"

CONTINUE THE STORY!

HEALERS' KISS II

KISS OF DESTINY

BOOKS2READ.COM/KISSDESTINY

GIFTS

Allure – naturally more likeable, possibly seductive; can lead to paranoia from overuse

Animal Speech – can speak to animals; socialize better with them than people; trouble with impulse control

Far-Sight – telescopic vsion; terrible near vision

Fire – can expel heat from body

Flight – can fly; large wings can be unwieldy on the ground

Healing – can heal others; compromised self-healing and immune system

Hearing – extremely sensitive ears

Ice – can absorb heat into body

Invisibility – cannot be seen by others

Listening – always reads everyone's thoughts

Memory – can never forget anything

Near-Sight – microscopic vision; terrible far vision

Night-Sight – enhances light for constant nocturnal vision; daylight painful

Seeing – receives visions of the future; no control over visions

Speech – can speak any language; cannot identify languages

Speed – can move at incredible speed; eats four times as much

Stone-Skin – skin is armored; also lacks emotional sensitivity

Strength – has the strength of four men; eats as much as two men

Transformation – can turn into a known mammal; can go insane from overuse

Water-Breathing – can breathe underwater; cannot leave water for more than a day

ACKNOWLEDGMENTS

I would like to thank God for giving me the mind and imagination to write and Mom for telling me I should.

Thanks to all my critique partners and beta readers, especially Sean, who read the my raw first draft (you poor, brave soul), and my friends in the Just-Us League, whose anthologies got me started in publishing.

Thank you to my awesome business partners in Authors 4 Authors. Rebecca, your editing and scene brainstorming are invaluable. Renee, thanks for keeping me on track when I get too stuck on the details.

Whitney, thank you for my first edition cover. Your ribbon of intent illustration lives on in my logo.

GIFTED HEARTS
SHORT LOVE STORIES OF CARUM SOUND
books2read.com/giftedhearts

SEEING THROUGH HIM

In a Beauty and the Beast retelling, the alluring Rosabella meets the invisible Leandro and strikes up an unlikely friendship. They must both overcome their insecurities to remain friends, but can they overcome their differences to become more?
books2read.com/seeingthroughhim

HER DEAREST TREASURE

In a retelling of "The Peasant's Clever Daughter," Sonia takes up the challenge of King Basil to win his heart. After their marriage, he discovers she has not told him everything.
books2read.com/herdearesttreasure

I LOVED YOU TOMORROW

An original short story: A mindreader meets a woman who sees the future—a future they are meant to share. Rhonwin must overcome his fear of her farfetched visions of him, and Moira must reconcile the fact that her love is not yet hers.
books2read.com/ilovedyoutomorrow

THE VEILED QUEEN

In a retelling of "King Thrushbeard," Queen Barbenia visits Boscada in search for an economic deal via marriage, but comes away with a royal-turned-deckhand after Prince Elio pushes his father too far. Queen Barbenia, known to Elio only as Captain Thrush, teaches Elio the meaning of hard work.
books2read.com/theveiledqueen

ABOUT THE AUTHOR

Brandi Spencer's love stories of Carum Sound are heavily influenced by the beautiful Pacific Northwest, where she lives with her husband and two sons. The scenic views of Puget Sound and the Cascades provide plenty of inspiration for her superpowered fantasy romances. A Western Washington University alumna and former cosmetologist turned work-at-home mom and homeschool teacher, she writes in between family life and work for A4A Publishing. She loves crafting, baking, and video games and spends far too much time researching for her stories.

Follow her online:

www.BrandiSpencer.com
Twitter: @Meriverian
Facebook: @Meriveran
Instagram: @Meriverian

AUTHORS 4 AUTHORS PUBLISHING

A publishing company for authors, run by authors, blending the best of traditional and independent publishing

We specialize in speculative fiction: science fiction, fantasy, paranormal, and romance. Get lost in another world!

Check out our collection at https://books2read.com/rl/a4a or visit Authors4AuthorsPublishing.com/books

For updates, scan the QR code or visit our website to join our semi-monthly newsletter!

Want more fantasy romance? We recommend:

FYR
by Lisa Borne Graves

At seventeen, Toury arrives in Fyr, where magic is power, a prince's love is deadly, and female autonomy is a dream. Alex, the Prince of Fyr, has to face his father's ailing health, the expectation to marry soon, and the hidden necromancers trying to take over the realm by exploiting his dark curse. At least there's hope in a cheeky savior, but Earth girls aren't so easy. Can they trust each other enough to save Fyr? Or will everything they hold dear turn to ash?

books2read.com/fyr

www.ingramcontent.com/pod-product-compliance
Lightning Source LLC
Chambersburg PA
CBHW020717130726
47899CB00011B/360

* 9 781644 771181 *